MW00701006

THE
LIMITS

The

LIMITS

Nell Freudenberger

ALFRED A. KNOPF

NEW YORK

2024

LIBRARY OF CONGRESS CATALOGING-IN-PUBLICATION DATA
Names: Freudenberger, Nell, author.
Title: The limits / Nell Freudenberger.
Description: First Edition. | New York : Alfred A. Knopf, 2024. |
"A Borzoi Book."
Identifiers: LCCN 2023005984 (print) | LCCN 2023005985 (ebook) |
ISBN 9780593448885 (hardcover) | ISBN 9780593448892 (ebook)
Subjects: LCGFT: Novels.
Classification: LCC PS3606.R479 L56 2024 (print) |
LCC PS3606.R479 (ebook) | DDC 813/.6—dc23/eng/20230221
LC record available at https://lccn.loc.gov/2023005984
LC ebook record available at https://lccn.loc.gov/2023005985

Jacket photographs: (NYC) Christopher McLallen/Millennium
Images, UK; (Tahiti) Antoine Boureau/Millennium Images, UK
Jacket design by Kelly Blair

Manufactured in the United States of America
First Edition

For Cleo and Nic

Now I live here, another island,
that doesn't seem like one, but who decides?

ELIZABETH BISHOP, "CRUSOE IN ENGLAND"

THE
LIMITS

1

She was already underwater when the sun came up. Twenty-five meters down, the first light hit the rose garden in patches, like a hand-colored photograph. Plated clusters of *Montipora* resolved from gray to green, brown fingers of *Acropora* blushed pink. The fish woke up, like birds. You could hear them snapping and grunting, crunching the coral between the steam puff and gurgle from the regulators. A trio of black-tipped reef sharks passed in the distance, propelling themselves with subtle, muscular flicks. They ignored the divers, who were so close to each other that Nathalie could feel the surge from Raffi's fins. She put space between them, then indicated some coral outcroppings a little farther on, where the coastal shelf descended, then dropped off sharply to blue.

Nathalie would have preferred to dive alone. This was her favorite hour of the day, when her time was completely her own; something was lost, even with Raffi. But things were done correctly at CRIOBE, and she was scrupulous about protocol, as well as the research station's equipment. No pleasure on earth was worth risking the place she'd made for herself here.

They backpedaled a moment to admire a school of yellow-tailed demoiselles wake up and start to feed. The damselfish avoided the white patches among the green, yellow, and purple of the reef, but the bleached coral wasn't dead. It was only empty. Either the tiny algae that lived in its transparent tissue would return, restoring the coral's healthy color, or that living tissue would shred away and die, leaving the calcareous skeleton.

Raffi touched her shoulder: a moray was emerging from underneath a rock. It was the same muddy green as the kelp and she had to admit that she wouldn't have seen it without him; Raffi had that gift for spotting what other people missed. The jaws of the eel gaped and closed, gaped and closed, his tiny eyes perhaps as useless as her own without the mask. An iridescent bluestreak cleaner wrasse darted toward his head, safe in its knowledge that the moray wouldn't eat its sleek servant.

Jardin des Roses was a beautiful name, but not entirely accurate. The *Montipora* looked more like mushrooms than like roses, and there was nothing cultivated about the landscape beneath them. It looked haphazard, but everything existed in precise balance with everything else; the plan had arisen according to the needs of each creature there. And not only the creatures. She really believed that the beauty was mathematical in nature, derived from the cycling of nitrogen and carbon through the living and nonliving components of the reef. The idea that it could be gone in a few years was sick.

When they came up there was only 20 bar left in her cylinder, and 'Ōpūnohu Bay was dark turquoise. Small waves whipped the surface, which had been still and silver on the way out. A sleek white cruiser was approaching the mouth of the bay, while a tug-style supply vessel she didn't recognize, RV *Persephone*, sat at anchor inside the pass, under a Danish flag. Vertical cumulus clouds sat over the water like greater ships, throwing blankets of shadow on the steep, bottle-green hills. Mount Rotui rose up in front of them with its elongated ridge, as if it had been dragged toward the coast. There was some local legend about theft.

"Seven-forty," Raffi said.

"Shit." She was giving an informal tour to a research analyst from Pew, on vacation in the area. She thought briefly about having her exemplary German student, Gunther, start the tour, but these relationships with funders were crucial, and it really did have to be her.

They were chugging slowly toward the underpass, where

the channel ran under the road to the station. Two children were standing on the shore, one eight or nine, the other barely more than a toddler. They were stooping and straightening and then stooping again, picking at something in the sand. Shells maybe, or unlikely treasures from the piles of sun- and salt-bleached plastic chips that washed up with the tides. Once she had picked a single diamond earring off a ledge, shed by some unlucky tourist; on shore another time a plastic baby, the size of a thumbnail, brittle and pink, its features washed away.

The older girl shaded her eyes to watch their boat coming in. There was nothing remarkable about a couple of divers returning on the skiff, and so she was surprised to see the younger one waving her arms over her head. Demoiselles, like the fish, traveling in a shoal—free, this early in the morning, from chores. Perhaps that was what made them so ebullient and friendly. She waved, and they redoubled their greeting.

"Professeure! Professeure!" Jumping up and down as if they'd won the lottery. Local girls whose parents ran fruit stands, fished, cleaned hotels. What did they want with her?

She thought she would start the tour outside, show the analyst the bay and say something about the dive this morning, before moving into the lab. If you were used to an air-conditioned office in D.C., you might enjoy the view of the mountains from the thatched Polynesian pavilion called fare pote'e. The American scientists at the station next door had a larger one, where they often took photographs, perhaps because they liked to think of themselves as more locally attuned than their French counterparts. Her friend Marie-Laure called the pavilions "un peu Disney."

Raffi guided the boat under the road and into the green channel. They anchored at the CRIOBE dock. It was ten of eight, and they worked quickly, unloading the gear and hosing down the boat. She had a dry shirt and shorts in her dive bag, and she pulled them on over her damp suit, running her fingers through her wet hair. No time for coffee, but at least the delay would be short enough to excuse.

But the girls had followed them. They'd crossed the road in record time; the older one was now scampering alongside the channel, pulling the baby after her. She was wearing a red Hello Kitty tank top and a ruffled denim miniskirt with rick-rack edging, a pink headband that secured a smooth topknot.

"Telephone for you! At the reception!"

Now she recognized them—the older, at least, was a relation of Veronique, who worked at the reception. Tahitian, emaciated, of an indeterminate but advanced age, and dressed always in bright local fabrics, Veronique nevertheless seemed, in her sour disdain for nearly all the lab's employees, more French than anything else. It especially irked her when the friends or family members of the researchers who'd failed to reach their mobiles called the station, and Nathalie wasn't surprised that she'd sent these emissaries rather than venturing out herself.

"An emergency," the girl continued politely in French. "She's waiting."

Whether the "she" who was waiting was the caller or Veronique, Nathalie wasn't sure. But there was no reason to panic, except with regard to the funders. She thanked the child, who smiled shyly from under her heavy thatch of bangs, and texted Gunther. Then she picked up her cylinder and BCD.

"Leave it," said Raffi, "in case it's Pia." He spoke French with Nathalie but English with her daughter, who'd learned the languages simultaneously and had no preference. Nathalie had remarked on it when she first heard them, because French was certainly easier for Raffi. But Pia said pointedly that Raffi had referred to French as a "shit language" and would rather speak English. She said it with a sidelong look, as if she thought she might offend or shock her mother. Nathalie had long since learned not to react to that kind of thing. More likely, Raffi was just using Pia as practice for his tourists.

One afternoon stuck in her mind. She'd happened to be standing outside the reception and had seen them coming in from a dive on the boat. Pia had been wearing a black Speedo, a modest suit that nevertheless showed every detail of her body, the high breasts, the oval of tanned thigh and slice of buttock. They were struggling; she'd been standing carelessly, and he was telling her to sit down; while Nathalie watched, unobserved, Pia covered his eyes with her hands, laughing, forcing him to push her off.

Regarding Pia, she trusted Raffi completely. It was her daughter's behavior she worried about, because that was the way she herself had always been. It wasn't age so much as knowledge; she fell in love because a person knew something she didn't.

"Go," Raffi said, shouldering both of their vests and taking a cylinder in each hand. "I've got it."

She walked on the dock, then jogged. People got excited about nothing here, any contact with the outside world. It was two in the afternoon in New York, and so Raffi was right: it was likely Pia, likely with something that only a fifteen-year-old would classify as an emergency. It was the last day of the year, but, like her, Stephen would certainly be at work.

The reception had an unpleasant, unreal feeling, the way places you knew well sometimes appeared in dreams. It was overlaid with an emotion, which she identified as fear only when she looked at Veronique, who indicated the landline on the desk with a gesture that was uncharacteristically respectful, almost sympathetic. It was early for her to be in; maybe she'd stopped in the office for something, was on her way somewhere else, had answered the call only by chance? Veronique seemed to confirm this by picking up her cigarettes and her purse before leaving Nathalie alone in the small office. For some reason Nathalie focused on the souvenir calendar pinned to the bulletin board above the desk, which featured, for December, the spectacular and ecologically devastating red lionfish.

"Pia?"

But it wasn't Pia, nor was it her father. It was his wife, who was pregnant. When was her due date? The thought occurred to Nathalie that Kate was calling to tell her Pia had a sibling.

"Nathalie?"

"Yes?"

"I'm calling because I can't reach Stephen." She sounded panicked, hysterical, a quality Nathalie despised, especially in women. "And Pia's supposed to be at Maxine's. But she isn't there."

It didn't seem to Nathalie like such an emergency. Weren't there a million reasons a teenager might not be where she said she was? They'd had an argument, and so she'd left. She'd left to see another friend, or because she felt like it. Pia was independent, unlike American teenagers who traveled everywhere by car, whose parents kept track of them with GPS. She'd walked around the neighborhood on her own at nine; had taken the metro with her cousins as a young teenager in Paris.

"Have you tried calling her?"

"Of course. She went out to Maxine's on Saturday, with another girl. She hasn't been home since then."

Whether or not the new apartment where Stephen lived with this younger wife was Pia's home—well, that was debatable. "She is supposed to be staying at Maxine's?"

"Out in East Hampton. Maxine's mother just called."

"Yes, okay."

"I tried, but I couldn't reach Stephen. He's at the hospital."

"But what am I supposed to do?"

There was a long pause. "I don't know." Her tone had changed. Now the woman sounded like what she was—a secondary school teacher, those dry and rigid women Nathalie remembered from collège. Correct and self-righteous, perfect for Stephen. "I thought she might have been in touch with you."

"No."

"Maxine's mother said the girls haven't seen her since Sunday morning."

Now something clutched in her chest, an unpleasant pressure not unlike becoming unexpectedly low on air while diving. Today was Thursday. Thursday afternoon in New York. No one had seen Pia for four days?

"But you've only learned this *now?*"

Kate made a noncommittal sound, which Nathalie took as an admission of guilt. Who the hell was watching her child? Stephen was in the thick of the worst public health emergency in a century, but Kate was at home all day. It was hardly difficult.

"How is that possible?"

"They were with the housekeeper. Maxine's mother is afraid the other girls were covering for her. She thought Pia could be with you."

"Of course she's not with me!"

"I know that," Kate said. "I saw her on Saturday."

Nathalie tried to be patient. Sometimes, when you wanted something from someone, no matter how urgently, you had to stop and imagine things from their perspective. It was something she practiced all the time with her colleagues at the station.

"I know this must be . . . hard for you."

Kate didn't say anything, and so Nathalie pressed on. "This situation. And your pregnancy."

"Excuse me?"

She was on the point of mentioning what Stephen had told her. But had that been in confidence? In any case, this woman wanted no comfort from her.

There was a long silence, so that Nathalie thought there was a problem with the connection. "Katherine? Katherine! Can you hear me?"

"I can hear you." A frosty, fuck-you voice.

Nathalie modified hers, dripping politeness. "Do you have any idea where Pia might be?"

"I have no idea," Kate said. "I'm not her mother."

2

The day Pia arrived had been so thick and hot that at two o'clock, Kate still hadn't left the apartment. She looked at the brick face of the condominiums across the street and saw shimmering strings of light. The smart thermostat kept the apartment in the Laureate at exactly 72 degrees and so she'd postponed going out, until now it was too late. The message from Stephen said that Pia had just landed, but that he would be held up at the hospital for at least another couple of hours. He was sorry, and he loved her.

When they moved in together, she'd felt a mixture of excitement and guilt. She told herself that her marriage to Stephen didn't mean that everything in her life had to change. It was true that their apartment was a significant distance in every sense from the one she'd shared until recently with Benji and May on one floor of a subdivided brick rowhouse in Gowanus. Although they'd taken turns borrowing from each other at the end of the month (Benji was the worst offender), Kate had never thought of herself as anything but solidly middle-class. By some of her students' standards—63 percent of whom had household incomes low enough to qualify the school for Title I funding—she was rich.

Since she'd married Stephen, she was rich by anyone's standards. The first time her sister had seen the apartment, she'd drawn in a breath. Kate had looked forward to impressing Emily, who lived in a three-bedroom house in Lake Grove and was a stay-at-home parent to three boys. Her sister recognized the difference between her own suburban comfort and the objects in Stephen's apartment, the artwork and the hush in the lobby downstairs. She'd said to Emily that the Laureate took some getting used to—but that was a lie. She'd gotten used to it immediately, as fast as you got used to a nice hotel room or an upgrade on the plane.

It was just that she'd never imagined spending so much time here. Her natural tendency was not toward caution, but Stephen often pointed out the total lack of data on the virus and pregnancy. He was still at the hospital all the time. This morning he had been "almost positive" he would be home when his daughter arrived, but Kate was learning that this signified something like a 40 percent chance. Her parents, his biggest fans, often pointed out her good fortune over the phone. In their telling, the marriage wasn't so much a love story as a piece of divine intervention that had swooped Kate up and landed her at the Laureate, an act of God.

When the pandemic began in the spring, Stephen had speculated that his ex-wife—living on a Polynesian island that was difficult to reach in ordinary times, conducting a study of deep water coral bleaching—was possibly among the safest people in the world. He said that in the blank and factual way that he always spoke about Nathalie, whom he mentioned only in the context of their daughter:

Pia will stay with Nathalie's sister in Saint-Cloud while Nathalie is in Polynesia. Nathalie has changed her mind, because French schools have closed. Pia is going to her mother in Moʻorea, since she can now attend school remotely. Nathalie wants to speak to me about Pia's options for next year.

"It would be crazy to bring her to New York," Stephen had said, after one of these phone calls with his ex-wife. No question mark.

"Now," Kate said. "But when the worst is over?"

He looked up, as if he hadn't considered it. "There'll be a second wave."

"But you're going to miss her this summer."

What was that thing that couples did, where they each argued for the thing the other wanted? It felt familiar from other relationships. In other relationships, though, the stakes had never been this high.

"Christmas won't be possible."

"Isn't it your year?" According to the custody agreement, Pia spent alternating holidays and one month of every summer with her father.

"Flu season is too risky—I'd feel safe buying a ticket for August. But she can be a handful, and I'll be at the hospital."

This was in the spring, before she was pregnant, when he was less worried about her health. Putting the burden of his teenage daughter's supervision on Kate made him apprehensive, almost pleading. It was at that time very unusual for him to be asking her for a favor.

"I have some experience."

"That's the thing about you!" her new husband said, with unconcealed delight. They never made this type of comparison aloud, but she knew Stephen believed she was more suited to him than Nathalie had been. Stephen had once told her that he was suspicious of people who cared a great deal about their pets or gardens, with the implication that loving animals and plants somehow signified a failure to love other human beings. Kate wasn't sure about that—she liked dogs, just had never wanted the responsibility—but she enjoyed being complimented by Stephen, who seemed to find virtues even in her weaknesses. Of course, they'd only been together two years. Coral, she had recently learned, was an animal rather than a plant, existing in symbiotic relationship to certain algae. Its future was so precarious that children being born today were unlikely ever to see it, except in an aquarium.

She wrote back now to tell Stephen not to worry. She and Pia would be fine on their own for a while. The gray speech bubble appeared, then disappeared, then appeared again. "I really appreciate it," he wrote. "I love you." It wasn't out of character for him to say it twice in two texts. He felt strongly about the two of them not taking each other for granted.

Stephen was always either going to be her husband or nothing. This wasn't only because of his age, although her former roommate Benji had persisted for a while in referring to him as "Dad" (Stephen was thirteen years older than she was), or because of his schedule—busy even before Covid—but because of a certain quality that was apparent even in the early days of their relationship, an unusual mixture of pragmatism and naïveté. He would chat pleasantly with Benji and May, while Kate got ready in her closet-sized bedroom in the apartment in Gowanus. The bedroom had an odd interior window to the living room, fitted with a frosted glass slider; through it she could see only Stephen's blurred outline on the couch that was covered with a piece of fabric Benji had brought back from a music festival in Tanzania. It wasn't that he looked out of place so much as that he was on a different schedule than the rest of them, clearly sitting there for a purpose. When she came out, Stephen would smile at her in a way that no one had ever smiled at her before: a way that made it clear that she, Kate, was the purpose. Benji and May sometimes looked like they were trying not to laugh, but Stephen didn't care about what they thought at all.

Stephen was one of those people actually from New York, the son of a lawyer and a doctor. It was Stephen's mother, Frances, who had practiced medicine; now in her early eighties, she lived nearby, in an apartment overlooking the park. The first time Kate had visited, she had come away with the impression that all the rooms in the apartment were painted dark red, but that was wrong. On subsequent visits she'd seen that Frances's bedroom was blue, and the dining room was wallpapered in toile, and it was only the "library" that was that color, a color that seemed to emanate from Stephen's mother herself. Now that Frances was retired, she was reading the classics. She was on the board of the New York City Ballet. Frances had admired Nathalie, but she liked Kate better *for Stephen;* Kate knew this because Frances had told her the second time they met. Frances was nothing if not direct.

Frances had been an obstetrician, and Stephen was a cardiologist, specializing in heart failure, who had begun caring for Covid patients in March. He said at that time that there was nothing to be gleaned from the CDC, and so he'd held meetings with his colleagues, his residency group, and even his medical school class, impromptu online gatherings of physicians from all over the country. He read journal articles from China, then Italy, then Seattle, and then spent hours on Twitter responding to them. Once it started for real, he insisted on taking his and Kate's temperatures every morning, followed by a reading from each of their fingers with a pulse oximeter. Kate's classes went online. Groceries were delivered, as well as coffee beans that Stephen had been in the habit of grinding himself. She took that over. The machine was very loud in the apartment, which was even quieter than usual during the many hours he was away, except for the astonishing increase in birdsong.

In mid-May, when the numbers finally started going down, Nathalie had called from the station in Mo'orea to say that Pia wanted to go back to her old school in New York. This was the bilingual school that Pia had attended until her parents divorced, when she was ten. She wanted to do this in the fall, because the Wi-Fi on Mo'orea was inadequate, because she needed the socialization of her peers, and because she had decided to go to college in the States. The look on Stephen's face as he heard this news made it abundantly clear to Kate that she had won the argument. It wasn't a question of whether Pia was coming but when.

Almost exactly two months later, at six-fifteen in the morning, Kate took a pregnancy test. She had been taking them with embarrassing frequency, unbeknownst to Stephen. They were trying to have a baby—one baby was the deal. Before she met Stephen, she hadn't been sure she wanted a baby; didn't she spend her life around kids? Benji and May were adamantly anti-marriage and child-free, generally opposed to what Benji called "all the bougie trappings"—trappings he and Kate were more familiar with from their respective childhoods in suburban Cleveland and Long Island than May was, having grown up as the daughter of Thai immigrants in East Hollywood. Their arguments were convincing. But it annoyed her when people, her sister, for example, made it about Kate: if you haven't decided by now, you're probably not doing it. Or, would you really want the hassle? The idea was that Kate was the youngest, Kate wasn't serious, Kate had been a wild teenager. (Truth be told, that phase of her life had lasted well into her twenties.) In her family mythology, Kate was the fuck-up, the one who was a little damaged, and it didn't matter that neither her adult friends nor her students nor her new husband saw her that way.

The second line on the stick that morning was faint, so faint that she turned it from side to side in the light. Did the faintness mean that the hormone level was very low, perhaps because the pregnancy wasn't viable? Or was it just early? She took a second, and thought the line was a little darker; in any case, it was there. She almost called out to Stephen, who was watching footage of hospitals in Miami, Houston, and Los Angeles on CNN in the bedroom while he was getting dressed. New cases were over sixty thousand per day. Across the country there was a spike in gun violence, and shootings in New York were up 75 percent from the previous year.

"It's only going to get worse," Stephen said from the bedroom, half to her and half to the screen.

Kate put the stick back in the empty box and put the box back in her medicine cabinet. It seemed like the wrong moment to make an announcement. There were two separate cabinets, each lit with three zinc-coated bulbs. Stephen was the last man in the world to look into someone else's cabinet. Kate looked at her face in the mirror, unchanged: the same mass of sandy hair gathered in a bun on the top of her head, the same freckles and narrow hazel eyes, the same space between her front teeth, a feature that had once humiliated her in eleventh-grade English (the only class in which she could remember paying attention) when her teacher, an Irishwoman passionate about Chaucer, had remarked that the gap had been interpreted in the Middle Ages as a sign of sexual appetite in women, and half the class had turned around and looked at Kate. This was before everything that happened senior year, because of course her reputation had preceded the event.

What was so terrible about liking sex? Not only in high school and college but sometimes even now she heard women complaining about it: he wants it *every day*; I just looked at the ceiling; do you want to hear me fake it? She'd pretended to understand, but—especially when she was young—had thought there was something wrong with her. She almost always wanted it, and preferably not over and over again with the same person. It was fascinating to see the way different boys were different, what kinds of things turned them on. She thought it was like sports, like soccer, which she had played in high school, and which was another thing a lot of women didn't get. They didn't understand that sex was a game, which you agreed to do with another person, for which you had to prepare yourself mentally but then, in the moment, had to let go and allow your body to do the thinking for you. Stephen had once made a similar comparison between athletics and medicine, and she'd almost brought up this idea—except that she'd learned from experience that no man, even those who seemed to take the most delight in her lack of inhibition, wanted to hear that she'd been equally unrestrained with a long list of people before him.

That evening he came through the front door in dark blue scrubs, the pair he stuffed into his bag before he left, so that he could change into a clean set before coming home. She was standing at the end of the hallway, and at first he didn't notice her. He was still looking at his phone as he worked the key from the lock, and the three deep lines in his forehead were very distinct. His hair was flattened from the paper cap he must've been wearing all day, along with the visor, the masks, and the gown. He looked as if he wasn't ready to be without all that equipment, somehow smaller than when he'd left that morning, his face exposed and pale, like the inside of a nut.

"Guess what?"

He dropped his keys into a dish on the table by the door, an ornamental dish with a scientific drawing of an octopus collaged into sea green glass. The recessed bulbs in the ceiling cast their dimmable light on a pair of narrow mismatched Persian rugs that had once belonged to Frances, and a squat walnut storage bench with a yellow velvet cushion, very old, with two carved arms that terminated in lions' heads. On the wall above the bench was a dark etching on dun-colored paper of a medieval hospital interior, identified in an antique font as *Hôtel Dieu*. Stephen looked up.

"Hi there—hang on."

He wasn't expecting it, and so she couldn't blame him. Or she couldn't blame him because he was still at the hospital in his head, where he'd told her that the fluorescent lights and windowless ICU now more than ever made him feel as if he were spending his days underground. After work, he had to claw his way up to the surface. She waited while he showered—an excruciatingly long shower—and changed into a second set of fresh clothes in the bedroom. When he finally came out, and she told him, he looked as if he were blinking his eyes in the light, so much so that for a second she worried he'd changed his mind. Suddenly he pumped his fist in the air, a goofy, boyish gesture she'd never seen before, or rather, that she'd seen mostly from her students. *No school Friday!* It was so silly that she made a face at him, but it was clear she had done it: the gloom had lifted for a moment. He took three long steps, put his arms around her, and actually lifted her off the ground.

"Damn am I happy," he said. Then he put her down and kissed her on the mouth, a deep kiss like the ones they'd shared on sidewalks outside tiny, expensive West Village restaurants where he'd once taken her on dates. That night they ate at home, spaghetti with a Bolognese sauce she'd made from one of his cookbooks, and had a conversation about the worst names one might give a child. Kate had grown up with a Chevy—not for the actor but for the truck in which his parents had allegedly conceived him—and at school she'd taught two girls named Chastity. Stephen swore that Pia had once played with a toddler in Amagansett called Lemon. They were laughing, but Kate could see whatever had come in the door with him creeping back. At first he'd refused wine in solidarity, but when she offered again, he accepted.

"It was a bad day," she suggested.

He shook his head automatically. "The best day. Now."

"But what happened?"

But he wouldn't say. After dinner, he called his sister, Maggie, in Boston, and left a message for his brother, Jesse. This wasn't to share the news—they had agreed to wait—but to determine if anyone was using the house in Amagansett they jointly owned. A week later, Kate was on her way to the beach, where Stephen believed she would be safe, or at least safer. The idea was that he was now too much of a risk to her and to the developing fetus. She had argued a little; she didn't want to leave him, but it was hard to insist when he was the one with all the information and experience with the disease.

The first summer they were together, they'd spent every weekend he wasn't on call at the house. It's like camping, he'd told her, very basic. A one-story shingled cottage, no AC or anything, but right next to the sea. She teased him for saying "sea," a word no one in her family would have used. And it wasn't anything like camping; he'd overstated the simplicity, presumably so that she wouldn't be expecting anything on the order of the apartment in Manhattan. But it was true that the house was run-down. He said it had been built in 1930, and renovated for the last time in the late '70s. Disagreements with his siblings about improvements had left everything untouched, apart from a few kitchen appliances and emergency work on the roof. The floors were linoleum throughout, the furniture mismatched; even the dining chairs weren't identical, although they were all in the Shaker style, some bare wood and others painted a flaking sage green, two black and shiny, embossed with the Princeton crest. There was an old upright piano, and what you might call a reading nook, with two sets of shelves where a collection of thirty-year-old puzzles faced a complete set of leather-bound volumes, *The Journals of George Eliot*, paperback fiction shoved in around them. Someone's library card was pinned to a corkboard by the back door, next to flyers for pizza and tick and mosquito control. The bedroom where they slept did have a window unit, as well as wallpaper patterned with sprigs of lilac, bedside ceramic jug lamps, and, bizarrely, an old oak church pew with the St. George cross carved into the wood.

"It's my hot Hamptons bachelor pad," Stephen said. "Do you like it?"

Of course she loved it, even before she saw the beach. The house sat in a depression in the dunes, down a long gravel driveway, surrounded by shrubs and dwarf pines that had grown almost up to the front door. You entered through the back door, where a rusted oil tank listed against the side of the house, variously sized bikes and boogie boards propped up around it. Wild turkeys and white-tailed deer were often foraging when you drove in; the turkeys stalked off disapprovingly at the sound of the car, but the deer would stop and stare, before darting into the surrounding vegetation, as if something were about to happen.

This was the summer that her father was recovering from the procedure Stephen had performed so successfully, and still seeing Stephen for the monitoring of his LVAD, the electrical pump designed to assist his heart. She had sat in Stephen's office in the Irving Center on 165th Street with her mother, whose respectful nods and murmuring gratitude were completely out of character; the only person Kate had ever seen her address this way was Father Carr from St. Pat's.

During the conversation, Kate had taken notes on her phone, mostly to avoid looking directly at Stephen. He was so competent, confident without being at all arrogant. He seemed to understand that they would want all the details, and if there was something they didn't understand—her mother was worried about the possibility of internal bleeding as a side effect of her father's warfarin—he would always say something like "Good question, I should've explained that better." Kate did allow herself to look at his hands, which never stopped moving, at least while he was talking. He didn't wear a ring, but many married men didn't. It was only once he began calling for daily updates on her father's condition that Kate started to wonder whether he was the most attentive cardiologist in New York, or if her feelings might be reciprocal.

When she woke up in the cottage, most mornings, the sun was already streaming into the room, falling on a quilt with a complex pattern of cotton hexagons that remained folded at the bottom of the bed, stitched by some inhumanly patient female forebear of Stephen's. He always woke up earlier than she did, and when she rolled over in the morning, she would find him staring at the ceiling, one hand behind his head. Unlike her most recent boyfriend, Benji's morose and critical bassist, Thomas, Stephen liked having sex first thing, and that summer they did it many days, as soon as Kate woke up.

One morning, though, he stopped her, not pushing her away exactly but making a space between them. "Hold on," he said.

"Are you busy?" she teased, touching him. "Do you want me to make an appointment?"

He moved her hand. "I'm serious."

She was confused and a little offended, and she pulled away, wrapped the sheet around herself. His shoulders were burned from the beach, the hair on his chest a mix of black and gray. His skin was warm and freckled, and smelled like salt.

"What?"

He put on his glasses. "I just need to know if you are."

"If I'm what?" She didn't like to talk a lot before she'd brushed her teeth.

"Serious," he said.

She hadn't hesitated. Her mother had once told her she was too transparent, and that men appreciated "a little mystery." But there was Stephen, in his glasses, looking as if he needed to be reassured, and there was nothing more appealing than vulnerability in a person who seemed always to have everything under control.

"Of course I am."

Then he gave her that disarming smile, sudden, like a kid. "Great," he said. "This is great news!" And asked her if she wanted to meet his daughter.

"It's a test," Kate's mother had said from her kitchen in Bay Shore, which she frequently used as an office. She was sitting on a stool surrounded by numerous manila folders, her earbuds in her ears and her laptop open in front of her. Now that she was retired, Nancy was always working. With a younger nurse from Bay Shore Senior, she'd started a business packaging medications for residential summer camps, an endeavor that had been so successful before the pandemic started—they'd contracted with hundreds of sleepaway camps and boarding schools across the country—that she'd been planning to renovate the kitchen.

Because of her father's condition, and because it was easy to stop on the way out to see Stephen, Kate visited Bay Shore that summer more often than she had since she was a college student. Her father, thinner and paler, sat in the den, watching soccer on fuboTV. Her paternal grandfather was from Tallaght, and so European men's soccer was something her father and Stephen had in common, a potential point of connection, although Stephen's team was PSG, a loyalty developed during a study-abroad program in college. This was where Stephen had learned to speak French, he told her, because his childhood nanny Conchita, who was from the Basque region of France, had used her own language only when she was scolding them. Kate wondered whether the kitchen might be renovated before Stephen had an opportunity to visit, and then was ashamed of that thought.

The house was a well-kept eighties-era ranch, and Stephen wasn't a snob. Or he wasn't a snob about people. It was really only the French proverb that someone—probably her mother's book club friend Elise, who had recently rebranded herself as a decorator—had encouraged her to have emblazoned on the wall above the mahogany veneer cabinets: *Mangez bien, riez souvent, aimez beaucoup.* There was nothing wrong with the sentiment, only the wall decal, the fancy script, the French. Also it was hard to imagine a less fitting expression, given that her mother did the bare minimum in the kitchen, no one in their family cared much about food, and she was pretty sure that "aimez" alluded to sex, which she was positive French Catholics thought about differently than American ones. They did laugh sometimes, mostly (and perhaps unkindly) about people like Elise, since her mother normally had little patience for pretensions of any kind.

"It's not a test," she had told her mother. "Pia's only here one month of the year. This is the only time I could meet her."

"He never spends Christmas with her?"

Her mother had an unerring instinct for holes in people's arguments; you had to be always on your guard. They'd already established that Stephen wasn't Catholic, wasn't much of anything, but had attended an Episcopalian church once in a while as a child.

"Every other."

"So this isn't his year?"

"I don't know." It was his year, but Stephen had wanted her to meet Pia right away.

Her mother frowned and entered something into her Excel spreadsheet. A campful of kids with insufficiently labeled baggies of prescription drugs from home was a nightmare for nurses; her mother had identified this very narrow problem, and her younger partner had brought the idea into the digital age. It had been a struggle for her mother to keep up with the technological aspects of the business, but she had developed a system that worked for her, with the manila folders and the spreadsheets and sheer force of will.

"Be prepared for an uphill battle" was all she had said.

By contrast, the summer she got pregnant was lonely at the beach. Her sister and the kids drove out twice for the day, and her college roommate Abby came on her own for a weekend from Philly. When Kate apologized for the shabbiness of the house, Abby looked at her like she was crazy.

"This is paradise," she said. "When I think about how I won't see the kids for three days, I want to cry."

"You miss them that much already?" They were standing in the kitchen, packing some snacks for the beach. Abby laughed.

"God, no. I just can't believe I'm going to have to go back in a couple days."

Kate added some salt-and-vinegar chips, and then some nectarines to compensate. She wanted to tell Abby, but they hadn't confided in anyone but family yet.

"We're trying," she said instead. "But I feel like I should be doing something to prepare."

Abby tucked her hair behind her ear. It had always been curly, cut to her chin, medium brown but now with an inch of gray roots. Her friend leaned one hip against the counter and looked out the window over the sink to the driveway, where two deer were nosing in the shadows under the trees.

"Just enjoy being alone," she said finally. "I don't mean alone-alone—I'm glad we're hanging out. But psychologically, at least until it happens. Just enjoy not having to love anything that much."

Kate was relieved when Stephen began coming for weekends in August. Cases were way down, although Stephen said they were in a "liminal zone," waiting for things to change again. He felt strongly that she should put herself on the list of immuno-compromised faculty who would continue to teach remotely, while others went in a few days a week for the hybrid, and Kate emailed the principal with a mixture of guilt and relief.

Twice, thrillingly, she had a virtual OB appointment, but these ended up being only a series of questions with a prac-titioner who was clearly eager to get to the next ten-minute appointment. Was she wearing a mask? Was she eating? Was there bleeding or cramping? The baby was big enough to see on a sonogram screen, but she had already been told that this would happen only twice in person, due to the restrictions. Stephen assured her that this was unfortunately standard pre-natal care under the circumstances, but she couldn't help feel-ing like it was a punishment meant specifically for her.

"Terrible timing," her mother remarked, when she drove out for the day in the middle of August. She was unimpressed by the state of the house, which confirmed certain biases she had against summer people. Kate knew her mother would have been equally critical of one of those houses with a spar-kling pool, a white marble kitchen, and an immaculate series of empty guest rooms—"mansions in the potato fields," she called them. The waste associated with seasonal residences was one of her canonical topics. Twenty-three Sandpiper was more modest, but it was falling apart. The state of the oil tank in par-ticular appalled Nancy; she wouldn't be surprised if you could poke a finger right through the rusted steel. If Kate didn't do something about that at least, and soon, it wasn't likely to make it through another winter. Kate reminded her mother that the house was jointly owned by three people, none of whom was her, and that she and Stephen had been married for less than a year.

"I'm just saying that if there are things to deal with, you should deal with them now. Soon you're not going to feel up to it."

"I thought the second trimester was supposed to be better," Kate said.

"It is," her mother said darkly. "I just want everything to go smoothly this time."

When she told Emily about this comment afterward, her sister said that if this was the only time their mother alluded to Kate's previous pregnancy, she should consider it a small victory. And she had to agree that her sister had a point. But the ease with which Emily offered her opinion made her suspicious. Were her mother and sister in the habit of going over this ancient history, when they couldn't think of any fresher material?

Nancy had been there only a few hours before she asked about Pia. She was cutting a pineapple she'd brought with her from the ShopRite in Bay Shore, ignoring the perfectly round, seedless watermelons Kate had gotten from the farmstand. Cut open, they revealed startling yellow flesh. Now she stopped what she was doing and stared.

"For the entire year?"

"Indefinitely," Kate said. "If it works out."

Nancy made a sound with which Kate had long been familiar.

"Girls that age . . ." her mother began, and was diverted, searching for the trash to discard the rinds.

"Here, I'll take that."

"You, yourself," she said, not relinquishing the rinds. "Holy mother of God. You think I don't remember?"

3

8-20-20

I'm writing this from the "field," LOL. Inès gave me this note-
book before I left, because she knows I love graph paper. So
I could keep notes. (Not a diary. "Diary": cringe, vomit, etc.
etc.) Now that I have a reason, it's not so bad to go back. I told
R that I was doing it for him & he laughed like it was a joke.
Because he doesn't think I'm serious.

"Étudie bien, Ruheruhe," he said.

PPT–LAX. LAX–JFK. Dad was going to meet me at the
airport, but he had to be at the hospital. He said just to use his
card and Uber. He didn't say not to tell Mom, but I know he
hopes I won't. Honestly it's fine with me, because the whole
airport welcome thing is so awkward. I'll see him at the new
apartment instead. Maybe she'll be out.

The first time was at Sandpiper, when I was 13:

DAD: Pia, I want you to meet Kate.
ME: . . .
HER: Pia, it's SO nice to meet you.
ME: Yeah . . .

Her hair was dirty-blond, not blond. Hippie dress & gladiator
sandals, like the demi wives R makes fun of at Caraméline. She
was so nervous around me.

HER: I don't know if your dad told you, but I teach high
    school.
ME [then]: I'm in middle school.
HER: Your dad says the French system is very challenging.
ME: School isn't that hard for me.

True then, except for science. M. Joly said I wasn't trying & he
knew I could do better because he knows my mom. So unfair.
Inès was just as bad & he was like, Mais la littérature, c'est ton
fort, faut dire . . .

D: The LVAD is a device that assists the lower left
    ventricle of the heart in pumping blood to the rest
    of the body. [That's Dad, giving you all the not-
    important details.]
HER: He invited me for a coffee in the hospital cafeteria.

Realized they were actually telling me their meet-cute story.
Also, their meet-cute story takes place in the HOSPITAL.

D: I go to get the coffee, but I want to give her something.
    So I see this bear at the register.
ME: Like a stuffy?? [Then I'm embarrassed that I still call
    them that.]
HER: Yes! Because they have a few things from the gift
    shop. At the cafeteria.
D: Only I get it back to the table and realize it says "Get
    Well Soon."
HER: And so I ask if it's for my dad?
D: And then I realized I was making a mess of it. So I just
    ask if she'd like to go to dinner one night.
HER: And I said yes!

The whole time I was thinking of how I was going to write it
down to tell Inès bc that was after Perpignan and I knew I was

going back to Paris end of summer. But I didn't have this note-book then. But obviously, I remembered. And Inès was dying when I told her.

    I: What'd you say?
    ME: I just stared at them like, you idiots, why are you
        telling me this?
    I: hahahaha

But really I laughed and said that was funny and did she still have the bear? & of course she LOVED that.

    HER: Yes, I do! I'll always keep it.

I don't care if she likes me, so why did I do that?

It's only been four hours, so four more to L.A. If you look at the flight map, it's blue all around the icon. Same if you look out the window, no land anywhere. South of here is Point Nemo, the "most remote place on Earth." No one lives there. If you did, your closest neighbors would be the astronauts on the International Space Station. In 2031, the ISS is actually going to fall into the ocean right there. They call it a "space graveyard," because the astronauts don't want their space junk to hit anyone.

    R says Tahitians don't think about it like that. Oceania isn't many tiny countries in a big ocean but instead one big family whose home is the ocean, which is like a living thing or a god. So it's even worse to dump trash there than it is on land. Nemo means "no one" in Latin. Like the captain in <u>20,000 lieues sous les mers</u> and the fish in the cartoon. In 2031, I'll be 26.

4

The bad habit of writing to Nathalie had begun with the pandemic and continued into the summer while Kate was away—one morning at 5:15 for example, when he was drinking espresso, trying to counteract the pounding in his temples and the sand behind his eyes, due to a serious error in judgment that had led him to consume either two or three vodka tonics the previous night when he got home from the hospital, while watching FC Bayern beat PSG in the Champions League final. The second (or third) was in celebration of a beautiful attacking header by Kingsley Coman, to score off a bounce in the upper right quadrant. Coman had trained at PSG, and then come to Bayern via Juventus to face his former club, a fact that had seemed relevant last night to Stephen's own life—some significance he couldn't now recall.

"Dear Nathalie," he always began, as if she were someone he vaguely knew in procurements, responsible for logging the most recent shipment of gowns from Guangzhou. "How are you?" She used to make fun of his formality, the way he might call her at midnight when he was leaving the hospital, after they were officially together, but separated by their respective careers, and ask, how are you? "I am well, and you, Stephen?" She said he was her high school English textbooks come to life. He explained that it was his mother's training; Frances believed in ritual, in the power of language to accomplish things in the world. You don't take a woman for granted, and you've already eliminated 75 percent of your rivals. This wisdom hadn't made the least impression on his brother, Jesse, who was decidedly in the other 25 percent of men—who took women for granted all the time and were nearly always successful.

"S," Nathalie addressed him, which made him feel like a different person, more unusual and mysterious, possibly even dangerous:

> We read about the mental health of doctors. I tell Pia you are like the tiki of Hiva Oa, sur qui on peut compter, but she worries. And I'm working so much. I worry about her without real friends here. This is nothing compared to our worries about you. And I hope that you will write to me honestly, at least: truly, how is it going for you?

That message came in April, in the worst of it. He took a car back to the apartment, where Kate might be on Zoom with her students, or struggling with some aspect of Google classroom. She had a verbal tic that he found slightly irritating, using "meanwhile" as a transition to an entirely new subject. *Meanwhile, this link is broken. Meanwhile, what should we have for dinner?*

Meanwhile, three more ICU nurses had contracted Covid. Sometimes from the window of his Lyft, he saw Vivek running out the Fort Washington exit, back to his girlfriend's place downtown. "Running it off," he told Stephen, and it made him feel like shit. His apartment was only a few miles away, and he at least might have walked; many mornings, he would take a gym bag to work, only to return home with it in the car. Meanwhile, he was gaining weight. Of course Kate didn't say anything. He could tell she wanted him to share more of what went on, but if he didn't tell her, there was at least one part of his life where it wasn't happening. Instead, behind the tinted windows of the car, a sheet of heavy plastic separating him from the driver, double masked and with his earbuds in, so that no communication was expected, he relaxed into his phone and wrote to Nathalie:

We're burning through 1000 gowns a day. At this rate, we'll be out
in ten days. We're likely to get more before that happens, but what
about Elmhurst in Queens, or SUNY Downstate in Brooklyn? Do you
remember Vivek, my brilliant resident? He says he's thinking of going to
India and staying with his grandparents, who live in—I can't remember
the city. Doing public health over there. (So far India is a success
story, maybe because it's such a young population.) He's talking about
abandoning his career, everything. I said that we all had thoughts like
that these days, and that I felt like going to Rangiroa in the South Pacific,
where I once spent some time. But I think his doubts are more serious
than mine. Or he's still young enough that he can imagine another life.

They had a history of written communication. Six months
after they were married, she'd left to do postdoctoral research
on Rangiroa. He'd been studying for his cardiology boards
anyway, and he said that knowing he was getting on a plane
to Tahiti immediately afterward was what had gotten him
through it. It was just something he said, though—he would've
felt the same if Nathalie had been doing postdoctoral research
in Buffalo or Newark. That was the way he felt about her then.

People said that long distance was dangerous, but they'd
decided that was a cliché. They were both too busy to do much
besides work, and it felt great to know that this other part of
their life was settled. He thought it was better than if they'd
been two residents sharing a cramped apartment near the
hospital, and maybe even better than being two biologists on
Rangiroa. When he described his work to her—the difference
between an atrial fibrillation and a flutter, for example—her
interest made it wonderful again; maybe it was the same for
her, when she sent a grainy photo of herself in the research
station, holding a settlement tile of infant coral from the genus
Pocillipora. "Regarde, les enfants!" she wrote, but it was hard to
appreciate purple blobs on five inches of terra-cotta tile next to
Nathalie's eyes and giddy smile in the other half of the frame.

Now, for the first time since Nathalie got the job at Woods
Hole and got pregnant, and they began living together for

real—now that they were divorced and separated by more than six thousand miles—they were writing to each other again:

> I was looking at the case numbers for your area—I guess you know there's nothing on Mo'orea yet, and I saw it was the same for Rangiroa. Tahiti is predictably worse, but they're doing all the right things with testing and the moratorium on cruise ships. Have you heard whether the Pension Tamatuamai is still there? I'm guessing yes, and that our bike taxi guy is still sitting at the bar with a Hinano, yelling at any lucky couples who got stuck there.

They had been heading down to see the sunset and escape the pounding New Zealand hip-hop at the bar, when the taxi man yelled after them in heavily accented English, "Too much love will kill you!" Nathalie had been offended, until Stephen explained that it was a song. Then she had wanted to discuss that lyric deeply, much more deeply than Stephen (and perhaps even Brian May) had ever considered it before. Rangiroa wasn't an island but a coral atoll, a circlet of volcanic rock with an interior lagoon. The atoll wasn't especially sandy but was one of the most diverse and plentiful habitats for coral in the world. Nathalie studied *Acropora*, *Pavona*, and *Porites* corals, but her specialty was the brush or "cauliflower" genus called *Pocillopora*, from Latin words meaning "opening" and "cup."

When he first met her, he'd been charmed by the contradictions between the stereotypical Frenchwoman he held in his head and Nathalie, who didn't care about clothing or style in general, who didn't read anything but marine science, and who loved American action movies, especially the Fast & Furious franchise. She genuinely enjoyed the food at Chipotle. The one thing about her that seemed particularly French to him was the seriousness with which she considered human relationships, as if they were concrete objects that could be studied and understood. She liked to ask him about the biology of the brain—she understood, at least, the silliness of locating human emotion in the heart—how electrical impulses might translate into the desire to see someone every day, or to let one date turn into another, which they got in the habit of doing soon after they met, spending every moment of their overlapping time off on the phone together. He was accustomed to the kind of relationship in which you did activities with a person who attracted you, made veiled references to that attraction, had more than usual to drink, and went to bed together. If all that went well, you continued sleeping together without discussing it much, because by then you were a couple.

With Nathalie it was different. They had met at a birthday party for one of his med school classmates, Tanya. The party was at a Burmese restaurant, and the owners had set up a long table in the back garden, underneath strings of lights. It was summer and she was wearing a white dress and green plastic flip-flops, which she made a reference to right away. She said she was wearing "tongs" because she had forgotten to pack anything but running shoes. He said that he was wearing this shirt because nothing else was clean, and got her to laugh. (Actually he'd chosen that blue linen shirt with the mandarin collar because he thought it was his most casually stylish.) She said that she had come to the States for a fellowship at Woods Hole, and that her specialty was coral reproduction, especially under the stress of climate change. She told him that coral could reproduce sexually or asexually, and that most sexually reproducing stony coral were capable of producing both male and female gametes.

"This is called broadcast spawning. Most people think that it is triggered by the moon, but actually the lunar cues are only preparing them to spawn."

He found it immediately touching that she believed in the existence of a large population of people deeply interested (but unfortunately misinformed) about coral reproduction.

"Then the sunset triggers the release of genetic material."

"So the moon just puts them in the mood." He remembered he'd felt mortified by this attempt at playfulness. It was so rare that he had the opportunity to socialize at all, and now he had somehow found himself talking about sex, sort of, with a beautiful French marine biologist in a white sundress, and he was ruining it because he had no practice.

"Yes," Nathalie had said. "Then the polyp releases a bundle of eggs and sperm into the water. Like ejaculation." Then they sat down to dinner.

Dear Nathalie,

There's a woman named Carmen. She's 32 and she's four months pregnant. Her husband and her mother keep calling me for updates, because she hasn't been picking up their calls. All she wants is me, and all she wants is to ask over and over again whether we can take the baby out now. I told her that from what we knew he was safe in there. I said it was like the best possible PPE, and I wished we could all walk around in amniotic sacs, but she just sort of looked at me, like, how could you be joking about this? She said it's not a boy, it's a girl, and her name is Violeta. That was yesterday or maybe the day before. Today we had to put her on a ventilator.

This happened two months before Kate told him she was pregnant. They were pregnant, was what she'd said. That locution had been popular around the time Pia was conceived, but Nathalie would have none of it. *Ah, toi? Tu n'es pas enceinte, pas du tout* was how she actually said it. Nathalie's pregnancy had come at an inconvenient time; she was supposed to be going to Sumatra to assess damage to reefs around an island called Weh, due to the tsunami. The initial reports about the coral were hopeful, in contrast to all the other reports about the tsunami. There was continuing danger due to all the debris in the water, and the runoff from Banda Aceh, but the stony corals affixed to the seafloor had actually survived the hundred-foot waves, and the reefs would recover, in the absence of other stressors.

Nathalie had laughed at that: in the absence of other stressors. In an imaginary world in which there are no other stressors. He couldn't remember if she'd said that in English or in French. She just wanted to dive. She read him bits of articles, anecdotal evidence about diving during your second trimester, as opposed to the first or the third, when it was clearly inadvisable. Casually, testing him out. He didn't say anything, because it wasn't a real debate; he was a doctor for god's sake, and there was absolutely no reason to take that kind of risk.

When Pia went through her Little Mermaid phase, about six years later, he had to be the one to watch it with her: Nathalie hated both the revised ending of the Disney version and the unflattering depiction of coral polyps, imprisoned in the sea witch's garden. He had to disagree. He thought the songs were great, and that the movie made a valid point about obsession. He himself had married a kind of mermaid, one with no intention of trading in her fins, who needed those periodic trips underwater in order to maintain her equilibrium.

S,

Here we are infuriated by news about the mining companies going ahead with exploratory missions. There are three types of seafloor mining—nodules, cobalt crusts, and sulphides from hydrothermal vents—but they amount to the same thing: destruction of an ecosystem about which we know almost nothing, with technology whose impacts we cannot predict. Almost every time the technical divers go down, we find something new. We believe there are between 500,000 and 10 million species down there, most of which we've never seen. This is like finding another Amazon basin and destroying it before anyone has walked under the canopy.

You will be interested in this. A team near Kiribati has discovered immunosilent bacteria, living alongside deep water corals and sponges. You'll read about it in a few months in your journals, but this is something my colleague on the expedition says no one expected. To the human immune system, these bacteria are aliens—so strange they are invisible. With these silent microbes, we could deliver immunotherapies that would normally be rejected by a human host. You see what this means, don't you?

She was dejected and then she could turn on a dime—she'd always been that way. But who, he wondered, was "we"? Raffi was the name that came up most frequently, sometimes described as her "fixer," other times as Pia's diving instructor. Just because she mentioned him so freely didn't mean anything. She asked about Kate in the same overt manner, and although he didn't like it—he would have liked to keep the two women entirely separate in his mind—he could hardly fail to answer her questions, especially once it was decided that Pia would come to New York.

When Nathalie called, Kate was often in the room. She always offered to leave, and he always declined; he liked the idea that everything was clear and aboveboard. He and Nathalie were all business on the phone, anyway; they talked about the airline tickets, the forms for school, the things Pia would need. As if by agreement (though they hadn't agreed) they didn't mention the emails, their pen pal relationship. The letters were in fact written by different people, younger people who expressed themselves only in that form. Otherwise, he thought, it was as if those people no longer existed.

Today was a bad day. We went back to a site where we haven't been for some time. In 2010, after the cyclone, we lost 50% of the forereef. From that time it was able to recover. But now this section is covered with macroalgae. Okay, no surprise. Mais ces coraux scléractiniaires me font pleurer. Because they just came back, and now they are dying. Have you ever cried underwater? You can't feel the tears, and so it's like your whole body is crying. No, I am not (as you accused once) comparing. It is not the same. But do you talk to your colleagues about this woman, Carmen? To your wife? I think I have seen you cry only in movies, Stephen.

The night before Carmen went on the ventilator, he found her awake. Her eyes had been closed, and then, as he checked her oxygen, they fluttered open, two wet, black stones.

"Mrs. Mejia, how are you feeling?"

"Tired, Doctor." Her voice was deep as a man's, full of gravel.

"That's to be expected. Your oxygen is good." It was 93 percent, but he knew better than to let that reassure him.

"Y el oxígeno del bebé?"

He'd never learned Spanish, but he understood that much.

"No need," he said. "We don't think you can pass it to the baby."

"You don't *think*," Carmen picked up.

"We think the baby is safe even though you're sick. Your body takes care of the baby first."

She looked at him as if she were the doctor, he the patient. "Sí, claro," she said.

He was grateful that they'd decided not to talk about the pregnancy yet, because he didn't relish letting Nathalie or Pia in on that piece of news. For one thing, he didn't want Pia to know before she arrived, in case it changed her mind. Pia's feelings about New York were much less enthusiastic than Nathalie had initially represented them, something he discovered in their glitchy and difficult weekly calls. Pia was always sitting against a yellow wall, with a small wooden crucifix to her left, next to a piece of heavy pink drapery that presumably covered a window or sliding door. He jokingly asked if she were calling him from church.

"Our landlady is Catholic."

It was crazy the way she suddenly sounded so grown-up—terrifying.

"Kate was raised Roman Catholic," he said. Kate was the subject sitting heavily between them, and in accordance with his new strategy of all-around transparency, he was trying to mention her as much as possible.

"Is she religious?" Pia asked lightly.

"Oh—no. Not at all. As a child, I meant. Kate's like us."

"Like us," Pia repeated without expression.

He couldn't tell if her skepticism had to do with the comparison, or with the idea that there was still an "us" to compare with Kate. Like you and me, he had meant, but increasingly that unit seemed to have little meaning for his daughter. He often sent her texts, since she didn't communicate via email, and it still seemed miraculous to him that his message could fly almost six thousand miles from New York to Moʻorea, and wind up in the palm of her hand. "I love you," or "How's paradise?" or "Just walked past Levain and wish I could send you one of those chocolate peanut butter cookies you used to like." To which Pia normally responded with a "reaction," the heart or the thumbs-up or the exclamation mark, and only very rarely with actual words, for example: "ça fondrait."

Pia normally spoke to him in English, although for a while when she was little, he and Nathalie had tried to conduct the entire household in French. That had gradually shifted, and he wondered sometimes if things would have worked out differently for them, if they'd stuck with her language. Sometimes, during their worst arguments, she would revert to French while he continued in English. He'd joked about that later to friends: we were *literally* speaking two different languages. Divorce was one of those things that everyone loved to talk about, whether they were married or divorced themselves. Often these sympathetic friends would say that divorce was "like a death"—in the sense that the parties involved should be given time and space to grieve. But one way that death was different from divorce was that no one ever wanted to hear about it.

The patient named Carmen died three days after she went on the ventilator. The OB team had tried, but the fetus wasn't viable. He was the one who spoke to Carmen's husband, Jimmy, and he sensed relief about this outcome at least. Stephen didn't blame him: with two other children at home who'd just lost their mother, a newborn in the ICU during a pandemic was too much. He wanted to tell Kate about it; he'd been working up to it. And then he came home one night, and she was standing in the hallway with her news.

He had been able to see she was excited about something, and disappointed when he put her off in order to execute his routine: both the dirty scrubs from his shift and the clean ones he'd worn home into the wash, and then another shower. He didn't think of it consciously, but there might have been a part of him that knew what she was going to say, because he stood in the shower a long time, furiously scrubbing his ears. He had a weird conviction that the aerosols from the ICU had made their way in through that organ, and were now replicating in his cells. He'd just read a study out of UCSF about a drug called zotatifin that could slow down the translation process, in which the virus hijacked healthy cells and used their machinery to crank out copies of itself. Just like people, viruses made mistakes when they tried to translate things, and the research group thought they could exploit those errors to slow down the disease before it mutated into more deadly strains.

Even if they found a miracle drug, it was of no help right now. He had felt almost as if he were in a dream as he exited the shower, wrapped a towel around his body, and changed into a T-shirt and sweatpants. The waking self was screaming at him to get out of the apartment, go somewhere else—anywhere. But his dreaming body continued performing the activities of ordinary life: toweling off his hair, taking clean clothes from the drawer, checking his phone. Coming out of the bedroom to find his wife, who had momentous news. Embracing her, still conscious of his ear pressed against her cheek: an ear that could not get clean enough, where stray particles might fatally linger. Now that she was pregnant, Kate's immune system was suppressed. It wasn't fanciful to think that he could be infecting her right now, and through her, their child. That would be the appropriate punishment for what he had allowed to happen to Carmen.

The only person in whom he'd confided this fear was Frances, when she called to ask how he was doing. It was much easier for him to talk to his mother than it was for other providers. He didn't have to use layman's terms, and there was no way to soft-pedal the danger. She was reading the literature, and she got it right away.

"It used to be—there was you, and then there was the patient. And now there's you and there's the patient, and you lay your hands on him, and then tomorrow you're the patient." This was on the phone, since his mother disliked FaceTime; she lived ten blocks away, but he hadn't gone near her in person since it started.

"Right."

"And then you worry about Kate."

He didn't say anything. He hadn't told his mother about the pregnancy either, although he suspected she would've guessed, given her training, had she been able to see Kate in person. Maybe she had guessed already.

"I've been reading about hell," Frances continued, and for a moment he was lost. It turned out that her classics book group had gone online, and they were making their way through the *Inferno*, again. "We chose it before the pandemic—because of the Abomination." His mother did not say the president's name on principle. "I never read introductions, but I have so much time on my hands these days. I can't remember the scholar's name, but listen to what he says: 'The exchanges with the damned serve to call into question all of the comfortable conventions that most of the time serve to mask from us our own mortality. Hell is a limit situation, like the prison camp or the cancer ward.' I can't get that out of my head."

It occurred to Stephen that his mother's obsessive thoughts

were only slightly less grim than his own. "What does that mean?"

"In hell you're powerless. As you travel through it, you're stripped of your illusions."

"Huh." He thought you were definitely powerless in the cancer ward, or the Covid one for that matter. He wasn't sure about losing your illusions.

"Anyway, what are you reading?"

A question only his mother would ask at that particular moment. He could remember her coming home from the hospital in the middle of the night, or very early in the morning. He was six, or seven, or eight, and she would come in the garden level of their townhouse on Seventy-First Street, trying not to wake anyone. She would go up past his and Jesse's room, and Mags at the other end of the hall, to the bedroom she shared with his father on the third floor. Stephen would wait a little while, then creep out of his room, just to make sure it was really her. She'd be angry if she knew he was up, and so he just peered between the smooth black balusters, so that he could see her behind the bedroom door she left slightly ajar, up on one elbow against the pillows within the low light from a gooseneck lamp, reading a little before she slept.

"Twitter," he said. "It's the only place you can get any information."

"Still," Frances said. "You need to escape a little."

"You want me to read the *Inferno* after work?"

His mother considered. "Maybe something lighter. The *Metamorphoses*? It's all about rape, of course—but otherwise it's a lot of fun."

"I can't focus on anything. I keep thinking about this woman."

"You feel responsible."

Stephen choked up unexpectedly. He cleared his throat, and excused himself, but he didn't think she was fooled. A very slight and uncharacteristic gentleness entered her voice.

"I'm skeptical, because I know you did what you could—"

"We don't know what the fuck we're doing."

"Nevertheless."

"People are bringing it home. It's happening all the time—we have doctors out now, nurses."

"So you think it's going to be an eye for an eye, with this woman?"

It sounded stupid when she said it out loud.

"Forgive me, but this is why I mentioned hell—or at least the introduction. This interpretation says that the whole point of the journey is education. The pilgrim becomes the poet, Dante becomes Virgil, or becomes himself. The reader feels sorry for the damned, just like the pilgrim does. The punishments seem to us cruel and unusual. But the distance between his feelings for the damned and what happens to them is how he learns."

"That's interesting, but—"

"But she's still dead."

"With her baby."

"Yes," his mother said, "she is."

5

thyna checked the change purse again. It was green pleather, shaped like a frog with a pink zipper for a mouth, the first place she'd ever had to put her own money. Her nana had given it to her on her fifth birthday, with five dollars inside, and she could remember at the time feeling like that settled it: she was grown. She still kept it for the laundromat, but now, somehow, it was empty, even though she'd been sure she had at least a ten. She also had two bags of laundry and her nephew, Marcus, who had been complaining about the heat all the way to the laundromat, because he'd insisted on wearing his Spider-Man costume.

It was crazy, stupid hot, like hell was rising underneath Targee Street, and the devil himself was frying the pavement on his flaming fork. At least the AC was good inside, which was why they'd walked to this one. There was a problem with their own washer, and Athyna's mom wanted to wait until next month to get someone to fix it. Her sister, Breanna, was at work, and that was how Athyna had Marcus all day.

Marcus was four and, Athyna had to admit, really sweet. He was never mean, and he didn't have tantrums. There was nothing wrong with her nephew except that he did everything a little slower than the average kid. Sometimes that was good, because he could play a long time by himself at home without getting bored or needing anything from Athyna. But if you had to go somewhere, it was a nightmare. Everything was interesting to Marcus: the phone repair place, a nasty-looking pit bull attached by a leash to a nasty-looking man, even the mica in the sidewalk, which she too had once thought was diamonds. The difference was that she'd believed whoever set her straight the first time. With Marcus, it was like *but maybe* over and over. It was on one of these endless stops, outside a deli with a coin-operated machine that offered plastic toys in plastic bubbles, the nylon cord from the laundry bags cutting into her shoulder, that she absently read the tabloid headline on the wire shelf of papers: STATEN ISLAND PEDO USED TREATS TO LURE TOTS. Why did they always have to write it like that, like it was exciting news?

"That one," Marcus said, pointing at one of those rubber balls with the swirling colors, which she actually still liked herself.

"You wouldn't get that one," she said, taking his hand.

There were three people in the laundromat: another girl her age on her phone, a lady with a shopping cart who looked about a hundred and ten, and the nicer of the two women who normally worked at Laundryland. Everyone was wearing a mask, although the girl kept pulling it down to take selfies. Who wanted everyone to see them at the laundromat? Like, MIRL #dirtyclothes, or @Laundryland rn! She and her best friend, Krystal, had decided to be off social for the summer and they didn't even miss it.

"Get me some Cheez-Its, please, Teetee?" He couldn't say the *th* sound, and so he'd always called her Teetee, which she didn't mind. Even adults sometimes had trouble with her name. If her mother was going to name her Athena, because she'd gotten really into some book about Greek mythology, she wished she'd spelled it the regular way, so people would know. A-thigh-na was the most common mispronunciation, and also the worst because of potential rhymes. The goddess of wisdom, though—she had to admit, she really liked that.

Of course Marcus liked Cheez-Its, of all snacks. He was such a weirdo. Even Breanna thought he was weird, which was part of the reason Athyna was patient with him. When Breanna heard she was having a boy, she'd started expecting some kind of little version of his daddy, Elijah, some kid who would come out wearing tiny Kyries. The joke was on her, because Marcus was way more like Athyna and their mom than he was like either of his parents, more likely to sit around eating Munchkins and drawing monsters than to be dribbling a ball or tearing up the climbing structure at the playground. Marcus hadn't walked until he was almost fifteen months, and her sister had been freaking out about what was wrong with him.

There were vending machines in the corner, so of course Marcus was begging.

"Teetee doesn't have money," she said. "We have to go home and come back."

He did understand then, and she saw his crying face starting. She couldn't stand it when he did that, especially because he didn't do it that much, and it was justified. She should've checked the green purse before they went out. It was almost a hundred degrees in the sun, and Marcus was wearing a long-sleeved costume. She rolled the sleeves and pulled up the legs to make shorts.

"But I'm hungry," he said. "And thirsty."

"I told you, I don't have money."

The attendant was a woman her mom's age in a navy Laundryland polo, with a plastic name tag that read Altagracia. Dominican, maybe. She reached under the counter and took out a paper cup. "You can get him some water."

Athyna went to the laundry sink outside the bathroom and brought the water for Marcus, who cheered up. She overdid it on the thank-yous, and then used it as an opening. "I forgot my change at home."

"We have a machine."

"I mean, I have to go home for money."

Altagracia shook her head sympathetically. "This weather."

"It's just, with him . . ." She indicated Marcus, who was sitting on a molded plastic chair, looking up at the shopping network on the ceiling-mounted TV. There were clear beads of sweat all around his hairline, but you could see he was cooling down. There was no reason to take him out again. "I could leave him here and run back. It's just around the corner."

Even Altagracia was on her guard then.

"I'm not watching him," she said.

"He doesn't need to be watched," Athyna assured her. "He's just going to sit here with my phone. For like ten minutes." She thought it was closer to fifteen, especially because she wasn't sure where there was any cash in the house, and would have to look. "Hey, Marcus," she said, before the woman could argue. "I got to go home and get money. Want to watch *PAW Patrol* on Teetee's phone?"

That little blank stare while the information was processing, and then, "*PAW Patrol* is onna roll!"

"You don't talk to anyone." She wanted to tell him to ask Altagracia if he needed anything, but she was listening. "Just look at the show till I get back." The show was twenty-two minutes, and she could definitely be back with the money by then. "You have to go potty?"

Marcus shook his fat cheeks solemnly. Her mom had just given him a haircut, and his face looked even rounder than usual. His belly made a convex shape under Spider-Man's cut red abs. "Just sit here," she told him. "Don't move. I'll be right back." She gave Altagracia a little wave of thanks, which she only very slightly acknowledged. Then she opened the glass door, into the breathtaking street.

Athyna was going to be a senior in the fall, and maybe her mom and her sister felt sorry for her, because who wanted to be a senior this year? She was doing her STEP program online, and her mom told her to focus on that and not to bother looking for a job—mostly because there weren't any. That was nice of her, and she was thrilled not to go back to the Burrito Bar, where she'd worked last summer for Mr. Thomas, the manager, the less said about him the better. But it was annoying when Breanna said she could "just look after Marcus," as if that was some great gift she was bestowing on Athyna. Her sister, who used to say that the sight of blood made her faint, now worked as a phlebotomist at a fertility clinic in Manhattan, and she and their mom both congratulated themselves on having a skill that had become even more useful during the pandemic.

Breanna blamed the conception of Marcus on their dad passing, like she was crazy from grief and couldn't help getting pregnant. Neither Athyna nor her mom bought that story, and her mom barely talked to Breanna for five out of nine months of the pregnancy. She did talk in Breanna's presence, however, delivering little homilies on the subject at hand. She had gotten pregnant young, but not as young as Breanna. And, unlike Breanna, she'd been married at the time. Did anyone, including Elijah's mother, who was a security guard at PS 57, really think Elijah was going to act like their own father, who had always worked so hard for them, who had stayed with them until the end? Their father was probably looking down from heaven at Breanna's belly right now and crying. Athyna had to admit that her sister's silence during these onslaughts was impressive, at least until the night she and their mother finally had it out. They'd been at each other's throats when Athyna gave up and went to bed, and when she got up to go to the bathroom around two, her sister was still crying in the living room, their mother's voice insistent, but too low to hear.

But the next morning, all the tension in the house was gone and her sister and her mom were talking about the med tech program in phlebotomy. That was a relief, but there was a part of Athyna that resented it, because during the time her mother and her sister weren't speaking, she'd been like an only child. She showed her mom her drawings again, like when she was little, and they had sometimes done baking projects on the weekends, because they both liked decorating cakes. They had a full set of pastry tips from Ateco, Liqua-Gel food coloring in twelve shades, and all kinds of Wilton edible decorations. When her dad was alive, they'd only done it on special occasions, but after he was gone they went crazy: a cake that looked like Hogwarts for no reason, with upside-down sugar cones dipped in melted chocolate for the turrets, and sparkling silver chocolate rocks they ordered online; cupcakes for Marcus's birthday that each looked like a different Marvel superhero—her Hulk especially impressive, with black licorice hair—and the one she did alone for her mom's birthday, a traditional white layer cake with complicated orange roses. Orange roses were what her dad had brought her mom every year on her birthday, and when her mom saw the cake, she put one hand over her eyes and said, "Teena baby, you *didn't*."

Once her mother and her sister were on good terms again, they spent a lot of time talking about Breanna's health, and how sugar was bad for the baby, and most of the baking stopped. Her sister didn't even mind their teasing about her belly, because Breanna was one of those people who didn't gain weight anywhere else, and there was also the implication that her looks were what had gotten her into this mess in the first place. Back then Elijah was working for a fancy event company in Rossville, being sweet to Breanna and taking her out for her favorite lychee bubble tea at the place on Forest Avenue. Breanna showed Athyna some Instagram celebrity with a sick body, in black lace underwear cuddling her baby. "That's some fucked-up shit," Athyna said at the time, but Breanna said, "It's possible." "If you're some piece of trash married to a movie star, maybe," their mother said, but in fact it was possible, because Breanna's body was back to its annoyingly perfect shape just a few months after Marcus was born—she was that vain. Athyna's mom said the two of them would cut down on the sweets as well, and also that she was a good girl about whom her mother didn't have to worry. Which meant, Athyna knew, that her mother didn't think they had to worry about her getting a boyfriend and winding up with a baby.

She'd meant to run, but it was too hot. And then inside the house she had to go through Breanna's bureau and her mom's nightstand before she finally found a five and four ones in the junk drawer in the kitchen. She reached in her pocket to check the time, and realized her phone was with Marcus; the clock on the stove said 11:11, which meant it was only five minutes until his show finished. She booked out of the house, dropping her keys in the process and having to fish them out of a clay pot on the other side of the railing, in which her mom had once planted purple mums. By the time she was back on Targee, she could smell herself, the sweat in rivulets from her neck down to her bra, the sleeves of her T-shirt slick and tight under her arms. It was so hot her glasses were fogging, and she thought for a second that she was imagining things when she saw the attendant hurrying in the opposite direction, yelling in rapid Spanish into her phone.

Athyna called out, "Hello, ma'am? My nephew?" But either the woman didn't hear, or whatever she was discussing on the phone was too important to be bothered with a teenage customer. And there was no reason to think the emergency had anything to do with Marcus, and the laundromat was not on fire, at least as far as Athyna could see. She was almost there, just half a block, jogging and willing him to be there, her nephew in jigsaw pieces behind the signs on the glass door, the red one that marked the hours and the green one instructing you to wear your mask, bent over the screen laughing at Rubble and Chase. She pushed away the image of the soft-jowled white man in the mug shot—they all seemed to look like that—who might grab a little boy from a laundromat in the time it took to say, *Come here,* or *Look what I have for you.* Was there a kid on earth more trusting than Marcus, or less likely to run? She saw it so clearly that when she burst through the door into the frigid air, she wasn't surprised to find the orange chair empty, except for the black brick of her phone in its dirty rubber housing. Marcus nowhere in sight.

"The little boy," she yelled. "Did you see a little boy?" But TikTok girl was gone, and it was only the ancient woman by the dryers, who turned to her quizzically, either because she was deaf, or because she didn't speak English, or because she no longer had any clue what was going on around her.

"A little boy this big," Athyna insisted. "Niño, niñito."

And then the woman pointed, and Marcus stepped out into the aisle, from where he'd been hidden behind the washers, no doubt drawn by the captive snacks and sodas in the illuminated machines against the wall.

"Didn't I tell you?" Athyna screamed at him. "*Didn't I?* I said stay in that seat right there! What're you doing up? See if I get you *anything*!"

It was crazy because he was only four, but he could read her. He knew when to worry and when everything was going to be okay. He also knew better than to smile, but he wasn't crying. He just stood there looking at her with his giant brown eyes.

"Thank you," she told the woman, because she really was grateful and also because she hated the idea, held by adults of many races whom she encountered on mass transit, that all Black teenagers were rude and wild. "Thank you so much." As if that old lady was the reason he was still here, instead of abducted by some psycho for curious strangers to sigh over tomorrow in the *Post*.

Her hands were shaking as she put the bills into the machine, one by one. "I don't know if I'm gonna have enough," she told him, but her anger was already giving way to relief as she crouched in front of the machine, taking extra care, inverting his little shorts and briefs, her sister's tank tops and her mother's yellow nightgown, like her own hot blood was slowly being replaced by something cool and turquoise blue, like the aloe vera gel Breanna rubbed on her skin after they got home from a day at South Beach. She got him his Cheez-Its and told him it was his last chance, and he settled happily in the chair. A moment later he was watching the rest of the show, so absorbed that she could rest her hand on his knee, still dimpled like a baby's, without it seeming too much like giving in.

6

As soon as Pia left, Nathalie moved back to the station. The lockdown was technically over, and it was easier to move around the island. The curfew could be reinstated at any time, though, making it a hassle to get between home and work. Living at work eliminated that problem. She gave up her lease on the cottage in Ha'apiti that she'd taken because it was Pia's favorite spot. Now she had a plain double room at the station to herself. The rooms were spartan: two single beds, a dresser, a tiny bathroom barely bigger than the stall shower, but she didn't mind. She mostly ate at the picnic tables around the station, or at the roulottes; once a week, she drove to the Super U Aré in Maharepa for breakfast supplies: coffee and granola and yogurt, star fruit, mango, and bananas from the vendors outside. She felt as if the pandemic had shuttled her back to her life as a graduate student, before she met Stephen, and she had all kinds of ideas. She woke up thinking about them.

Her two other students had gone home five months ago, when everything first shut down, but Gunther had correctly surmised that having the station's resources, the reef without the normal touristic pressures, and her full attention virtually guaranteed that he'd receive his PhD ahead of schedule. Not to mention the choice between spending the pandemic in Hamburg or Stuttgart (or wherever he was from—she could never remember), as opposed to on a pristine South Pacific island. Or no longer pristine, but still more beautiful than nearly everywhere else in the world. What more could you possibly want?

Gunther had dark, curly hair that didn't change color no matter how much time he spent in the sun, and a small, round face at odds with his lanky figure. He reminded Nathalie of a Modigliani, purposely distorted. He was successful because, unlike many students who thought they wanted to be marine biologists, he already had the personality of an engineer. He was a workhorse, an obsessive tinkerer who also had a knack for the machinations involved in securing funding. They communicated easily in English, but the conversation never seemed to progress to the personal. She didn't know anything about his family at home, or whether there was a romantic partner who resented his extended stay on Mo'orea. She didn't think it was a language thing, since his English was almost as fluent as hers. He spoke enough French to get by, but wasn't popular with the Tahitian staff at CRIOBE like some of the graduate students were—even the Americans, who rarely spoke any other languages. She thought it was his single-minded energy that turned people off; she could respect and even encourage it, but it was plain that he ran on an internal combustion engine for which the fuel was pure ambition.

They were working side by side in the lab one morning soon after Pia's departure, when Raffi walked past their open door carrying a brand-new gray Pelican case, of the type used to keep sensitive equipment dry on the boats. This wasn't unusual in itself. When she'd first started coming to Mo'orea, Raffi worked for the station's technical staff on an as-needed basis, maintaining the buildings and grounds as well as the boats. His expertise in the water had soon led him to start supervising dives for visiting scientists, who were inevitably charmed by his knowledge of the island. After the American station opened its cultural center, in partnership with the island's most prominent Tahitian cultural ambassador, the French had attempted to compete by building an auditorium for community programs and a spectacular new biodiversity museum. Giving Raffi the title of cultural liaison was a move Nathalie had enthusiastically supported, and not only because it looked good to the funders. His knowledge of Mo'orea's ecology—the intricate web of relationships between its flora, fauna, and human occupants—was the deepest and most genuine of everyone she'd worked with on the island.

He raised his right hand.

"Ia orana," Nathalie called out—the Tahitian greeting was culturally more significant than the utilitarian French and American versions, and so she tried to use it even in an international context like the lab. Raffi responded and Gunther looked up, following him with his eyes. She regretted suddenly the decision to put her student in charge of their inventory. Raffi rarely took anything without signing it out in the log, but she knew Gunther suspected (probably correctly) that the Pelican case would be used for business unrelated to the research station. If you didn't know Raffi, you might think he hadn't noticed Gunther taking stock. But Nathalie knew that nothing escaped him, a quality that made him invaluable on a boat full of preoccupied scientists, dive tanks, gear, computers, and other expensive instruments, all of which had to remain in perfect order. Raffi knew exactly what Gunther was thinking, and the set of his heavily inked back and shoulders—visible under a purple Lakers jersey as he walked down the breezeway—said that he didn't give a shit.

"DreamDives.com getting an upgrade?" The sarcasm was evident, but she noticed that Gunther waited until Raffi was out of earshot.

"I don't think so." It was the end of the worst tourist season in memory, and Raffi's side business had always come from direct referrals by the managers of small hotels and guesthouses. Nathalie suspected he was spending most of his free time on his biofuel project: a private endeavor that didn't have anything to do with CRIOBE, and that Raffi felt strongly about keeping separate. Gunther was right, though, that noses would be put out of joint if it was revealed that she'd turned a blind eye to lab supplies being misused.

"I'll talk to him."

"Okay," Gunther said, pushing his glasses up on his nose. The glasses had delicate steel frames, and he was never without them. He wore a prescription dive mask that he kept in his bungalow for fear of it getting taken by another diver. "I just hope la directrice doesn't decide to pay us a visit," he added, in a way that made it clear he hoped for nothing more.

"Focus on tank five," she said sharply.

The real problem was a personality conflict between Raffi and Gunther that Nathalie traced back to an early-pandemic dispute about sharks. In April, Gunther had come up with a secondary project that involved monitoring the rays and reef sharks that were in the habit of gathering at the stingray flat inside the lagoon, waiting for the dive boats to come and drop tuna heads into the water. A group of biologists in the Philippines had already demonstrated that shark feeding altered the ecosystems in which it took place, encouraged plant- and plankton-feeding reef fish to broaden their ecological niches and gobble up bits of tuna that the sharks—messy eaters—let fall from their subterminal, lipless mouths. The practice was technically forbidden in Mo'orea but tacitly allowed, since it enabled profitable tourist expeditions to swim with sharks and rays.

Now that there weren't any tourists, Gunther wondered how long it would take the sharks in particular to learn that the free lunches were gone. What would it say about their cognition, and their ability to adapt to the vicissitudes of the Anthropocene? It was outside Nathalie's area of expertise, but it was interesting, and she'd told him to go for it. Gunther had become increasingly excited as, over a period of weeks, the pod of blacktip reef sharks diminished and then stopped arriving in the lagoon altogether, just as he'd predicted. He had begun monitoring the associated reef fish when the sharks suddenly and without warning returned. She knew that Raffi had been present for several of Gunther's monologues on the subject, his incredulous speculation about what could be bringing the predators back to the lagoon now that there was no one dropping bloody fish parts into the water.

After one of these frustrated rants, she suggested Gunther contact the authors of the Philippine study and describe his problem. Maybe one of them would have an idea. It was only after he hurried inside to send that email that Raffi spoke up.

"But they are feeding them."

Nathalie looked at him in surprise. Raffi was methodically rinsing fins and suits in the turquoise plastic tub that sat in the corner of the open-air dive shed. His wetsuit hung loose at his waist, revealing the traditional tattoos that covered his back and right arm. Among younger people the tattoos were cool again, a return to an ancient practice once restricted by the Catholic Church.

"Who's feeding them?" Nathalie asked. "There's no one here."

"No tourists."

Nathalie started to understand. "Those Blue Lagoon guys—who run the shark tours?"

"They were afraid they wouldn't come back after the pandemic."

"The tourists?"

"The tourists will come back. But the sharks? They want them to be ready on day one. So they continue to feed them."

Nathalie couldn't help laughing, but it was disbelief more than amusement. Gunther had spent a lot of time on the sharks, when he could easily have been working with her corals. The crazy thing was that Raffi and Gunther were actually on the same side of the issue. As a scientist, Gunther would certainly have preferred that the shark feeding didn't take place. He would rather have set up a project that investigated the reef sharks' behavior in their unsullied natural environment. Raffi wasn't a trained scientist, but his ecological agenda was very clear; he was suspicious of strategies that relied on new human interventions to correct for earlier impacts. Both of them made compromises that the dire climactic times demanded—Raffi looking out for the tour operators and Gunther examining the impact of the feedings—but both also would have preferred that the compromises weren't necessary.

"So the Blue Lagoon guys are feeding them," Nathalie confirmed. "Do they also get in the water and pet them?"

Raffi gave a rare smile. The tourists were always eager to touch the rays. It didn't seem to harm the rays, who were also so accustomed to the tourists that almost no one got stung. The tour operators got paid; the tourists got dramatic underwater photos with dangerous creatures; and the rays got fed. It was a profitable arrangement for everyone involved, and she could understand why Blue Lagoon wanted to ensure its persistence through the pandemic.

"But why didn't you say anything before?"

Raffi was hanging the suits on the rail. An iron mesh screen, painted red, let air in under the roof, which had been retrofitted with photovoltaic panels. The suits drip-dried onto the smooth concrete floor, headless figures gently swinging in the breeze, knees bent and rumps extended, ridiculous in the way she thought the scientists sometimes appeared to the local people.

She thought they were right to be skeptical, especially of those scientists who dropped in and came out, publication in hand. She'd heard elders criticize their own young people for forgetting the science that had always been here: navigation, the lunar cycles, husbandry of land and fish. When you found someone unconventional, like Raffi, you admired him; you admired yourself admiring his more traditional values. But recently Nathalie had a creeping suspicion that what she was really admiring were her own values, circling like currents around the globe. Or maybe an ideal version of her own values, cribbed from an idealized Polynesian past—written over so many times as to be unknowable, at least to an outsider. In the philosophical morass of such questions, was it better to be like Gunther and engage only so far as was necessary to do the work you'd come to do?

"I didn't know you were interested in sharks," Raffi said.

"I'm not—but Gunther is. You know he's obsessed with this."

"Yes."

"But you didn't want to tell him?"

Raffi gave an innocent shrug. "He never asked."

7

The Laureate's front desk rang on her phone. Kate reminded herself, as she did every year on the first day of school, that teenagers were much younger than they looked, that there was a yawning delta between their brains and their bodies. A book she'd read for her certification argued that adolescents sometimes met the clinical criteria for psychopathy, in spite of not having any kind of personality disorder, simply because their emotions were so out of sync with their ability to control them.

"Your daughter is here."

It was the new doorman, Yuri. Probably Pia had said she was here to see her father, and Yuri hadn't made the distinction.

"Thanks," Kate said. "Please send her up." Her hand went to her abdomen, where their potential daughter or son was now decidedly both here and not. Kate didn't look pregnant yet, her mother had opined the other day over FaceTime, just "puffy."

The elevator played a female British voice when you pressed the button: *fourteenth floor, going up,* a mechanical affectation that made Kate grateful that the pandemic prevented friends from visiting her new apartment. She thought that British voices probably had a different resonance for Pia, conjuring up a different set of stereotypes.

"You're very welcome, Mrs. . . ." Yuri hesitated, because he was still learning the names.

"Kate," she said.

"Mrs. Kate," he said. "She's on her way."

It took her a moment to synthesize the child she remembered with the girl standing before her in the long, empty hallway outside 14C. It was her hair more than anything; it had been cut, maybe by Nathalie, into a sort of '70s fringe that would have been a disaster on anyone other than a fifteen-year-old who looked like Pia, and on Pia was vaguely reminiscent of a young Patti Smith. Except that someone (Kate guessed Pia herself) had also bleached the ragged cut to platinum. The contrast was especially striking with Pia's dark eyes and deep tan.

"You made it—hi! Come on in," Kate said. The fact that there was no question of hugging, now, was probably even more of a relief to Pia than it was to her, although their masks made an awkward moment even more so. Pia had been tested before the flight, but Stephen had stipulated that they would all wear masks in the apartment's public spaces, at least until the end of her quarantine. "Why don't you just leave that there."

Pia let go of her black rolling suitcase reluctantly. She was dressed for a climate-controlled aircraft rather than the weather either at her point of origin or her destination: oversized green fatigues cinched with a riveted black belt, a white hooded sweatshirt that read *Los Angeles*. Her shoes were the same Air Force 1s popular with Kate's students—amazing how adolescents the world over could agree on sneakers—but much more worn than her students' dignity would permit, maybe because of the island's dirt roads.

"My mom took me on the ferry to the airport, and then I flew from Pape'ete to New York, with a stop in L.A."

"You must be exhausted."

Pia shook her head but gave a little shiver. "I slept on the plane."

"Is it too cold in here?" Kate was now always warm.

"It's the AC," Pia said politely. "I'm not used to it."

"I'll turn it down," Kate said. "Do you want something? Juice, or tea? Or if you want to nap? Your room is ready." Like a hotel concierge, she thought. Shut up.

"Is my dad—"

"On his way," Kate said. "He got held up at the hospital." She had a flash of anger at Stephen, who might've relayed that information to his daughter himself. But at that moment, Pia's phone rang, a foreign ringtone that put Kate in mind of an emergency signal.

"Maybe that's—"

Pia glanced at the screen. "My mom." There was a flurry of French, in which Kate recognized only the word for hospital. Pia had the phone between her ear and her shoulder, and so Kate started to wheel the bag toward her room. "It's okay," Pia said. "I got it." And then into the phone, a series of negative responses. Pia was exasperated with her mother, although she wasn't making a big deal of it in front of Kate.

She retreated to the kitchen, to give Pia her privacy, but although Pia went into her bedroom, she noticed the girl didn't shut the door. Maybe she felt the language was enough of a barrier. Kate absentmindedly opened a bag of pita chips, then added extra salt—flaked sea salt that came from a white box. *Eight-dollar salt*, she heard Benji say, out of nowhere. *It's a stressful time*, she responded in her head to Benji, with annoyance—although of course that wasn't fair, since the real Benji was nowhere nearby. Who was it, noticing the eight-dollar salt, distinguished by its crystalline shape?

Pia's head popped out of the room again. "She wants to talk to you."

"Your mother?" She had never spoken to Nathalie directly, although she'd heard the voice at the other end of Stephen's phone on many occasions. Rising and falling with greater frequency than an American register, she thought, but maybe that was simply the way anyone would talk to their former partner, with whom they had to navigate the minefield of transnational parenting. Now Pia crossed the room and handed Kate the phone with an innocent expression.

"Allô? Katherine?" No one called her Katherine, certainly not pronounced in that way. And of course Nathalie was accustomed to saying hello in English.

She went with an aggressively American pronunciation: "Hi, Natalie."

"Thank you *a thousand times* for being there when she arrived. It's such a relief to me."

"Stephen wanted to be here."

Nathalie gave a chipped little laugh. "Oh, believe me. I know."

Kate had the urge to defend him against his ex-wife's sarcasm, in spite of having been annoyed herself. "His time isn't his own. He's hardly had a break since March."

What did Nathalie know of this past spring in New York, from her extraordinary perch in paradise? The constant worry about Stephen, and Kate's knowledge that her worry was selfish. The time she'd driven three hours to bring her father a prescription, and then watched her mother retrieve it from the porch, in mask and gloves, blowing a sort of kiss to Kate but clearly afraid of whatever else she might be bringing into their yard. The guilt when she logged on for class and found that Laila wouldn't turn on her camera because of an argument happening between her parents, who both had Covid, or that Ciara, who did turn it on, was wrapped in a blanket because the heat hadn't gone on in her apartment, and was apologizing to the class for not having had time to do her hair.

Pia had opened the refrigerator, and was standing there just as long as an American teenager would, staring at different varieties of flavored seltzer. So much for ecological education in the South Pacific.

"You poor things," Nathalie said. "You have been through hell. My sister in Paris, also." She sounded genuine, and Kate wondered if she'd reacted too quickly. But only for a second. "But this is the thing with Stephen, isn't it? Doing everything so completely. Never cutting corners."

"That's why he's such a good physician."

"Exactly!" Nathalie exclaimed. "You understand him."

He's my husband, Kate only barely kept herself from saying. She managed this restraint because Pia was still standing right there, having finally selected a raspberry-lime seltzer. Then she headed back to her room, closing the door this time. Now that she'd passed her mother off to Kate, she seemed remarkably incurious about what was being said.

"That kind of precision is perfect—in the hospital. But no one can get through ordinary life that way. There is too much disruption, chaos, especially now."

"Well," Kate said. "We got through the worst of it." She was conscious suddenly of sounding like her own mother, who became more resolutely plain-spoken in the face of people she thought were putting on airs. What was Nathalie getting at? Talking to Kate about Pia was one thing—you could make a reasonable argument that it was now necessary for them to speak directly—but trying to commiserate about Stephen was another. She yearned for him to walk through the door now, so that the evidence of his ex-wife's boundary-crossing would be incontrovertible.

"And you'll be teaching your students from home?"

"Yes," Kate said. "I'm remote for the time being." There was some tension between the teachers who were going into school in person and those teaching entirely online. The list of exemptions was public and hers only said "immunocompromised," but everyone knew she was pregnant. Her friend Norma said that no one was criticizing Kate, although they all thought James's obesity was total bull; he's chubby, Norma said, at best. But what teacher wouldn't welcome a year totally remote? To have it happen this year, Norma had said, was the silver lining of all silver linings; she might think she wanted to commute to Brooklyn now, but just wait until she was six months along. Kate and Stephen had talked about how much time she and Pia would be in the apartment together, but she wasn't sure she'd fully considered the reality until now. It had been less than fifteen minutes, and already she felt like she needed a break.

"Just to know that you'll be there," Nathalie said. "Because I'm so far away."

The picture of Nathalie she kept in her mind was one she'd found online, in the early days of dating Stephen. She was sitting on the edge of a boat with a landscape of choppy gray water behind her, a darker gray island in the distance, wreathed in fog. The location might've been tropical, but stormy weather made it look more like some kind of Nordic sea, cold and drained of color. Nathalie was wearing a high-necked black wetsuit, her dark hair pulled back tightly but escaping around her face, revealing an elated smile; clearly she couldn't wait to get into that forbidding water.

"I'm here," Kate said.

"Is she just there?"

"I'm sorry? Oh, you mean Pia—no, she's in her room."

"I should tell you—it has not been easy for her." Nathalie hesitated a moment. "First with me here, then New York, then the divorce and Perpignan, then with my sister in Paris. And my sister is a real—something."

"Mine, too."

"So you understand. And finally back here on Mo'orea. No school, no friends . . ."

"I understand."

"Now she has rebelled."

"You mean her hair?"

Nathalie dismissed this with a noise that seemed particularly French, a sort of *pfft*. "I am saying that you cannot trust her. She hides things."

As eager as Kate was to get off the phone, this seemed important. "What kind of things?"

"She is smart—this is the problem. Her life has been unstable—mostly my fault. I take responsibility. She is in many different environments, so she learns to adapt."

Kate was familiar with this parental tack, a way of complaining that was really designed to brag about a child's special skills or qualities. She found it more in people with the leisure to manage and analyze their children's experience. The parents with less seemed comfortable allowing chance into the equation, acknowledging that kids weren't born with equal talents, and that talent in the end mattered less than accidents in determining eventual outcomes.

But it was easy to say what other parents were doing wrong. Kate was holding Pia's phone in her right hand, her left hand gripping the granite countertop. Sunlight flooded the peaceful living room. Was there really something alive inside of her? She felt nothing but a dull ache, like her period coming.

"She seems very bright," she told Nathalie.

"Oh yes—but you have to watch her. She's an excellent liar, unfortunately. A storyteller."

"Well," Kate said, "we'll take things a day at a time. Stephen will keep you posted."

Nathalie seemed to take this hint, at least.

"I won't take any more of your time."

"I'll tell him you called."

A moment later, Pia wandered out of her room. She had changed into a pair of green-and-blue plaid pajama pants, and taken off her mask. Kate had done the same, without thinking, to talk to Nathalie.

Pia put her hand over her mouth.

"It's okay," Kate said. "I forgot, too."

Pia took her phone, then disinfected it with one of the wipes Stephen kept on the counter. "My dad says your immune system is weak?"

That was just like Stephen, to be medically precise even when lying.

"Not exactly," Kate said.

Pia nodded. "You shouldn't believe everything my mom says, either."

Kate frantically ran through her end of the conversation in her head. But even if Pia had been able to hear Kate through the closed door, she couldn't have heard Nathalie. Was it just a typical teenager's reaction to her mother? Or had she somehow guessed what Nathalie had said?

She tried to steer the conversation away from Nathalie. "It must feel strange to be here. This probably isn't what you expected."

Pia looked around at the apartment: the open-plan room with its French doors onto the useless, decorative balcony over Seventy-Sixth Street, the modern gray sectional on the Turkish rug, the mahogany dining table, and the dark green granite island, over which hung two frosted white pendant lights.

"It's what I expected."

It occurred to Kate that although the apartment was new to Pia, many of the objects in the room would be familiar: the rug, the Sam Francis lithograph above the couch, and an antique cherry armoire, a family heirloom in which Stephen stored his record collection. Now Pia opened the chest, running one finger across the sleeves as if she were looking for something. A moment later she removed one of the albums—Perez Prado's *Exotic Suite*—which featured a monumental stone head with blank stone eyes, Aztec or Incan, and a long-haired naked woman in soft focus, praying—the whole unlikely image lit with a red glow.

"I just mean—the situation," Kate said. "That your dad isn't here."

Pia looked up quizzically, as if Kate were a passerby on the street, who had taken an incomprehensible interest in her personal circumstances. "It's not *your* fault."

"Right," Kate said. "I mean . . ." But she didn't continue. The lower half of Pia's face was remarkably like her father's; the full mouth, bow-shaped and definite, looked feminine on him, while the strong chin was masculine on her. It gave her prettiness a stubborn edge.

"You must be eager to see your friends."

Pia's school was operating this year on a complicated seven-day cycle. She would have four in-person mornings, followed by two days of remote and one independent-work day. There was a fully remote option, but Stephen said that not many families had chosen it. This was in contrast to Kate's school, where the principal, a flinty and terrifyingly efficient woman named Jane, who always wore her Yale sweatshirt on College Day, reported that few students had committed to the hybrid that BEST was offering. Fear of the disease, responsibilities at home, and long commutes for many students were the reasons Jane offered, and even the teachers who would be in school part-time spent most of August preparing to teach virtually.

Kate had fantasized about the rapport she and Pia would develop during their time alone together in the apartment—and about Stephen seeing the rapport she had created, against all odds. She realized now that she had been picturing this relationship as it might develop with one of her students, whom she could assume, even before she got to know each new class, would be similar to those who'd come before. With those kids she had two advantages from the beginning: the authority of a teacher, and the solidarity of the school itself, a small public high school that ran on the Expeditionary Learning model, to which many of the students had transferred from larger and more chaotic environments. The irony of attempting to implement a project-based, collaborative, and community-focused pedagogy in the current moment wasn't lost on the principal or any of Kate's colleagues.

"Your school is beautiful," she told Pia, if only to make conversation. To get to the office of admissions for the interview, she and Stephen had entered through an elegant glass and stone exterior, then walked past immaculate classrooms and high-ceilinged science labs where students in goggles worked at rows of laboratory benches, a gym with a balance beam and actual climbing wall. Stephen had said that it wasn't the facilities but the bilingual education that he liked, since that was so hard to find in the U.S. She thought about saying that

her twelfth-grade students came from at least a dozen countries, and spoke many languages, but that would've sounded
moralizing and petty. Who wouldn't want their kid to go to a
school like the Lycée Français, if they could afford it?

"You've seen it?" Pia asked.

"At the interview."

Pia, whose whole manner had been unfocused, either because she was tired or because she was wary of Kate, suddenly
snapped to attention. The guardedness immediately fell away,
and she sounded like any American teenager. "They inter-
viewed *you*?"

"I went with your dad." Another thing about teenagers was
the hunter's sense for vulnerability or evasion. The passion for
accuracy. She knew Stephen had called his daughter to describe
the interview, how much they wanted her back. She'd intentionally not eavesdropped, and so she didn't know he'd omitted
her from his account. It made sense, though. The school had
wanted to meet with them both, but Pia's face clearly displayed
what she thought of that, and Kate didn't really blame her.

"Anyone living in the home, I guess," Kate said. "I guess
they wanted to make sure I'm not a psychopath."

Pia's mouth twitched up, a beat too late.

"It's really nice. Really serious academically, it looks like.
And I know it's hard to get in."

"You teach in a public school."

"Yep."

"Did you tell them that? At the interview?"

"They asked—yeah."

"What did they say?"

"They said, 'That's wonderful.'"

Both of them laughed nervously, maybe for different reasons. But some tension left the room.

"I hate it there," Pia said.

"At Lycée?"

She nodded.

"Oh." There had been some miscommunication. According to Stephen, the decision had been entirely Pia's. He had it from Nathalie, who'd said she'd selected it over other options. Remote schooling from Mo'orea wasn't sustainable, but Pia might have gone back to the aunt and cousins in Saint-Cloud.

"You wanted to go back to France?"

"I wanted to stay in Mo'orea." The dark circles under Pia's eyes were only partially camouflaged by the sunburn. She scratched at a bite on her neck.

"With your mom."

"And Raffi."

Was that someone Kate was supposed to know? "But your dad said there were issues with the Wi-Fi. And I know your parents wanted you to be with people your age."

"There are people my age in Mo'orea."

Were they in an argument? And if so, whose part was Kate taking?

"Your school's schedule sounds good," she said, attempting to move toward more neutral territory. "Some of my students are hybrid, too, but we're not sure how long it'll last."

But Pia wasn't listening. "I enjoy diving," she said.

"Scuba diving?"

"I do it with Raffi."

"That's—"

"My instructor."

"I've always wanted to learn."

"Do you always date older men?"

It was so casual, so unexpected that her chest constricted. *I am saying that you cannot trust her.*

"We're married, Pia."

"Right," she said. "Sorry, I forgot."

"But no. Your dad is the first."

Pia turned her back to replace the album. Kate saw that she had slightly lifted the sleeve to the left of the Perez Prado, in order to return it to the correct spot. Then she tapped both down so that the row was even, an echo of her father's method.

"That's why my mom sent me. She thought I was spending too much time with Raffi. Because he's, like, thirty. She thought it was un peu trop." Pia paused, giving Kate time to catch up. "That means 'too much.'"

"I got that."

"If it were anyone but Raffi—"

"She doesn't like Raffi?"

"Oh no, she's crazy about Raffi. That's the whole problem."

"I see," Kate said, although she didn't. Pia had a crush on her diving instructor? Nathalie disapproved because he was older, or because she had a thing for him herself?

"I'm going to the store to get something for dinner," she told Pia firmly. Stephen preferred that she order everything rather than go into businesses, even masked, but Kate felt the need to get out. "If there's anything you want?"

"No, thank you," Pia said, but when Kate had shut the door, forgot her mask, and come back in to grab one from the box on the table, next to the octopus plate, Pia stuck her head out into the hallway.

"Actually, chocolate—if you could. And anything with caramel. Oh, and graham crackers! Especially those cinnamon sugar ones, if they have them."

"Got it," Kate said. "I also love sweets."

"Mm-hm," Pia said, glancing at Kate's lower half in a way that made her wonder if the girl could tell. But no—of course she was only thinking that Kate had less leeway to eat junk than she did. She tried not to take offense.

"And for dinner—I was thinking some simple fish, or pasta with pesto."

Pia pursed her lips, raised her eyebrows and her shoulders slightly, an adult gesture of ambivalence perfectly mimicked, but not authentic.

"Which would you prefer?"

"I want everything." Her dark eyes met Kate's under the shock of white-blond hair. "I'm starving."

8

8-23-20

She's gone. How can this apt be quiet in the middle of the city? SO TIRED, but then Frances facetimed, and I felt like I should pick up. Who calls their grandma by her name? Inès and Emma say Mamie, and here it's usually Grandma or Nana or something.

F: Well this is anticlimactic.

What grandma says "anticlimactic"? She's sitting in the red room in her apartment that I used to love, with the gold samovar that's just for decoration, and the painting of lemons. Behind her is a wall of bookcases. She's wearing a white sweater, and her eyes are milky blue, like Dad's. I can't see her hands but I used to always look at them, because they were so bony and the veins stuck out. Then later I thought about how she had actually put her hands in all of those vaginas, to pull the babies out. She wears a stack of rings, one with an emerald, & I thought, does she take those off??

ME: I guess.
F: At this rate we might as well have talked while you were in Moʻorea! I wish I could give you a hug.

She's not a big hugger. She didn't make cookies (American) or Sunday dinner (French) but I remember when I was little she would take me to Serendipity and get one of those giant frozen hot chocolates. She would get two straws but never drink it herself. She told me "frozen hot" was an oxymoron, like "giant shrimp." She used some examples from Shakespeare instead of the shrimp. "Cold fire" is the one I remember. It was from Romeo and Juliet, and so I guess it's about love. But for some reason it reminded me of mom. That was the first time I heard the word "oxymoron," and it sounded so crazy to me that I thought she made it up. But later some English teacher asked us, and I was the only one who knew.

I told Frances that Dad says maybe there'll be a vaccine soon.

F: No doubt. It's very hard on you.
ME: . . .

I love Frances, but I hate when anyone feels sorry for me. I felt like saying, it's hard for you, because you could die from going to the grocery store. But that would be too mean.

F: Are you looking forward to seeing some of your old friends from Lycée?
ME: Yeah. [Like anyone even remembers who I am.]
FRANCES: That was a stupid question.

She doesn't cook, but sometimes she can read your mind.

FRANCES: I'm sure you're missing Mo'orea. I've done a lot of traveling, but never to the South Pacific. I had a friend who went, though. She went on a cruise, and before it was over she'd dated both the captain and the first mate. She was blond and very popular.
ME: What happened to her?
FRANCES: She married someone in Los Angeles. Did good works. Strangely that is what happens to popular girls, ordinarily—you would think some of them would become celebrities or something, remain beloved by

many? But in general, they chose marriage. At least in
my day.

ME: I'm never getting married.

F: That's a sound decision. What are your priorities, then?

My priorities! Dad would laugh. That's my mother, he would
say.

ME: I don't know.

F: That's fair.

But then she has a way of looking at you that makes you feel
guilty. Her hair is pure white & parted over on the side, so it's
like a very smooth cap, just past her chin. "To hide my wattle,"
she says, which is kind of funny. What do I want to be when I
grow up, does she mean?

ME: I think I want to work on TV shows. Maybe be the
director or something.

F: That's very wise. TV isn't going anywhere, I think we
can safely say. And working as a team is wonderful,
having a community of work. That's the thing I miss
most.

ME: A community of work?

F: I don't tend to get bored. But I do get lonely. We'll see
each other outdoors, your father says.

ME: He's never going to be home.

F: I know he wishes it were otherwise. You and I, though.
Let's plan on it.

8-24-20

Dad's priorities: Covid
Mom's priorities: Coral

My priorities:

1. Get R's gift

I told Inès what he calls me & she was like, rouéroué? I told her it was Tahitian for "my darling." But it isn't. It means "juvenile tuna." In Tahitian, the fish has different names at all its stages, as if I was Pia when I was little, but Pauline when I was a teenager, and then Paige in my twenties etc. etc. But R never changed the name. He's been calling me Ruheruhe since I was five and went to the Montessori with the climbing structure like a ship.

2. Get some experience
3. Get ticket

Also:

4. Don't talk to HER. Esp not about R. Why do I do stupid shit like that?

8-26-20

Open water: 18m/60ft

Advanced open water: 30m/100ft. My level, but R says I'm ready to do deep diver specialty, if I want.

Rescue diver/Deep diver: 40m/130ft

Divemaster: Same depth limit as rescue, but you need to have logged 60 dives. R says he'd probably done that by the time he was 12, spearfishing with his uncle on the reef.

Technical diver: 100m/350ft. That's without a submersible. In a submersible, people have gone a lot deeper. Last year a rich American guy named Victor Vescovo went to the bottom of the Mariana Trench, 35,853 feet down. He found an animal no one's ever seen before that looks like a stingray made out of glass. (He also found candy wrappers and plastic bags down there.) Vescovo said his mission wasn't just about science but about "testing the limits of human endeavor." The submersible is made of titanium and cost 37 million dollars. It's named the Limiting Factor.

9

He let himself into the apartment quietly, a few minutes before five in the morning, and went to the kitchen, where he found his daughter standing behind the island brandishing one of his Japanese cooking knives.

They'd paged him just after two a.m.: a sixty-three-year-old male with cardiac tamponade from a ruptured aortic aneurysm, whose ECG had shown low voltage in all leads. He'd volunteered to be on call because they were staying in town for Labor Day weekend, and some of the second- and third-year fellows could use a break. He told them it was trial by fire, and if they could get through this, etc., etc. But it was equally possible that this was the new normal, and all of them knew it.

Kate had to work in the days leading up to the first day of school, and at first he'd planned to take Pia out to the beach, just the two of them. He'd thought they could go swimming, take out the Sailfish, get lobster rolls. But Pia hadn't been interested. It became clear later that she had plans with a friend on Saturday night. He was vaguely hurt, but Kate had told him he was being crazy: it was great that kids were finding ways to socialize, and even better that Pia had been invited, before she even started school.

"It's just Maxine. She knows her from before."

"Old friends, new friends," Kate said. "Who cares? It's a big deal having friends at all right now."

"They won't stay distanced."

"It's outside." Kate put her hand on his shoulder, squeezed. "Give them a break."

He didn't have to be on call, but it was nice to relieve the grateful night fellow, during the lull in the midst of everything. He didn't even mind when he got the page, especially because it was an ordinary instance of pericardial effusion, unrelated to the pandemic. The patient's husband was sure he had Covid, but the rapid test was negative, and Stephen explained that the dyspnea associated with heart failure could look like congestion in the lungs. He did the pericardiocentesis, which went smoothly, although they would keep the catheter in for twenty-four hours to make sure fluid didn't return. Overall, the whole episode was satisfying, and Stephen was in a good mood, not even very tired, when he came in the door and found Pia with his knife.

"Jesus—Pia."

"Oh," she said. "It's only you." She replaced it on the magnetic strip, and returned to her Tupperware of cold spaghetti.

"No one could break in with Yuri down there."

Pia shrugged.

"I was at the hospital."

She was attacking the spaghetti as if they hadn't fed her for weeks.

"Toujours en décolage horaire?" The phrase had just popped into his head. And at five a.m., after performing a procedure on a man in critical condition. Here was the proof that he wasn't too old to have another baby. "Any chance you want a walk around the reservoir, when you finish that?"

"Décalage," she said. "But yeah, okay."

The streetlamps were still on as they walked around the shadowy bulk of the Museum of Natural History. A man sleeping on a bench picked up his head to yell something at them as they passed.

"Did he just call me a wormy old boat?"

Pia giggled, and he realized that he was not above taking advantage of the unhoused and mentally ill, if he could make her laugh.

"A germy goat?"

They used to like to tell Pia that she'd spent nine months in the museum while Nathalie was pregnant and completing a fellowship there, but Pia was like most children in that she had very little interest in her parents' life before she'd arrived in it. She liked the dinosaurs, and was happy to be taken through the Hall of Ocean Life by her mother, but the thing that had stood out to her were those (incorrect and now relabeled) dioramas of ancient people. She wanted to know where the Native American kids were, what they were doing while their parents traded with the Dutch. Could they take her in to see? She was maybe three or four, not old enough to understand that the scene didn't continue outside the frame.

They entered the park at Eighty-First and walked up the bridle path to the reservoir, still and silver green at this hour, flat as glass. On the east side, the gray clouds were touched with vivid pink, and the black fringe of trees was resolving into its individual forms. The towers of the El Dorado loomed, the windows starting to glow, but the sky above them remained a saturated, nighttime blue.

"It's nice to have some time just with you." They walked east on the running path. The birds were going crazy.

"She sleeps a lot."

"Kate?" But who else would she be talking about. "It's pretty early."

"I mean in general."

"An average amount, I think." He thought that if Pia were to ask, he would tell her. It might be easier that way, more natural.

"Mom never sleeps."

"She's always been like that." He didn't want to talk about Nathalie. He didn't want to talk about Kate either. He wanted Pia to offer something of herself, but he didn't want to push.

Was she okay? Did she dislike Kate already? Was it normal that her first thought in the event of a break-in was violent retaliation, with the help of his state-of-the-art Kanpeki knives?

"Only since she had me. She said you never woke up, so she had to get used to it."

He demonstrated restraint in not contesting that. Maybe when she was an infant that had been true. But what about when she'd had the phase of nightmares every night, at seven years old, and Nathalie had been in Woods Hole half the week? What about the year after that, when Pia refused to go to bed before midnight, because her mother was away on another of her solo sojourns on Mo'orea? Who'd gone to Pia then?

"Are you excited about school starting?"

She gave him a look.

"Are you nervous?"

"*No.*"

"Okay. It would be normal, given everything that's going on. And having been so far away."

"I feel more far away now."

That took him a minute. "From there?"

Pia seemed actually to be thinking about her answer. "From everywhere."

She felt far away from everywhere in New York City, but not on an island in the South Pacific?

"It's the pandemic," Stephen suggested. "We're all in a state of suspended animation." But everything looked and sounded normal in the park, where you could still hear the traffic from the west side. It was now about a quarter to six, and they stayed close to the fence to accommodate the first joggers, men and women with complicated shoes and impressive calf muscles, those who didn't fuck around. None of them were wearing masks at this hour, but he was tempted to tell Pia to put hers on. They'd admitted a guy Stephen's age in April, who had eyeballed okay, was walking around and telling anyone who would listen that he'd run eight miles two days earlier. Even Vivek was taken in. But by the following morning, he was in the

ICU. People would recover and then crash again. You couldn't take solace in any improvement, or even trust your observations because the disease itself was so fast and unpredictable—like a stranger in your apartment with a knife.

"Who did you hang out with when you were there, apart from Mom?" He wasn't prying, or at least, he wasn't prying into Nathalie's life. It was just that Kate had said that Pia had said that her mother had said that she was spending too much time with her dive instructor, whose name Kate had misremembered as Roman. Which sent him later and in private to the internet, where he couldn't find anyone associated with the labs, or the neighboring American research station, called Raffi or Raphael.

"Mostly mom's boring friends," Pia said. "I don't know which ones were more boring, because French people and Americans are boring in really different ways."

"It's a good point." She'd done that as a kid, too, sometimes escaping punishment for bad behavior with a joke or an observation that made her sound older than she was—an only child thing, maybe. It was nice to see that quality persisting underneath the brittle adolescent shell. But what did it mean that she mentioned the dive instructor to Kate, rather than to him? Was Raffi simply a functionary at the station, someone whose name came up because he performed essential services? Or was he Nathalie's boyfriend, a fact Pia was keeping from him, but wanted to advertise to Kate in some attenuated form of competition? If he knew the man's age, it would help. Was he young enough for Pia to develop an infatuation, or worse, a reciprocal crush?

He trusted his ex-wife to handle all of Pia's physical needs, to take care of her in a remote location, to keep her safe from sunburn and stingrays, decompression sickness and sharks. He had much less confidence in her ability to talk to Pia about love and sex, because Nathalie combined a too-casual attitude about the magnitude of sexual interactions with a lot of genuinely frustrating hang-ups about sex itself, so that they'd sometimes joked that she would prefer the spawning and brooding of the corals she studied to the fraught and messy copulation of human beings. A joke that concealed the problem under its know-it-all sophistication.

Given all this, the idea that it was somehow "American" of him to have been upset when he learned that she'd had an affair with a visiting professor from the University of Copenhagen was infuriating. From his point of view, they'd gotten divorced because Nathalie was unfaithful, full stop. He was otherwise not the type of person to get divorced, and it was another maddening fact that she saw it differently, believed in a convoluted explanation about her career and their "cultural differences." Frankly, it might have been the thing that kept Stephen from letting go entirely. Maybe he wanted to write to her in a way that he didn't want to write to anyone else because there was something he needed to make her understand.

That along with, of course, Pia. Pia had been nine years old, at home with him in New York, when the man named Martin came to Mo'orea and had sex with his wife. They had been collaborating on a project about striated sea hares (Martin's specialty) and their relationship to coral (Nathalie's). Pia thought that the sea hares—so called because of rabbitlike appendages on their heads—were cute, and liked to see Martin's photos, which her mother blithely emailed for Stephen to show her. In one photo the man himself appeared, in scuba gear, several of these creatures on his outstretched palm. The reality was that Martin was tall and broad-shouldered, probably at least six-three, but with very little hair. The reality was that sea hares were aquatic slugs that ate toxic blue-green algae called cyanobacteria.

It wasn't about sex, Nathalie had told Stephen after Martin left; you know how I am about sex. It was about *intense intellectual collaboration*, she said, as if that was supposed to make him feel better. Sex was something that happened or didn't happen depending on local conditions, about which the only possible attitude was laissez-faire. Which was exactly the wrong attitude to take toward a stranger fucking his wife, it seemed to Stephen—not to mention the potential love life of their teenage daughter while she was marooned on a South Pacific island.

"Did you do a lot of diving?"

Pia shrugged. "Mom always wants me to go."

"But you like it, right?"

"Depends who you go with."

The hair was really disconcerting. It made her look, in the still-deep shade of the trees on the path around the reservoir, like some kind of sprite, an otherworldly being. Every single person they passed at least glanced at her.

"And you mostly went with Mom?"

"The problem with Mom is that she only wants to look at her thing. She's like, obsessed. There could be sharks after us, and she'd be like, 'Regarde, Pia—les cils très très fins!'"

Her imitation was, of course, perfect. "The very thin what?"

She thought for a second. "Cilia?

"So they're all excited about proving that the *Pocillipora*—those are the spiky ones that look like Covid—can change because of all the bad stuff that's happening in the ocean. It's getting warmer and more acidic, and so the coral, like, *choose*, to have these red larvae instead of green ones. The red ones are supposed to be tougher, or something. But why does it even matter if companies are going to send robots down there to scoop everything up and get metal for our phones?"

"Your mom was talking about that, too. But I'm interested in the larvae—how are they tougher?"

"Like, they can swim faster, but they don't settle down as fast. They're looking for someplace better."

"Got it," Stephen said. "That's a good description."

Pia did a dramatic mock yawn. "I mean, I've heard enough about it. Not just from Mom but from Marie-Laure, and Gunther, the world's most irritating grad student."

"What makes him so irritating?"

"He's always talking about *larvae*. And he worships Mom."

"Oh." He didn't know the grad student, but he remembered

Marie-Laure, a tall, athletic-looking specialist in ocean acidification, with whom they'd once eaten Thai food in a restaurant in Falmouth, where Nathalie was spending half of every week at the time—when it still seemed like he could do his job and she could do hers, and they could have interesting friends, and raise Pia and stay together forever. He didn't know whether Marie-Laure had been there when Nathalie had met Martin. Would she have advised her against it, or encouraged her to destroy everything for a couple of tropical fucks with a balding slug specialist? Who destroyed his life in a matter of weeks, and then went home, and whom Nathalie professed not to care whether she ever saw again.

"They call it 'parental effects,'" Pia said. "Then they all argue about whose name is going to be on the paper, and then they write the paper, and then they publish it. But I mean, so what?"

"That's how scientists communicate their findings," Stephen said. "By publishing papers."

"And then they feel all happy and have Hinanos in the fare to celebrate."

"We should talk about drinking," Stephen said. "Now that you're back in the city."

Pia put one hand over her eyes. "Dad."

"Yes?"

"I'm saying, how's a paper going to change anything?"

Was she trying to distract him from the topic of alcohol? Was drinking with her friends what she wanted to stay in the city to do? Or was he naïve to expect her problems to be so familiar and concrete?

"When I was a kid everyone was worried about acid rain," Stephen said. "But now it seems like they've got that under control."

"I don't think this is going to be like that." She was walking slightly ahead of him, her legs scissoring faster and faster. He thought he might have to break into a jog to catch up. Suddenly she stopped abruptly, and he put out his hand so they wouldn't collide. Her shoulder was so small under the bulky sweatshirt. He could feel the sharp protrusion of bone—acromion.

"Sorry."

"It's okay."

It was strange how little physical contact they'd had since she got back. He didn't know if it was her natural reserve, now that she was older, or something that had happened to him in the past year, so that now he was afraid of touching anyone.

"Even if the coral does disappear, I'm glad you got a chance to see so much of it—probably as much as anyone your age."

"I don't really care about coral. Or at least, not like Mom does."

"That's fair."

"It's just so stupid, the way adults do things."

"You're probably right." They were coming back around the south side of the reservoir. Kate would be waking up and wondering where they were.

"Raffi says deep sea mining is the new nuclear testing."

He snapped to attention. But he was careful to keep his voice casual. "How old is Raffi?"

She hesitated. "Mom told you about Raffi?"

"Of course."

"Thirty." Without missing a beat.

"Isn't that an adult?"

"I just mean *those* adults. The scientists. He doesn't think all their projects are so important—even though he's friendly with them, because he needs to keep his job."

"What's Raffi's job again?"

"Now he's the liaison culturelle."

"What's that?"

"It's bullshit—that's what he said. Really he works on the boats and the dive gear and stuff. For the researchers." She looked up at him, and for a second she seemed younger than she had since she arrived. "Raffi makes sure no one gets hurt."

When they got home Kate was already in the kitchen drinking coffee, frowning at her clunky, school-issued Chromebook. He had recently suggested maybe tea for the duration of the pregnancy, and from the look she gave him had decided not to make any more suggestions. She usually slept in a tank top and flimsy shorts, but this morning she was wearing an oversized BEST T-shirt and a pair of his pajama pants. It probably wasn't because of the pregnancy, not yet very visible, but because she knew how a girl Pia's age would feel about her new stepmother's body. It wasn't exactly fair to Kate, in her own home, and she was doing it anyway. He was filled with love.

"Are there Frosted Mini Wheats? I missed those so much."

"There's Shredded Wheat. I'm trying to buy the healthy stuff."

Pia didn't say anything, but walked around the stool where Kate was sitting and started opening and closing cabinets, not gently.

"Above the toaster," Stephen said. She found the cereal, and kept hunting, until she uncovered an old box of confectioner's sugar. Then she poured the cereal in the bowl, dumped an egregious amount of sugar on top, and doused the whole thing with almond milk.

Kate laughed. "That's one way to go."

"I'm supposed to gain weight," Pia said, in a voice with a shrug built into it. She was leaning against the counter, eating standing up even though there were four stools, and she wouldn't have had to sit right next to Kate.

"It's not great for your skin," he said. They were going to have to tell Pia about the baby, maybe even this weekend.

"I think that's a myth," Kate said, without looking up. "Chocolate maybe, but not sugar."

Stephen thought that if he had to be the bad guy in order for her to like Kate, he was happy to play that role.

"Meanwhile, only three students have submitted summer reading challenges. And only this one shows any real effort."

Stephen noticed that Pia couldn't help glancing at Kate's screen, at the mention of someone her age. Maybe it was the effect of an extended period without much socialization, like Nathalie said. He preferred that explanation for anything that might be going on with Pia, not least because it exempted him from responsibility.

"Athyna with a 'y,' " Pia read over Kate's shoulder.

"They were supposed to apply the ideas from the introductory packet about feminist theory to their reading of *The House on Mango Street* or 'The Man Thing.' I wonder if that was too much to ask, for the summer?"

"Nobody does that stuff till the night before school starts," Pia said, but with slightly more warmth.

"You're right," Kate said. "There must be a way to make the assignment more interesting."

"Maybe there's an app? Where it's like a contest?"

"That's an amazing idea," Kate said. "I'm actually going to bring that up in my meeting later."

Pia brightened, and Stephen thought for a beautiful moment that everything was going to be fine. Nuclear families were on the way out, anyway. Artificial. They could be the new kind, loving but flexible.

Then his daughter turned to him. "Remember that awesome thing Mom did in Jamaica? With the high school kids and the—what are those trees?"

Mangroves, Stephen thought. They'd developed a two-year curriculum around threatened mangrove forests, to teach the kids how valuable they were. It was Nathalie's idea to give them actual seedlings so that each student could take ownership of several trees. She'd come back from Jamaica elated, and had resolved to start traveling and doing more fieldwork again. Really it was the mangroves that had initiated everything.

"I don't remember," he told Pia now.

"I should get myself together before I really sit down with all of this," Kate said. Pia was standing perfectly still, holding her bowl and spoon, watching Kate gather her papers and laptop from the counter, as if she were some kind of exotic animal. No one had used the word "stepmother" yet, not so much because of its nasty connotations as because it seemed absurdly intimate for the approximately two weeks the two of them had so far cohabited.

"This is always an exciting weekend for teachers," Kate continued. "And also terrifying. But it's hard to feel much at all about the first day of school on a screen."

She was pointing it out, but she wasn't down about it. It wasn't her whole life: that was the difference between his ex-wife and his present one. It was a good thing for Pia to see. Kate was moving toward their bedroom when his daughter spoke.

"Mangroves! They're trees that grow in salt water, and tons of fish need them to survive. Plus they keep the coastline from eroding. It was cool because the kids actually got to raise their own trees from seedlings, and then plant them in the wild."

"That sounds incredible," Kate said valiantly.

"They did a news story about it in France. My mom was on TV."

"Wow," Kate said, with slightly less enthusiasm.

"I wish I could've gone with her," Pia continued. "But I was in school."

This was complete bullshit, because Pia had never shown a shred of interest in any kind of conservation program. He thought she would last about eleven seconds planting seedlings on a hot, mosquito-infested Jamaican coast. He guessed that many of the Jamaican kids had felt the same way about the program, noble as it was.

Kate looked from Pia to Stephen, not blaming him but letting him know that she understood what his daughter was up to. She looked tired, as if the baby was the one doing all the sleeping, and for the first time he imagined with real clarity what it would be like to have a newborn and a teenager at the same time. Pia watched Kate disappear down the hall, shutting the bedroom door firmly behind her. Before Pia arrived, they'd still been at that stage in their relationship when closed doors were unusual. He turned to his daughter, who shoved a huge bite of the cereal into her mouth, but her eyes—very much her mother's huge dark eyes—creased at the edges as if she were laughing.

"What are you doing with yourself today?" He couldn't help the edge in his voice.

"I have to read Greta Thunberg's speeches before school starts."

"That sounds good. Especially because you're so interested in climate science these days."

Pia smiled. "Mom already gave me the highlights. Did you know Greta Thunberg doesn't buy any new clothes? She just takes old stuff from people. And she sailed across the Atlantic instead of flying."

"And I bet she takes short showers and hangs her clothes to dry," Stephen suggested.

"No one in Europe has a dryer. It's a total waste of energy."

"Give it a rest, Pia."

"What?"

He wanted to say that she needed to go easy on Kate, but he was worried Kate could hear them from the bedroom. Kate would hate him defending her, and it wasn't likely to work anyway.

"You know what."

Incredibly, and not artificially, Pia's eyes suddenly filled with tears. Apart from her wild blond hair, she looked exactly as she had as a child, in their former apartment, when he'd chastised her for leaving her dress-up clothes all over the living room floor. She had so many toys, especially those designed to encourage proficiency in science and math: building materials, a chemistry set, a circuit board. But all she wanted were Nathalie's and his mother's old clothes. If there was a costume within a mile radius, she would find it and put it on.

Pia put her bowl in the sink, then reconsidered, turned back and washed it, with the maximum amount of noise and water. Then she dropped it in the drying rack so roughly that he thought it would break. It was one of the very thin ceramic bowls in robin's-egg blue, imported from Finland, that Kate's parents had given them as a wedding present. She'd said at the time that they were trying to impress him.

"*Sorry,*" Pia said. "Sorry I'm in your way so much. I told you I didn't want to come!"

"Pia—" he began. "That's not it at all. *Pia—*" But before he could think how to continue, both his wife and his daughter were barricaded in their rooms.

10

They'd gone to the beach, and now her sister and Elijah were fighting. She could hear them in their room upstairs, not yelling yet. She knew what it was about: Elijah, who'd been laid off from the event company at the beginning of the pandemic, was supposed to be applying for a job driving a van for Amazon that paid seventeen dollars an hour to start. But when they got back, he hadn't been home, and her mom had quick-changed to go to work, because this weekend was double overtime. It was seven and Marcus hadn't eaten since a snow cone from a cart at about three; he was starving and cranky from the sun and the water.

It had been nice, though. At first when they'd gotten to the bus stop and seen all the people waiting, Athyna had wanted to go home. But her mother and her sister would've killed her, and she would've had to spend all day with her brother-in-law in the hot house. When they got on the bus, the paper mask seemed too thin to keep out all the germs, even with the windows open, and Marcus's mask was too big and always slipping off his nose. A strung-out young white guy was spitting into his phone, over and over, *didn't say shit, didn't say shit,* only a few seats away. Her mom and Breanna rested the beach umbrella in its carrying case between them, and talked about what they'd brought to eat as if nothing was wrong, and Athyna let her mask fog up her glasses, which was better, like being partially blind.

From the beach, you could see the inverted arches of the

Verrazzano, its cables disappearing against the gray water. They'd learned in school that the city had misspelled the Italian explorer's name, and Athyna could relate. The water lapped on the shore, and Marcus screamed and ran in and out like any other kid. The air was humid and smelled like salt and asphalt. Breanna lay on her stomach in the shade of the umbrella, and released the S-closure of her bikini top, attracting the attention of a group of young men walking past. An ancient white lady in a white strapless suit, tanned deep reddish brown, lowered herself into a green-and-white-striped beach chair. A blond lifeguard who could've been on TV stared fixedly at the water from under an orange umbrella, two red rescue cans standing up in the sand at the base of his chair. First her mom fell asleep, then Breanna, so as usual Athyna was in charge.

Her mom and Breanna could relax and unplug, but she and her dad were live wires. They worried, and so they had trouble sleeping. When she was little, she'd find her dad up early, coffee on the table, mopping the kitchen floor with bleach. This was when they were in Brooklyn, in East Flatbush. She and her sister were hardly allowed out in that neighborhood, and you heard gunshots, especially at night in the summer, but inside everything was spotless. Her father had a thing about roaches, even though they lived in New York, and he'd take everything out of the cabinet under the sink once a week and Clorox the hell out of it. Her mom thought he was crazy, but they never had any bugs.

That was before he went to school to learn hyperbaric welding. She had a photo of him on his graduation day, with six or seven other guys, holding up his certificate in front of a banner that said DIVERS INTERNATIONAL. He was wearing the dive watch that her mom had gotten him for a graduation present, which was now in a navy blue leather box in Athyna's bureau drawer. Her mom said that it made her too sad to look at it. She had a bunch of videos of him, too, one that even showed him working underwater. In it, her father extended his wand

and lit a trembling ball of white flame. Breanna had laughed when she called it a "wand," but their dad just corrected her: it was actually called a "stinger." The stinger carried the electrode inside the chamber, supplying the power for the job. A hose filled the chamber with oxygen, pushing out the water. Then the chamber was dry enough to light an underwater fire. How was it possible?

Her father wore a bright yellow dive helmet with a glass plate riveted across his eyes. He wore a suit that kept him dry, but if he was down there a long time, there was a machine to pump hot water through the suit. In the video, you saw her father from the side, through thick glass, doing his work. Then whoever was taking the video—a Long Island accent, like a lot of the guys her father worked with—shouted something that was hard to hear. She'd played it enough that she thought she understood. *Are you cold?* Then you could hear them say, *Look at the window*, and her father obligingly turned, a sharp black hammer in his right hand. The hammer was attached to a line. With the other hand he took a narrow brush and tried to clear the glass. It looked as if her dad were inside a glass box, but actually it was the other way around; the men filming were the ones in a tank, and her father was in the open sea. You could pause the video and zoom in, but with the helmet and the murky green water, there wasn't enough resolution to see his eyes.

They didn't go to the beach when her dad was alive. By that time they were in their first apartment on Staten Island, on Winter Avenue, and it was the last thing he wanted to do after a week of work. Once he sent a picture of himself on a pebbly beach in front of a long, dark gray house, its windows reflecting light, with a pin to show them where he was: Sands Point, Port Washington. When she googled the house, where her father had been employed repairing a dock for Jet Skis, she saw that it had six bedrooms and had been purchased for more than five million dollars. That wasn't the kind of thing about which her dad would comment. Mostly he talked about how much he loved diving, and how grateful he was. When they moved to Staten Island, he was grateful, and when they found the three-bedroom house by the expressway, where they still lived, he was more grateful still. You have your positive men and your negative men, her mother said; you look for one who starts out positive, because there's enough negative coming at you after a while.

She thought of that when she heard her sister and Elijah arguing upstairs. This was something she'd figured out about beauty. Her sister was beautiful, and Elijah was fine, and that made it harder for both of them after they got together. Each thought they were giving some gift, and they couldn't take it when the other wasn't dazzled by what they had to offer. Athyna didn't think she and Breanna were opposites by nature; she was considered more responsible, and better in school, but maybe that was just because people admired Breanna whether or not she showed up on time or made good grades. Maybe on another planet, where the aliens loved Athyna's nearsighted round eyes instead of Breanna's almond ones, the skin she'd inherited from her dad instead of the color Breanna got from their mom, her tight 4C curls for Breanna's 4A, then all their other qualities would be reversed, too.

These thoughts were interrupted by Marcus, who was hungry. Athyna got the box of mac and cheese out of the cabinet and then wished she'd found something that could go in the microwave. To keep him quiet while the water boiled, she gave him her phone, but now Breanna was screaming about how Elijah had had the whole day, and she was watching Marcus even though she worked all week, so he could call about the job. That was all he had to do, and as usual, he'd fucked it up. And then Elijah was calling her a bitch, and Marcus was listening, even though he was also looking at the screen, moving his little body back and forth in the chair.

"What are you playing?"

"Fishing."

"Like those guys we saw today." Off the pier, opposite the rec complex. "What do you think they were trying to catch?"

"Fluke," he said.

Every once in a while, Marcus really surprised you. "Really? How do you know?"

"Asked Nana."

It was weird how you could hear someone's voice but not the words. Breanna's was at a pitch that signified trouble.

"You want Teetee to take you one day?"

Her nephew blinked, then nodded. "Away, where?"

"Oh—" He'd misheard. Honestly, it didn't sound bad. "We could go to Coney Island." As long as she was pretending, she might as well be creative. "We could go to Florida. Take an airplane. We could go to Disney World."

There was a crash, and then a yell from Elijah. Marcus gave her a look. His looks were way beyond his vocabulary, and she was very familiar with this one: his eyes blank but his bottom lip hanging open, revealing his square, perfect teeth. "We'd stay in a hotel."

"We gonna sleep in the same room?"

"You think I'm gonna get you your own hotel room?"

"In the same bed?" He was still sad about her move to the couch.

"In a big bed with a lot of pillows. A feather bed."

Marcus smiled. He seemed to like the word, and repeated it under his breath several times, almost singing the first syllable: "*Feath*er bed."

They heard Breanna's feet pounding on the stairs, and then the water running in the bathroom. Bree was fixing her face to go out. Athyna knew she wouldn't come in the kitchen, and she was glad. She didn't want Marcus to see his mother crying, and she also didn't want to comfort Breanna herself. If her sister thought Athyna got some pleasure out of watching things fall apart with E, she was wrong. Breanna's bossiness annoyed her, but it was also uncomfortable when power flowed the other way between them. She didn't want to have to feel sorry for Breanna any more than her sister wanted to be pitied by her.

They were out of milk, but Marcus didn't care. He was happy with the cheese powder mixed with some butter and the macaroni. They heard the front door slam after Breanna and, after a while, E went out, too.

"I need to pee," she told Marcus. "Be right back."

Athyna went upstairs. Their bedroom door had a lock on it, but only from the inside. She hadn't been in Breanna's room for a long time, and she'd forgotten what pigs they both were. There was clothing all over the floor, mostly Breanna's, but also some of E's T-shirts and boxer briefs. Breanna made a face and called him ghetto when he drank Colt 45, but she hadn't done anything about the collection of empties next to his side of the bed. Her makeup was scattered across the top of the dresser, along with a couple of old tissues she'd used to blot. There was a framed picture of the two of them on the wall, taken at the boardwalk in Coney Island in front of a crazy sunset, E holding her sister from behind, both of them looking 100 percent in love, but also straight at the camera. The picture was in a thick, black frame that was a little crooked on the wall, maybe from the force of the crash, which Athyna could see now had come from a candle, one of those scented candles that some people liked, this one red wax in a thick glass jar, smelling too strongly of cinnamon. She remembered Breanna buying it at Bed Bath & Beyond, right around the time E moved in; otherwise she wouldn't've have been able to identify the shards that were everywhere on one side of the bed.

Athyna looked for a mark where the candle would've hit—her sister could barely throw a ball, so she was unlikely to launch a missile E couldn't easily dodge—but the pale yellow paint that her dad had rolled onto the wall nine years ago was marked in a bunch of places. What must've happened was that her sister had accused E of wasting the day, and Elijah had fought back—*I don't got time for this shit*, and You *don't got time? Seems to me you got nothing* but *time*—and then E must've said something that made Breanna pick up the candle from her bedside table, the candle she must've bought because she imagined the two of them in this bedroom in some kind of cinnamon-scented love haze, and thrown it at him. The thick red cylinder of wax had separated from the glass and rolled into the dust under the bed. Athyna felt like Dr. Tara Lewis on *Criminal Minds*, putting together the evidence, except that E wasn't a psychopath, just a bad boyfriend. *Fiancé,* her sister always corrected, because they were planning to get married after the pandemic, but Athyna personally thought it wasn't bad that they had to wait. Maybe Bree would come to her senses and ditch him.

She felt dizzy suddenly—it happened when her period was coming—and sat down on the bed. What would Bree say if she came home suddenly and found Athyna in their room? What would E say? It would be different, that was for sure: E would use it as an opportunity to make fun of her somehow, and her sister would flat out kill her. Athyna kicked off her flip-flops and lay back on the unmade bed. It was sort of nice to be trespassing, almost as if she were in a stranger's house. She stared at the picture from Coney Island, which had been closed since the pandemic started. There was a man she'd seen there once, with hair styled into two fat twists, which were then looped into a spiral on either side of his head to resemble ram's horns. He was wearing a red tracksuit, and had three different women with him, women in leather miniskirts and boots, wearing wigs and neon lashes. It had been years ago that she'd seen that group making their way down the boardwalk as if it were a parade and they were the main attraction, but she still sometimes thought about them, especially when she was thinking about sex. Sometimes she was one of the women, and sometimes she just watched. Sometimes the face of the man with horns changed and became a face she knew: Javier or her sixth-grade math teacher, Mr. Bronson.

It wasn't as if her sister and Elijah didn't owe her a moment of peace in their room, which for all its chaos felt kind of familiar and homey, the smell of L'Air du Temps overwhelming everything else. E's cast-iron hand weights (he didn't like the plastic ones) were in their rack against the wall, underneath an orange rectangle of light, and you could smell the charcoal from someone's barbecue. Except for the orange patch, the wall looked gray now, all the yellow draining away with the light. Crazy to think her dad's hands had rolled the yellow onto that wall for her and Bree, probably imagining it was the first of many paint jobs he'd give that room. She could picture him in here in his sweatpants—the ugliest dark gray Old Navy cargo sweatpants—and his Giants T-shirt, crouching on the floor to do the baseboard, a towel next to his knees to wipe his face, Luther Vandross on his portable CD player, the window open because the fumes could give him a headache. Her father got migraines, which he was embarrassed about because people thought it was a female thing. He never called it a migraine, but would say he had a "three-Bayer headache." After the headache passed, he was always really tired.

She was nine or ten when her father painted the room, after they put the down payment on the house. Their own house. No way her father was thinking that in less than ten years the room would belong to Bree and Elijah, and that Marcus would move downstairs, and Athyna would flee to the couch; that while the walls upstairs stayed yellow, in defiance of flying objects, the hands that had held the foil pan and pressed the roller would remain only in a framed picture in the living room, one selfishly covering the other, hiding it forever.

"Teetee!" Marcus called, as if thinking about him summoned him, as if the two of them were connected by an invisible string. "I'm done!"

"So play something," she called down. "My phone's right there."

But there was no response, and she wasn't sure he'd heard. This was the year she was going to apply to college, get out of here, get some space of her own. The question was, what would happen to Marcus? If she hadn't been here, would her sister have gone out? Would E have come down to the kitchen, made the mac and cheese, sat there while Marcus ate it and talked about *Animal Crossing*? Would he have forgotten and left Marcus in the kitchen, wondering what had happened? She thought of him calling her name and hearing only what she was hearing now: the background drone of the expressway, Shawn Mendes blasting from the yard with the barbecue, a dog barking.

"I'm coming," she called out. "Marcus, I'm coming!"

11

The first time she met him, Raffi was cleaning a fish. It was the first year she was on Mo'orea full-time, when Pia was five, and they were at a barbecue in honor of the American station's new cultural center, in front of a dormitory at the edge of Cook's Bay, dark green and struck through with white sparks as the sun went down. The most senior Tahitian man at the party later grilled Raffi's catch. The huge parrot fish, with its iridescent turquoise scales and rainbow fins, its bulbous beak perfectly evolved for crunching coral, mesmerized her daughter, and she'd stayed close to Raffi all night.

Everyone was drinking, and Nathalie thought later that her first impression of Raffi had been wrong or misleading. At that age he was what Tahitians called a taure'are'a, a young man out with his friends, testing his freedom, and his habitual guard was down. He'd told her a story about asking his mother for a birthday present. He'd been twelve or thirteen, and all he'd wanted was what kids in Nathalie's generation had called "un blaster," a boombox to play cassettes. Instead his mother had given him a speargun.

"I was a bad kid," Raffi told her, half bashful and half proud. "I'd already started drinking and getting high, getting into all kinds of shit. But I'd been fishing since I was little—first in the shallowest water with my hands, then with a little bamboo pole. This speargun she got me was the real thing, better than my friends had, and eventually I started going out on the fore reef at night with my uncle for emperors and snapper. That's when I got addicted, I guess you could say. When I'm in the water at midnight, I can't be partying." He laughed. "So yeah, she knew what she was doing."

Nathalie liked the story, but she liked even more his irreverence, his ability to make fun of himself. Over the last ten years, she'd watched his transformation from adolescent rebel to island ecologist under his mother's influence. She didn't know if back then it was the spectacular fish or Raffi's inked shoulders, but Pia couldn't take her eyes off him. As a child Pia normally had refused to eat fish, but that night she'd put away a whole plateful, picking it off the bones with her fingers in the local style.

One morning, soon after Pia left for New York, Nathalie was checking her tanks in la dalle—the indoor-outdoor workspace behind the dock, named for its slab of concrete flooring. A gap between the translucent plastic walls and corrugated roof let in light and air; simple benches around the perimeter were mostly occupied by Plexiglas aquaria. Her surviving baby corals from the larval fluorescence study sat in between Ann's nudibranchs and the Swiss ecologists' cyanobacteria. The Swiss were playing some kind of house music over in their area that made it hard to think. Martin, she remembered, had favored jazz piano while he was working, while she and Gunther preferred silence when they could get it. Still, the place was a hive of activity, the kind of environment that had made her want to do science in the first place.

She looked up from the aquaria to see Raffi and a man she didn't know dragging one of the skiffs up from the dock. She watched as they transferred it from the trailer dolly to cinder blocks on the broad gravel path between la dalle and the dive shed. Then Raffi knelt to examine the motor. A visiting fellow—not one of hers, happily—had hit coral coming around the point from Ha'apiti the other day.

She stepped out of the shaded workspace onto the gravel, into the heat of the day.

"Is it okay?"

"The prop's fine but the skeg is damaged," Raffi said. "We'll have to replace it."

"Oh," she said. "Thanks." She watched him for a moment, but engines weren't her thing.

"Pia's there?"

He had a habit of asking questions out of nowhere. "She arrived safely—I talked to her."

"That's good."

She wondered if her daughter had messaged him. In most ways Raffi was exactly the kind of person she hoped would influence Pia, direct her attention away from herself and toward all of the fascinating problems that might engage her attention one day. On the farm in Paopao, just for example, he was working on the tamanu project. The tree was native and grew in the sandy soil on the coast; its fruits yielded an exceptionally clean biofuel that was already being used in southern India. At the moment, Raffi produced only enough oil to run his own irrigation pumps, but his goal was to expand and eventually export his product. She wasn't especially preoccupied with where Pia would go to university, but there was no doubt that a series of summers on Mo'orea working with biofuel would look impressive on an application one day. Plus, it would be a way to guarantee Pia's presence on the island during those months.

"And my husband wrote to me," she told Raffi. "My ex— we've been in touch a bit more." She was immediately embarrassed about revealing a fact that couldn't possibly interest Raffi, who had met Stephen only a few times, ten years ago now. Maybe it was only that he was an easy person to tell; in the unlikely event that he had an opinion about her increased communication with her ex, he wasn't about to offer it up. She herself wasn't sure what she thought, except that Stephen's note had touched her and done something to mitigate her regret about Pia's departure. "Just a quick email to let you know she arrived safely, although I know you spoke to her." He hadn't mentioned the conversation with Kate, although she was sure he'd heard about it. "She's still getting over the jet lag, obviously. But I can't tell you how happy I am to have her here. It makes everything else bearable, if you know what I mean." He might have left it at that, but as often happened between them recently, he continued:

I've been thinking about when she was little. Do you remember how frustrated she used to get? Especially if we did something for her that she wanted to do herself. And then you'd say, all right then, you shut the door. And she'd start wailing because she wanted to do it "that time." You remember, we used to joke about that? It reminds you that time is just something we invented.

It was amazing that they were divorced, a quarter of the globe between them, and having the same thoughts. She too had been thinking of Pia's early childhood—not only the parrot fish but the way their daughter would start in on some story or question as you were trying to leave her room at night, anything to distract you and keep you there another few minutes. That was in New York and it used to drive her crazy, because nights were when she was able to sit down and work on a paper without distractions. She would snap at Pia that she didn't have time for it, and close the door, and then often she would hear it opening again, Pia's feet padding into the living room to try her father. It had seemed like life or death then, keeping the bedroom door shut and preserving her time to work. But what had been so important, that she'd been trying so urgently to get down?

"I miss her," she told Raffi now.

Raffi tucked a rag under the carburetor to catch the spillage. "But the school will be better."

"I thought you hated French schools." She was just teasing him, but as often happened when she tried to joke, Raffi took her seriously. She'd seen him laughing with his cousin Yannick, and guessed that she might miss what amused them as well.

"But for her, it's better."

"You haven't heard from her?"

"A WhatsApp," Raffi said.

"Saying?" She couldn't help it; she was so eager.

"That at the airport in Los Angeles they didn't have the candy she was looking for."

Nathalie laughed, relieved and disappointed. She'd been hoping for something of significance; at the same time, she was glad Pia wasn't raging to Raffi about being sent away. "I'm sorry she bothers you so much."

"No bother."

She didn't want to embarrass him by talking about what she believed was Pia's crush. At the same time she wanted the two of them to acknowledge and then dismiss it.

"She attached herself to you, perhaps because Stephen was so far away."

Raffi straightened up as one of the Swiss crossed the path, making his way toward the lab buildings. "I told her to focus on her studies."

"Thank you," she said. And then on an impulse: "You're lucky with your family. Everyone together—getting along."

Normally Raffi lived here on Moʻorea with his mother, his sister and brother-in-law, but if he had business in Tahiti, he would sometimes crash at his cousin's apartment in Papeʻete. Once, when she was especially sick of her colleagues at the lab, Nathalie had gone to a party in that apartment, gotten ridiculously high; but privately she'd found Raffi's cousin coarse, a heavy drinker with terrible teeth, far beneath Raffi in intelligence or sensitivity. She much preferred his mother and his sister Hina, who lived in a house surrounded by fruit trees, up on a hillside in the Paopao valley.

"Together, at least," Raffi said now, with characteristic circumspection.

"Not getting along?" she asked.

Satisfied with the state of the engine, Raffi retightened the bolt on the carburetor and removed the rag. "It has to do with my sister's placenta."

She thought she'd misheard him. "Hina's what?"

"Pūfenua in Tahitian. You know we bury it."

"And plant a tree," Nathalie said. The tree then belonged to the child—or maybe "belonged" was the wrong word. The child was meant to learn to care for it as they grew up. It was a tangible connection to their land, although now people had to be flexible, because most didn't own their own land the way Raffi's family did. So much of it had been bought up by outsiders, Europeans and now Chinese developers.

"It's such a lovely custom."

Raffi made a sound that might have indicated agreement or boredom with this observation. "It matters where you do it. My brother-in-law's family is from Hitia'a."

Nathalie was starting to understand. "But your mother's people are from here."

"She would like it on our land."

"And Hina?" Nathalie said. "What does she want?"

"We're all waiting for her to decide," Raffi said. "There's a lot of tension."

"Your father's family is from Hitia'a too, right?"

Raffi looked at her for the first time. "That's right," he said. "And so it's complicated."

His father had been dead now almost five years. Nathalie had never met him, because he'd been sick already that first year she was in Mo'orea, but she knew the details: it was cancer of the throat, oropharyngeal, and had started in his tonsils. It was stage three by the time he was diagnosed, because it took so long for him to visit an oncologist, one of the few in Tahiti. After the second appointment at Ta'aone Hospital, when they'd seen the X-rays, Raffi told her that the doctor attributed the cancer to smoking, and seemed skeptical when his father said that he'd never used any kind of tobacco. It was painful to speak by that point, because he had a constant sore throat. The growth in his neck that had alarmed them turned out to be one of his tonsils, swollen to the size of a plum.

It wasn't until the end of the appointment that the doctor asked his father where he was born. Raffi had spoken for him, telling the doctor that his father had been born on a farm in Hitia'a, on the northeastern coast of Tahiti, near the famous waterfall in the valley of Papenoo. He had lived there, the youngest of seven siblings, until he married Raffi's mother. The doctor was particularly interested in his life as a boy of around eight or nine, and took detailed notes. In subsequent appointments, Raffi noticed, he stopped asking about cigarettes and seemed more solicitous of his patient, a development that pleased Raffi's father, who had great respect for doctors.

Raffi's father would have been born in 1965 or '66, in order to have been eight or nine when D'Estaing had authorized the last aboveground nuclear test, code-named Centaure. The bomb had detonated above Moruroa, in the Tuamotus, to the southeast. In the defense department models, the mushroom cloud ascended eight kilometers, before drifting north over the open ocean. In fact it rose only about five kilometers, and on July 17, 1974, the wind at that altitude pushed it west toward Tahiti. At the time Nathalie had read that there were 85,000 people living on the island, almost all of whom would have been exposed to more than 1 mSv of ionizing radiation.

Nathalie had learned all of this because she was the one who'd encouraged Raffi to apply to the CIVEN, the agency that offered compensation for injury or illness resulting from the nuclear tests. She had helped with the ridiculous paperwork, the requests for nonexistent healthcare records; she'd written several letters, but had been unable to complain in person because the commission didn't maintain an office in Tahiti. Its decisions were based on data from a baroque web of agencies, ministries, and special investigative committees, each with its official acronym. The CEA, France's atomic energy commission, had written a report, independently evaluated by the IAEA—but those physicists reviewing it hadn't been able to verify any of the calculations about the local population's exposure because at the time the French defense ministry hadn't declassified the relevant documents.

Nine months after his father's death, Raffi's mother, Monique, had received a letter from the compensation agency. Raffi had brought it to the lab to show Nathalie. The letterhead was decorated with the profile of Marianne, *Liberté, Égalité, Fraternité*, and gave as the reason for the rejection of the claim his father's inability to prove an exposure to radiation over 1 mSv, because his childhood home was unfortunately not close enough to any of the twenty-six designated radiological surveillance points on the island. Also, and again unfortunately, some of the surveillance equipment in that area had proven faulty. It was with regret that they informed the family of the outcome of their case.

Nathalie had offered at the time to keep fighting, but she was relieved when Raffi declined.

"My mother would not be opposed to Hitia'a, if Rahiri's family owned land there. But they don't."

"Rahiri's your brother-in-law?"

Raffi nodded. "His family has a house but no land. My mother doesn't want the kid to be a hotu pāinu."

"That's a seed?"

"A waterborne seed. Drift fruit, like mangroves or coconuts, or tamanu. Also an insult—for someone who's forgotten where they're from."

She left him to finish with the boat and returned to the office. But instead of tackling the prospectus she was supposed to be working on, she opened her email:

S,

Thank you for writing to let me know all is well. Has she said anything about school, especially socially? I expect she will be fine academically. It's funny to hear you've been thinking of her babyhood—moi de même. Today I remembered the first time she saw a parrot fish up close, how amazed she was (peau brûlée variety, *Chlorurus sordidus*). Perhaps there's a science gene in there somewhere? More likely it was his colorful costume that enchanted her. Lycée Corneille was not much for dramatics (ironie du sort) and so I hope she may be able to be part of some production this year. I believe it is a healthy release for her. I am not opposed to the arts, as you once accused—just hopeless in that department. You I remember used to make elegant drawings while you were thinking, on scraps of paper next to the laptop. A man in a hat, an old car—a rabbit once, running. It would be nice if we were granted several lives in which to try things, no?

12

The thing she noticed about Athyna was that she kept her camera on. It was rare. They were required to have them on for classes, but you would use up most of the period if you took the time to ask each one for an excuse. *My camera's broken. I'm eating breakfast. My sister's naked.* There was a barrier that normally went up once a high school student had put on clothing and left the house, traveled by car or bus or subway to reach a classroom. Now that transition had been eliminated, and in Kate's opinion it was mostly terrible for teaching and learning. It was as if everyone—herself included—had told themselves that, given everything, all they had to do was get through this.

They had gotten through three lessons on the personal essay, beginning with Toni Morrison's Nobel Prize address. The kids always liked the weird, fairy-tale setup at the beginning, and the way the bad kids become the moral center at the end. Some of her best classes had been on that essay in the past. But it was so different when she couldn't be in the same room with them. Now they were supposed to be meeting in small groups on Zoom to discuss the topics for their own essays, but only Athyna and Hernan had shown up in the breakout room, and Hernan said he'd just logged on from his phone to tell her he was late for work.

"We need to set up another time to discuss your essay," she direct-messaged him in the chat. Hernan responded with a row of yellow thumbs, but without any further commitment. Athyna was in her normal spot on the bottom bunk, leaning against a white wall that she'd decorated with memorabilia: an aging blue paper certificate from middle school band, glossy magazine photos of Baby Rose and Stephen Curry, an impressionist painting of a rowboat against a riverbank full of flowers. The light from the window, mostly obscured by the bunk bed, gave her surroundings a greenish glow.

"Some of the boys at this school are—" Athyna shook her head. "But Hernan's okay. He's writing about his grandmother."

Kate noted *Hernan: grandmother* on a Post-it next to her computer. In general, grandparents weren't ideal subjects for college essays, unless there was something spectacularly unusual about them. "What's going on with his grandmother?"

"She died."

"Oh—I'm sorry to hear that. Did she have Covid?"

"No," Athyna said. "I don't think so. I think she had cancer, but then there wasn't room for her in the hospital because of Covid."

"That's terrible," Kate said. They observed an awkward Zoom pause in honor of Hernan's grandmother.

"Let's talk about you, though—about your essay."

Athyna gave a theatrical sigh. "I don't know." She was wearing her hair gelled back in a tight bun, which made her eyes look even bigger than usual. Athyna's eyes were gorgeous, dark, alive to everything, the kind of eyes that held you accountable when you were standing at the front of a classroom. But the lens on the Chromebook gave everyone a fishy expression. "I was going to write about seeing a therapist for my anxiety, but now because of Covid I don't."

"We could all use some therapy these days," Kate said.

"Yeah I know! But the insurance stopped covering it. And now I don't have anything to write about."

"Well—if it makes you feel better, I don't think that's a great essay topic."

Athyna's face snapped back to the camera, a little hurt.

"I mean—it could be a great essay. But for college I think you're going to want to show them your best self—not that your best self couldn't be anxious." She was screwing up. If she couldn't manage her students or her stepdaughter, how was she going to be a mother?

As if on cue, Kate felt the familiar popping, just below her ribs. She'd started telling a few close friends, including Abby, over FaceTime. Abby's kids had been fighting in the background, and the room behind her looked like some sort of severe weather event had just occurred. Her friend apologized for the chaos, which was due to the fact that there was no camp this summer, and no playdates, and that this condition had begun three months before the summer even started. When Kate confided her news, Abby had started to cry, and she'd been moved that her friend could be so happy for her in spite of the circumstances—but now she wondered about those tears. No one was going to tell you it was a stupid time to have a baby, or catalogue the ominous facts the way you might point out a sky that was darkening literally to someone who had blithely proposed an outing.

"What?" Athyna was shouting to someone off-screen. "No, not under the broiler." She turned back to Kate. "Jesus, who does that?"

"Someone's cooking?"

"Donuts. My brother-in-law. Not making them, just heating them up."

"The broiler does seem wrong for that."

"Right?" But Athyna was distracted by someone. "You see I'm in a meeting here. Weren't you napping? You tell your dad to do that." She sighed. "Okay, come here. Meet my teacher. This is Marcus."

Marcus was a round-faced little boy with eyes exactly like Athyna's. He was wearing a Spider-Man costume, or half of one, because he needed help zipping it up the back. A pair of pull-up training pants printed with cartoon characters showed where the arms of the suit were hanging limply at his sides.

Athyna did some magic, removing the wet pull-up without taking off the suit.

"Come on," Athyna said. "Help! I can't do it if you don't get your arms in the sleeves."

"Hi, Marcus," Kate said. "Nice costume."

"He never takes it off."

"How old are you, Marcus?" Kate asked.

"How old are you?" Athyna prompted. "You tell her." But Marcus just stared at Kate, his belly exposed to the camera.

"Let me guess," Kate said. "Are you five?"

Marcus grinned. Athyna shook her head. "Tell her."

"Yes," Marcus said.

"You are not," Athyna said. "He's only four, but he's big." She gave Marcus a light shove, but he wormed his way between her legs, leaned back against her chest. He'd lost interest in Kate on the screen, and was playing with an action figure, half man, half machine, twisting one of its limbs around and around in the socket. Athyna adjusted her body to accommodate his. "He's *bright*," she said, as if Kate had suggested otherwise. "It just takes him a minute. Sorry he's here—my sister's at work."

"It's okay," Kate said. It was rare that anyone, student or teacher, wasn't interrupted by family.

"And my brother-in-law—Marcus's dad—" Athyna mouthed the word "useless."

"Got it," Kate said. "So if you're not going to write about the therapist . . . ?"

Athnya shrugged but stayed mute. Often the students resented the idea that they should write about challenges and how they overcame them. They were proud, and they wanted to stress the things they had rather than what they lacked. And why should they be forced to do a song and dance about hardship in order to get into college? But if Pia were to come to her in a few years and say that she wanted to write about anxiety, Kate would caution strongly against it. And if that were true, shouldn't she give Athyna the same advice?

"Maybe you could write about Marcus. About taking care of him and doing school at the same time?"

"Teetee takes care of me." It surprised Kate that he was following the conversation.

"I can see that."

Athyna was nodding slowly. Considering. "I thought of that. But do you think that's kind of like—making excuses? Like it's so hard for me and shit?"

"Well, it has been hard," Kate said. "Hasn't it? Not just for you but for everyone. We were talking about paradigm shifts when we read Toni Morrison's essay. You remember the old woman and the bird?" There was a light knock on the door. "Hang on a second," she told Athyna as Pia stuck her head in the door.

"Hey," she said. "How was school?"

"Sorry," Pia said. "I didn't know you were—" The way the screen was angled, Pia could see Athyna but not the other way around.

"You can say hi," Kate said. "If you want."

To her surprise, Pia came and stood at her shoulder.

"Hi."

"Pia's a sophomore this year," she told Athyna. "Athyna's a senior."

"Wow, that must be stressful," Pia said.

"No kidding."

"What are they doing for graduation?"

Athyna shook her head. "We don't even know. Can you believe it? They're like, working it out. No disrespect," she said to Kate. "But this is a lot of bullshit. Like, I don't even care about prom. Okay? I mean, I do *care*, but not like some people. But do you know what I really want? A senior picture. Just like—a picture of myself in a cap and gown. And now they're saying we might be taking pictures with our damn *iPhones*, and they're going to do something like photoshop a cap and gown on there. And I'm like—*nope*. I'm not doing that."

Kate hadn't heard anything about senior pictures, because it was the other ELA teacher who did the yearbook. She made another Post-it: *Senior pictures—ask Nick.*

"When I told my mom, she started to cry."

"I don't blame her," Kate said.

"But it's nice," Pia said, "that your mom cares about something like that."

Kate couldn't help glancing up at Pia. Was that for Kate's benefit somehow, some game she was playing, or did she just feel comfortable connecting with someone her own age on a screen?

"Oh yeah," Athyna said. "She still has my sister's in a frame in the living room."

"I'm sure there are going to be senior pictures," Kate said, trying to express more confidence than she felt.

Pia took a step back. "Well, I'll let you—"

"We'll be done in a minute," Kate said.

"That's your daughter?" Athyna asked doubtfully when Pia had closed the door.

"Stepdaughter."

"Oh—yeah," Athyna said, but whether that signified simply the lack of family resemblance, or an awareness of the complications inherent in the relationship, Kate wasn't sure.

"We were talking about paradigm shifts in response to the Morrison essay, and I was going to say that Covid has shifted a lot of paradigms. Our lives are really different."

"Uh-huh," Athyna said, but she could tell that she'd lost her. When they ended the call a few minutes later, Athyna wasn't any closer to an essay than when they'd logged on. Kate stood up, stretched, felt dizzy, and sat down again. She ran her hand over the slightly curved shape of her belly. She felt bloated more than anything. Many years ago her aunt had told Kate that she got pregnant like every woman in their family: straight to the hips.

Pia's door was half-open. Stephen had furnished the room as soon as he knew she'd be living with them full-time: a glossy white bed and desk set, a beanbag chair, and a tie-dyed blue comforter. The night before she arrived, he'd appeared in the living room with a well-worn stuffed polar bear and a delighted expression, and she had thought for a second that it was for the baby. *I knew I'd kept this somewhere,* he'd said, and went to put it on Pia's bed.

Now Pia's folders and papers covered the desk, scattered around the Chromebook, iPad, phone, and assorted chargers. A cold mug of coffee or tea with a white skin rested on top of a trigonometry textbook, and Pia's clothing overflowed from the suitcase still sitting open on the floor next to the closet. Ripped jeans, plain cotton underwear, the sweatshirt she'd worn on the plane, as well as a long, brightly colored sundress Kate had never seen. Apart from clothing, the only things she seemed to have brought with her were a framed photo of herself with two girls around her age, clowning for the camera, and a poster featuring a Polynesian reggae artist called J Boog. The polar bear was no longer in evidence.

"Hey," Kate said, peering in. "How's it going?"

She'd been writing something in a notebook, but shoved it under the pile of schoolbooks. She was dressed in the school T-shirt and athletic shorts, her hair pulled into a tight, short ponytail.

"It's nice you met Athyna."

"She was cool. Not like the assholes at my school."

"Oh," Kate said. "But not all of them, right?"

Pia raised her eyebrows and said nothing.

"It's hard to switch," Kate guessed. "You probably miss your friends in Paris."

"Not really." Pia shifted her position in her pneumatic desk chair, and glanced at the picture on her nightstand. "I miss my cousins."

Kate looked at the photo. It was a selfie, the girls posed against a graffitied wall, wearing dark eye makeup and pouting for the camera. There was a distinct family resemblance, especially because it had been taken when Pia's hair was still dark.

"That's them?" Kate guessed. "In Saint-Cloud?" She knew she was getting the vowels wrong, but she felt stupid trying.

"*San-Clue*," Pia corrected. "Yeah—that's Emma and Inès."

But no other information was forthcoming, and Kate didn't want to seem as if she were seeking information about Nathalie's family.

"I wanted to see if you needed anything. When you knocked?"

Pia frowned. "Never mind."

"Are you sure?"

Her lips were pressed together, the same gesture that Stephen used to express frustration, but when she spoke, her voice was syrupy, almost shy.

"It was about a pregnancy test."

Kate sat down on the edge of Pia's bed, because there was nowhere else.

"What?"

"I took some."

In the kitchen, the dishwasher beeped three times to tell them it was finished. There were no voices, no hammering, only the hum of the air conditioner and the very faint sound of traffic in the street fourteen stories below. Kate couldn't feel the baby.

"I mean, I took a pack of yours."

"Oh. Why did you do that?"

Pia looked directly at Kate. "I was embarrassed to buy it from a store."

"Right," Kate said. "I get that. I mean—"

"You mean, why did I need it?"

"You don't have to tell me that," Kate began, but this conversation was so much more personal than anything they'd discussed up to this point that for a moment she hesitated.

Pia shrugged. "I don't mind—as long as you don't tell my dad."

"No," Kate said. "No, I wouldn't."

"I was worried I could be, so."

It was very far from the most distressing thing a teenager had told her, objectively. At school she always stopped a student who was on the point of sharing something, to remind them that she was legally obligated to report anything that could be classified as abuse or neglect. It was unfair to teach them that they could write about anything without reminding them of the consequences, especially to their parents. She'd had kids who said, with breathtaking maturity, that life had been hard on their mother or father, and they didn't deserve to be punished for one mistake.

With sex it was different. She generally discouraged this type of confidence from girls who came to her, although she was allowed to keep it to herself as long as a student wasn't in danger. Now she tried to remain neutral and unsurprised.

"You haven't been here very long."

Pia had a way of starting to laugh, then cutting it off. "Oh— it didn't happen *here*. I mean, where would I even?"

Kate laughed too, releasing nerves. "Right," she said. "I've read that teen pregnancy is down—not because of the pandemic. It's been going down since I was in high school."

Going down, but not gone, as the existence of Athyna's nephew proved, or a girl named Grisleni, whom she'd known at her last school, in the Bronx. Grisleni had been one of her favorite students ever, funny and hardworking and talented. They'd bonded, and she'd gone to the baby shower in a community hall in Mott Haven, decorated with lavender paper bunting. She'd tried to keep up over email, but eventually Grisleni's Hotmail had begun returning messages to sender. Sometimes on the train, before Covid, she'd imagined she saw her: a young woman with her student's long black curls and heavily lashed dark eyes, trying to maneuver a stroller over the platform gap. Then she would realize that it had been eight, nine, ten years since she'd left that school, and that the baby girl Grisleni had been carrying would be almost a teenager herself.

"It was harder to get a test there. I would've had to hitch into town."

Whereas here, you can just snoop in my bathroom, Kate thought. One of the many boxes she'd bought, probably uncovered in the cabinet underneath the sink.

"So—you took the test?"

Pia nodded in a way that made Kate think it would be very difficult, as a teacher, to know what she was thinking.

"And?"

"It was negative," Pia said.

"Oh—great," Kate said. "That's great." There was an awkward silence. Pia frowned at something on her desk.

"You should still be tested for STDs, though. I can set that up for you, if you want."

For the first time in this strange conversation, Pia looked genuinely alarmed. "Oh," she said, "No—my mom made me go to the doctor."

"So your mom knows that you're sexually active."

"Uh-huh."

"Then we don't have much to worry about."

Pia didn't register a yes or no to that. Instead she got up suddenly from the chair and began rummaging for something in the still-unpacked suitcase. Maybe it was the first time Kate had seen her legs uncovered: they were thin and tanned, with the stalky fragility of girls who developed late, but from the middle of the right thigh almost to the knee was a wide, straight gash, still covered with a dark brown scab. The skin around it was puckered and shiny.

"You hurt yourself," Kate said without thinking.

Pia stood up, covered the wound instinctively with her right hand. "Coral," she said. "It's really sharp."

"I've heard that."

"It doesn't hurt anymore."

"That's good."

There was a flutter, but it was in Kate's chest. The baby was completely quiet. Dead, maybe. Stephen believed that her previous experience was an anomaly. He said they were at the point that they could stop worrying—but in spite of all his knowledge about the body, he was wrong. There was no magic about the second trimester, no point past which you were safe, even once the child was out of the womb. Kate thought about getting up to go.

"There was a girl in my high school who got pregnant." The moment she said it, she wondered about her own motivations. It wasn't because she thought it would deter Pia. If kids wanted to fuck each other, they did.

Pia stood up and pulled a pair of track pants over her shorts. "What did she do?"

"She left for a year. Supposedly she was on a service trip with her church—in Honduras."

"But she wasn't?" As if casually. She perched on the housing for the radiator, painted white with a lattice screen.

"Of course not," Kate said. "She was in Ohio with her aunt and uncle. Everyone knew."

"What happened to the baby?"

"She was supposed to put it up for adoption—she did do that. But it was born too early. It died."

"Oh." Pia kicked gently against the steel screen of the radiator cover with her bare feet, first one foot and then the other. Each time, there was an unpleasant clang.

"Can you—"

Pia stopped.

"Thanks."

"You don't need them?"

"What?"

"The tests."

"Oh—no. It's okay."

"Because you are already?"

Kate thought she felt a faint cramping. Her whole body felt tight and hard.

"What?"

"Pregnant."

She and Stephen had agreed that they wouldn't lie. If she asked, they would tell her. It was just that every time she'd imagined that scene, she and Stephen were doing it together.

"Yes," she said. "We wanted to wait to tell you until we were absolutely sure."

She thought it was the answer that Pia had been expecting, so she was surprised to see her head jerk to attention. But that was something that happened. You suspected something, and then you asked, and then you were startled when your suspicions were confirmed. Probably Pia had sought out the tests for exactly that reason—only pretending to need them herself. After the initial shock, her eyes narrowed, and her chin lifted just slightly.

"The baby's due in March. We were going to wait to find out the sex, but if you want to know—"

Pia picked up her phone and started scrolling. "Gender is a construct."

"I'm sorry if you're upset."

"I'm not."

"Oh—okay. Good." She waited, but there was nothing—crickets, as her students would say. "I'll tell your dad we talked."

Pia looked up. Her jaw pushed forward, her chin pocked with tension.

"I meant, about the baby. I won't tell him about the other thing."

"I don't give a fuck what you tell him."

"Still. I'll let you talk to him about that, if you want."

Pia took an audible breath. Then she put the phone down on the windowsill. "What happened to her?"

"Who?"

"That girl from your class."

Kate hesitated, because Pia's interest was prurient. But she was the one who'd decided to tell the story.

"She came home. But that was the middle of the year. So she had to wait until the next year to reenroll."

"She didn't graduate with her class."

"Right."

"That must've sucked."

"I'm sure it did."

"And then what?"

"I don't know," Kate said.

Pia nodded, as if that was what she expected. "You didn't stay in touch."

13

When he got home, Kate was lying on her back on a mat in the bedroom, one hand on her stomach. A woman on the iPad propped up next to her head was counting her breaths, or probably not only Kate's breaths but those of a group of pregnant breathers all over the city. It could even be nationwide. *You are not the only one who feels overwhelmed. All you have to do right now is breathe.*

"Oh, hi," she said, opening her eyes. She was wearing one of the hospital's *Amazing Things Are Happening Here* T-shirts and a pair of salmon-pink leggings. Her hair was in that topknot that he'd always liked, and her cheeks were flushed.

"You look beautiful."

She narrowed her eyes. "Maybe in a sort of miracle-of-life sense. Not in the conventional sense."

"In both senses. Are we alone?"

Kate looked slightly alarmed. "Didn't you get my text?"

He reflexively pulled out his phone.

She sighed. "I'm right here. I told Pia—I had to, because she asked."

He tried not to show his relief that he hadn't had to do it himself. "How'd she take it?"

"Not great."

"That's what we expected."

"I don't think it was the best idea—me telling her."

"She had to find out somehow." A part of him had hoped that Pia would be excited. He could imagine her pushing a toddler on the bucket swings at the park, maybe a little boy to whom they would give a solid name without the slightest French resonance. He liked Ben or Jack or Gus.

"Where is she?"

Kate shook her head. "I heard her go out a while ago. She's probably in the park with her friends."

He'd loved being a dad on the playground. He was the one who'd gotten up early with her on Saturdays so that Nathalie could sleep. He and Pia had a whole routine. They'd stop at Levain for a coffee and a blueberry muffin for him, a cinnamon brioche and orange juice for her, but they wouldn't sit in the bakery. They took it to the Diana Ross Playground in the park and sat on the bench to eat. She would get distracted from her food, want to play right away. Athletic, and small for her age, which enhanced the appearance of coordination. And that very delicate little face that was mostly her mother, except with his mouth—a feature he'd always hated, until he saw it on his daughter. Her clothes were distinctive in a way he couldn't quite name—simple, because Nathalie wasn't into frills, but a little foreign. Other parents noticed her, and although these judgments were superficial, he couldn't help feeling proud.

He tried tracking her on his phone, just in case, but Pia wasn't sharing her location. His best guess was the Great Lawn, so he walked in past the Delacorte, where a brass band had attracted a group of elderly people. They looked like tourists, but he couldn't be sure—were groups of old people actually visiting New York? The band was fronted by a young Black woman in pink overalls playing a French horn, and a baby-faced white trumpeter in a newsboy's cap; the old people were masked, but the musicians, of course, were not. When he got up to the lawn, he started a methodical circle along its western edge, betting that a group of high school students wouldn't walk any farther than necessary before dropping to the grass to consume their after-school candy and soda.

As often happened these days, he was immediately distracted by public health—in particular the unevenness with which his neighbors were taking precautions. Groups were well spaced, but within those groups almost no one was masked; it was a beautiful day, more like summer than fall, and he didn't blame them. Or at least, he understood. The sunbathers and the readers were probably safe, but the earnest talkers—the group of students, the boomer political group, the group that looked, from its perfect diversity across all categories, like AA—were worrisome. He felt like some lunatic or freak, and had a crazy image of himself clambering up one of the green hawthorns at the edge of the lawn, whose red fruits were now staining the soles of his shoes, to deliver a message no one wanted to hear: *Winter is coming! Beware, beware!*

She wasn't there, or at least she wasn't along the periphery, and it would be too obvious to wander the center of the lawn looking for her. She would kill him, or at least become even angrier with him than she already was. He exited at the top of the lawn and took the bridle path back down toward Eighty-First, passing through the arch. Riders in velvet helmets were taking advantage of the beautiful weather. Was it eerie to see people looking at their phones on horseback, or was he just getting old? He didn't intentionally take the path that led to that playground; he just wound up there, admiring the simple seventies aesthetic, the blocky wooden climbing structure with its chain link spiderweb. He looked until he saw a mother looking back, scowling at him, because lone men staring dreamily into playgrounds were suspicious.

He'd given up and left the park when he saw her, in a crowd exiting from underground. She was climbing the stairs out of the subway at Eighty-First Street, and at first he didn't recognize her, both because of her clothing and because he hadn't expected her to be coming from the train. She was wearing a long, Polynesian print sundress, and her hair was held back from her face with a cotton band. The utilitarian black straps of her school backpack looked strange against her bare shoulders. Thank god she was wearing a mask—one of the N95s he kept in the drawer by the front door—but it made it hard to read her expression.

"Pia!" He had to call her several times before she stopped, although he was pretty sure she'd heard him the first time. She waited for him on the southwest corner, opposite a construction site where a length of orange PVC funneled steam from the pipes below the street. The air smelled like laundry and a deep organic rot.

"I was looking for you!"

There was some kind of pity on her face, or amusement. "I went downtown."

"We should talk about the subway."

Instead of responding, she dropped the backpack to one shoulder and extracted a pack of gum from the smaller zippered pocket. She pulled down the mask, unwrapped three neon yellow sticks, and put them in her mouth at once.

"Hollywood," he said. "I haven't seen that in a while."

"It's my last pack."

She started to say something else, but two ambulances screamed by, one after the other. They dodged a phalanx of dogs barking crazily at the emergency vehicles. A heavily tattooed dog walker, her keys on a carabiner at her waist, reined them in, yelling over the sirens.

"The train just seems unnecessarily risky."

"I take the bus to school."

"School is one thing, but—"

"I had to get a souvenir for a friend in Moʻorea."

"You couldn't order it?"

"If I could've ordered it, she could have."

He was relieved it was a female friend. According to her mother, she hadn't had any. "What kind of souvenir?"

Pia didn't answer, maybe because he'd crossed a line. It was just that he'd missed a couple of years, during which the threshold for privacy had changed.

"Sorry," he said. "It doesn't matter."

"Magnets."

"What?"

She sighed and reached into the backpack, which looked empty without the load she normally carried to school. The box was about half the size of a shoebox, unwrapped, one of those executive desk toys with a row of spherical magnets hanging from a frame.

"I didn't even know they still made those."

"It's called a Newton's Cradle."

"Why does she want that?"

Pia shrugged. "She saw it in some movie? It's weird what people get interested in."

Her tone had softened, and he was encouraged. "I know what you mean. I remember this guy your mom knew on Rangiroa always wanted us to bring him Mallomars."

She laughed, more than he expected. He tried to use it to his advantage. "I don't mind you getting around on your own. I just thought you were with kids from school."

"Those assholes."

"I get it," Stephen said. "But it's early days."

"I want to go remote."

"Out of the question." Probably he should've given her a chance to make an argument, but she'd come halfway around the world to go to school in person. The school was actually making it work.

"I knew you'd say that."

"You used to love Lycée." He could remember the little blue smocks that buttoned up the front, that they used to wear for art and outdoor play. They'd looked just like the girls from the Madeline books.

Pia expelled an exasperated breath.

"What?"

"Nothing."

He waited, but she didn't elaborate. "I didn't know it was that bad. Why didn't you tell me?"

She looked at him. The white headband revealed a patch of

acne normally hidden under the platinum fringe, the darker roots now showing under the blond.

"You mean 'cause we never keep secrets from each other?"

"Pia," he said. But he'd walked right into that one. "I'm sorry I didn't tell you myself. We were waiting—"

"Yeah," Pia cut him off. "She told me."

They stopped at the light on Amsterdam. Around them people hurried through their errands, not making eye contact. It was different from the scene in the park, not only because clouds had moved to cover the sun.

"I guess it's not that much of a surprise," he said.

"Maxine said you would, but I didn't believe her."

"Maxine?"

"She said when people marry someone that young, they always do."

"Kate's almost forty."

"That would be like me dating a two-year-old."

"I can understand why you're upset."

Pia shrugged, glanced both ways this time before starting across. "I'm not *upset*. It's just kind of embarrassing. Like— guess who's going to be a big sister?"

He was happy she'd used the word, at least. "I could get you one of those shirts, finally." He thought he saw a slight smile. There had been a period of years when she'd asked almost daily. Most of the other children she knew either had an older sibling or were getting a younger one. It was rare to find another family with only one child. Nathalie pointed to the ecological advantages, and more immediately, to the fact that they lived in Manhattan, at that time in a two-bedroom apartment in a prewar brick co-op on West Eightieth. The maintenance was enough to pay rent on a whole house in almost any other city; here it got them five rooms, including the bathroom, with scuffed oak floors and distempered radiators, a building full of families who kept their shoes, strollers, and athletic equipment in the halls.

When his father died, Frances pointed out that they might

trade up. His mother even paid for Pia's schooling, and so their expenses should have been minimal; he was secretly proud that he'd married a woman who cared as little for consumer goods as he did. Given that, though, their credit card bills had always surprised him; they each had certain indulgences. Nathalie might not spend money on her own clothes, but she ordered Pia's from Europe and thought nothing of dropping three hundred dollars on cosmetics at Caudalie. And he had to admit that the amount they spent on car services, groceries, and takeout was obscene. In spite of all this, in the context of her school— where paparazzi occasionally appeared on the sidewalk, trying to catch the movie stars picking up their kids—Pia actually had felt herself to be at an economic disadvantage.

It wasn't as if he wished to go back to that apartment now. He looked forward to the silence of the lobby, the power of the mirrored elevator whisking them upward, the calm British voice saying *fourteenth floor*. It had been a pleasure to walk Kate through the empty rooms of 14C with the broker, who deferred to her as if she were the one paying for everything. Kate showed a reserved admiration: she might have been looking at an apartment for a more fortunate couple whom she nevertheless refrained from envying. She didn't despise those people, the way Nathalie might have, but he didn't think she really believed she would be living there until they were unpacking the boxes.

They reached the massive glass and steel awning just as the rain was starting, the LAUREATE in brass relief under a filigreed design that might have been a crown of golden leaves.

The door opened as if by magic. "Dr. Davenport."

"Hi, Yuri," he and Pia said together. She gave the doorman a radiant smile, and he thought she was as adept at concealing her emotions as her mother was transparent.

"It's nice here," she said, as they waited in front of the marble-paneled elevator bank.

"I'm glad you like it."

"Lots of kids are still remote."

"I think only when there's a medical reason. And I don't think you can switch mid-stream—only at winter break."

"I think anything is possible," Pia said. "When parents ask."

He had to admit that might be true. The elevator was taking longer than usual, maybe because people were now loath to share the cars.

"So you'll ask?"

"I'd have to discuss it with Kate as well."

There was Nathalie: not only the identical dark eyes but that stubborn insistence, steamrolling over counterarguments in pursuit of what she wanted. But at the same time there was his daughter, who looked so lonely.

"Yes," he said. "I'll ask."

14

9-21-20

Crossed off priority #1. I went to this huge Home Depot on 3rd Ave. The guy who helped me was an asshole. He asked what I wanted it for, like it was his right to know. I thought about saying it was for a science project, but I wanted it to be nothing like the actual reason.

> ME: Art project
> HIM: What's your art about?
> ME: ??
> HIM: Is it about your FANTASIES?

Why can't I ever think of what to say back? What do you call that? Oublie pas ta langue, Aunt Sonia wrote to me when she heard I was moving back, but now I'm forgetting everything. Then I went to Barnes & Noble & bought the toy. They asked me if I wanted it wrapped. Glad I said no because on the way back, I ran into Dad and I had to show him the box.

9-23-20

No, my ART is about nuclear war. L'esprit de l'escalier = when you think of a comeback too late. We found out today that there won't be an Upper School play this year, because of Covid. Or maybe they'll have one online, if we're lucky. Everyone sitting in front of a Zoom saying lines, wearing whatever costumes we can find at home. M. Dupree was like: Sucks, that. He's cool. Today in class:

MAXINE: My mom is such a cunt.
MD: That word, interestingly, comes from the Latin: cuniculum. Does anyone know the meaning?
ALEXA STRAUSS (of course): It means "burrow."
MD: Exactly. So in the Middle Ages, "rabbit" was slang for a woman's genitals.
MAXINE: Ma mère est vraiment un lapin.

LOL = MDR.
But there still isn't going to be a play.

9-26-20

"Lloyd's is the world's leading insurance and reinsurance marketplace, with a common purpose; to understand and share society's risk. Together with our customers, business partners and communities all over the world, we are building a braver future—one that is more sustainable, resilient and inclusive." (lloyds.com/about-lloyds/our-purpose)

9-27-20

Dad found a box of books for the baby. He's like, Do you remember these? The one I remembered was We're Going on a Bear Hunt. There's the father and three kids on the cover, the baby in pjs on his shoulders. Maybe because I always wanted brothers and sisters. And then the mom is in it too, but they draw her like a kid. I remember I was confused—was that the mom, or an older girl? When Mom was planning to go away, she'd say, "I'm going to have to spend some time in the field," and for a long time, I thought she meant an actual field. LOL. But when we were looking at the books [Dad all nervous because we're like ACKNOWLEDGING the impending arrival of his baby] I realized that it was that actual field I used to picture. From the bear book. Grass! Long wavy grass! We can't go over it. We can't go under it. Oh no! We've got to go through it! Even after I went to Mo'orea. It makes no sense because the picture is a field in the country somewhere, maybe England, with grass up to the dad's armpits, up to the kids' chins. Swishy swashy! Swishy swashy! Wildflowers & no ocean anywhere. It's weird how when you're a kid you can think something for a long time after it's logical—le Père Noël, etc. etc.—and then suddenly realize, Oh right, no.

15

There was always a period of relief after her daughter left, and then the loneliness set in. She'd been secretly glad last spring, when it had become clear that French schools weren't going to reopen until the fall. Her daughter had arrived from Paris in May, and they'd quarantined for two weeks at a gloomy airport hotel in Faʻaʻā. Then they'd moved to the cottage in Haʻapiti. Pia hung out in the office during the day, doing her remote school when the Wi-Fi allowed. When school was finally finished for the year, Nathalie thought she might make herself useful around the station, but it turned out that what Pia most wanted to do was to dive with Raffi. They worked out an arrangement where he took her out when he wasn't occupied with the scientists, replacing a bit of the income he normally made from tourists on the side. Nathalie and Pia had dinner together in the evenings, and sometimes watched a TV show together: they liked *Dix Pour Cent*, *Ted Lasso*, and the Polynesian comedy *SIS*. Mostly Nathalie wanted to work after dinner; she thought Pia ought to use that time to read—novels, or something. But Pia argued that Nathalie never read anything outside her work, and insisted on spending her evenings on Snapchat and TikTok and Instagram.

During the months they'd spent together in Moʻorea, Nathalie had made a point of asking about Pia's phone calls with Stephen. She thought an adolescent girl's relationship with her father was crucial, perhaps for Pia in particular. If her daughter was in a certain mood, she would accuse Nathalie of trying to extract information about Stephen's life, and especially his new marriage. She just barely kept herself from saying that she had no need to get that information from Pia, because Stephen had started writing to her himself. She had been surprised, also not. The pandemic was his excuse to forget about Martin and reestablish some of their former intimacy. Since Martin, he'd related to her in an emotionally frozen way that she thought of as particularly American. The idea of Americans as loose and freewheeling was absurd, a creation of Hollywood.

Pia had a way of responding to questions about her father that Nathalie had to admire. She blinked her eyes, appeared not to understand. Was there a reason her father shouldn't be fine? Was there a reason she was inquiring? Was it odd to have moved four times between the ages of ten and fifteen, from New York with both her parents, to a marine research station in Perpignan with her mother, to a Parisian suburb with her aunt and uncle, and then back with her mother to another research facility in the South Pacific where she had once spent a year as a child? Was she supposed to have feelings about it? Pia didn't actually ask these questions; it was all in her face, which was such a perfect mask of diffidence that Nathalie thought she might someday go onstage. She was certainly never going to be a scientist.

People often exclaimed at the physical similarities between the two of them, but neither of them agreed. Pia would respond that she was short (she was petite, like Frances, her paternal grandmother), and Nathalie always said that Pia was much more beautiful—which she was, if only she would occasionally smile. The real difference, Nathalie believed, was that she had always known what she wanted to do with her life. She had known ever since a family holiday in Camaret-sur-Mer, where they'd walked among the tide pools and her father had bent down to show her how she might put her finger in the mouth of a purple-tipped anemone, then gently pull it away—*tac!*—unstuck, but forever attached to this phylum of creatures, the Cnidaria. Whereas when you asked Pia what she hoped to do in the future, her daughter had no idea; she seemed to think there was something wrong with the question itself. For this reason, Pia would do better in the American system, where they allowed you to waffle and deliberate well into your twenties.

Now she thought that they should have used those four months together for conversation. She had a new appreciation for what Stephen had gone through on the phone. She tried to take a break around three in the afternoon every day in order to ask her daughter if she could talk; more often than not, Pia said she had too much homework. Every few days they did manage it over WhatsApp, Nathalie sitting at the picnic table near the reception, where she could hear the splash of the water wheel aerating the shrimp beds across the road, and sometimes catch the particular heavy sweetness of the tiare blossoms that grew on manicured bushes planted by the former director all around the lab. In New York it was nine p.m. and Pia was in her room doing homework; usually the Wi-Fi was good enough for them to have a genuine conversation. Or at least, the Wi-Fi wasn't the problem.

"Tell me your classes, again?" she asked one day, struggling to get her daughter to talk. The transformation effected at Sunset Coiffure in Tiahura was ebbing, her natural dark hair starting to reassert itself. Nathalie thought the tan was fading too, although it was hard to tell from the phone's camera. Pia was lying on her bed in the apartment Nathalie didn't recognize, against pale blue cotton pillows, the kind of innocuous bedding you might select for a teenager you didn't know. Stephen had asked before she arrived whether Pia wanted to choose some things for her room, and Pia, in one of her moods, had said she didn't give a fuck. Nathalie had translated that by saying that Pia would wait until she got to New York, and so she thought the wife must have picked out the essentials in the meantime.

"I have English literature and history in English. And also the sexual health workshop. French literature, chemistry, economics, and math are in French." They spoke in French, but Pia inserted the names of the English subjects in her American accent—a way of speaking that had been a marvel to Nathalie when her daughter first acquired it.

"Why history in English but economics in French?"

"No idea."

"What do you learn in the sexual health workshop?"

"Oral sex, reusable menstrual products, pornography."

"How useful!"

"Truly," Pia said drily. "Zac had to name four types."

"Four types of pornography?"

"That would've been no problem for him. But it was four reusable menstrual products. He only knew two."

"I don't think I know of any?"

"Oh, and Mandarin. Mandarin is in Mandarin."

"Mandarin!"

"I hate it."

"Why did you choose it?"

"Dad chose it."

"Why did you allow him to do that?"

But Pia was no longer interested. Nathalie felt a sort of panic. In a moment, Pia would say that she had to go, and Nathalie might not reach her again for three or four days. It was incredible to think that if Stephen's wife wanted to see Pia, she could simply walk into the next room.

Behind her daughter's head were the blue pillows, and behind the blue pillows, an empty white wall. "Have you decorated your room?"

"No."

"Have you taken the things from the suitcase?"

"No."

"I see." Was there a part of her that took pleasure in Pia's failure to adapt? She decided that no, there wasn't. The station wasn't the right place for Pia, nor was her sister's family, where she would be forced through the ruthless machine of the French school system. Not everyone encountered an anemone that revealed her future. And it wasn't so terrible to grow up a little, before you decided how you wanted to live your life.

That first year they'd spent together in Moʻorea, she was five. Stephen was able to join them twice for only a week each time, and so Nathalie always felt unkind saying that it was the happiest period of her life. That year, when she finished her work, or as a break if she had to go back to the lab, she would ride her SYM along the coast to the Montessori in Temaʻe near the airport. She would wait outside the gate with the other parents for the children to finish singing their songs—"Ah, les crocodiles!" and "Tourne, tourne petit moulin," but also some in Tahitian, including one about the crown-of-thorns starfish—*Acanthaster planci*—the corallivorous echinoderm whose devastating effects she was studying at the time. In the song, the sea stars ate the coral, and then they went down to the bottom of the sea and the coral revived: everything in its own time, in a cycle. She loved the idea, but the evidence was against that kind of recovery continuing indefinitely into the Anthropocene. Blissfully unaware of these facts, the children would emerge, taking their backpacks from a row of wooden hooks. The children were Tahitian, French, American, and British; you heard at least three languages as they embraced their parents and caregivers. The fenced play area had swings and a tiny climbing structure shaped like a ship, not a canoe but a cruise ship, with a fin-shaped stabilizer accessible by a ladder, from the top of which you could see the glittering turquoise water of the public beach.

She felt like the perfect mother when she picked Pia up from the Montessori, and she wanted to hear all about it. But like most children, Pia wasn't inclined to give a detailed report of her day. And so she always asked the only question that prompted a response—a question she thought she might as well try now.

"Did anything funny happen today?"

Pia remembered. Nathalie could see it in the half smile, even on the screen. The mouth was Stephen's, but Stephen would never suppress a smile that way. He either smiled or he didn't.

"Someone ate a bee."

"What?"

"Jacob is his name. I think? Or maybe Jules."

"Was Jacob-or-Jules stung?"

"It was dead."

"Why would anyone eat a dead bee?"

"That's what the teacher asked."

"And?"

"He thought it would be funny."

"Boys are quite young at your age."

"Obviously," Pia said. "Oh, and I guess this is also funny— Dad's having a baby."

There was silence, which Pia finally filled with a nervous, yelping laugh. Startlingly, incredibly, Nathalie had never even considered it. She knew Kate's age exactly; she was thirty-seven, and so, of course. Nathalie had been thirty-four when Pia was born, but later she thought she could've waited, especially since they'd decided they would have only one. Now, apart from her, unbeknownst to her, there would be a baby.

"Wonderful."

Her daughter was watching her closely. "You knew?"

"No." She wished for a moment they weren't on camera. She tried to keep her face calm, but she didn't have that gift. "This is the first I'm hearing of it, but I'm not surprised."

"Dad's so old."

"Not so old."

"Sorry, I meant—"

"Oh, it doesn't matter!" The idea of her daughter feeling sorry for her was insupportable. Honestly this woman was doing her a favor. She always thought it would've been better for Pia to have a sibling, but she hadn't wanted to do it herself. Pia and the baby would be far apart in age—but barely more, it occurred to Nathalie, than Stephen and his new wife. It was almost funny. There was no reason Pia and this child couldn't someday be close.

Nathalie changed her tone. "It doesn't matter how old the father is. And fifty isn't old in New York. Plenty of your friends had fathers that age—Zoe or Chloe, or whatever her name was."

"There was one of each."

"Are they still there?"

"The old Chloe and a new Zoe."

"Is your father having a boy or a girl?"

"They don't want to know. Unless I want to know, she said—then she'll find out."

She noticed that Pia avoided using Kate's name, and so she used it on purpose. "Kate said that?"

Pia glanced toward the door, lowered her voice conspiratorially. "Weird, right?"

Nathalie laughed. She'd resolved a moment before to be 100 percent adult about the situation, generous and unperturbed. She had to be. But it was hard to resist the rare intimacy with her daughter. "Somewhat weird. But what did you tell her?"

"I said I didn't care."

"Like Pierre."

"What?"

It amazed her that Pia didn't remember. At one point the miniature box set with its red cloth covers had been their favorite. She had always thought that Americans wrote the best children's books, because they were like children themselves.

When they hung up, Nathalie went back to the office and worked through the afternoon. Ann invited her to her bungalow for dinner—the brilliant Norwegian theoretician, Andreas, was making chicken curry—but Nathalie excused herself on the grounds of a grant she was writing to bring colleagues from Perpignan next summer. When she finally locked up for the evening, she thought she really ought to go into town for something to eat. Instead she decided to have a drink. There was a mini-fridge where she normally kept a few Hinanos and a bottle of duty-free Diplôme left over from the last resident. Personally she couldn't stand the taste of juniper. But she remembered now the bottle of blanc de blancs that Marie-Laure had left her when she went back to Paris in April. She'd been saving it—it was sort of crazy to open it for no reason, and alone, given the expense of good wine on the island. However.

Nathalie took the bottle outside to the red concrete porch. Insects swarmed around the light from the room next door, where two of the young Swiss ecologists cohabited. Mosquitoes, midges, and dull brown wax moths beat their wings against the screen, and the house geckos chirped under the steep green slope of the corrugated roof. She decided to sit in the fare. Would anyone walk by and see her drinking alone? But the only person likely to be around was the security guard, who was no doubt sitting on his plastic stool at the entrance, chatting with a relative on his phone. And why did she care? Were her colleagues really thinking what she imagined they were thinking: about the affair with Martin, the divorce, her petulant teenage child, soon to have a sibling? It was much more likely that everyone was too involved in their own domestic dramas to give more than a passing thought to hers.

She was no longer in touch with Martin, but he was the one who'd first alerted her in 2017, when the Danish shipping giant Maersk made a $25 million commitment to a Canadian start-up, DeepGreen. He'd forwarded a press release announcing that the company would supply two ships as well as "project services" to a series of exploratory voyages in exchange for shares in the new venture. The exploratory voyages, according to the company's CEO, were a necessary step in moving from the exploration to exploitation phase of a mining program. The company worked through a subsidiary in the tiny island nation of Nauru, which was also necessary in order to secure rights to two of the richest swaths of the Clarion-Clipperton Zone, on the abyssal plains between 4,000 and 5,500 meters below the surface. With no evidence, the CEO baldly declared that mining the sea floor—less than one percent of which scientists or any other human beings had ever seen—was a responsible solution to a projected scarcity of metals like cobalt, copper, nickel, and manganese, and would avoid problems with terrestrial mining, such as pollution, deforestation, and child labor. It was laughable that CEOs of mining companies had suddenly become passionate about deforestation—not to mention child labor in Africa—at the moment that a fortune was set to be made from potato-sized lumps of metal sitting on the darkest regions of the ocean floor.

She made her way to the small, thatched structure, sat down not at the empty picnic table but on the grass with her back against one of the wooden supports. The question was how you could make people understand what was down there. There was the Casper octopus, ghostly white and not yet named, that laid its eggs on the very nodules the mining companies wanted to take. There was *Vampyroteuthis infernalis*, mischaracterized as a squid but actually the only living member of a family as old as the dinosaurs, and 270-year-old Greenland sharks that didn't reach reproductive maturity until the age of 150. But none of those more familiar creatures had anything on the Cnidaria: corals alive today that had been around when the pharaohs ruled Egypt, sponges that had inhabited that cold, lightless world for eleven thousand years, since the end of the last ice age. The soft-bodied octocorals, suspension feeders, could be starved by a plume of mining sediment, and they'd only just identified a new species of stalked glass sponge growing on the cobalt-crusted seamounts, concealing crabs and worms like shy apartment-dwellers in its lacy perforations. A whole miraculous world that had been undisturbed because nothing had changed there—not the darkness or the pressure or the clarity of the water—for all those thousands of years. And with one swipe of a robotic claw, it could all be gone.

Nathalie popped the cork, pouring generously for herself into a purple Duralex water glass from a set she'd bought at the Carrefour in Fa'a'ā before Pia's arrival. She wasn't good with the heavens, but on clear nights in Mo'orea it was impossible not to look up into a night sky that seemed to catch the island in a spangled net of stars. She could pick out Sagittarius and above it Capricorn, with a large bright body near the vertex of the triangle closest to the horizon—Saturn, she was almost sure. She lifted a glass to the genderless baby. *Bonne chance, mon petit,* she may or may not have said out loud.

16

Sometimes she told her mother about her symptoms, but after a while her mother just said, "Oh, Athyna," and so she stopped. It was worse in the mornings anyway, when her mother was mostly sleeping because her shift at the hospital ended at midnight. Her sister left before Marcus woke up, and even if E was awake, it wasn't like he was going to come down and make sure Marcus sat on the toilet, get him his cereal. She was usually pretty happy to see Marcus anyway, even when he woke her up by lifting the comforter on the couch and putting his head under there, blowing in her ear: *Teetee*. His body was moist with sweat but he didn't smell—or he smelled like Johnson's Baby Shampoo. He talked to his Cheerios while he ate, a stream of nonsense that she guessed was always running on a loop in his head.

Once, when she was little, she'd asked her nana who the guy outside the Foodtown was talking to. Of course she knew he was crazy, but there was a thing she did with her grandmother where she pretended to be younger than she was, so her nana would treat her that way. Her nana saw through it, but Athyna was her baby, the youngest of all her grandchildren. She had waited to ask about the crazy guy until her grandmother was inside the store, at the meat fridge, picking up packages of ground meat to check the dates. To the angels, she had said.

And who was to say it was nonsense, anyway? Maybe the reason Marcus didn't walk or talk for so long was that he was busy with some great creative project, and he would grow up to be the next Spike Lee or Jean-Michel Basquiat or Walter Dean Myers, who wrote a story that they read in school last year and that she really liked. It was all about stepping up and being a dad to your kid, and she actually gave E the photocopied packet when Breanna wasn't around, and said he should read it. And he took it and was like, *Yeah, Tee. Cool.* But of course he didn't.

Not Basquiat, because he died. Sometimes she worried she would accidentally have a thought and then it would come true. That worry was one she'd confided only in Rosalie, her old therapist, and it was what she really wanted to write about, but her teacher said it wasn't a good idea. She thought everyone would write about anxiety during the pandemic, and it made Athyna so ashamed to imagine her teacher thinking of her as unoriginal or boring that she couldn't even explain in the moment. Then the teacher's freaky-looking daughter—stepdaughter—had come in and they'd gotten distracted. What she would've liked to explain was that the symptoms of Covid and of what Rosalie had told her was anxiety were the same, and that made it completely stressful every morning when she woke up with a stomachache and a sore throat. Her chest felt tight a lot, too, and so when her mom brushed her off, she would go to Breanna, ask her to take her temperature, in case she was somehow doing it wrong. But her sister had even less patience than her mother. She would roll her eyes and be like, *Thyna, you are* fine.

What if she complained so much that when it was really Covid, they missed it? There were kids who got it so bad that they couldn't go to school for months, or play sports, or even remember the stuff they'd already learned. She'd been planning to try out for the volleyball team, and work on the yearbook again, because she liked laying stuff out on Adobe. It made you feel calm to move the photos into the right places, and create the right-sized box to fit each senior's memory. She'd been working on it since she was a freshman, and never once had she thought that anything could happen to keep a professional photo of herself in a maroon-and-black cap and gown from appearing next to a box of text about what BEST meant to her.

This morning, Marcus hadn't woken her. He'd been playing on the floor near the couch, and she'd almost shouted for E, except she didn't want to wake her mom. She could smell Breanna's L'Air du Temps, and so she knew she'd already left for work. It made her crazy to think of her sister breezing through the living room, past the sleeping lump of Athyna under the ugly plaid comforter, getting out of there for the entire day. The walls of Half Moon, Breanna's clinic, were the color of chocolate, with glossy white moldings, modern upholstered couches, and glass tables with fresh flowers and fashion magazines. The couches were the same pale pink as Breanna's scrubs, which she put on every morning to offer sympathy and hormones to sad white women who wanted to get pregnant. Maybe they weren't all white; Athyna had never asked. Rich women in any case, because IVF was crazy expensive and most insurance didn't cover it. After Breanna welcomed them with compassion—this was something her boss had said about her, which Breanna repeated proudly, as if compassion were some kind of talent and Breanna was the Simone Biles of assisted fertility—she ducked into little rooms to take their blood.

Sometimes they're like, do you have kids, Breanna confided in Athyna. *And I can't be like, oh yeah, I have a son and I wasn't even trying.* Her sister had an expression that was supposed to indicate helplessness or surprise, but it was really just another way of looking pretty. Athyna thought that it was probably possible to avoid lying and also keep people from feeling bad, if Breanna was really so compassionate. It wasn't like she was the one actually helping to make people pregnant, either. There was, in fact, no difference between what her mother and her sister did for a living, except that her mom made more money and worked shitty hours in a hospital. Also, most of the people whose blood her mother drew were waiting for bad news—

HIV or cancer or diabetes—and not getting ready to spend tens of thousands of dollars to have a baby.

"Hey, little man," she said to Marcus. She touched her phone but it had died in the night, as usual. What time was it? She found her glasses on the floor, and dragged herself off the couch, crouched next to Marcus, and ripped the side of the pull-up, so heavy it was almost dripping. If it broke, the little plastic beads would drop onto the carpet and be impossible to fish out. And they'd be walking on Marcus's piss forever. "Come on and wipe," she said, because she didn't want him to get a rash. Of course someone had let the toilet paper in the bathroom run out, so she took the edge of her sister's blue towel and wet it, added a little of E's Men + Care body wash, and wiped Marcus's ass and his little penis, which was circumcised. Her sister had said there was no reason to do it—someone at work had talked her out of it—but then she changed her mind because she said that E said that he wanted his son to "look like him."

That was ridiculous, because no nasty grown dick looked anything like the bare little mushroom sprouting between Marcus's legs. She'd seen two others. Her dad's, when he was alive and she was little enough that he didn't care if she walked in on him in the bathroom. And then last year before Covid she had her first boyfriend, but she and Javier hadn't done any more than fool around. She could tell he was getting tired of it, and he was going to break up with her, and so she'd done it herself over text. Jada had organized a bunch of girls to give her shit about it, and she almost felt bad until of course Jada got with Javier herself. Then it was like: okay, whatever.

"Run and put on your big boy pants," she told Marcus. "Hurry up. Teetee'll get your Cheerios."

But first she poured herself some coffee. At least her sister had the decency to make a full pot. E didn't drink it, was always talking about how caffeine fucked with your brain, which was funny given how much weed he smoked. She put in some cream and two sugars. It wasn't until she'd fixed Marcus's cereal and some orange juice that she thought to look at the clock on the microwave. It was 8:48; her class had been online for almost twenty minutes and she hadn't even realized.

Just then Marcus trotted into the kitchen, looking for his breakfast, with his father right behind him.

"I'm late," she told E. She almost told him why, but it wasn't really anyone else's fault this time. If she hadn't been too lazy to plug in her phone before bed, she would've been in class already. She lifted Marcus onto the stool by the counter, and then made for the bathroom. She could at least smooth her hair back with Bree's new organic coconut gel. But E was blocking the way.

"Stop playing," she said.

"Try and get past me."

She couldn't help laughing. "I'm serious, E. I gotta get to class."

"On the iPad?" The doorway was narrow enough that he filled it just by putting his forearms against the frame. When she tried to duck under one side, her head met his elbow. He hadn't been smoking; he smelled like the Dior Sauvage her sister bought him, and his arms were ripped from the pull-up bar in their room. She was conscious of her hair, which was crazy, and the fact that she wasn't yet wearing a bra. Behind them Marcus was suddenly silent, which meant that something had actually gotten his attention.

Then, without warning, Elijah stepped aside, sending her stumbling into the empty living room. Or empty except for her father's picture, which looked this morning as if he knew a secret.

"Go, Teeny, go," E said, which was annoying as shit. Also, why did everyone in her house call her something different?

When she logged on from the bottom bunk in Marcus's room—because no one needed to know she was sleeping on the couch now—they were talking about the election. Some of them would be able to vote for the first time, and everyone was voting the same way, except for maybe Edison, who wouldn't talk about it. Edison was that kind of green-eyed handsome Caribbean guy you saw in advertisements; he'd once told them his dad liked Trump because he wasn't a politician and he said what he thought. And Alicia was like, "Dude, your dad's from the D.R., right? Doesn't he know Trump wants to put him in a fucking cage?" And Mercedes said that Trump had taken away DACA, and he was going to send her and her sister to Honduras, where they'd never even been. And Michael, this geeky white kid from Queens—the one you might actually suspect of being MAGA—said that Trump ignored the virus until it was too late. And then Hernan was like, "Yeah, Trump killed my grandma," and everyone was quiet.

Since then, Athyna could tell that her teacher was trying to keep it about civics: How long do representatives serve in Congress, and who can tell me what is the filibuster? Some of the kids were actually in the classroom, and even though they all said it sucked, Athyna envied them. She searched out Krystal in the grid, and then sent her a private chat, which Kate had forgotten to disable. Krystal turned on her camera, and gave Athyna a little wave. Athyna had digital copies of everything they were reading: *We the Animals*, *A Streetcar Named Desire*, *We Should All Be Feminists*, and *Going to Meet the Man*, but it was different to see all the new spines on the shelves behind Krystal, each title a different color. Her mother and Breanna said she'd be crazy to commute during Covid if she didn't have to, and she argued; she threatened to sign up for the hybrid at the next transition period, just so E could see what it was like to be responsible for Marcus on his own.

But the fact was that her heart sometimes started racing on the way to the deli, and she had a sudden fear that the people brushing past her on the sidewalk, pods in their ears and masks on their faces, weren't people at all but giant insects, an infestation that had happened while she'd been hiding inside. On those trips, it was a relief to get back into the house and

see the beige living room carpet with the heart-shaped coffee stain near the base of the radiator, and even the hideous
plaid comforter, which she always folded neatly over the back
of the couch, next to the glass-topped end table with the large
framed portrait of her dad. It had been taken at her youngest
aunt's wedding in New Jersey, and it showed her father in a
light brown suit and open-collared white shirt, much less gray
in his fade than she remembered, looking into the camera with
an expression too serious for a party guest, as if he somehow
knew that this was the picture that would sit on top of the
white coffin at First Central Baptist twelve years later. Having him there reminded her how, even more than her mother,
he was the one who'd insisted on the house being picked-up
and tidy, who straightened the pile of mail before he put it on
the kitchen table, who washed the car himself in the driveway
every Saturday.

"Athyna?" her teacher said.

"Sorry," she said. "I'm sorry I was late. I was watching my
nephew and I didn't see the time."

Everyone laughed, and she understood that she'd missed
the question.

"I was asking if you could come to the party," Kate said.
"I was saying that we got school funding for a pizza party, in
Prospect Park."

"Like just for seniors?" Athyna asked, and this time no one
laughed because maybe everyone was wondering the same
thing. Were they actually getting something special just for
them?

"By homeroom," Kate said. "So we'll stay podded together.
But it should be fun. I'm hoping we can all be there."

Prospect Park, Athyna thought. The ferry, and then at least
two trains, different from the ones she normally took to school.
Her throat was hurting again; she wasn't imagining it.

"Yeah, I guess," she told her teacher. "I have to ask my mom."

17

He thought of himself as someone who was good under pressure. There was one incident in particular while he was doing his residency in internal medicine. The patient was an overweight white male in his early seventies, in critical condition. When their group came in, he was sitting hunched forward in the Emergency Department, waiting for a bed in the hospital. His pulse was thready, and his skin was a strange gray. The attending confirmed pericardial effusion with an ultrasound probe, and a nurse had brought a 60cc syringe. But it was clear almost immediately that the amount of fluid was more than usual—the attending said he'd never seen anything like it—and Stephen had in the moment come up with the idea of a vacuum bottle, normally used to remove large volumes of fluid from the stomach rather than from around the heart. He'd been allowed to perform the procedure himself, not elegantly; he'd sort of jammed it in through a sub-xiphoid incision, since the kit wasn't made to be used that way. It wasn't the kind of thing they taught you in the classroom, and yet it had worked; the man had come back. He'd done it all while his classmates watched, impressed and a little envious.

"Your father is a cardiologist," the attending had confirmed afterward, and Stephen had explained that his father was a trusts-and-estates attorney, but his mother was an ob-gyn. The attending had written Stephen's recommendation for his subsequent fellowship in cardiology, which he'd followed with another in heart failure. It had seemed right to him at the time, but now he sometimes wondered—was it really just that incident that had determined how he would spend the rest of his life?

For the long weekend, Stephen decided they would go out to Amagansett, just the three of them. At Pia's school the holiday was now Indigenous Peoples' Day but the governor had come down on the side of Columbus, on the creative rationale that he represented the city's Italian American heritage. Now the NYPD had a van permanently parked by the limestone statue at Columbus Circle, behind its metal barricade, amid calls for its removal. At the hospital it didn't much matter what you called the holiday, because New York City had just hit fifty thousand cases for the second time, and everyone was gearing up for something as bad as or even worse than the spring. He thought it might be his last chance to leave the city before the second wave began in earnest, and he wanted to take full advantage of it.

For this reason it was frustrating to see how unenthusiastic his wife and his daughter were. He was up and ready by six-thirty, which didn't seem out of line on a holiday weekend when you were planning to fight traffic on the LIE. Every time he refreshed the map on his phone, Google added several minutes to their drive.

"If we go now, it's still only three hours," he called out from the hall. Kate was in the kitchen, slamming cabinet doors and putting food into a bag.

"Don't worry about taking a lot of stuff," he said. "The farm's still open. We can have squash and beans, like our native ancestors."

He was referring to a commercial they'd heard on the radio last summer, for a sporting goods store that advertised learning to paddleboard "like our native ancestors." Whose native ancestors, Kate had asked.

When she didn't respond now, he added, "And I can go to the IGA."

She appeared with her shopping bag, wearing jeans secured with an elasticized hair band around the button and a red-and-white striped maternity top that emphasized the new bulge of the baby. "I'm hungry now," she said.

Stephen factored in a stop at Levain. Would it be faster to walk to the bakery now, or get the car and put on the hazards while someone ran in for croissants and muffins?

"Pia!" Kate said. "Are you ready?" There was a muffled bumping from Pia's room, but no response. Kate sighed loudly.

Stephen looked at her in surprise; he'd clearly missed a transition in their relationship during all the hours he'd been spending at the hospital.

"You two okay?"

Kate gave a sarcastic laugh. "Oh, wonderful. The best was when she came back from hanging out with your mother and asked me if I was a fan of the new Supreme Court nominee. Because, you know, we're both Catholic."

"Ugh," Stephen said. Frances had been texting him more frequently than usual, not only on the subject of Justice Ginsburg's death and the vacancy on the Court, but on the president's weekend at Walter Reed. *The Abomination seems to have survived, thanks to casirivimab. Wish he'd tried the bleach.* That was his mother, pulling no punches and up on the generic for the antibody cocktail, even in retirement.

"Your daughter can't stand me," Kate added.

"I'm sure that's not true. She wouldn't be asking to go remote otherwise."

"Go remote?"

"I said I'd have to ask you."

Kate gave him a wondering look. "But isn't that the whole reason she's in New York? To go to school in person?"

It wasn't, he thought, the whole reason. The whole reason was that his daughter had wanted to come, or her mother had said that she might want to come, and that was all he'd needed to hear.

"Yeah," he said, "you're right. I guess it just hasn't been what she thought it would be."

"Well, that's the general human condition right now—isn't

it? It's not that I mind having her here," she added quickly, but she wasn't looking at him. She was frowning at her hands as if they somehow displeased her. "My fingers are swollen."

"That's normal."

"I know it's normal!" She took a breath. "It would just be easier if you were around more."

"It's just that the caseload right now—"

"I know," she said, cutting him off. "It's an impossible situation."

"Pia!" he said, more sharply than he intended. "Let's go!" A moment later his daughter wandered into the hall in her pajamas, as if baffled, an actor entering the wrong scene.

"I was just going to take a shower?"

When they finally turned onto Sandpiper, after almost five hours on the highway, it was early afternoon. The house had a musty smell that he associated with the beginning of the summer, the first Friday they would get out there for good. His father would open all the windows, and his mother would put clean sheets on the beds. They would sometimes go to Bostwick's for dinner, lobsters for his parents and fried clams and ice cream for the kids.

His parents both returned to the city during the week, and he and Mags and Jesse had been in the care of one or another teenage girl, rarely very engaged. Before his parents left every Sunday, Frances had always issued strong warnings about the ocean, but she'd allowed them to figure out the rest on their own. There were no organized activities, no camps or summer tutors. On the weekends, his father taught them to use the Sailfish, and eventually they could take it out themselves. He and Mags liked fishing for perch at Louse Point, and they all played tennis at the free and weedy courts across the lane. Jesse could beat him by the time he was nine, even though he was a year and a half younger; eventually he went on to tournaments at the Maidstone Club, bringing home trophies. The teenage sitters told Jesse he was going to be a heartbreaker one day, Stephen was "a sweetheart," Mags, "a handful."

There were bitter arguments—stretches when they weren't speaking—but oh the feeling of waking up on Sandpiper, knowing you had the whole day. Froot Loops for breakfast, careful not to drip the sweet, Technicolor milk on his comics, which no one took away in order to hurry him out the door. The beach only when he was ready, no sunscreen that he could remember, Mags dragging him to the wet sand by the water for some project: an underground city, or drip castles. Returning starving to hot dogs boiled by the babysitter, and then hearing the ice cream truck at the top of the lane. Then back to the beach after lunch, followed by evenings in front of reruns: *Knight Rider, The Facts of Life, Family Ties.*

He wished now that Pia had had a similar experience, but he and Nathalie had always shared the house with his siblings; even if they'd owned it themselves, parents didn't leave their children for the season anymore. Probably that was for the best. But he could see that the blue dirt bike in the beach grass, leaning against the oil tank, gave her nothing like the feeling he was experiencing, a wave of nostalgia so powerful that it almost took his breath away.

"How about a walk on the beach?" he asked, when they'd put the bags in their rooms. Pia had chosen the one his mother pretentiously referred to as "the Narcissus room," because of the daffodils on the wallpaper. He suspected she'd picked it not for the décor but for its location at the very end of the hall, as far as possible from him and Kate. He'd broken the news about the remote option in the car, and although he'd presented it as his decision—his and her mother's—her eyes in the rearview mirror had told him exactly whom she was going to blame.

While Kate did her sciatic exercises and took a bath, Stephen dealt with his inbox. His eyes lit on Nathalie's name in the midst of all the others as if it were in bold. That was a marketing strategy no one had invented yet: advertising embedded in emails from your exes. Someone could make a fortune.

He answered the others first: anxious messages from his patients through the portal, the weekly scheduling email, a missing diagnostic code from billing, and a request for a recommendation from his least favorite fellow. While he was answering, a message came in from the attending, Craig, who wanted to know if Stephen could cover for him next Wednesday afternoon in clinic with their residents, so he could watch his son play flag football. Stephen wondered if the baby might someday play flag football, and whether he would seem particularly aged among the fathers on the sidelines. He had tried with Pia, but he'd missed a good number of sporting events, assemblies, and concerts; it had always seemed as if there would be time to do better. If he'd known she would be spirited off to France at ten, he would've gotten there.

He opened the one from Nathalie last, telling himself it was a final chore rather than a reward. Who was he kidding? But there couldn't be anything underhanded about it, because he was sitting in their bedroom with Kate in the ugly pink tub in the bathroom, the door slightly ajar. She was listening to a podcast she loved and he hated, in which hyper-informed young men reinforced each other's liberal opinions at interminable length. He mostly agreed with their arguments but couldn't stand the style: ostentatiously insidery political and economic vocabulary sprinkled with self-conscious profanity. They weren't going to beat the red hats by sounding like grad students at a bar.

"Is it too loud?" Kate called, and he told her not to worry. He opened the message from Nathalie, which had no subject line:

S,

I hear you have some news. Toutes mes félicitations! I was surprised to hear it from Pia—did you think I would be upset? On the contrary, I've always wanted a sibling for her. She didn't tell me when the baby is due, so you'll have to—early spring is my guess? Hopefully the situation will be more stable then.

To me it sounds as if Pia isn't settling? Of course I'm not there, so this may be an impression she gives to me—maybe even intentionally? As if I might be hurt if it's easier for her there? Please try to convey to her the opposite. No one wants her to be happy in New York more than I do. Then I will be able to stop worrying. Have you seen the cut on the back of her thigh? That was her own doing. She had a sort of crise—a panic attack, I guess you would call it.

Here we are proposing work with the new cryogenic technology, in collaboration with researchers in Australia. Previous cryopreservation focused on sperm only—and so we were dependent on spawning events to unite them with eggs. With this technology, we could freeze larvae (like our hardier red-fluorescing Pocillopora) and biobank them for future rewilding of the reef. Do you remember our first conversation on this subject? You were so embarrassed! Wearing that terrible shirt à la Chairman Mao. But I thought: okay, this American man blushes to think of sex between corals—how bad could he be?

Please do keep me informed about your observations. I have no doubt that a brother or sister will eventually be to Pia's benefit. I am only worried about the path from here to there, if you understand— Katherine's pregnancy, just as Pia was trying to get to know her. This possibility is something I think you might have mentioned, before we made our decision. Your wife will be utterly distracted for years, and that is her right. You must support her, Stephen, and as you say, "be there for her." Having a baby in these times can't be easy. We didn't know how lucky we were.

Nx

His brother was coming, and so he went grocery shopping. Normally he would've knocked and asked Pia to come along, but he wanted some time to think before he brought up the matter Nathalie had raised. Cutting, for god's sake? Wasn't *that* something Nathalie should have mentioned, before they made their decision?

He ended up getting everything from the fish store and the farm, although it was more expensive. Local milk and butter, swordfish, baby lettuce, and butternut squash. Fresh sage and rosemary, and the pickle bread Pia loved for breakfast, several cheeses and crackers and the addictive salt-and-vinegar chips. At the last minute, a plum pie and some honeycomb ice cream. He thought they all deserved a treat.

As he was waiting in line to pay, he admired the pump-kins, an overwhelming variety arranged in wooden bins, from tiny, misshapen yellow gourds, to green speckled swans, to 50-pound giants, both orange and white. They were so hope-ful in the hay-scented fall air, just like any other year.

He thought maybe he had overreacted to Nathalie's email. It wasn't cutting, if you didn't use any implement; self-harm wasn't good, of course, but that kind of behavior was common in adolescents, and you couldn't throw a stone in their neigh-borhood without hitting an excellent psychologist. There was a woman named Rachel, whom Pia had seen during the divorce.

On an impulse he chose a big pumpkin he thought Pia would like: ghostly white, but with a healthy green stem and one unmarred side that left plenty of room for a face. He had to put his basket down to pick it up, and he was aware he looked foolish, kicking his basket forward toward the front of the line while he cradled the giant gourd. But he didn't care. He would take it home to the city and carve it himself, if no one else was interested.

18

She was making comments on her students' essays when she heard her brother-in-law's voice. *My mom and I have never gotten along because we are such different people.* Pia had heard Jesse coming as well, and was welcoming him with more enthusiasm than Kate could remember her showing for anyone since she'd stepped off the plane. She heard them walking around to the patio under the pergola in back, where Stephen thought the four of them could safely eat outdoors. She should stop immediately and join them, or it would look rude. *She grew up in Mexico with six brothers and sisters, and I am a modern Brooklyn girl.* Kate inserted a comment: *Can you be more specific? What do you mean by "modern"?*

She changed her blouse, then checked her reflection in the spotted bathroom mirror, her freckles more pronounced in the unflattering light, against the background of a pink plastic shower curtain. There were things she thought Stephen and his siblings hadn't changed just to spite one another. Still, being in the house reminded her of those first vacations together, when he was nervous about everything. If he went to the store, he got two kinds of milk for their coffee, because he wasn't sure which she preferred. He made plans: a picnic in the Walking Dunes, an outdoor movie in the Square. (It was *Footloose*, which somehow neither of them had seen. The audience laughed through many of the serious scenes—it was objectively absurd—but Kate thought the laughter was a little wistful, for a comforting, mythological America now entering its final throes.) Once, they went whale watching in Montauk. She had been accustomed to men her age who wanted to split the check at restaurants and then bemoan the state of the country. She didn't disagree, about education and ecology in particular, but she thought there were reasons to be hopeful—for example, the sight of two humpback whales breaching together right off the side of the boat. Look at that, Stephen marveled: they're playing. Then he asked the captain about the changes in the fishing regulations that were bringing back the whales and listened carefully to the answer. He didn't need to be right or to know more than another man. When the whales shot out of the water, in their terrific, straitjacketed majesty, he took her hand.

Kate made her way through the living room toward the patio, where she could see Jesse through the warped screen door. He was several inches taller than his brother, with broader shoulders and a ragged haircut. He was wearing a yellow plaid shirt, the sloppiness of which only served to highlight his extreme good looks: the features chiseled without being vapid, the body that advertised a life spent outdoors. Stephen was what her mother would call "a nice-looking man," whereas his brother was a person you couldn't pass on the sidewalk without noticing. In the past she might have been distracted by a man like Jesse, but not now. In spite of her mother's and sister's predictions, here she was in her floral maternity top, expecting a baby, having chosen the right brother.

The back patio was secluded from the road and the surrounding houses by a thicket of dwarf pines. The night was warm but very dry, and the shrubs around the patio looked as if it hadn't rained in months. Clumps of stiff brown leaves hung from the living branches of the bayberries, and the patio was littered with desiccated pine needles. Stephen had dug out the fat wicks of citronella oil candles in buckets, left over from the summer, and coaxed them to light. Each tin bucket gave off a twisted tail of pungent mineral smoke. Pia was standing between Jesse and her father, laughing at something her uncle had said. She didn't look at Kate when she stepped onto the patio. Stephen said he was going inside for the drinks.

"I'll go."

"You stay and chat."

"Kate!" Jesse lifted his elbow in greeting, while managing to look as if the elbow thing—and maybe the restrictions of the pandemic in general—was a party game someone else had initiated. Silly, but he would go along with it for the sake of the group. Maybe under his brother's influence, Stephen had agreed that it would be okay to take off their masks outside.

"Congratulations."

"Thank you." Kate responded to Jesse's obligatory compliments on her appearance, his obligatory questions about due date and sex. The bugs were bad in spite of the candles, and she killed a mosquito on her arm.

"We were just talking about spies," Jesse said. "Pia was telling me about an undercover operation in New Zealand."

Jesse was interested in exotic information, the further outside his own experience, the better. The first time they'd met, he'd asked about her students in so much detail, with such a flattering degree of attention, that she'd told Stephen his brother was one of the few childless people she'd ever met who were genuinely concerned about the city's public education system. Stephen had laughed and said, that's my brother, in a way she didn't understand at the time. Now she thought he might have meant that Jesse's interest wasn't fake, but that it was situational and temporary; if you became too passionate about any one subject, he might find you a little ridiculous.

"Tell her about it," he encouraged his niece now.

Pia blinked, as if she'd only just noticed Kate was there. She was wearing a black top that exposed most of her stomach, about which Stephen had asked Kate anxiously when it first appeared. Was it appropriate? Did her students wear anything that revealing?

"Which bombing?" Kate asked.

"The *Rainbow Warrior*," Pia said, but offered no further information.

"This was in '85," Jesse said. "In my advanced age, I actually remember it. Frances was passionately antinukes, of course, so she'd been following the story. It was a Greenpeace boat," he explained for Kate's benefit. "Protesting nuclear testing in the Pacific."

Pia suddenly turned to Kate. "You don't remember?"

"I was a toddler, so no. But I remember learning about the tests in the Marshall Islands. Bikini Atoll, and everything."

Pia's eyes narrowed. "Did you learn about the jelly babies?"

"Jellyfish?"

"*Babies*. Like all their organs were jelly. They were born but they were just blobs. And then they died right away."

The leaves skittered across the patio in a sudden breeze, as if they were raking themselves. "I haven't heard of that," Kate heard herself say.

"Terrible," Jesse said. "But why is it called 'Bikini' again?" What Jesse had was grace. Any tension in the conversation, and he stepped in to neutralize it. Kate thought the value of that shouldn't be underestimated.

"The bathing suit came out the same week as the first nuclear test," Pia said. "Raffi—my friend—he says that the bathing suits were banned on beaches for years. They were too shocking." Then, as if Kate was too dim to get it: "The *bathing suits*. But not the tests."

Kate was glad Stephen was in the kitchen. He had concerns about Raffi.

"The *tests* went on for twenty years. And that was just the Americans and the British. The French kept going until the nineties."

"Incredible," Jesse said. "But was it the Americans or the French who bombed the ship? That's what I can't remember."

"French spies," Pia said. "Opération Satanique, secretly authorized by Mitterrand. A frogman put a bomb on the hull."

Stephen was opening the screen door with his shoulder. He had a bottle of wine and one of cider under his arm and four stemless plastic wineglasses in one hand.

"A Satanic frogman!" Jesse winked at Kate, then moved to help his brother. "Why do they never teach the interesting stuff in school?"

"You should ask the teachers," Pia said.

"What about teachers?" Stephen said, smiling at Kate. But he'd missed too much of the conversation. Kate wanted a glass of wine more than she ever had, but accepted the apple cider he was offering.

"Business is good, I guess?" Stephen asked his brother.

"We won't be able to keep the tastings going this winter," Jesse said. "But yeah. Orders are up everywhere."

After dinner and dessert, when Jesse had gone, Kate asked Pia to help her with the dishes.

"I can do it," Stephen said.

"No," Kate said. "Pia and I can handle it." A small sound of protest escaped from Pia, and Stephen gave Kate a look like, *You don't have to do this.* But she wasn't going to let Pia get away with it—either the hostility earlier or the avoidance of house-hold chores. At her age, she and Emily had cleaned the kitchen almost every night.

"I'll wash, you dry," she said when they got into the kitchen. The first few minutes were silent; Kate wanted to give Pia a chance to speak first. But Pia wasn't biting.

"That's awful about the nuclear tests. I didn't know the extent of them."

"Don't take it from me," Pia said, picking up an ancient terry dish towel with a pattern of ivy leaves. "Take it from Kathy Jetñil-Kijiner."

"Kathy—"

"She does these video poems. There's one about the jelly babies."

"That sounds intense."

"Tiny beings with no bones," Pia said. "I remember that. Also when she says, 'I'm not mad at all, really. I already knew all of this.'"

"But she is mad," Kate guessed.

"That's the whole point."

"Maybe this is something my students could watch," Kate said. "We're always looking for Indigenous voices."

Pia let out an exasperated sigh. "I wouldn't bother you, you know. You'd like, never see me."

It took Kate a moment to follow the sudden change in topic. "If you were remote, you mean."

"I'd just be in my room."

"That's what I'm worried about."

"You're *worried*?"

"I'm worried that it would be depressing. I see it in my students all the time. A lot of them live too far to take advantage of the hybrid. It's really hard on them, in the house all day."

Pia banged a plate down on the stack. The plates were heavy brown-and-white speckled stoneware, unbreakable. "So fine," she said. "I'll talk to my dad again."

"Maybe we could all talk together."

Pia picked up a serving fork and without warning, launched it across the room. It hit the washing machine in its louvered recess and clattered to the floor.

"Maybe you could go fuck yourself," she said. And then she left the room.

"Everything okay?" Stephen called from the bedroom. "I heard a crash."

"We're good!" Pia sang out. "Nothing's broken."

Kate picked up the fork and dried it on the dish towel. The kitchen was cold and damp, and the pressure between her legs made her feel vaguely nauseated. There was a word for whatever it was, which you were supposed to avoid by performing Kegels. They were so simple—do them anywhere!—but she was already forgetting, missing days. If she couldn't do what she was supposed to be doing now, how could she hope to raise a child, much less a child who didn't throw cutlery?

The trick would be to do things right from the beginning. Of course, their parents had done right by them. They'd worked and saved and dragged them to church. They had stayed together, and no one had died. But then, someone had died. She had held someone in her arms. If the baby had been a real, finished baby, it would have been taken away immediately to give to the new parents. Doug and Judith Nowak. Who had come to the hospital at the news that Kate was giving birth prematurely, but who did not want to see the baby. Who had gone home to comfort each other when they heard.

He was a boy. Did she want to hold him? She couldn't remember saying yes, just the baby wrapped in the white blanket on her breast. The wizened face and the breathing that seemed too loud for its doll-sized chest. Doll-sized, but nothing like a doll, with the translucent red skin stretched over the ribs, thin as pins. The closed eyes and gasping mouth. The black clots of her own blood on the blue plastic sheet that someone quickly bundled and took away.

19

10-12-20

I'm postponing priority #2. Not because of LL's stupid story. I knew that was her. In Ohio with her aunt and uncle, etc. etc. Knew about the baby too, or sort of. Mom didn't know though—I could tell.

Mom says, sois gentille, Pia, bc it's so hard for Dad. Dad is so stressed because he had a patient who died. He kept emailing Mom about it, because he couldn't tell LL. I guess because she's pregnant? Or maybe he just thought Mom would understand better. She was telling me but honestly I was distracted by their names, which were so beautiful. The mother's name was Carmen, and the baby was Violeta. Some people think it's unlucky to name babies before they're born, but I can see why you would. Because you wouldn't want someone to die without a name.

10-20-20

Now I'm doing remote days with Chloe and Maxine at Maxine's house, because her parents are never home. Escape from LL, LOL! I told them about priority #3, and Chloe was like, maybe we can steal jewelry from our moms to buy your ticket! She is not the brightest.

CHLOE: You could take something from le lapin!

We're all calling her that now, thanks to Maxine.

> MAXINE: Le lapin probably doesn't have anything.
> CHLOE: Take her engagement ring! My mom always leaves
>   them by the sink. Like when she's putting on lotion.
> M: That's not going to work. Where would we even
>   sell it?
> C: At a consignment store!

But then there was this awkward moment because of Maxine's grandma, who got taken by a con man. She was this society lady and he was a younger man—but not that young, because she was 80 or something—who moved in and married her and then started selling her stuff to consignment stores: gowns, jewelry, and even paintings. Then after she died Maxine's parents had to hire lawyers—lawyers other than themselves—to get him out of her apt on Park Ave. Everyone remembers because there was a big story in NY Post etc. etc.

> M: Like what happened to my grandma, you mean?
> C: Sorry.
> M: Tu dis du mal des morts??

First C looks worried—me too—but Maxine is always kidding when she speaks French outside of school. She likes to make fun of Mme Martin, who isn't French—just married to a French guy—and is always using idioms. Like look at me, I'm so fluent.

> M: Who's going to believe three teenagers selling
>   expensive jewelry? We'd probably get arrested.

Maxine doesn't care about grades, but she's smart. Chloe's so stupid that once on the roof—where we have to eat now, even when it's raining—Miles was like, "Hey Chloe, name five countries outside the U.S." And she was like, um, "France, England, Africa" . . . And everyone starts laughing and she's like, "What?" And the thing that's really insane is that she likes being stupid, like she's a baby everyone has to take care of. She's doing it with Anders, and tells us about it, which is so gross. Maxine says this guy Dylan at Choate is her boyfriend. I don't know if anyone believes her, but no one says anything because Maxine is popular for real, not because she's pretty— she's not—or rich—she is—but so is almost everyone at Lycée. It's like this weird kind of confidence.

> M: Oh, wait—I'm a genius. I'm fucking Annalise Crillon.
> C: You're fucking Annalise Crillon?

I'm pretending I know who that is. Maxine can tell though, because she's smart like her parents, like a lawyer, and she usually knows when I'm lying.

> M: She graduated last year. But she was perfect. Perfect hair, perfect boobs, nice to everyone & center on varsity volleyball, as like, a freshman. And so no one was surprised when she got 20/20 on her bac.
> C: She would not be fucking Maxine, like, ever.

Maxine hits Chloe, not lightly.

> M: I mean I just THOUGHT of something genius. IN THE MANNER of Annalise Crillon. [Maxine pauses dramatically.] Rewards points! I literally just heard my dad say we have a zillion. Because we get them from the credit card and we can't go anywhere now. I bet your dad does, too.
> ME: Steal them?
> M: I would say "make use of." Before le lapin does. They're a family asset.

I say that's a good idea, and it is. But then they start talking about R, and how I'm going to lose it in Mo'orea. Total mistake to tell them he was my boyfriend and esp to show them the picture.

> M: If you're going to lose it to a hot 30 year old Tahitian guy, I'm gonna need details.
> C: Maybe it could be under a waterfall?
> ME: ??
> C: That would be AMAZING for Instagram.
> M: [rolls her eyes] You get locked out for like, a sexy DANCE. It happened to that slutty senior in ceramics.
> C: [acknowledging] But like, before and after pix?
> M: [ignoring her] When do you want to go?

It has to be before the end of the year. That's when Yannick said it would happen, when we ran into him at Champion Toa. That was on the way back from diving with the Americans. And afterward R was like, "You know he's full of shit, right? You saw his cart?" The cart was full of cheap rum, like a lot of it. R said please don't repeat anything he said because we could both get in trouble and of course I said I wouldn't. But the way you know someone's lying is also the way you can tell if they aren't. It's about getting the small details right. And no one who's full of shit would know about international shipping insurance from Lloyd's of London.

> C: We can help you!

She's actually pretty nice. Is being dumb connected to being nice? And if yes, then what about the opposite?

> M: [winks at me] Aux grands maux, les grands remèdes.

11-1-20

1966: Aldébaran—61 million becquerels of fallout per square meter: "a degree of contamination which is rarely recorded, except during the world's most serious nuclear catastrophes." (https://moruroa-files.org) Detonated above the uninhabited "nuclear" atoll, Moruroa. French govt knew the cloud was headed for the inhabited Gambier archipelago. Did not evacuate.

1966: Tamouré, Ganymède, Bételgeuse, Rigel, Sirius

1967: Altaïr, Antarès, Arcturus

1968: Capella, Castor, Pollux, Canopus, Procyon

The French like to name nuclear tests after Greek gods, or stars.

1970: Andromède, Cassiopée, Dragon, Eridan, Licorne, Pégase, Orion, Toucan

1971: Dioné, Encelade—30x more powerful than Hiroshima. Rains right afterward over Tureia, the "worst case scenario." Scientific mission finds groundshine (radiation coming off the ground) and cloudshine (radioactive plumes). The groundshine and cloudshine contaminated public and private family cisterns. Residents not evacuated.

1971: Japet, Phoebé, Rhéa

1972: Umbriel, Titania, Obéron, Ariel

"On ferait ca à Paris?" is what people wrote on the protest signs. In Paris, Aunt Sonia's company does marketing for a parfumier that is planning to introduce a fragrance called Encelade in 2022. Encelade is supposed to smell like a "jungle fraiche à flanc de volcan." It will have "un magnétisme sauvage."

1973: Euterpe, Melpomène, Pallas, Parthénope, Tamara, Vesta

1974: Capricorne, Bélier, Gémeaux, Centaure, Maquis, Persée, Scorpion, Taureau, Verseau

1975–1996: Testing moves underground

2020: French military doctor reports cluster of thyroid cancers in the Gambier that "leaves no doubt" cancers are the result of ionizing radiation from the nuclear tests.

11-4-20

"The ** would be designed not to destroy ships, but to frighten their captains. Mere rumors that harbors and ports were ** could be enough to reduce shipping significantly" [7]. There was no need to ** a single ship. Lloyd's of London would pull insurance on ships going into ** harbors or increase insurance rates enough to discourage entrance into those harbors." (Sabrina R. Edlow, Center for Naval Analyses, April, 1997)

11-5-20

The name comes from limpets. Those are snails, basically. Mom told me one thing about them that is kind of cool. They use this very strong foot to dig into the rock. They actually EAT rocks, especially chalk, like that kid in pre-K at Lycée. (I actually used to love Lycée, which is funny now.) They dig into the rock until they make a kind of print of themselves in one spot, called a "homescar." They can leave to eat during the day, but they leave a trail so they can get back to their spots at night. And they don't take each other's homescars, so no one comes home and gets surprised by another limpet in her place.

20

She told herself that she had been too busy to respond to Stephen. Today, for example, she and Gunther were analyzing the photos of the mesophotic coral colonies at 30, 60, and 90 meters. A colony was considered healthy when fully pigmented with its normal color, "pale" when some of the symbiotic algae was visible, and "bleached" when completely white, with the skeleton showing through the tissue. When even the tissue had sheared away, then it was classed as "recently dead." At the outset, Gunther had proposed excluding colonies grown over with algae or boring organisms—those that drilled into the coral skeletons—since their death had likely preceded the study.

"Have you ever considered working with boring organisms, Gunther?" their departed British postdoc, Alan, had innocently asked. Alan was funny and creative but hadn't had nearly Gunther's discipline.

The work had seemed crucial last year when they began the study, but now Nathalie was impatient with everything that didn't have a direct application on the reef. What she really wanted to be doing was cryopreservation—freezing and storing larvae from the most vulnerable species—but the technology wasn't yet at the point where they could do it at scale. In the meantime, she'd been talking to colleagues about a coral nursery deeper than any they'd yet created, to protect species like the knobby *Echinophyllia* and the elephant skin coral, *Pachyseris*. On a recent dive they'd observed a metamorphosis in *Porites rus,* which formed branching colonies in the lagoon. When you went down to its depth limit, the shape changed; at 45 or 50 meters, it grew as flattened plates that sometimes combined with the fluted folds of *Pachyseris* in spectacular rose formations.

She hadn't given Gunther any more than an outline of her idea. While she had absolute faith in his work, she didn't entirely trust his academic integrity. If he had a chance to get ahead, she thought he'd take it, no matter whom he had to run over in the process. But she was going to need him if she hoped to realize a project on the scale she was imagining.

"I was thinking about substrates," she said now.

He picked it up right away. "There's a factory just outside Frankfurt. I did some research—they work with artists."

"Artists?"

"Sculptors, mostly," Gunther explained. "I was thinking of a sort of—installation."

"I was thinking of it more as a library."

Gunther nodded. "But at thirty or forty meters it's still accessible to recreational divers. You could get a famous artist involved."

"Could we?"

"Of course. It has cachet—eco-cachet."

Nathalie groaned.

"But really."

"It's a good idea," she acknowledged. Maybe even a great idea. Underwater sculpture covered with bleaching-resistant baby coral was the kind of thing that might make funders open their wallets in a big way. Maybe it would even help to bankroll their less-sexy cryopreservation efforts. She could imagine the counterargument of course, from those who opposed such aggressive interventions. But did anyone other than the coral specialists understand how drastic the times really were, how they called for the most drastic measures?

When they'd finished in the lab, Gunther went to get lunch. Nathalie stopped in the office, where only Marc was in the corner, wearing headphones, single-mindedly focused on his screen. Their colleague specialized in seabirds and their relationship to traditional navigation and was very difficult to engage on any other subject. This was useful, because it forced her to confront her mountain of email. But as she responded to a peer review invitation from *Frontiers,* a request from an American journalist, and a proposal from the director for a symposium to be held in the new auditorium, her mind wandered for at least the hundredth time to Stephen's message of several weeks earlier—all the more irritating for not really demanding a reply:

Thanks for your congratulations. The baby's due March 17. I'm terrified about what's coming this winter, and hope at least the second wave will have spiked by then. It could be as bad, or even worse, than last spring.

You should've told me about Pia. We have her back in therapy now with Rachel, who you'll remember. I had to pull strings to get her an appointment, which gives you a sense of how common psychological distress is among teenagers these days.

There is some brighter news that I thought would interest you, from your least favorite vacation community. We've been seeing more whales—the small ones whose species I forget, and some spectacular humpbacks right near the beach. I asked a few years ago, and it seems that the new fishing regulations are having some effect. There have been dolphins too, more than I can remember, even when I was a kid.

The small room was crowded with equipment: plastic bins labeled with the names of the scientists, an underwater sensor with lux and PAR meters that Ann had won in a competition, and some LED lights that her colleagues were using to evaluate phenotype plasticity in *Dascyllus trimaculatus.* She sat down in a wooden chair with her back to Marc. The window was so low that you could see only the top of Mount Rotui over the green-painted roof of the neighboring building, a dark ridge shrouded in fog. The small whales Stephen forgot were called minke, named for the Norwegian who first identified them.

About Pia, he was right that she should have told him. She hadn't wanted to say that they'd fought, and especially not why. If Pia wanted to be with her, that was natural: she was the mother. No one judged Stephen. But if Pia wanted to be with him, well, that meant there was something wrong with her. It was no secret that there was something wrong with her. But she'd imagined that she might keep it from her daughter, and that was why it was so hard when she saw the cut on Pia's leg.

This was in July, the last full month they'd spent together. Her daughter was fixing herself a bowl of muesli in the kitchen. They had wished each other good morning, but nothing had been said about the previous night. Nathalie had been wondering if they couldn't just move past it. Then she saw Pia's leg: an angry red gash about three inches long, perfectly straight and barely scabbed over.

"You cut yourself."

"By accident," Pia said. "On the corner of the desk."

This was not credible, but for a moment she hoped. "Did you put something on it?"

"Savlon."

"A few times a day at least," Nathalie said. "We don't want it to get infected."

Pia nodded, and that was it. She thought of pressing her, but it seemed too delicate right at that moment. Given what had happened the night before, it was a miracle that her daughter was speaking to her in a civil manner at all.

It had started when Pia told her she'd be going on a full-day expedition with Raffi and a few scientists who remained at the American research station, and Nathalie had brought up her daughter's summer assignments. This was an ongoing topic of conversation. Pia maintained that she'd just finished a grueling

French school year and had no desire to start an American one right away. She could read "those books" on the plane. Nathalie said that there was no way she could read the five books on the list from Lycée over the course of a flight, or even two flights totaling more than thirteen hours.

"I've already read *L'Étranger*. Like four times."

"I'm sure not four."

"The point is that you're responsible for what you do."

Nathalie heard a particular tone in Pia's voice that heralded bad emotional weather. She wondered if the argument was worth it. The site Pia wanted to visit with the Americans was interesting, an uninhabited atoll with an unusually healthy fringing reef, and it would be much easier to acquiesce. It was certainly better than leaving her moping around the cottage on her phone. On the other hand, the Americans would charge her for Pia's cylinder and seat on the boat, at exorbitant guest prices. She could take Pia on the same expedition for free, if she could wait until Saturday. The Americans were all strangers, adults Pia didn't know, so there was no social benefit to going with them.

"You won't know anyone but Raffi."

"Raffi's enough."

Nathalie looked at her. This was before Pia had cut and dyed her hair; it was dark and looped back in a messy bun. There were bright spots of color on her cheeks, and her chin jutted forward in an obstinate way. Her face was so symmetrical that it suggested a certain sweetness to people, who often smiled when they saw her. There was probably some biological reason for this response. In Pia's case, it was also misleading. At this point in the conversation, Nathalie could hear in the slightly accelerated pace of her daughter's speech that she was becoming dysregulated. No matter how innocent she looked, she was capable of a fully realized adult rage.

"Wait until the weekend," Nathalie said. "Then we can go together."

"What am I going to do until then?" They were standing in the living room of the cottage, a small room, a little run-down and claustrophobic at night when the blinds were closed, the pale yellow walls adorned with local art: an oil painting of a beach scene, a pencil drawing of the stereotypical vahine in a flower hei, her faintly seductive smile an invention dating back 250 years to the arrival of French and British sailors. A large conch—no doubt imported from the Philippines—formed the base of a lamp with a linen shade that left most of the room in shadow.

"Do your summer reading. Not *L'Étranger.* Read *Romeo and Juliet.* That might interest you."

"Oh my god."

"Read *Persepolis*—that's a graphic novel—it's only going to take a couple of hours. And it might make you appreciate your relative freedoms."

"You—" Pia stopped and shook her head, as if it wasn't worth explaining.

"What about me?" Nathalie thought she wasn't going to answer, and then Pia suddenly exploded.

"You make me laugh! Do you even know how selfish you are? My *freedoms*? You always do exactly what you want. And then we have to pay."

"Who is 'we'?"

"Me and dad! Like if you hadn't fucked that guy, we'd all still be in New York."

"That has nothing to do with it."

"Really? Isn't that the whole reason you got divorced?"

"I would still be here now, doing this study. Unfortunately this is just a fact of my job."

"To have affairs?"

"To do fieldwork. I study coral, Pia. There's very little of it in New York. Or Paris, for that matter."

"No shit." This, for emphasis, in English.

"I always thought it would be nice for you—"

"To have divorced parents who live six thousand miles apart?"

"I'm sorry about that. But the combination of Paris, New York, and Mo'orea hardly seems like a prison sentence."

"To *you*. Because those are the places *you* want to be."

"So where do you want to be?"

She was crying. Her cheeks were a blotchy pink and white under her tan, and the dark circles under her eyes stood out. Her nose was running, and she wiped it on the sleeve of her sweatshirt. Nathalie tried and failed to muster sympathy. She thought frankly that Pia was acting like a spoiled little horror.

"You know where I want to be?"

"Where?"

"Anywhere without you! Anywhere!" Pia grabbed a spray can of sunscreen and threw it—not at Nathalie but at the wall across the room.

Don't react, Nathalie thought. She'd read that somewhere, too: don't play along. It took two people to have a fight, even if one of them was a teenager. Pia picked up a bright purple pillow, gave Nathalie a look, and threw that too, this time at the shell lamp, which tottered for a moment on the flimsy rattan side table, and then crashed to the floor, landing not on the rag rug but on the tiled floor, shards of shell everywhere.

"Pia—Jesus Christ! That's enough!"

"Fuck you!"

"Enough!"

Pia gave the couch another desperate kick and ran into her room, where she slammed the door, a wooden door that shook the frame and bounced open again with a whine. Pia howled—an animal sound so loud that Nathalie was sure it was audible to the neighbors, a retired métropolitain couple who spent most of their time reading serious literature on modern steel outdoor furniture facing the lagoon. Had they heard everything? Pia slammed the door again, slightly more gently, so that this time it stayed shut. Then she'd clicked the button lock, and everything had become suddenly and completely quiet.

When Nathalie was a teenager, her own mother had sometimes locked her in her room. They lived in Cesson-Sevigne, a suburb of Rennes, on the Rue des Petits Champs, near the start of the expressway to Mont Saint-Michel. The name was nostalgic because there were no fields, or even substantial gardens; the houses were small, with gabled slate roofs and stone walkways, quimperoise lace curtains in the kitchen windows. Her father was a math teacher at the high school, and her mother worked for Hertz. By the time Nathalie was Pia's age, her mother had worked there for twenty years and had a cut-glass statuette next to a dish of hard candy on her desk to prove it. She hadn't been to university, or traveled outside of Europe, but she spoke decent English, which she'd taught herself from the *Éditions Assimil*, as well as subtitled reruns of *Dynasty* and *Baywatch*. She practiced it on the tourists, mostly British but also German, Australian, and sometimes American, who rented cars and drove north to see Mont Saint-Michel.

Pauline wore her red curls cropped short. She wore floral dresses and pumps to work every day, then came home and put on an apron to make dinner. Nathalie's father always had several glasses of wine with dinner, but her mother did not. Her own father had drunk himself to death, in her telling, and she preferred to abstain. *Your mother is naturally happy*, her father said, and it was true that Pauline was ferociously cheerful. She took pride in never losing her temper at work, even with the difficult Dutch customers, and only very rarely at home. The one thing she couldn't stand was a complaint. *In our life*, she often told Nathalie and her sister, *there is nothing about which one could complain.*

After Sonia went to university, Nathalie had her own room. It was at the top of the house, wallpapered in dark green baize. At one point she had covered it with posters of English bands: The Smiths, The Cure, Depeche Mode, and removed the collection of shells and sea stars that had sat on the top of her bureau for as long she could remember. They didn't go far, into a box in the drawer with her underwear, and when she was jailed in there, she sometimes dumped them out on her bed to look at them.

The first time, she hadn't understood what was happening. Even on the inside, the door didn't have an integral lock. Her mother had secured the knob to the adjacent bathroom door-knob with Nathalie's own bike lock. It was such an unlikely strategy that Nathalie understood that she must have tested it out in advance. She could remember realizing what had happened, yelling various threats through the door—she would break it down, she would set the house on fire, she would jump to her death—and then kicking the small plastic trash can across the room, where it cracked in a satisfying way. She had opened the casement window and leaned out; across the street, she could see the house of her sometimes-friend Sandrine, and beyond that, the gas station and Carrefour. It was a damp, gray Sunday afternoon in the fall, and the air smelled of leaves and diesel. The front door of their house was the same as Sandrine's, with two concrete steps that led down to a path of hexagonal concrete pavers, a wrought iron gate. Nathalie leaned out the window, trying to imagine herself splayed bloody on the pavement. She thought she might put on her kilt and fishnets, and make up her eyes. The cops would arrive, and all their neighbors would peer through their curtains, then step out their front doors. There would be whispers through the crowd as everyone realized who was responsible, and then it would be her mother who would have to lock herself inside.

Nathalie hadn't thought about her mother for a long time. It was strange to be doing it now, in the office, alone except for Marc hunched over the terminal in the corner. She thought of placing a call, but it was the middle of the night in Rennes. And how would she work up to her question, which was how her mother had called her bluff? How had she known with absolute certainty that all those threats she'd made as a teenager had been hollow, and that there was no way her mother was going to glance out the bedroom window and find her broken body on the pavers below?

"Probably I shouldn't even get into this," Stephen's email continued. Was it her imagination that the tone got more aggressive as it went on? "But you seem to have some strange ideas about Kate."

> Pia's just getting to know her, and it's been going very well. She's planning to go to an outdoor event for Kate's senior English class, in fact. The Lycée is great, but I think we agree, not exactly a microcosm of the city. A lot of Kate's students come from families below the poverty line, with all the concomitant problems.
>
> I've always thought Kate got into this work because of her own high school experience. She got pregnant at sixteen but her parents didn't permit her to get an abortion. She was sent off to live with an aunt and uncle for the duration of the pregnancy. They weren't especially sympathetic to her predicament, but the idea was to hide the evidence from friends and neighbors. The baby was born at five months and didn't survive. It was a small town, so of course everyone knew. You can imagine how this would make having one's first child traumatic, even in less uncertain times.
>
> And so to answer to your question, yes I am going to "be there for her." And for Pia and the baby. Best of luck with your larvae.
>
> Stephen

She wished for someone, someone other than Marc, with whom she might share the final part of Stephen's message, which felt like a kick in the gut. To go from his memories of Amagansett—which it was true she hadn't liked, with its clubby exclusivity, its private lanes and massive American homes, but where they had spent a great deal of time early in Pia's life—to this passionate defense of his wife, after Nathalie had ventured nothing except the guess that she might be distracted. For whom had high school been easy, after all? She knew of two girls in her own class (certainly there had been some she didn't know) who'd gotten pregnant before graduation. Both took care of it with a pill. They were, she supposed, the beneficiaries of a more civilized society.

But apart from Stephen's self-righteous commentary, the information about Kate was interesting. Stephen was inclined toward anyone he thought might need protection or aid. She thought that this grim idea of duty was Frances's legacy, more condescending than helpful to its recipients. In that regard Nathalie had been an anomaly, and perhaps her failure to need him sufficiently was the thing that had sabotaged them in the end.

She hadn't been planning to respond, but now she dashed off a few lines into her phone:

Thank you for letting me know about the therapist. Please keep me posted on Pia's progress, as well as any new concerns you might have. As for the rest of it, I admire your and Katherine's dedication to the less fortunate. I never had the confidence—I guess you could say the self-confidence—to believe that I could save anyone. As you say, I stick with my larvae.

She found most sign-offs ridiculous, and so she left it at that. It wasn't as if he didn't know who she was.

21

Athyna picked the route with the most buses. All of a sudden, she hated being underground. It was like she was from the country somewhere, or Jersey. It wasn't that she was afraid of getting Covid, like her mother and Breanna thought, but that she was afraid of the train stopping in the tunnel, the cutting off of the air and maybe the lights, an announcement over the derelict speakers that would be impossible to make out. Once she'd been stuck like that for twenty minutes. At the time it had been only a pain in the ass, but the thought of it now made it impossible to fill her lungs completely, as if someone had put a cage around them. It seemed better not to go to the party, even though she was dying to see Krystal in person.

Her mother disagreed. "You're not going to the hybrid—okay. But you have to show your face or they'll forget you exist."

It wasn't the nicest way to put it. "I went out yesterday," she pointed out. Yesterday her mom had gotten off work early to vote. She'd picked Athyna up in the car, and they'd gone to PS 57, where they ran into Elijah's mom. She came over to them right away and started asking about "her baby this" and "her baby that," and Athyna's mom had said coolly that Marcus was shopping with his mother while they voted, and that it was Athyna's first time. Elijah's mom made a big deal over that, and then her mom asked if Sandra had voted yet herself. Sandra said she wasn't sure if she could—there was some problem with her registration.

After she left them to go back to work, Athyna's mom shook her head. If you can't get it together this time, then God help you, she told Athyna, and the lady behind the table for their district gave her mom a look like *Mmm-hmm*, even though she couldn't say anything because she was a poll worker. When you looked at the map of Staten Island, there was a band of blue at the very top, because that was where there were Black people. The rest of the island was red. Athyna filled in the bubbles completely, as they'd been taught for the Regents exams, and then she fed her ballot into the machine. Another poll worker smiled and offered her a sticker, and then it was over—somehow she'd thought it would feel like a bigger deal. She asked when they would know, and her mother said it could take weeks.

"And it's going to be a beautiful day." They were in the kitchen, and her mother was making chili. Wednesday was her day off, and she always went to Costco in the morning. Then she cooked two giant meals and froze them for the week, supposedly because she was responsible for two, and Breanna was responsible for two, and Athyna for one. The way it worked out, her mom cooked two; Breanna made elaborate plans— she was going to make Vietnamese pho or enchiladas verde— but she and Elijah often ended up springing for pizza on their nights, and Athyna stuck with either spaghetti or eggs.

"You never know," Athyna said. She'd been looking at the weather all week. It had started out cold on Monday, not even 45 degrees, but now it was in the low 60s, and Saturday's high was supposed to be 73 degrees. The chance of precipitation was 3 percent.

"I know you don't want to go," her mother said. "What I don't know is why."

She couldn't say that she was scared of the train. It was nice in the kitchen with the onions frying. Her mother added the meat and that rich aroma settled over the kitchen.

"Chili," Marcus said with satisfaction. He was playing on the floor with his Transformers—the one he called Birdboy, even though its name was Grimlock. She was going to have to make sure he used the right names when he went to kindergarten next year, or the other kids were going to laugh at him.

"How's Krystal?"

"She's good."

"She liking the hybrid?"

"Not really."

"But she's *going*."

"I thought you didn't want me going in."

Her mother added the tomatoes from a box—she thought they tasted better than the ones from a can. "I read an article."

"About hybrid school?"

"About agoraphobia. People are afraid to go outside."

Athyna decided to try a different tack. "Who'd watch Marcus?"

"His father."

"I thought E was getting a job."

Her mother sucked her teeth.

"You know he'll get something like, the minute I sign up."

"Beans," her mother said, and Athyna passed her the open cans, one at a time.

"It's not still the thing with Javier and that girl?"

"Whaaat?" she said, but her mother just raised an eyebrow at her. She shouldn't have told her, because her mother never forgot anyone's name.

"Jada."

Marcus got up suddenly, made a sound like a jet engine, and ran into the living room, holding the toy above his head: "Birdboy Geronimo Jackson!"

Grimlock," Athyna called after him. Where did he even get these things?

"The one who was trash-talking you," her mother said, not letting it drop.

"It wasn't like that. And they're not even in my homeroom."

"So?"

"I just don't feel like it."

Her mother added the chili powder, coriander, and unsweetened cocoa powder, her secret ingredient. "I feel you," she said with her back to Athyna, and for a moment Athyna thought she'd gotten herself out of it. "But the only cure for that is going."

To distract herself from the unholy screech and rattle of the R train, she thought about her essay. There was a list of prompts on the Common App, or you could just make something up. Somehow that made it harder. You were supposed to show the college your "best self," and whose best self was on display this year? One prompt suggested you write about something "you find so engaging that it makes you lose all track of time." That would probably be Marcus, because there was nothing that made her lose track of time like watching him—but she knew that wasn't what they meant. You were supposed to be really into outer space or music or something, which it was possible she might be (she had played the trumpet in middle school, and still loved drawing and baking, for example) if she wasn't always watching Marcus. "About an event in your past and how it affected you, and what you learned about yourself." Well, she knew what she'd write for that one. That was an essay about her dad, whom they used to worry about because his work was dangerous, but who had died on dry land, in a car accident on the LIE, driving back from his company's headquarters in Syosset.

Last year she'd come into the classroom to find the word "irony" on the whiteboard. The teacher said he'd heard them saying this or that was "so ironic," and he wanted to talk about what irony really was. Athyna thought she knew, basically, and she wasn't really listening, until the teacher, Nick, called on her to give an example. Right away that was the example in her head and she knew it was perfect. Instead of saying it, she shook her head in a way that made everyone laugh. Nick had sighed and moved on, and she felt kind of bad about it. But she wasn't going to let some teacher who didn't even know there had been a person named Marcus Jay Slocombe use her dad to define a vocabulary word.

She got off at 4 Av–9 St and waited for a bus. It was only ten, and so it was possible she'd get there early. She could picture herself standing there like an idiot—Kate had said there would be picnic tables—and people showing up and being like, *Who even is that?* Because it had been so long since she'd shown her face. It would've been way better to go with Krystal and Bianca and the rest of them, but of course they were coming from the other direction in Brooklyn. She could've taken the R to the 2, 3 to Grand Army Plaza and met them there, but it would've involved another train.

She was wearing a navy blue hoodie that said *American Eagle* in red script, her favorite black jeans, and her black-and-yellow Jordans. Her hair was slicked back in a tight knot, like she always wore it these days. Breanna had offered to take her to Fena for braids, probably so she could have an excuse to get hers done again, but Athyna had said she didn't feel like it. She'd seen her sister give her mom a look, so obviously they'd talked about her thing about not going out. But honestly what was less safe than sitting in the salon for hours, where you knew people would be talking and letting their masks slip off, falling back into the comfort of that?

There were already a few people at the picnic tables when she got there, thank god. Her teacher was setting up drinks—they had individual cans of soda instead of the big liter bottles—and individual bags of chips. She felt like BEST had gone all out, but maybe it was just because of Covid. They'd all have to put their hands in the pizza boxes anyway, when it came. She joined the other Crystal—with a "C"—and Mo and Tania and Maddie helping Kate, and it was actually sort of nice the way everyone was like, *Athyna! Hey, girl.* She'd always gone by her full name at school, so it was different from home in that way. Jada wasn't there yet, but Javier was throwing a football with Israel. He stopped and put his hand up, like *hi* or *peace*, and when she did the same he smiled and said, "You're 3D." For a second she thought he was being rude and then she got it; she wasn't on Zoom, for once.

And then Krystal came running down a path out of the trees and was screaming her name, saying to everyone who would listen, "This is my sister and I haven't seen her in, like, half a year!" And Hernan was like, "You're not sisters." But Krystal put her hands on Athyna's shoulders and touched her forehead with her own, was like, "Yes, we are."

"Let's try for six feet," Kate said. "But it's really nice to see you, Athyna."

"Thanks," Athyna said. "Are you—?" She stopped just in case she was wrong, and her teacher had just gained the Covid weight like everyone, but Kate laughed.

"Yes, I'm expecting a baby. That's why I've been remote."

"Is that why *you're* remote?" Krystal asked Athyna.

"Yeah. It's fucking twins." She put her hand over her mouth and looked at her teacher. "Sorry." Then she told Krystal, "You know why I'm remote."

"She lives so far I haven't seen her for the whole pandemic," Krystal said loyally.

"No one but me is having any babies," said Kate. "Make me a promise."

"Not me!" Krystal said, and Athyna nodded, but it was so weird talking about that stuff with her teacher, and Krystal was already pulling her over into the shade, where all the girls were sitting together for once. The boys started a football game for real, like it was some kind of Thanksgiving or family reunion. Down in the meadow below the picnic tables, couples were lying out in the sun. Parents, mostly white, pushed babies in fancy strollers, following kids on scooters. At the bottom of the hill was a pond with a crazy number of dogs splashing around in the shallow water; Athyna was glad Kate had decided to meet up on the hill. There were a lot of conversations going on at once, and it wasn't until they'd been sitting there for a while, Athyna listening to Krystal asking her in an undertone what she really thought of Israel, because he was texting her all the time and she wanted to get Athyna's opinion while they were all here in person, and also trying to remember which T-shirt she was wearing, and whether she wanted to take off her sweatshirt—it was getting warmer—trying to form an opinion about Israel but also kind of watching Javier—all the boys looked older, and some, including Javier, had new facial hair—that she noticed her teacher's stepdaughter sitting at one of the picnic tables by herself. What was her name?

She was reassuring Krystal that Israel was fine-fine, not just okay-fine, when they heard someone screaming. The boys stopping playing, and everyone was looking around; there was no change in the weather, but something had happened, because the people on the path had stopped in their tracks, and there was a sudden hush in the park. Then suddenly a woman started yelling, and other people joined in, and Hernan, who was looking at his phone, looked up and announced, "CNN said it! He lost!" Then all the girls started screaming and hugging each other, and taking selfies so they'd know where they were when it happened. Athyna looked around for Edison— had he and his dad really voted for Trump?—but he hadn't come to the party. A couple who'd been lying on a blanket was standing up now, one of them banging a drum, and from somewhere beyond the trees they heard singing.

"What are they saying?" Bianca asked, and it was hard to make out, but after a while they figured out it was "You're fired." Kate waved them all over to the picnic tables, and someone was like, "Speech, speech!" but like, as a joke, and Kate said, "I didn't win the election, but I do have a question." Everyone quieted down, and their teacher, who actually looked really pretty, wearing a blue-and-white flowered maternity top and those jeans that were made for pregnant people (Athyna could see the stretchy black band starting at her hips), asked how many of them were able to vote for the first time. That was a nice way to put it, because some people weren't old enough, and she was pretty sure Luis was undocumented. She raised her hand along with the others, and Kate said, "So you guys did this. Congratulations."

The white people in the meadow were not calming down. Now someone was banging on a tambourine—did these people carry instruments wherever they went?—and another group was chanting, "Ding dong the witch is dead." That sounded a little silly to Athyna. The troll was more like it, or the devil—except that the devil was clever. Was there an imaginary creature who whipped people up to a frenzy with lies, or was it only people who could be like that? Now you could hear horns from the street, celebratory: three short bursts followed by a long wail of automotive joy, as if everyone had agreed on a pattern.

"See if they all keep marching and shit after this, though," Jason said, and a lot of people nodded at the wisdom of that. Jason had a skinny neck and a big nose and a fade; he looked like a little kid still, but he was smart. Athyna looked at their teacher to see what she thought of what Jason had said, but she hadn't heard because she'd gotten on the phone with someone, maybe her husband. A bunch of Athyna's friends were taking calls as well, and so she looked at her phone: her mom had texted her a fist bump and a heart, and she got a selfie of Breanna with the nurse and the receptionist from the clinic, all in their light pink Half Moon scrubs. They'd added the sparkle filter and an American flag sticker.

The only person who wasn't celebrating was the stepdaughter, who was still sitting at the picnic table, her knees pulled up to her chest. Her phone was on the table, so maybe she'd gotten tired of looking at it, or pretending to; she had turned and was watching some kids on the ballfields below the brick building with the bathrooms, still playing soccer in shiny uniforms: blue vs. yellow. Athyna could see how it would be hard to be dragged to a party where you didn't know anyone. She felt like being nice.

"Hey," she said. "I met you on Zoom."

Kate's stepdaughter was wearing a black T-shirt that said

Paris in sparkly silver letters and had been cut off across the bottom to reveal her stomach. She had on a black denim mini-skirt, fishnets, and white Doc Martens. The half-dark, half-platinum hair was really shaggy now, falling in her eyes, but Athyna could see she was wearing heavy black eyeliner; honestly she looked like some '90s music video on YouTube.

"I'm Pia."

"Athyna. What grade are you in again?"

"Seconde in France," Pia said. "Tenth, here."

Was she showing off? If so, Athyna had no time for it. "Are you French?"

"My mom is."

"Does she live in Paris?"

Pia rolled her eyes, but it was clear it wasn't directed at Athyna. "She lives on an island near Tahiti."

"Whoa. That sounds nice."

"She's a scientist. She studies coral."

"That's cool."

"You want to see a picture?" Pia opened her photos and started scrolling. Suddenly the colors changed, from the regular stupid selfies to all kinds of green and blue.

"Go back," Athyna instructed. "Where's *that*?"

"That's Tetiaroa. It's an atoll—like an island with a lagoon in the middle. Marlon Brando owned it."

Was she supposed to know who that was? "Who owns it now?"

"A foundation. There's a hotel, but only celebrities go there—Kim Kardashian and Barack Obama."

"You saw them?"

"Nah," Pia said. "I just saw it on the news."

Athyna appreciated the honesty. "Does your mom do scuba?"

"Yeah. I mean, she's always done a lot of it. Sometimes tec divers help, when they need to go really deep."

"Uh-huh," Athyna said. She tried to remember if her dad had ever talked about tec diving. "My dad was a diver."

"But not anymore?"

Athyna could never say it and sound normal. Either it sounded like she was trying to get attention, or like she didn't care. "He died five years ago."

"Oh," Pia said. "Sorry."

"At least he missed all this shit."

"Was he, um, sick?"

"He was in an accident."

"Diving?"

She looked like this was the most interesting conversation in the world, and maybe that was why Athyna lied. The way it had really happened was just so stupid.

"Yeah."

"On vacation?"

"Out on Long Island. He was a commercial diver, so he worked on bridges and piers and stuff."

"That's cool," Pia said. "I think I'd like that. I like the diving more than the science."

"Do you do it a lot?"

"I used to—before I moved to this shithole."

"Hey!" Athyna said.

"I mean New York is cool," Pia said quickly. "But my school is full of assholes."

Athyna couldn't help laughing. There was something funny about the way she said it, like she was trying to be down. Without the clothes and the makeup, she would look about twelve. "So now you live with your dad and Kate." She tried to imagine her teacher in pajamas, or dressed up to go out. Someone said last year they'd seen her being picked up in a Benz.

"For now, yeah."

"I didn't know she was having a baby."

"Me either."

Athyna glanced over her shoulder at Kate, who had gotten off the phone. She was talking with Bianca, Tania, and Angelique, who were acting stupid, touching their teacher's stomach and suggesting names. Tania was always complaining about her much younger half-siblings, and everyone said it would be a miracle if Angelique didn't get pregnant before she graduated. Kate shouldn't be encouraging her.

Maybe because she felt Athyna watching her, Kate looked over. She made eye contact with Athyna and smiled a little, as if to say thanks for talking to her stepdaughter.

"I had to, like, guess."

"That sucks." Athyna felt disloyal, but at the same time she sympathized with Pia. She hated when her mom and Breanna hid something from her. "I didn't know why she was remote. I'm all-remote, too."

"I wish I was," Pia said.

"My mom says all the schools might close soon."

Pia tilted her head to one side and held up crossed fingers.

"Athyna!" Krystal called. "You want to go up to Grand Army? Maybe they'll interview us on CNN!" They were helping the teacher put all the garbage into black plastic bags, but it looked like everyone was about to take off. Athyna held up one finger to Krystal to wait.

"My sister had a baby when I was thirteen," she told Pia. "I was sort of dreading it, but now I'm really into him. She lives with us, so he's like my little brother."

"I always wanted an older brother," Pia said.

Krystal was waiting with Israel on the path. Javier was with them, not looking at her but waiting, tossing the football in the air and catching it.

"Hey," she said to Pia. "AirDrop me that picture of that island."

Pia tried, but they couldn't connect. "I can text it?"

So she gave Kate's stepdaughter her number. She glanced at her screen, where the picture had appeared. She could print it, add it to her wall. The water was a crazy green, like mouthwash.

"Is this a filter?"

Pia grinned. "Nope."

"Damn."

"Athyna—we are *going*. With or without your ass."

"I gotta go," she said. "Good luck with school and everything."

"Yeah," Pia said. "You too."

22

Mom says she & Dad have been emailing. And I'm like, about me? And she's like, not only about you, Pia, parce que l'inti-mité de mariage n'en finit jamais. Which honestly? Sounds like a line from that stupid show Aunt Sonia watches, Bazar de Whatever. I guess he also told Mom about Kate's teen preg-nancy drama—yawn—because again she was like: sois gentille, Pia. Why do I always have to be nice to THEM? Meanwhile, crazy conversation w LL on way to picnic.

> LL: Thanks for coming.
> ME: [Dad made me, so . . .]
> LL: I'm not trying to be a stepmom for you. I think it's a little late for that. And you have a mom.
> ME: OK.
> LL: But I want to be someone you can talk to. Like an aunt.
> ME: OK.

I already have an aunt. Sonia is just like Mom, if Mom worked at a marketing company in the 15th. They look alike, and they even move their hands the same way when they talk. The weird thing is when I try to picture Sonia, it's no problem, but Mom's face is like a moving soup of eyes, nose, mouth. Even though I saw her more recently than I saw Sonia.

Best thing about LL is I can get away with everything. Worst thing is how she jumps when I come in the room. This apt is so QUIET. In Moʻorea you can always hear the ocean or a radio or dogs barking or something. At Inès and Emma's, the floors are old wood and they make noise. Someone's always calling someone else or running on the stairs. But here I go to get a snack and LL jumps and then is like, "Oh, hey"—Mom says don't say "hey" in English because it makes you sound stupid—or "You startled me!" First time I was like, whatever, second time annoyed, third time had to go back into my room because I didn't want LL to see me cry.

Texted Inès I feel like a burglar and she was like, "MDRR-RRR!!" She couldn't tell about the crying because it was a text. And so far we've only made fun of LL together. Once I sent a pic of her butt when she was bending down to get something under the sink, & Inès was like hahahahahaha. Text sucks because when I feel like texting they're asleep, and when they feel like texting because they're going to XFT at Rambuteau (my favorite boba place) I'm in the middle of maths sans frontières.

11-10-20

1946: Operation Crossroads—Investigation of effects of nuclear weapons on warships. Names of bombs are Gilda (after Rita Hayworth's character in 1946 film noir) and Helen ("of Bikini"). Invited dignitaries and press found explosions "less spectacular than expected." But test animals—rats, pigs, and goats—placed on boats mostly destroyed. Public outcry is over animal testing. Picture of mushroom cloud cake being sliced by Vice Admiral William H. P. Blandy and his wife. Mrs. Vice Admiral Blandy smiling at the camera and wearing a mushroom cloud hat.

1948: Operation Sandstone

1951: Operation Greenhouse

1952: Operation Ivy—first hydrogen bomb test. Vaporizes Ālloklap (Elugelab). "The island of Elugelab is missing!" (Atomic Energy Commission chairman Gordon Dean reporting to incoming U.S. president Eisenhower)

1954: Operation Castle Bravo—projected to release 5–6 megatons of TNT. Scientists miscalculated and released 15 megatons instead. 1000x greater than Hiroshima. That's why they tested them so far from their home countries, because the scientists didn't really know what would happen. Bikinians had been moved temporarily to uninhabitable island Rongerik, then Kwajalein, then Kili. 66 years later, most Bikinians are still there.

1956: Operation Redwing

1958: Operation Hardtack 1

1962: Operation Dominic

Sometimes the names just go alphabetically: Able, Baker, Charlie. Sometimes the U.S. military gave the islands code names:

Enewetak = "Fred"
Bikini = "How"

But sometimes, it went the other way:

Christmas = "Kiritimati"

11-17-20

Dad's going to move out before Christmas. It's to keep us safe, he said.

11-23-20

It's a long walk from the station. Atlantic to Ocean to Sand-piper. Flag blown all the way around pole, Latino guy wrap-ping burlap over hedges, Amagansett Cemetery with crooked gray stones. LL thinks I'm at Maxine's. Logged onto the mining company's site and texted the press release to R, even though he probably won't write back. At the bottom of the press release there's this thing about Forward Looking Statements:

"Forward Looking Statements are accompanied by words such as BELIEVE, MAY, WILL, ESTIMATE, ANTICIPATE, INTEND, SHOULD, WOULD, PLAN, SEEM, SEEK, and FUTURE. Forward Looking Statements involve significant risks and uncertainties that could cause the actual results to differ materially from those discussed in the Forward Looking Statements."

What the mining guys mean by that is that they might fuck everything up the same way the nuclear testing guys did. And what their lawyers mean is that you can't blame them if they do. When I finished with the website, I didn't feel like doing any of my "independent work." Went to the beach.

Same sign as always: Restricted, No Access, etc. etc. Same wooden walkway. For some reason thinking about a bathing suit Mom used to have, black with white belt. Straw hat like any other mother. Today water & sky are both gray. Long ropes of kelp on the beach. Picked some up to squeeze the bladders. Quelle est la fonction de ces petites poches d'air? Qu'est-ce que tu penses? The brown kelp is the only kind with bladders. You can't choose what you remember.

No one there except two guys fishing. An old guy and his son, my age or maybe a little older. Drove their truck right on the beach—Mom's bête noir. Hernandez Bros HVAC. Asked what they were trying to catch and son said: sea bass.

og: You fish?
me: Sometimes
s: Where?
me: [can't say Tahiti] Gerard Drive
og: That's good for small bluefish. Also porgies.

Old guy introduces himself: Carlos. The kid's his nephew, not his son: Justin. Carlos has a long white ponytail & a brown hearing aid that wraps around his ear & squeals sometimes when he talks. He looks disappointed when that happens. He seems eager to chat, like he and his nephew have been alone too long. A lot of people are like that these days. Nephew is quiet like R when he fishes.

c: You live around here?
me: I'm just visiting a friend. On Mako Lane.

Stupid to tell strangers where you live, even if they're nice.

me: You?
carlos: He's from Corona. Not the virus, the
    neighborhood!

Justin seems embarrassed.

carlos: The cases are the worst in the city there. That's
    why he's here with me.
me: I heard about that.

Justin is packing their gear in the tackle bag. They're almost finished. Black Vans hoodie, jeans, Timberlands. Hair buzzed in back, long in front. Some pimples where I have them, right under my hair. Black eyes, dent in chin, maybe that's what makes me think of R. Some Latinx people look like Pacific Islanders. That's what made the Kon-Tiki guy think the Pacific was settled from S. America. Totally wrong, but everyone remembers him because of his raft. It's weird how the wrong things get remembered.

> CARLOS: He's staying with me until he can go back to school in person. But maybe he'll stay forever! Why would anyone want to leave?

The sun is coming through the clouds in these yellow shafts, like a painting in the most boring part of the Louvre. But it's real so I can see what Carlos means. Carlos introduces himself & Justin, so I have to say my name. I'm thinking it's not good to give my actual name. But for some reason I can't think of anything, and maybe it's because of the picnic, because at the last minute I say, "Athyna."

> CARLOS: A beautiful name for a beautiful girl!
> JUSTIN: [Something fast in Spanish. Uncle laughs, but Justin's mad. Uncle carries cooler of fish to truck.] Sorry. He's crazy.
> ME: Everybody's crazy now.
> JUSTIN: Ha. Yeah.
> ME: Is that your uncle's company?
> JUSTIN: Yeah
> ME: With your dad?
> JUSTIN: Nah. Just him. "Brothers" sounds better though.
> ME: [Laughing. It's not funny but I'm nervous. R never does that. If he doesn't want to react, he doesn't. Justin's taller than R, even though much younger.] Your parents are in Queens?
> JUSTIN: My dad passed.
> ME: [I'm lying already so I go for it.] Mine, too.
> JUSTIN: Yeah? From Covid?
> ME: No. A diving accident.
> JUSTIN: Wow
> ME: Did your dad die of Covid?
> JUSTIN: No

But he doesn't say how. Uncle calls him from the truck. Looks like maybe he's going to go so I say I have to go. He says see you around. I remember Hernandez Bros, but what am I going to do? Call and ask to talk to Justin?

·····································

Check texts on walk back to station. One from LL: how's it going? Big thumbs-up to that, Rabbit. Asked if I wanted $ this AM before I left. So she can give me Dad's $ and I'm supposed to be grateful? So I said no, thanks, and now I have no $. Only a CLIF Bar and I'm so hungry and the train is in 2 more hrs. Checked WhatsApp but nothing from R. People are different there and when you go away it's hard to keep in touch. Email and text aren't important, but gifts are. He's going to be so surprised.

Feeling guilty is like a magnet. You go to the guilty thing even when you shouldn't. So maybe that's why I text Athyna. Just like, hey, what's up, but she writes right back.

A: Your mom's kicking my ass w this paper!

Kind of cool she even remembers who I am.

ME: STEPMOM
A: ahahaha sorry
ME: want me to hack her laptop and give you an A?
A: [Thumbs up, brown one]

Is she done texting me?

ME: I'm out on Long Island.
A: No school?
ME: "independent work day"
A: LUCKY
ME: Told her I'm going to study at my friend's

I don't use "LL" because she might think it's weird.

> A: hahahahahaha
> ME: don't tell her!
> A: [Shh emoji]
> ME: Had to get out of there
> A: [Thumbs up]
> ME: Went to the beach
> A: [Meme of shivering SpongeBob]

I don't tell Athyna about SpongeBob. How kids laugh because he lives in "Bikini Bottom," but that Bikini is a real place. Actually Bikini was what the Germans called it; the Marshallese say Pikinni. After Castle Bravo, the Pikinnians could never go home.

> ME: It's not that cold! It's nice here!
> A: I [heart] the beach.

Then the dots are still there so I think she's writing something else. When it comes I have to click it because I'm on the train and there's no Wi-Fi. I think it's a meme but it isn't. It's a picture of a guy in scuba gear, respirator clipped to his belt with a carabiner. Flexing and grinning for the camera and suddenly I realize.

> ME: yr dad?
> A: yup

I feel really shitty even though there's no way she could know.

> ME: out here?
> A: Sands Pt. But idk where that is?
> ME: We cd find it if you want?

Then there's nothing. Probably she doesn't even want to see where her dad went. And also why would she want to hang out w a 15-year-old who doesn't even go to her school?

> ME: like if you want to skip HER class & come out here haha
> A: summer mb!
> ME: k!

But by then I'll be gone.

The fallout from Bravo also fell on Rongelap and Utirik. On Rongelap, there was a big flash of light. People came outside to see what was happening. Snow was falling from the sky! It fell on their hands and in their hair and on the coconuts and the fish hanging outside at the market. It fell in piles on the ground and little kids played in it. They put it in their mouths. The U.S. Army didn't get anybody out for two days. The snow was warm and dry because it wasn't snow—it was exploded bits of radioactive coral.

23

He found a one-bedroom Airbnb in a brownstone in Washington Heights, a five-minute walk from the hospital. He'd just emailed the host when Kate knocked on the door of his office. The plan was such a relief to him that he hadn't been prepared for her strong and immediate resistance, when he'd brought it up the previous evening. All morning she had been coldly efficient, barely looking at him, but he thought it was a question of giving her enough time to get used to the idea. He was sure that if he showed her the graph of hospitalizations—the one that really mattered—she would understand.

"Do you have time to talk?"

He couldn't tell for sure, but he was afraid she'd been crying. "Of course."

The home office was crowded because of the Peloton bike she'd convinced him to get in June. She was the one who used it, mostly. She picked out instructors she thought he would like, but their earnestness at the temple of physical fitness was too much for him. She insisted that anyone who loved data as much as he did could design an exercise program that worked for him, and he had to explain that he didn't "love" data. The hours he spent studying his own hospital's Covid logs, reading journal articles and long threads on Twitter from doctors in L.A. and Lyon and São Paulo, were essential because they were all in a new country now.

"I wanted to show you this." He'd printed it out. "See how it looks like a set of stairs? Now look at the graph from last April. The slope was exactly like this right before it got steeper—here."

But she barely looked. He had misread her state of mind; she was much angrier than he'd anticipated. She was practically vibrating with it.

"I can't stay here alone."

Her voice was deceptively even. It was an unfortunate consequence of the new bike that his now very visibly pregnant wife was sitting across from him at the desk, the only other unoccupied space, as if it were a consultation between doctor and patient. As if they were back in his office in the hospital, with her mother, talking about her father. The last thing he'd expected when he implanted an LVAD in a seventy-year-old contractor from Long Island, following his bypass surgery, was to sit down with the family and discover a woman who made it difficult to explain even the routine instructions he had to convey. At that first meeting, she'd been wearing a black turtleneck sweater that contrasted sharply with the mass of strawberry blond hair, tied up in a bun on the top of her head in what he had not noticed, but then suddenly did notice, was an attractive new style. He had to focus on her mother so as not to become distracted by the shape of the woman underneath the turtleneck, the modesty of the choice only highlighting what seemed to him the most vivaciously alive human being he had ever encountered. To find her in a hospital talking about possible bad outcomes for her father was like finding one of those red-and-purple Siamese fighting fish at the pet store in a tiny bowl. You would do anything to liberate something so wonderful from its woefully inadequate surroundings.

"Pia will be here," he said.

Kate shook her head in disbelief.

"I know it's not easy—" he began, but Kate held up one hand.

"I think you know I'm doing my best there." Each word broken off from the last, as over a bad connection.

"You're doing great."

"But she's not doing great, and she's not company for me. And she isn't even here very often. Do you even know how little she's here?"

"I know she's studying with the pod." He'd been delighted when she'd accepted his veto on the remote option without too much drama, and soon afterward asked permission to do her virtual days at her friend Maxine's. Truth be told, he couldn't keep Pia's complex hybrid schedule straight, but he was glad she had friends. He'd emailed the parents to confirm that Pia was welcome, and the mother wrote back from an address at Debevoise to say that both of them were back in the office, but that someone named Gisela would be there to "keep an eye on the girls." He hadn't been sure he trusted this person to make sure Pia and her friends kept their masks on, but the benefits seemed to outweigh the risk.

"But why do you say she isn't doing well?"

Kate made an incredulous sound—a sound that indicated she believed he was out of touch with his daughter, after bringing her all the way to New York to live with them. She was inferring from this failure possible future failures with regard to their own child. It wasn't completely unfounded, but it also wasn't fair to have this referendum on his parenting happening now, in the midst of the medical crisis of the century. There was also the fact that Kate had never had a child, and couldn't understand their tendency to spin out of the predictable orbits they originally followed, onto more distant and erratic paths—a tendency that made those early decisions about food and sleep and supplies that Kate read about every night in an oversized paperback with a purple cover, over which he too had once agonized, utterly irrelevant.

"I think she's cutting herself."

It wasn't that she took pleasure in telling him. But there

was a steeliness to the way she said it, an insistence that he confront certain facts. He'd had med school classmates who became light-headed during their first surgery rotation, had to sit down. It was a point of pride among those of them who didn't experience any of those reactions to the smell or sight of wet human tissue being sliced or burned. And so the sick feeling that rose in his esophagus now was a surprise, and he had to take a moment to steady himself before he responded.

"Why do you think that?"

Kate shifted position in the chair, trying to get comfortable. "I've seen it before. The stereotype is that it's all white girls, but boys do it, too. Kids of color of all genders. We don't know how many, because there aren't enough studies."

"You saw—more marks?"

"You've seen them?"

"On her leg." He didn't want to say how he knew.

"Exactly. And then I was looking for my nail scissors the other day, and I thought she might have taken them."

"I don't think she'd go into our bathroom."

Kate looked as if she were about to say something, then stopped herself. She was wearing an oversized gray T-shirt from some education conference that read *Envision the Future*, and her cheeks were very pink. "I found them in her bathroom. I thought they'd rusted, but it was blood."

"It could've been an accident. While she was cutting her nails?"

For a moment, she looked sympathetic. "It could've."

"But probably not," he admitted. "You think she wanted us to find them?"

Kate shook her head. "I had to look around. They were behind some other things in the medicine cabinet. Also, it's not something they usually do for attention. It's usually the thighs or the belly, the ankles—anyplace covered by clothing."

"I just meant, since she didn't clean them."

"I don't know if we can infer much from that."

It was true that Pia's room was a mess. Clothing everywhere, wet towels left on the bed, the empty coffee cups that drove him crazy, since he didn't think she should be drinking it yet. *Je ne grandis plus*, she said, when he brought it up.

"Okay," he said.

"It's not that I don't want to talk to her."

"No, it should be me."

A look of relief. "I think so."

His email was open on his laptop, and he couldn't help glancing at it. The Airbnb host had responded already.

"I can go." Kate stood up.

It could be an immediate no, because of his profession, or a generous yes, because of his profession. It was hard to know how people were going to react. Sometimes he heard them at seven o'clock, both here and at the hospital, banging their pots and clapping. Other times people moved away from him on the sidewalk, adjusted their masks, and he realized he hadn't removed the lanyard with his ID. Maybe the clappers and the sidesteppers were even the same people.

He was eager to check the message, but Kate was lingering.

"Is the baby moving?"

Her face softened. "Not now. When we were talking, but it always stops when I stand up."

"It's like, 'Whoa, where are we going?'"

Kate smiled faintly. "Will it be the bedroom? Or the kitchen?"

"It's hard on you."

She started to argue, but stopped.

"Anyway, I'll deal with this," he promised. "I'll email Rachel."

She was in the doorway, but she hesitated. "The therapist?"

Of course, the cutting had been the first thing he'd mentioned when he'd contacted the therapist for Pia. He just hadn't wanted to say anything to Kate. Maybe it had been naïve to think she wouldn't figure it out on her own.

"I just want to get some language," he said now. "I'm going to talk to Pia myself when I tell her about the apartment."

His wife's eyes narrowed. "You're really doing that?"

He thought that had been clear last night.

"Just an Airbnb," he said carefully. "Near the hospital. I asked about the first three weeks of December. I'd come home right after the second shot, for Christmas." He got up to embrace her but she took a step back.

"Did you do that for us?"

"Yes!" he said. "For you and the baby. I—" He thought that if he told her about Carmen, she would understand. Carmen and Violeta. But for some reason he still couldn't talk about Carmen.

Kate was shaking her head. "I mean, for me and my mom. Before we talked about my dad—did you get some *language*?"

"Oh—no." He heard the sarcasm, but tried to ignore it. "Because I have that conversation all the time."

"Right," Kate said. "It's your job." Then she went out, to the bedroom or the kitchen, closing the door firmly behind her.

He'd vowed to stop comparing them, but this was a way in which Kate and Nathalie were the same. Because everything he'd said had made sense, and she'd acted as if she'd understood. In the end, though, she was the one who'd walked out with the upper hand, and he was left sitting here, feeling like he'd screwed up.

                       ....

The apartment was on 172nd Street, only three blocks from the tower where he'd lived when he was a resident. The empanada bakery on Broadway, where he'd grabbed two shredded beef pastries more nights than he could count, was still operating, and even the sit-down place on St. Nicholas that specialized in chicharrón, where he'd once taken Nathalie, had survived the pandemic so far. His rental was a third-floor walk-up, simple and clean, if slightly dingier than it had appeared online, with narrow-plank pine floors yellowed by varnish. The galley kitchen smelled of Lysol, and the counter opened onto a living room with one exposed brick wall, facing a brown velvet couch and a mirror framed with pressed-tin salvage. The only other decoration hung in the tiny bedroom, on a cream-colored wall well scuffed around the baseboard: a small canvas print of a tropical atoll, the turquoise water of the lagoon fading out to darker green beyond the reef. During the three weeks he would spend in the apartment, Stephen would go back and forth as to whether this was an extraordinary coincidence, or simply an example of confirmed bias—one of the most generic images in the world, to which his life experience inclined him to impart significance.

In college he'd gotten to know an assistant professor in the classics department, who taught a class popularly referred to as Greeks for Greeks, a distribution requirement in history for nonmajors. The joke was that it was a gut class for frat boys, but in reality it was full of science majors balancing more demanding coursework in their own departments. (Frances, characteristically, had encouraged him to try something more challenging in that field, but Stephen was struggling through organic chemistry at the time, and he'd ignored her.) In fact the young professor was inspired, and the class was great; he'd looked forward to it every week as a break from his labs and problem sets. They read different versions of a few classic Greek myths, but the only one that stayed with him was the story of Phaeton, who lost control of his father Zeus's golden chariot and wreaked havoc on the world. The havoc came in the form of natural disasters like droughts, wildfires, and floods.

The professor held office hours in a diner off campus. Because of his long Greek surname, he'd asked his students to call him George. When Stephen arrived for their meeting, George told him that he was a vegetarian for health reasons, and then proceeded to order cheese fries and a strawberry milkshake.

"Don't judge me, Dr. Davenport," he said. "I had a rough weekend."

Stephen was a premed sophomore, and that was possibly the first time anyone ever referred to him that way.

"Dr. Davenport is my mom," he told George.

"Oh yeah?"

"She's an obstetrician."

George stopped eating, a fry halfway between his plate and his mouth, and made a sort of strangled chortling sound. Then he revealed to Stephen that a woman he'd been casually dating had just told him she was pregnant. She was planning to keep the baby.

Apart from telling Stephen he was getting an A in the class, the professor didn't touch on Greek mythology for the rest of their conference. Instead, they'd discussed George's problem. George told Stephen that he had a friend who'd grown up with her single mother, but whose father had sent wonderful letters throughout her childhood. Now that he was dead, she treasured them even more.

"So I thought I could do something like that?"

It was unclear whether George was as forthcoming with all of his students, or whether Stephen just happened to be in the right place at the right time. Either way, he'd been enormously flattered that the professor would confide in him about such a personal and adult problem, and even ask his advice. Stephen had just turned twenty at the time, and he'd given his enthusiastic endorsement to this fatherhood-by-correspondence plan. They hadn't crossed paths again after the class ended and Stephen's routine was increasingly confined to the campus science complex. He hadn't thought of the classics professor until many years later, when Pia had moved with her mother to France, and the memory had made him want to laugh and cry at the same time. Where were George and his offspring now?

24

The call from the bank came at the beginning of December, right after Stephen moved into the apartment near the hospital. There was a robot who put you on hold for a person. You called me, she wanted to shout, but of course that was pointless. She had put the clunky landline on speaker and finished the email, which she bcc'd to all the students who were behind on their personal narratives, stressing that she was happy to give them extra time for the assignment but that the Macaulay Honors deadline was fixed. "Please email me by the end of the day," she wrote, "and if you're not feeling well, or have other extenuating circumstances, we'll figure something out." She turned to Tania's essay, about being bullied in middle school and regaining her confidence through mixed martial arts, but the hold music was really distracting. What algorithm had decided that Men at Work's "Down Under" was appropriate for pandemic-era customers waiting for help with credit card fraud?

Finally a woman came on the line. She introduced herself as Wendy, and spoke English with an accent unfamiliar to Kate. Kate agreed to review recent transactions, which included $2.75 to the MTA, $212.36 to Fresh Direct, and $13 even to an empanada bakery near Stephen's rental.

"And $760.42 to Alaska Airlines?"

"What?"

"One economy ticket on December thirtieth, 2020, from Newark to Papeʻete, via Los Angeles?"

"No," she said. "Not that one."

"No need to worry!" Wendy said. "We declined the charge as a preventative measure. We will cancel your cards, and get another sent out to you right away. As a platinum customer, you are entitled to this service at no extra charge."

"No—" Kate said, "hang on, sorry. Please don't cancel the cards."

"Ma'am, in cases of fraud—"

"It was us," Kate said.

There was a pause as they veered off script.

"It was us but it was a mistake."

"You made the charge to Alaska Airlines for $760.42?"

"It was made by another member of the family. It was unintentional."

"You did not want to purchase the ticket?"

"We were only looking—to see the price."

"Ah, okay," Wendy said, slipping out of character for a moment. "Expensive ticket!"

"Yes—thanks so much for catching it."

"No problem," Wendy said. "We can remove the hold on your card. You may immediately resume using your card."

"We appreciate it."

"Is there anything else we can help you with today?"

"You're not going to believe what she did," Kate told May, who finally came to visit one Sunday afternoon. Pia was at Maxine's, as usual, and Kate prepared for her former roommate's visit as if for a date. She washed her hair and got cookies from the store, tea for herself and Coke for May, who was one of the only people Kate knew who still smoked and drank soda. May was wearing a hot-pink-and-brown argyle sweater that might have come from a fancy boutique in SoHo but was most likely from an excellent, under-the-radar consignment store. May dressed like she worked in fashion, but she was actually a social worker for the city's Human Resources Administration.

"Oh, okay," May said, when Kate showed her into the living room. "I'm moving in."

"Please," Kate said.

"Stephen will be thrilled."

"Stephen likes you." Stephen had always liked May; it was Benji he couldn't stand. "But we wouldn't have to tell him," Kate added, "since he's not even here."

"Just until the holidays, though, right?" May said. "I could use a monthlong break from Benji, at this point."

"Benji would never come here."

"Of course he would. He'd give you a hard time—and then he'd put his feet up on this great couch and eat all your caviar."

"We don't have caviar. But I got you some Coke."

"Awesome." May glanced at Kate's stomach. "I can get it."

"It's good for me to move around."

"You look great."

"You have to say that."

"Yeah, but you do—your skin, especially. Very dewy." But the hug she'd given Kate at the door was gingerly, as if she were afraid of inflicting damage, and she certainly didn't ask to touch her stomach. Instead, while Kate was getting the cookies, May walked around the living room looking at the art. "Is this a Sam Francis?"

"I wouldn't have known—but yeah."

"And look at all this vinyl. Can you hook it up to the Sonos?"

"I haven't figured it out yet. I still just listen on my phone."

May shook her head at this waste. "So what does the kid have to complain about?"

"Well—me, I guess. No one likes a stepmother."

"You're probably being too nice to her."

"You think?"

"My mom used to say all American kids were spoiled. No offense."

"I mean, my mom would say she's spoiled, too. I sometimes feel bad for her, though."

"Yeah," May said. "She's not going to get to go to Tahiti."

Kate laughed and sat down in a chair opposite May. "Well, her mom's there." It was strange to find herself defending Pia.

"She's like, a marine biologist?"

"Right—she studies coral."

"I didn't know anyone was actually a marine biologist. It's one of those jobs."

"She's one of those people." As if it knew something, the baby began a rhythmic drumming. Was the baby her ally against Nathalie? Did it have a sixth sense for danger?

"But he left her," May said.

"She left him, actually. Or at least she was the one who had the affair, and then he ended it after that."

"I admire someone who draws a line in the sand at infidelity," May said. "It's unfashionable. Now everyone's obsessed with that Belgian sex therapist."

It was loyal of May to compliment Stephen, to be on their side. She thought maybe she'd been too hard on him about the move. At night he always texted to see if she could FaceTime, no matter how late it was. For the first few days, she'd given him the cold shoulder, told him she was too tired to talk, but soon she was desperate for adult conversation. He made her laugh having imaginary dialogue with the baby, whom they had nicknamed Murray. "Dad, you suck," Murray would say. "Where the hell are you?" And, "I'm going to need a lot of burping to make up for this." Murray's affect was that of a domineering old man: "Get my diapers! On the double!"

Stephen didn't tell her much about the hospital, but he listened to what was going on with her students. Jasmine's internship at the aquarium had been postponed. There was a Zoom goodbye party for Khalil, whose family was moving to Troy. Sometimes he had to respond to a message while they were talking. Once he'd offered to call her back and she said she'd just rest her eyes; by the time he turned back to the phone, she'd fallen asleep. In the morning she found the phone in the bed next to her, and when she opened it, there he was, getting his coffee.

"Hey, good morning."

"You kept it on all night?"

"I wasn't watching you sleep," he said. "Or not much."

"I was probably drooling."

"Probably." He was already in his scrubs, an N95 around his neck. "But you were breathing quietly—for both of you. It was beautiful."

"It's not Stephen," Kate told May. "It's Pia. I honestly don't know what to do anymore."

"Far be it from me," May said. "You're the pregnant teacher. But I'd maybe try being a little tougher on her. Treat her like she's younger than she is."

She waited until the rare evening when they were both home at dinnertime. Pia now ate at Maxine's almost every night, even when she hadn't spent the day there. When she did come home, she would generally tell Kate she wasn't hungry. She'd done the same thing that night, but Kate persisted.

"Please sit with me," she said. "I've been staring at the screen all day. I need some company." Pia had been heading for her room; Kate saw the slight lift in her shoulders and thought she might refuse again. Or maybe argue that if they had allowed her to go remote, Kate would have had company all the time. Instead Pia shrugged and sat down on one of the stools at the island, as if she expected Kate to serve her there.

"Let's sit at the table, if you don't mind. I need a chair with a back these days."

Pia sat at the table, which was round and accommodated ten. Kate left one seat empty, and took the next, so they weren't exactly facing each other, nor were they side by side.

"How was your day?"

"Very academic," Pia said. She didn't inquire about Kate's. "I think we're going to go out to Maxine's house in East Hampton for the break."

"For all of winter break?"

"I'll come back while my dad's home. For Christmas and stuff." For once Pia looked apprehensive, as if she thought she might be going too far. But it made sense—what teenager wanted to spend time with her stepparent alone over break? And what had Kate thought they'd be doing—baking cookies? She tried not to take it as a personal rejection.

"Isn't this all a lot for Maxine's parents?"

"They don't care," Pia said. "They're mostly at work or whatever."

Kate could remember the care her own mother had taken to keep things equal among her circle of friends. A baked ziti dinner at one house, lemon chicken at another. Her sister drove Kate and her friend Annie to soccer practice in exchange for gas money, switching off with Annie's older brother. Nancy was especially careful not to take advantage of the full-time mothers just because she worked outside the home. It was almost a point of honor, and women who were careless about the division of labor got talked about in phone conversations Kate overheard, her mother with the receiver between her shoulder and her ear, chopping vegetables. *It's not that I mind, but* . . . There were, in their town at that time, no fathers Kate could remember who were involved in the distribution of childcare responsibilities.

"And we're all in the same pod, so we have the same classes. We help each other."

"That's great," Kate said. "I keep meaning to ask what you're reading in ELA."

Pia didn't look up from her plate. "We don't call it that. But we're reading *As I Lay Dying* in English, and *The Plague* in French."

"Really?"

"It's just a coincidence," Pia said. "Tenth graders read those books every year."

There was silence, in which the only sound was the clink of their forks against the plates. The plates were from Villeroy & Boch, mostly white but with a pattern of tiny botanical drawings. Kate was always nervous about putting them in the dishwasher. Pia was pushing the chicken cutlet that Kate had fried in cornmeal around on her plate. She thought maybe she should just get to it.

"I got a call from the bank."

Pia speared a large piece of chicken with some salad on her fork and shoved it into her mouth.

"They blocked a charge to Alaska Airlines, for a one-way ticket to Tahiti. On December thirtieth."

Pia did look up then. Her expression was blank. "Did you tell my dad?"

"Nope."

Pia relaxed slightly. "How do you know it wasn't him?"

Kate started to ask why Stephen would want to go to Tahiti, and thought better of it. "Your father would have known to alert the credit card company if he were traveling. Also, he would have mentioned it to me."

Pia shrugged, as if that were doubtful. She was wearing her white uniform blouse, thin enough that you could see a pale pink bra though the fabric, and a pair of track pants. Her roots were now a coppery brown, but the blond ends were still wild looking and dry from the bleach. She always wore the same earrings: a rose gold bar with a chain that looped around to the backing. Now Kate noticed for the first time a tiny silver starfish in the second piercing of her right ear.

"I know you haven't loved being back at Lycée. And I'm sure you miss your mom."

Pia stood abruptly. She took her plate to the sink, dumped a large portion of her dinner into the trash drawer, and put it into the dishwasher. Then she turned to Kate.

"Thanks for dinner."

"I get that you don't want to talk to me about it. I mean, I wouldn't either, if I were you."

Pia opened the cabinet and took a box of cookies.

"I'm just saying that I'm here."

Pia made a sound that might have indicated the redundancy

of that statement, but could also have been a reaction—positive or negative—to the caramel stroopwafels Kate had selected. She took the cookie out of its individual wrapping and leaned against the island. But she didn't leave.

"The thing about *The Plague* is that it's supposed to be this existentialist classic. About the human condition, blah blah blah. But there are like, no women in it."

"That's really interesting," Kate said.

"There's the doctor's mom, who basically just sits in a chair staring out the window." Pia spoke through a bite of waffle. "And the doctor's wife, who dies at the end."

"I'm afraid I've never read it."

"It's so boring," Pia said. "If Covid doesn't kill us, *The Plague* will."

Kate laughed, but she could tell it was a joke Pia had made before. She thought she would just ask—sometimes it helped to catch a kid off guard.

"You miss Raffi?"

Pia hesitated. "Now that I'm not coming, Raffi's fucked."

"Fucked in what way?" Kate said. "If you don't mind me asking?"

"He needs something from me." Pia balanced on one leg, resting the other instep on her inner thigh: tree pose. Kate had sometimes stood like that herself, before her entire center of gravity had shifted forward.

She got up and began clearing the dinner things. "What's that?"

"A part—that he can't get in Tahiti. He can build anything. He's harvesting biofuel."

"But I'm sure you're not the only person—"

"Also, he's in love with me," Pia interrupted casually. "You might not believe it, but it's true."

"Oh I believe it," Kate said. "It just seems a little problematic."

"It just happened," Pia said. "Are you going to tell my dad?"

"No," she said. "But I think you should stay here for winter break. At least until your dad gets back."

"Wait—what? I told you Maxine's parents don't care."

"I'm responsible for you," Kate said. "Whether either of us likes it. And I need to be able to trust you."

Pia affected shock. "That's like—*blackmail.*"

"Blackmail is something that happens beforehand," Kate said. "This is consequences."

Pia exhaled sharply and said something Kate couldn't catch—maybe in French. Then she turned and left the room.

25

To get to Raffi's family land in the Paopao Valley, Nathalie drove past the juice factory and the American station, before turning inland at the apex of Cook's Bay. On the way she stopped at the Super U Aré, since you never showed up empty-handed. She got a bottle of whiskey for the adults, and grabbed a coloring book for Raffi's niece as well. His sister Hina had invited her to stop by and see the baby anytime—probably because she was bored at home with her mother, her daughter, and the infant all day. But it was definitely weird to show up without telling Raffi in advance. Nathalie thought she might call and say she was nearby, and ask if it was a good time, but a trip into town wasn't unusual and didn't constitute an explanation.

Coming out of the supermarket, she squinted in the noon light and felt in her bag; she must've left her glasses on the dashboard. It was hot. Between the store and the parking, the fruit sellers fanned themselves under a blue tarp, calling out listlessly: "Mangue, papaye, carambole!" Normally she bought from them, but there were all kinds of fruit trees at Raffi's mother's place, and she knew that if she visited, Monique would press gifts on her.

"Not today," she told the fruit sellers in English—they preferred Americans, and with them she could pass. The fruit reminded her that she was hungry. It would be easy enough to tell Hina that she'd been meeting a friend for lunch, and it had just occurred to her to stop by and see the baby. She would call when she was close, but she wouldn't give Raffi enough time to say no. The day before yesterday, Gunther had pointed out two missing containers of ammonium nitrate crystals, not noted in the log. A Pelican case that she was sure Raffi would return was one thing, but chemicals were another. She wished she doubted Gunther's information, but she knew her student too well for that. The fact was that she had to talk to Raffi.

At the middle school, a paved road branched off the coastal route, and the curving dirt driveway off of that. The house at the end of it was long and low, all one level, painted creamy yellow. The roof was corrugated steel, unpainted but with white latticework decoration hanging from its underside, matching the trim on the slatted windows. Two shades could be lowered to protect the concrete porch from the sun; when Nathalie drove up, Raffi's four-year-old niece was there, lying on her stomach on a woven mat. Bougainvillea grew up a trellis alongside the window, and a row of young birds of paradise had been newly planted in front of the porch. The little girl got to her feet when the car appeared on the dirt drive and then scrambled into the house to alert the adults.

Nathalie parked in the deep shade of a mango tree, took her purse and string bag of gifts up to the porch. Something crunched under her foot as she approached the front door, a crayon that the niece—called Maeva, Nathalie was pleased to remember—must have been using when she pulled up. Maeva had left the front door slightly ajar, but Nathalie knocked anyway, stepping slightly to the left of the door, to get out of the sun. One burning oblong crept across the smooth concrete porch, the hull of a canoe. The only sound was the soporific drone of insects from the surrounding vegetation. As far as she knew, Monique's fruit trees and Raffi's tamanu were all the family grew on the land, which hadn't been completely cultivated since his grandfather's time. Raffi's father had served in the navy and had been making his living as a marine mechanic before he died.

The family was small by Tahitian standards; Raffi and Hina were the youngest of four. The older daughter lived in New Caledonia with her husband and children, and another son worked at the airport in Fa'a'ā. Raffi and his brother didn't get along; he'd told Nathalie that his brother had talked about building a house on the graded plot up the slope from his mother's. For that reason, Raffi had hastily erected a workshop to claim the site—three cinder block walls and an aluminum roof, one wall open to the weather. That was where he worked on the tamanu project, which his brother thought was foolish. His mother was more favorably disposed, although Hina had once told Nathalie that this was because Raffi was their mother's favorite. They both hoped Raffi would eventually tear down the workshop, get married, and build a house.

When she and Raffi were first starting the fluorescence project, there had been some gossip; Marie-Laure had repeated it to her. The fact was that there were relationships like that, but more with older white men and younger Tahitian women than the other way around. Of course she'd needed Raffi then for everything to do with the boats. It might even have been part of what inspired the thing with Martin, just to disprove any rumors. With regard to the compensation for his father's illness, she'd wanted to help, not because she was French per se but just because they were a nice family. She had always tried to stay out of politics, the debates of which seemed to her to rely on grand generalizations unsupported by data—a science only in name.

It was Monique who came to the door; as she opened it, Nathalie saw another door swinging shut inside. Monique's face was round and showed her Chinese ancestry. Her cheeks were like two brown fruits underneath the black crescents of her eyes, which had a knowing, appraising way of looking that was hard for Nathalie to decipher. She thought that Monique liked her, but she couldn't be sure.

"Come in, come in." Monique was wearing a red-and-white patterned pareo and house slippers, and had a tiare blossom in her hair; whether she'd changed because they had a visitor, or that was how she always dressed at home, Nathalie didn't know. "Hina is just feeding the baby."

It must've been Raffi's sister, then, disappearing into the bedroom for privacy. Nathalie had started breastfeeding Pia, because the data seemed to support it, but she'd given it up after five weeks, partly in reaction to the type of sanctimonious American mother who would expose herself anywhere—a restaurant, park, or airplane—just to flaunt her maternal or natural qualities. Personally it had made Nathalie feel like a cow.

"It's hot. You'll have some fruit?"

"Thank you."

A low stucco wall divided the kitchen from the yard, but it was really one extended space, with a sink, refrigerator, and another wooden table outdoors. Where Nathalie was sitting, at a small round mahogany table in the main living space, the floor was white linoleum streaked with brown and red. There were red curtains in the windows that filtered the light. She was always struck by the way that Tahitian houses were dark and cool, as opposed to the way the French designed, to take maximum advantage of light and views. She also preferred to see out, but there was something comforting about the womb-like dimness of this space. From around the kitchen doorway, Raffi's niece Maeva scowled at her.

"A present for you," Nathalie said, holding out the coloring book. Gifts were standard, but she could never do it naturally. The girl came forward eagerly to take the book, and her face fell.

"I have this one already."

Her grandmother looked up from the kitchen, where she was cutting a pomelo. She said something sharply in Tahitian, and the girl responded sullenly in French:

"Thank you very much."

"It's wonderful that you speak to them in both languages."

Monique brought the plate to the table. "My daughter's Tahitian is bad. But her other grandfather teaches at the Lycée Agricole. So Maeva's father's is good as well."

"I heard you," Hina said mildly, coming out of the bedroom.

"Well," her mother said.

Hina kissed Nathalie on each cheek. "But I have a Tahitian name," she continued. "Only Raffi's is French."

"He has one," Monique said. "But I also love 'Raphael.' I have a picture of him there." Nathalie looked, and there was indeed a small religious painting of an angel standing on a fish. She'd never attended any kind of church and wasn't sure whether Raphael had other maritime associations. The other piece of art she recognized: a local image of the javelin piercing Mount Mou'a Puta through its peak.

"He has a Tahitian name?"

"Tevaihau," his mother said. "Tevai means 'peace'; hau is 'water.'"

Hina laughed. "That's my brother, the peaceful angel."

"Is he—?"

"Up at the shed," Monique said, inclining her head. "He'll be down to see you."

"I'll walk up."

Monique protested, as if appalled. "It's too hot!"

Nathalie thought Raffi's mother must've been aware of the kind of work they did, out on the boats all day. She knew her skin showed it, too; it was something her own mother always commented on, on the rare occasions she shared a photo. But there was a kind of over-the-top solicitude for foreigners, no matter how much time you'd spent on the island. Maybe it was a way of keeping them at a distance.

"But the pomelo is so cooling." The weedy pink flesh was delicious, swollen with juice.

Monique smiled. "Not too sour?"

There would be no way to have the conversation she wanted to have with Raffi in front of Monique and Hina. They would have to switch to English, which would be both rude and risky, since she knew Monique wouldn't understand but was afraid Hina might.

"This is from your own trees?"

"We have papaya, guava, mango, banana, pomelo, and passion fruit," Monique said proudly. "Now the pomelo are sweet."

Possibly Raffi knew what she wanted to discuss, and would come to the house to avoid it. She wondered if he'd seen her drive in.

"I'll walk up with you," Hina offered.

"Mama!" Maeva had wandered out on the porch. "My crayon is broken!"

Hina sighed. "Never mind. Come take a walk to see your uncle."

"The purple one! I need it for her cape!"

Nathalie didn't hear whose cape it was, because the baby woke up.

"I'm going to kill her," Hina said under her breath. "Maeva! You woke your brother."

"Come, Maeva," Monique said, and to her daughter: "You get the baby."

This time Hina left the door ajar. The crib was catty-corner to the window, opposite a daybed covered with a solid yellow cloth. Someone had stored a stacked cardboard pallet of soft drinks against the wall, underneath the window. The baby hadn't really been crying, just alerting them with short bursts of sound; as soon as Hina picked him up and put him over her shoulder, he stopped. She bounced on her feet, patting his back and making a susurrant sound. The curtains—blue in this room—made blue lights in her long black hair. The baby's bald head, perfectly round, rested against the hollow of her shoulder. It was no performance, and Nathalie couldn't help watching. If she had nursed Pia longer, would they be closer now?

Hina came out of the bedroom with the baby in her arms. "I'm sorry," she said. "Now he'll be awake."

"He's beautiful," Nathalie said. "I'll get out of your way."

"I was looking forward to chatting," Hina said. "Is your daughter still here?"

"She went back to New York for school this year."

"I would love to go to New York."

"I'll have her bring you something when she comes—a souvenir."

Hina laughed, pleased. "No need. Such a pretty girl."

"She's hardheaded," Nathalie said.

"Like my brother. You'll find him up there." And then as an afterthought, a bit of her mother in her, she indicated a hook on the wall. "Take a hat."

When they had graded the plot of land on the hill, they'd laid two paved tracks that followed two switchbacks from the house. Now weeds had grown up between them. Nathalie went through an open gate, stepping carefully over a drainage channel covered by an iron grille. She wore Monique's wide-brimmed palm-leaf hat, but the sun had gone behind clouds. The air was humid, not unpleasant, and she wondered if it might rain. Fat green papayas hung like decorations around each spindly, silver trunk, under each umbrella of leaves. Behind them were some lower, fuller trees with clusters of pale and mottled guavas. She shaded her eyes: the roof of Raffi's shed glinted a watery gray, but it didn't look like anyone was up there.

It wasn't until she'd almost reached the shed that he heard her and stepped out. Raffi shaded his eyes, and Nathalie waved. He lifted his hand briefly, then went back inside. Why did she immediately assume he was hiding something? It was Gunther who'd put that idea into her head. Resentments grew like weeds on this small island. Along one side of the shed, where you might put a yard if it were a house, were four rows of spent tires, evenly spaced, where he'd planted the tamanu seedlings. She'd been to see them once before, almost a year ago; now they were thin stalks with full pinnate leaves. Behind them were the family's mature trees, already flowering. Just seeing them reassured her.

"Ia orana," he said, coming back outside. "What a surprise."

She tried to sound nonchalant. "I was in town." She didn't mention lunch with a friend; better to keep it simple. "I wanted to come see Hina and the baby."

Raffi just looked at her. He was wearing a familiar pair of blue-and-orange board shorts, a T-shirt from the new eco-museum, and a baseball cap. He could have been a surfer on some beach in California.

"The trees are growing well."

"Not really. They should be bigger now. That's why I'm doing a new fertilizer."

She should've grabbed her water bottle from the car before walking up. Unlike his mother, Raffi hadn't offered her water or a chair.

"Fertilizer?"

"I'm making it."

Now she understood. He was answering before she could ask. "So you needed ammonium nitrate from the lab."

"These trees are supposed to grow down by the water."

"I know that."

"The fruits can travel miles across the ocean. Little voyagers."

Nathalie thought they were getting off track. "Why didn't you just buy it?"

"More expensive," Raffi said. "I need a lot."

A dangerous-looking hacksaw with a yellow plastic handle was sitting on a three-legged wooden stool, just inside the shed. Underneath the stool: a pressurized can of liquid rubber. She was going to ask what it was for, but thought better of it. There was no need to pry further than necessary.

"People have been fussy about the logbook."

"Your student." He didn't bother with Gunther's name.

"He's a pain in the ass—but a great researcher."

"Research," Raffi said thoughtfully.

The anthropologists had shifted their game decades ago, turned their gaze on themselves, at least in theory. But for a long time the biologists had been exempt. Now it was—what are you doing with the community? Who are you bringing on board? Every funding agency wanted to hear the word "Indigenous," but did they really care what happened here? It was a trend, like anything else. It would be insulting to Raffi and his neighbors to pander to them in that way.

"I know what you mean," Nathalie said. "But this would go beyond research. Now we're starting to understand which larvae are the strongest, and the cryopreservation people are having more and more success. If we can start scaling that up, it's going to be possible to create a bank of species—not dead specimens in a museum, but living larvae that can be reanimated when conditions are ideal. Or at least when they're likely to have the best chance of survival."

Raffi's mouth twitched up on one side. "And put them on the fake reef."

She stared at him. "How did you know about that?"

He shrugged, as if the question was beneath him.

"Gunther's just doing some preliminary research. To provide an attractive substrate, resistant to algae. We were thinking of ways we might get it funded."

"An art project."

She decided to stop fighting it. "That would bring tourists. A win for us and a win for you. Scuba tours, at thirty or even forty meters. It would be a way to showcase the coral diversity at that depth. And maybe fund some of the cryopreservation work."

Raffi turned his back to her. He knelt by one of his plants, examined it. But unlike the first time, when he'd shown her the seedlings with an enthusiasm that made her smile, she had the feeling this was an act.

"What?"

Unlike a lot of Tahitian men, he kept his hair cropped short. The skin between his hairline and his T shirt was darker from the sun.

"I think it's better to keep it in the lab."

She was surprised—both that he'd offered his opinion, and by the opinion itself. She'd always thought he was bored by the less practical aspects of their work. "In the lab—really?"

"In the lab, it's science. On the reef it's just another disturbance."

"That's fair," Nathalie said. "But we would be cautious. We're talking about coral recruits, not mining equipment."

"Gardening."

She looked around them, at his neat rows of trees in their tires. "Isn't that what you're doing here?"

"But this is a garden."

"Okay," she said. "I take your point. The ocean is not a garden."

"Or a bank."

Raffi had been squatting by the tires, but now he stood to his full height. He was only a couple of inches taller than she was, but his shoulders and chest were as broad as those of any man she'd known. Did that physiology have a relationship to lung capacity? Free diving, he could stay down almost five minutes.

"I've seen pictures of the mining vehicles," he said. "It'll be another Moruroa."

She wouldn't argue with that, of course; it was just that she didn't think it was the scientists' fault. Those were different scientists, first of all, and even the men whose intellect made it possible to build the bomb were hardly the ones who'd endorsed fifty years of testing in the Pacific. She wasn't an apologist for her own or any other government. There was no excuse for what they'd done. But she and Raffi were on the same side.

"I couldn't agree with you more," she said.

He looked at her, assessing.

"Look at the Solwara project. That was an unmitigated disaster—ecologically, financially, and culturally for the Papuans."

He brushed the soil from his hands.

"It makes me so angry, I want to murder someone," she continued. "And the worst thing is, most people would agree with us. I think most people have this fantasy of another chance. If we could just go back to the way things were, do things differently. And now we *do* have the chance—one more chance. There's a pristine paradise, untouched, that's been hidden from us until now. But the moment we have the tools to explore it, they want to ruin it. If only people could see what's down there, they would start to understand. That's why I think a"—she was careful with her choice of words—"*repository* of species—"

"Not murder," Raffi interrupted, smiling slightly. "That would be going too far."

She laughed. "Honestly, I don't know sometimes." There was a breeze. In the distance you could see Mou'a Puta, shot through with the hole in its peak. White clouds moved fast across it, and another grayer mass covered the sun. In the sudden shadow, the air smelled thick and green. It was going to rain.

"Well," she said. "I'm going to get back to the lab."

He nodded. "I don't need any more of it."

It took her a moment to understand that he was referring to the chemicals.

"I can fix the log. Just, next time—"

He nodded slightly.

"And be careful with that stuff, okay?"

He ignored her. As soon as she started down the path, he'd gone back to the saw. On the switchback she looked up the hill, and saw that he was cutting through a 5-gallon drum, of the type he collected to store his oil. The sound of the saw biting into the metal was horrible, but she marveled at his skill with his hands. He could make anything, from a basket out of leaves to the workshop from concrete and rebar. It had seemed to go up overnight. What drove her crazy were those silences. If he was angry, why wouldn't he just say something?

When she got back to the car, the house was quiet. Maeva was no longer on the porch, and the front door was closed. It felt impolite to leave without saying goodbye; on the other hand, the baby might be sleeping again. Most likely, Nathalie decided, everyone was napping.

She walked up to the porch and left the hat on a plastic chair with a flowered cushion. The crayons were still lying on the porch around the patterned pandanus mat, and so she picked them up, including the broken purple one. She arranged them neatly, next to the hat. Then she got in her car and drove away.

26

It had been a regular Sunday morning. Her mom had gone to church, and Elijah had taken Marcus to the playground. Bree was at her friend Andrea's wedding shower. Their mom had tried to get Athyna to come to the service, but she said she had homework. She did have homework, but she was distracted and kept looking at her phone, and hadn't made much progress when E came in.

"Where's Marcus?"

E stuck his head in the fridge, looking for juice. He was sweaty, coming from the courts. "Thought you were sick of watching him."

"Where is he, though?"

E shook his head. "Bree came and got him after her thing. They're at the store." He carried the jug of orange juice upstairs, and then she heard the shower. When he came back downstairs he was wearing only a pair of jeans, holding a blunt in one hand.

"Want some?"

"Light that in here, my mom'll kill you."

"It'll help you chill."

"*Excuse* me?"

"You heard me."

"I'm chill."

E raised his eyebrows. "Then what was the shrink for?"

"I have anxiety," Athyna said, then felt stupid. Who wasn't anxious? But Rosalie would say: *We're talking about you, Athyna.*

"Fine," E said. "Just offering. Because you look stressed."

"I have a lot of work."

"This is good shit."

"No, thanks," Athyna said.

E shrugged. "You do you." He went out the back door, from the kitchen, to sit on the steps that faced the strip of weedy yard. They'd had big plans for a garden when the pandemic first started, but her mom and Bree had been working so much.

The thing about anxiety, Rosalie said, was that it could make your mind play tricks on you. It could invent a crazy worry, what Rosalie called a "tall tale"—that someone had poisoned the cereal she'd had for breakfast or that she was going to get locked in the bathroom at school overnight—and get her to believe it. The trick was to get Athyna to focus less on her worries and more on the things that were important to her: drawing or cooking were Rosalie's examples. But she was getting sick of cooking, especially for Marcus, and her drawings were really just doodles, like the one she was making in the margin of her math notebook right now, a field of mushrooms, instead of looking up how to graph multivariable equations. The worst thing about doing math on the app was that it timed you, and the clock made Athyna so nervous that she gave up before she'd even started. That was why she was drawing mushrooms in red pen, bulbous caps all different sizes, in the style of a Japanese cartoon. Once she'd seen a white layer cake covered with meringue mushrooms just like this, red with white spots, beautiful and frightening at the same time. She thought she wouldn't mind making that, if she had all the time in the world.

She was focused on her drawing—the tissue-thin partitions on the underside of each cap—and so she didn't even hear the door open.

"Jesus, you scared me," she said, but E didn't say anything. He looked as if he'd been thinking something sad out there; it made him somehow younger than usual. Just like the last time, he filled the kitchen doorway with his body. But instead of teasing her, or blocking her way, he came toward her, looking right through her, as if there was another girl behind her on another couch.

"Hey," Athyna said, but she was so confused about what was happening that she didn't even move. This was something she thought about a lot, later. There would have been plenty of time to get out of there, in the moments between E standing in the doorway and E putting one hand on the arm of the couch, the other on its back, pinning Athyna between them.

The muscles in his arms flexed, hard from lifting. Was he trying to kiss her?

"What the—" she began again, turning her head away.

"Come on, Teeny," he said. "Sweet Teeny." Then he put one hand on her back and jerked her down, so she was on her back on the couch.

"No," she said then—she was sure she did. Then "No!" again. But you couldn't just lie there saying it. You had to move. It was like starting to wake up while your dream was still there. It was bending over you and you couldn't move.

He had one hand on her shoulder and his knee between her legs by the time she finally pushed him off. He had to relent first, because there was no way she was strong enough. He sat back on the couch and laughed at her.

"Last chance to get some action and you blew it," he said. "Poor Teeny." Then he grabbed his jacket and let himself out the front door.

Athyna locked herself in her bedroom. Her former bedroom, now Marcus's. Then she started throwing stuff into her back-pack. It was the one she used to take to school, and there was all kinds of junk at the bottom: her creased copy of *In Our Time*, which she still had to return, an empty container of ICE BREAKERS with a tampon and an eraser shaped like a taco inside, and a folded note from Krystal that said, *you better wait 4 me!!!* That was all from last year, before the pandemic even started. She didn't throw it away but she did text her friend, because it sort of seemed like a sign, and until that moment she hadn't known where she was going to go.

She asked if she could come over, and Krystal was like, "u ok???" Her friend knew something was wrong because it was weird to be asking if you could go to someone's house these days. They used to go home with each other all the time, usually sleeping over because they lived so far apart. Their moms approved of each other and almost always said yes. Instead of answering Krystal's question, Athyna typed back carefully that no one in the house was sick, and that she'd barely been outside all week, but if Krystal's mom wasn't cool with it, nbd. Then she waited for her friend to answer. She was so focused on her phone that she forgot she was going to need her toothbrush, not to mention more than two pairs of underwear. That was all that was clean in the dresser she still shared with Marcus, but she should have taken the dirty ones and washed them later. While she was feeling around in the back of the drawer, her hand touched the leather box with her father's watch. No one would miss it, so she slipped that into the backpack, too.

She had to get out of there before everybody got back. The house was totally quiet but she knew E could return at any time. She didn't want to see her sister, but her mom was the real danger because she always knew when something was wrong. Athyna stared at her phone, willing it to light up. *C'mon Krystal.* But it was really Krystal's mom, Cherisse, who had to decide. Krystal's parents were from Trinidad and Athyna loved them—especially Anton, her dad, who wore his locs in one of those Jamaican caps, played cricket on the weekends in Marine Park, and always greeted her with an enthusiastic *How ya goin', Teena,* as if she were some kind of bright spot in his day. When she came over in a regular way, he used to walk out to buy mangoes from the lady on the corner and make them juice with lots of ice, just because he knew they loved it. He was the opposite of her own father, who had planned even a trip to the grocery store like he was a lieutenant responsible for a whole platoon, and also the opposite of Cherisse, who was nice but so brisk and organized that it was sometimes a little scary. It was completely possible that she could say no.

Her stomach dropped when she heard the door, and she was relieved when it was only her sister and Marcus. She waited for her nephew to call out, but for once he didn't come looking for her. That was divine intervention—or maybe just hunger—because a minute later she could hear Breanna yelling at him in the kitchen. The thing to do was just to leave and then figure it out. If Krystal didn't come through, she could always try Maddie or Tania—although her apartment was crazy, all those kids. She checked again. What would her dad say if he could see her, scared to walk around in the daytime? What would her dad say about all of it?

Finally she heard Breanna going upstairs to look for E; that was her chance. She opened the bedroom door, but she'd forgotten about Marcus, who'd finished whatever Bree had given him and was playing with his toys on the rug.

"Teetee!"

"Hey," she said. "You don't have to yell."

"Why you got your backpack?"

"I have to go out."

His face fell. "Go where?"

She didn't have time for it. "Out, okay? I'll see you later."

He was going to cry; she could tell. She knelt down and picked up Grimlock, who was having some interaction with the yellow Power Ranger, who had boobs and a tiny waist. What was the point if even the superheroes looked like that? She flew the two of them around and said something about Grimlock getting rescued by Yellow Ranger—that was "inverting the paradigm"—but it was uninspired. Just switching the roles around in the same stories wasn't going to do it. She was sweating under her hoodie.

"That's Birdboy," Marcus said, sullen now.

She had an idea. "Look," she told him. "I gotta go out and get your Christmas present."

"Santa brings my presents."

"Yeah, but I'm gonna go to the North Pole and get this one. He can't bring it 'cause it's big." That did it. Marcus's attention was totally focused on her.

"How big?"

"Like, really big. He asked me to come get it."

"You talked to him?"

"No, silly. Santa doesn't have a phone. He wrote me a letter. But he said I have to come tomorrow, and it takes a day to get there."

Marcus nodded, calculating. "So you'll be back tomorrow?"

"And then a day to get back. And I have to stay overnight."

"At his house?"

"At a hotel. Then I'll be back."

"Okay."

"Be good, okay?"

Marcus nodded.

"We don't want him to change his mind."

He wasn't wearing the Spider-Man costume, because Breanna didn't like to walk around with him in that. He had on a little Champion sweat suit and a new Nets cap that was too big, stiff at the brim. She took it off and kissed the top of his head.

"I won't tell anyone," Marcus said.

Athyna glanced at the stairs. "You can tell them later," she said. "When they ask." She was out the front door and down the steps when he opened it. "What now, Marcus? You know you're not supposed to open that door."

But he was holding something—her coat. "I don't need it," she told him. It was, like, 60 degrees. What kind of weather was that for December?

Marcus frowned. "But it's gonna be so *cold* when you get there."

For a second she didn't know what he was talking about, and then she had to laugh. She went back up the steps and took it from him, and gave him a hug. "Be good," she said, and then she closed the door and locked the top lock, so there was no way he could follow her. Then she took three deep breaths, in through the nose and out through the mouth the way Rosalie had shown her. And then she left.

The weird thing was that she couldn't tell Krystal what happened. Her friend had come through for her for real—she'd texted that it was okay to come even before Athyna got to the ferry. Krystal even took the train into Manhattan to meet her, and they rode out to Mill Basin together, just because she knew how Athyna felt about the subway. When they got to Krystal's apartment, though, Cherisse had already talked to Athyna's mom, who'd guessed in about ten seconds where she was, and sent Athyna about four hundred texts. She and Cherisse had agreed that Athyna could stay for the first half of the week, because she and Krystal hadn't spent time together in so long, but that she had to be home by Thursday. And she's certainly no trouble, Cherisse had said, winking at Athyna over a bag of groceries she'd just set down on the counter.

Anton was the cook in the family, and his food was great; on the first night she stayed with them, he made his curry crab and dumpling stew, which was a Trini thing, his "specialty." Athyna had seconds, but Krystal complained that it was too heavy. Cherisse was at work at the day care during the day, and so Krystal and Athyna logged onto school from the dining table, which was in between the kitchen and the living room. Anton had some kind of security job at night, and so he slept through the mornings. When he walked past them with his coffee a little after lunch, he kissed Krystal on the head.

"*Dad*, don't do that! Thank god I'm off camera."

"Turn it on," Anton said mildly. "Respect your teacher."

Krystal rolled her eyes, but turned it on. "Our teacher's having a baby," she said. "She probably wishes she was off camera, too."

"What's prettier than a pregnant lady?" Anton said, before settling himself in front of the TV with his coffee.

When Krystal asked why she'd come, Athyna just said everyone was being mad annoying; she couldn't take it anymore; they were dumping Marcus on her all the time. All of that was true, but she thought Krystal might sense she was leaving something out, might push her until she had to tell about what had happened on Sunday morning. She'd thought it would be easy to talk once they were together in person, but things were different since she'd gone remote. For one thing, Krystal had gotten back on social in a big way, and was all over TikTok with Bianca in some videos that Athyna privately thought were trashy. Bianca had always been the best dancer in their grade, but Krystal was faking it, dancing more with her ass than anything else. She'd straightened her hair like Bianca's, and was wearing a lot more makeup. Bianca was always calling, and Krystal's voice changed when she talked to her.

"Yeah, Athyna's staying with us for a while. Yeah, it's so good to see her—" She looked up: "Bianca says she thought you were never coming back."

"I was at the pizza party, wasn't I?" Athyna said.

They were in Krystal's room. That was the plus of being an "only." The apartment was on the second floor, right over the red metal awning and the front door Athyna loved, with its oval of colored glass. Krystal's room was just the same, with the beige shag carpet, the bulletin board full of middle school photos (including the strip of the two of them from the photo booth at Chuck E. Cheese), and the old-fashioned bureau with brass knobs, supporting two souvenir dolls in West Indian dress. Krystal was lying on her bed with the animals she'd had since elementary school—a dog with a plaid ribbon around its neck and a monkey holding a heart that said *Forever*—and Athyna was sitting on the brightly colored exercise mat where she put her sleeping bag at night. She was careful to put it away in the morning, and put the mat under the bed, and Cherisse commented on how neat Athyna always was, in contrast to Krystal.

"My mom likes Athyna better than me," she told Bianca, eyeing Athyna on the mat. And then, "Yeah, you better, bitch." But she didn't repeat whatever else Bianca had said. "Love you."

When Krystal got off, she said Bianca was auditioning for an actual Broadway show.

"Is there even Broadway now?"

"It's like, for *after*." As if Athyna were questioning Bianca's talent.

She tried to explain. "But how long do you think it'll be? I mean, with all the stuff they're saying about different variants?" This was in the category of things that Athyna worried might come true if she thought about them. She just wanted Krystal to say that of course the pandemic was going to end, that her mom had told her it would be over in—whatever number of months. Athyna didn't care. Just that it wasn't one of those things where there was a before and an after, and you could never go back.

Krystal got up off the bed and opened her closet door. Her dad had hung a full-length mirror in there so she could see herself top to bottom. Her friend leaned in toward the glass, then ran her pinkie finger under her right eye to fix her liner, being careful of the nail. She was wearing press-ons, because no one was getting manicures now.

"You know, you're kind of freaking me out, Athyna," she said.

<hr />

She woke up so early on Thursday morning that it wasn't even light yet. Cherisse had said the snow would stop in the night, but it was coming down even harder: huge flakes like chips of soap. She got up and went to the window to be sure, keeping the sleeping bag around her, and in the cone of light from the streetlamp right outside Krystal's window, you could see it, racing rather than drifting, covering the street and the cars. The bare trees were thickly frosted, but there was wind, too; while she watched, a branch dumped its heavy, silent load. The street was perfectly quiet, no cars or sirens or music or voices.

She looked at Krystal, who was sleeping all curled up in the fetal position, the comforter up to her chin. Her face was visible, and she looked different than she did when she was awake. She looked worried, like a little kid, the way Athyna always felt. She wished Krystal would wake up and see Athyna standing at the window, and tell her to get in the bed the way they used to when they were kids. They would lie with their knees up to their chests, their foreheads almost touching, and try to scare each other. *There was once a girl who wore a key around her neck*, or *Four friends went on a camping trip in the woods*. Athyna had been the best at making up stories. "I have one," she'd tell Krystal. "Listen to this."

Krystal sighed and shifted, and Athyna thought she was waking up; instead her friend rolled over to face the wall. Athyna left the window and lay back down on the mat, which had cooled off immediately without the heat of her body. She zipped up the sleeping bag around herself and her phone. There were two winter storm warnings on the home screen, for Brooklyn and Staten Island, a "nor'easter," the news was calling it. It occurred to her for the first time that if there was enough snow, she might not have to go home. And then that she wouldn't even have a coat, if not for Marcus.

What she really wanted was a message from Bree, letting her know everything was okay. No way would E say anything—he wasn't an idiot—but thinking about it made her feel sick anyway. She wished her sister would write something like, *hey girl, what you doing at Krystal's?* Or even *Marcus misses his Teetee*, the kind of bullshit she used all the time to get Athyna to do what she wanted. It was like how she'd sometimes go back in the house to check that the knobs on the stove were off, even when she'd already checked them once, or flip the light switch an extra time. Those rituals only worked for a little while, but they allowed her to get on with her day. Any normal message from Bree would be enough to tamp down her worry, at least temporarily. She thought about snapping her sister, but would that be suspicious? It was weird enough that she'd left for no reason in the middle of Covid without telling anyone where she was going.

She still had Rosalie's number, and the therapist said she could always get in touch. But she wanted Rosalie to think she was doing fine and that was why she'd stopped the therapy, not because the insurance had run out. It was way too early to text Rosalie anyway. Even if the snow continued all of today, the trains would be running by tomorrow. The ferries could take until Saturday, Sunday at the latest. What was she going to do then?

The sky was getting lighter, grayer. The black branches stood out behind the glazed window. Cold seeped in around the frame, so Athyna was grateful for the nylon bag's puffy hood. Maybe it was the trees or the uncanny quiet of the morning, but she started thinking of how her dad used to call them from the car, when he was driving outside the city. Once he told them about a whole bunch of seals playing right near where he was working in the bay; another time he swore he'd seen a bat with a wingspan as wide as his windshield, diving across a country road just after the sun went down.

Kate's stepdaughter had invited her there. There was a house. She'd said anytime, and Athyna had gotten the sense she meant it. She probably didn't have any friends. Worst case her teacher found out, but Athyna couldn't imagine Kate getting angry. She liked Kate, but there was no getting around the fact that she was the kind of white woman who got all worked up over unimportant shit, like whether she should encourage them to use Standard English in their college essays. That meant taking out the gottas and adding "are" and "is" before the verbs—she always wrote that way in school, but not everybody did. On the other hand, Kate said, she didn't want to *suppress their voices.* She wanted them to *express* themselves, because she knew they had so much to say.

Well, some of them did and some of them didn't, and it didn't have a lot to do with what kind of English they used. The thing about Kate, and about teachers in general, was that they all held an insane belief that putting something awful into words was somehow going to make it better.

"Hey," she wrote to the stepdaughter, just to see. It took a couple minutes, but Pia wrote back.

> hey

It was sad to think she slept with her phone on, just in case.

> I was thinking about what u said

The dots appeared and disappeared.

> how we could go out there

This time the response came right away:

> thinking of going this wknd! w my friends. but I'm not staying w them.

Yeah, Athyna thought—*all your friends.*

> u cd come? stay at our place?
> sat?
> yes!
> you think trains running?

She added the snowflake and the goggle-eyed, tongue-out emoji to say the weather was crazy.

> my friend's dad cd drive us

Maybe she did have friends. Or maybe it would be her own dad, in the Benz. Naturally, rich people could do whatever, even in a nor'easter.

> or we cd meet at LIRR on Mon?

She remembered her dad taking it, when his car was in the shop.

> u just get a tkt online . . . it's easy

It might be easy, but it wasn't cheap—her dad had almost always driven. On the other hand, she'd already decided she was getting Marcus a sled, which was big like she'd promised, and also only $9.99 from the Home Depot on Targee. The thought of Christmas with everyone made her queasy.

> but how wd we get to yr house?
> 23 sandpiper ln—we cd walk fr there

Athyna gave that the thumbs-up.

> awesome!!

"Awesome" was a thing Kate said, too. It could be a nightmare, but it wasn't like there were a lot of choices. And anything was better than going back home. The question was what she was going to tell her mom.

"K," she wrote to Pia. "I'll text u if imma make it." Then she rewrote that in Standard English, because she didn't even know this girl or how she thought. Although it didn't seem like a real plan, and Athyna had committed to nothing, Pia wrote back with exactly where they should meet, and at what time, like it was all set.

27

Two weeks into Stephen's self-exile, they had twenty patients in the ICU. Five of them were critical, although one was in significantly better shape than the others. His name was Arvind, and he was the youngest, forty-six, an IT professional from Brooklyn. Before he was moved to intensive care, he would joke with the nurses, and took a particular liking to a very efficient practitioner named Donna, who was also very pretty. Once Stephen came into the room and heard him stage-whisper to an elderly and especially uncommunicative man in the next bed, "Donna's here. Could you please try to mention my yacht in Florida?"

Now Arvind was intubated and could communicate only with his whiteboard or the notes app on his phone. In fact they all used whiteboards because the ICU had been retrofitted for negative pressure, and the machines were very loud. In the ICU they followed the "3 Ps"—proning, paralysis, and patience—which he explained to Kate at home as flipping the patient onto his stomach, heavily sedating him, and then crossing your fingers and waiting. It wasn't as bad as in the spring, when they'd been so short of respiratory therapists that he'd been fiddling with the ventilators himself, learning to operate the different models sourced from various facilities, even from out of state. The party line was that Covid patients required a lot of "tinkering," but the respiratory therapists tended to disagree. Over and over he would summon a therapist because of some worrisome number and be told that in RT "less is more." It wasn't his favorite philosophy. One anesthesiologist reminded him that with Covid the numbers weren't going to be perfect; what they were going for was "good enough."

One night, about an hour into his shift, Stephen heard the code blue for his building, fifth floor. His pager buzzed a second later; they needed an assessment on bed 3 for possible use of ECMO. Stephen rushed down the hall, although he was sure the nurse had made a mistake. Arvind was the one in bed 3, and it had to be one of the other four who required the emergency life support; he was betting on the diabetic woman in bed 2 or the man on dialysis in 5. But when he got to the ICU, it was indeed Arvind who was in trouble. He was unconscious, and his skin had the familiar blue-gray tinge.

Stephen was immediately worried about ARDS; the pink sputum in the endotracheal tube wasn't a good sign. He did the echocardiogram bedside, and while he was scanning the heart, Donna suggested that they call the family. He gave her the okay—he should have thought of it himself—and she found the number. On the first ring, someone picked up.

She was a young woman in a red silk shell, the kind an office worker might wear under a suit jacket. She called out to the room in what Stephen assumed was Hindi or Bengali, and a whole family seemed to crowd into the screen. The old man behind her right shoulder was the father, and he spoke first, pulling a toddler into his lap as he did so.

"Thank you for calling, Nurse. Please tell us?"

"He's not doing well all of a sudden," Donna said calmly. "The doctor is here with me now, looking at his heart." She angled the screen so that they could see him.

"This is unfortunately characteristic of the disease," Stephen said. "Things change very quickly. We're going to put him on the ECMO machine, which is our most advanced form of life support."

Donna took over with the family so that he could focus on the images of Arvind's heart on the monitor. She flipped the camera to the patient's face, obscured by tubing.

"We want to make sure you all have a chance to speak to him now."

A gasp from someone off camera let him know that everyone understood the gist of that message. The father spoke to Arvind, and then they passed the phone from relative to relative. The young woman who'd picked up the phone was last to speak.

"You've got to pull through this, Bittu," she said sternly. "We expect nothing less." Her accent was British-inflected. "Mami would not survive it."

The ventilator could be heard under the sound of the machines, the push of air, followed by two beats, followed by another push.

"Bittu, is that clear? You hear me?" Her voice changed when she addressed the nurse, almost plaintive: "Do you have his board?"

Someone had tossed Arvind's whiteboard on the tray table attached to Stephen's side of the bed.

"Hang on." Both his hands were occupied with the ultrasound machine, but he could see that the scribbles were mostly illegible, probably written as the sedation was taking effect. There was the word "cant" without the apostrophe, then something Stephen couldn't read inside a heart, then, suddenly much more clearly, as if he'd put all of his effort into it before going under:

Will I d

Arvind had only made it through the first letter of the last word, but Stephen thought it was clear enough. Before passing the board to Donna, he took his hand off the controls of the machine for a moment and rubbed a finger through those six letters, smudging them out.

"There's not much here," Donna said, taking the board. "He was under sedation." But the older woman began pointing, and then talking excitedly to the other family members, repeating one word. "Love, love," Arvind's mother translated for them, "Pyar means 'love.'"

"He's sending you his love," Donna said, but the young woman in red, Arvind's sister almost certainly, looked troubled. Had she seen him erasing something? Possibly her brother's last words? She deserved to have them—but how could the mother have stood it? In his place, wouldn't she have done the same?

"What's the prognosis, Doctor?" The family went quiet around her.

What had Nathalie written? *I never had the confidence— I guess you could say the self-confidence . . .*

"Arvind is in critical condition," Stephen said firmly, into the camera. "But we're doing everything we can to help him."

Based on the images, he sent out the ECMO alert. He did it reluctantly. The average times on ECMO had increased as the pandemic persisted. Even in a hospital like theirs, with experienced teams, the mortality rate was somewhere near 40 percent. Arvind was young for a Covid patient, but of average age for this particular therapy, which was so invasive and so expensive that it was rarely used on anyone over sixty-five. The longer Arvind remained on it, the worse his chances would become.

After the procedure, Stephen went to the nearest call room, next to the bathroom, a tiny, depressing space with a steel storage cabinet, an empty desk, and a single bed. Normally he might have gone to the cardiology office, maybe had a conversation with a colleague, but they were trying to distance as much as possible. He thought of lying down, but he wanted to be alert if there was any change with Arvind. There was also always the possibility that another of his patients could code; there was no rule against it happening at the same time. All they talked about was the unpredictability, the quick declines—and yet, he was still surprised when it actually happened. Arvind was the one he'd thought was going to make it.

To keep himself awake, he looked at his phone. There was a message from Kate about some mail for him that looked important. And the co-op board wanted to ask his advice about health protocol in the lobby. Could he join a Zoom next Tuesday? The messages sort of shimmered with strangeness, as if he'd entered another dimension. He switched to his email, but just as he did so, a message came from his daughter: "R u at the hospital?" He checked the clock over the cabinet; it was 12:20. But he couldn't deny he was happy to hear from her. There was something about the teenage dialect that restored air to the room.

> You're up late.
> can't sleep
> Me neither.
> haha

He wished she would ask him how he was doing, but he knew better than to expect it. It wasn't as if he was going to tell her either way. "I miss you," he typed instead. "I can't wait to see you for Christmas."

> me too!

Immediately, with an exclamation point.

> hey is it ok if i go out to maxine's house in EH for winter break?

So maybe it was because she wanted something. You had to keep in touch with them somehow, and especially in his situation.

> For Christmas?
> week after? when u go back 2 work?
> Kate says you're spending a lot of time with Maxine.
> what does she expect me to do??

Ok. I'm just asking.

we're a POD

Was she impatient with his limited grasp of her schedule, or had she accidentally hit caps lock?

Her parents invited you?

The gray dots indicated she was responding. She stopped and started again.

yeessssss

Okay—just wondering. Who else besides you and Maxine?

Chloe

Do I know her?

He tried to remember all the little girls from her class before she left. There was the blond one with glasses who was always dressed up and liked to talk to adults. There were the Korean American twins who swam competitively, and the snub-nosed redhead Pia hated, whose mother was an actress divorced from some French politician.

nope . . . like none of those kids are still there

I'm glad you're making new friends

Pia sent a crazy-eyed emoji with a lolling tongue, whatever that meant. She was wildly excited about her new friendships? It was a wildly uncool thing to say? But he'd learned a long time ago not to try to be cool.

she said i couldn't tho

Chloe?

no, duh. kate

It took him a moment.

Kate says you can't go to Maxine's?
I KNOW RIGHT?

He guessed the caps served all different purposes.

Let me check in with her about that.
it's like, my ONLY socialization.
Maybe it was a misunderstanding.

The next emoji he understood: it meant "hmm." And he had to agree, because as far as he knew, Kate wanted Pia out of the house as much as possible. His pager buzzed, and he took it off his belt, so he had one device in each hand.

"Got to go," he texted as he walked out of the call room. Arvind was stable for the moment, but they wanted him back in the ICU. He texted as he hurried down the hall:

I'll talk to Kate. I love you.

In return not just one heart but a whole string of them, bright red, as if full of beautifully oxygenated human blood.

28

12-14-20

Notes for a diagram of the RV Persephone:

Dimensions: 90 m x 18.5 m

Draught: 7.1 m (The draft or draught of a ship's hull = the vertical distance between the waterline and the keel, including appendages such as rudders and propellers.)

Main engines: 23500 BHP
   4 x MAK 9M32C

Thrusters: 2 x CP main propellers
   2 x bow tunnel 2040 BHP
   2 x stern tunnel 1200 BHP

Accommodation: 60 persons

Flag: Denmark

Navigational status: Active

12-21-20

In Paris it was a fat embroidery needle that I dropped into my pocket at BHV when we were shopping for Aunt Sonia's birthday. Had money but didn't want Inès to see. At the Laureate just nail scissors, but I was thinking about the knife when Dad came in. Had to pretend I thought he was a burglar LOL. At Sandpiper I couldn't find anything so I used the keys to the apartment that LL made me when I got here. They're gold and sharp because they're new. I used to think I wasn't really doing it—like other people really did it and I was just pretending. But the blood is real. It's drops on a string, like a spiderweb after it rains.

R was the first person I saw with the really authentic tattoos. That was when I was little and I guess I was staring. Mom was like, if you're curious just ask. I remember that. He said this style is from the Marquesas & these are shark teeth & these are linked ancestors. He said that Tahitians used to have their tattoos carved into their skin with a chisel. Then they blackened them with charcoal. Girls had their butts tattooed to show they were ready for marriage. (Vomit!) When someone died, their relatives would scratch their own skin with a shark's tooth to show their grief.

I called Hernandez Bros and it rang a bunch of times. Then it went to voicemail so I was like, hi this is—I almost forgot—Athyna, from the beach, and I was wondering if Justin could give me a call. My jeans have holes in the knees and so while I was leaving the message I put my finger in there and felt a scar. You cut in, but you get a ridge. You get something from nothing. While you're doing it, you're perfectly focused, like seeing a math problem on a test and knowing exactly how to solve it.

He called back pretty fast and so I said I'd meet him at the same place. He can drive! First I thought his uncle brought him, but then he was the one driving the truck. I climbed in and he was like, hey, like we were already together. And for a second I was scared because he looked older. He asked me if I wanted to go somewhere and I almost jumped out. But then I saw he was jiggling his knee (the left one, not the driving one) like he was nervous, too. So I said, where? And he was like, whatever you want. But he looked miserable. So I said Gerard Drive? And he was happier all of a sudden, like, yeah I know where that is.

It was freezing and the sky was overcast. Gerard Drive has the bay on one side and a marsh on the other. In the summer the grass there is very bright green, and you can see white egrets standing in it. Now the grass is tall and yellow (swishy swashy, swishy swashy) and there are some ospreys' nests on top of the wooden platforms. There were some guys fishing on the bridge and they waved (old guys so maybe they thought it was Carlos in the truck) and Justin waved back. We drove to the end and there was only one other car there, and a guy walking his dog on the beach. Justin turned off the motor with an actual key—it's an old truck—and was like, why did you call, I mean, I'm glad you did.

ME: I was bored out here.
J: Visiting your friend again?

I nodded. But Maxine was still in the city. I'd been thinking maybe Athyna would text to say she was coming after all, but of course she hadn't.

ME: I don't like her that much.
J: Why do you visit her then?

The inside of the truck smelled like gasoline, but I like that smell. I used to have a thing about smells. Sometimes, not every time, when I passed someone on the street I would shiver. It was like I was inside their life for a second, like I SMELLED their life. I once tried to explain to Inès and Emma and Emma was like, t'es cinglée? So I didn't try to explain to Justin.

ME: Getting away from my mom

Had to say mom because if I don't have a dad, why would I have a stepmom?

J: I miss my mom.

Then I kind of felt bad because I wanted to say me too.

J: My sister and brothers are young, so she's mad busy.
ME: Yeah
J: Do you want to, um—
ME: Ok
J: —take a walk?

Then I was so embarrassed because I thought he knew what I thought he was going to say. And I said yes! So I think I was all red, and I was like, WE CAN TAKE A WALK! But then he was like, or we could . . . and he sort of pulled me over to the driver's seat so I was on his lap and he was like, you're so pretty. Then we kissed and his mouth tasted like the watermelon Ice Breakers I saw on the dashboard, and then he put my earlobe in his mouth and that was kind of crazy. Like I wanted to do everything. And then he put his hands under my shirt. He took my shirt off over my head and put his hands under my bra. Then he stopped all of a sudden and I thought omg he thinks I'm too small bc I'm like 32A.

But it wasn't that. It was the guy with his dog—a white guy my dad's age with gray hair and a Patagonia vest. And J was like, oh shit. And instead of just looking away like a normal person he came RIGHT UP TO THE CAR and KNOCKED ON THE WINDOW and was like GET OUT OF HERE OR

I'M GOING TO CALL THE POLICE. I wasn't wearing my shirt and the old guy is shaking his head like I'm disgusting but looking at me at the same time. And I wanted to say mind your own business, asshole. And also call Dad, if I could've called him without telling him anything else about the situation. And I was almost like, my grandmother is Dr. Frances J. Davenport, because he looked like someone she would know from the Maidstone.

After that we just drove around for a little, until it was time for my train. I was supposed to eat dinner at Maxine's in the city, with her parents this time, and Kate might call to check. But I told Justin I would be back next week.

J: With your friend you don't like?
ME: Not because of her
J: Because of me?
ME: And also because I'm going to be away after that

I was glad he didn't ask where. We hadn't even gotten each other's contacts so we did that. And then he was like, bye, and I was like, bye, and he tried to kiss me but it was so awkward and our teeth clicked. And then he was like, wait, try again, and it was better.

It wasn't until I got out at the station that I even remembered we were in his uncle's truck, with Hernandez Bros HVAC on the side. And I wondered if the guy would have even come up to us if we were in, for example, my dad's car.

29

On the day of her appointment, the first day of winter break, Kate woke up before six. She was lying in bed a half hour later when she heard Pia in the shower. She was clearly planning to go early to Maxine's again, but Kate didn't have the patience for another argument with her stepdaughter. Especially an argument without caffeine. She couldn't have coffee because of the gestational diabetes screening that afternoon; instead, a miniature pink glucose drink waited for her in the refrigerator. The screening was only one of the tests the doctor would perform at this appointment for which she'd been waiting six months—the only time she would see her fully formed baby before it arrived.

Last week, in preparation, she'd called Abby.

"What should I ask?" she asked her friend. It was a voice call, because Abby was making sandwiches for four kids at the time. She'd worked out a system where she traded days supervising remote school with her brother-in-law, a stay-at-home dad.

"A SAHD," she'd told Kate. "That's what he calls himself. But the kids like his days better. You have a doula?"

"We lined one up." Something clattered, and there was the sound of two children screaming.

"Oh, shit."

"What happened?"

"I forgot to take the dog out." Now Kate could hear frantic pop music in the background. "Jack! Do you have to do that here?"

"You sound busy."

"It's online P.E., if you can believe that. What about a lactation consultant?"

"You think I'll need that?"

"Most likely," Abby said. "How is it possible I'm out of juice?"

It was hard to wait until afternoon. When she finally got to the office, many of the chairs in the waiting room were marked DO NOT SIT. Everyone was masked, and no one made eye contact. It was a bright December day, but it would be dark in an hour. The light slanting through the windows of the radiology department, on the sixth floor of a six-story white-brick satellite of the hospital, was already tinged with orange. She needed to pee, but was afraid she'd miss her name being called.

Her OB was a skinny white woman in her forties, Dr. Frankel, whose curls were contained by the elasticized bands of her N95. Her affect was cheerful as she greeted Kate, but she looked exhausted. The questions began with Kate—nutrition, sleep, and exercise—and moved on to the baby. How often was it moving—how many times per day, and how much? Kate regretted her failure to keep some kind of record, but her inability to provide exact answers didn't seem to surprise Dr. Frankel, who simply proceeded with her list. Had Kate signed up for childbirth classes, parenting classes, or infant CPR? What was she thinking about breastfeeding, and did she want recommendations for a pediatrician or a night nurse? Was she bleeding, spotting, leaking fluid, dizzy, constipated? How much caffeine did she consume? Was she depressed?

"I mean—"

"It's a difficult time," Dr. Frankel said. "Let's weigh you."

It was a mechanical beam scale, and the larger iron weight had moved to the next 50-pound increment. "That seems like a lot," Kate said, fishing for reassurance.

The doctor shrugged. "It is what it is. You could lay off the sugar a little."

"Did the glucose test—"

"We'll call you if there's any concern—but not if the results are normal. Now, let's take a look at your baby."

Now that the moment was here, she felt as if it had come too soon. A part of her wanted to get up and leave. Instead she lay down on her back and exposed her abdomen, hard and white with visible blue-gray veins. There was a porcelain pitcher webbed with gray cracks that had sat in the living room of her childhood home. It had belonged to her mother's grand-mother, but at some point someone had broken it.

Dr. Frankel was washing her hands for the second time since she'd come into the room, and so Kate took the opportunity to call Stephen. She was relieved when he appeared on the screen in his office in the hospital, and she could introduce him to her doctor, whom he'd never met.

"Hi, Dad," Dr. Frankel said, absurdly peppy. "We're just going to take a look at your—" Then she looked at Kate's phone and her voice changed to a normal register. "Oh, are you at Columbia?"

"Right—Irving."

"I thought so! I did my residency there."

"Feel free to come back anytime," Stephen said. "We can use you." They laughed together, without amusement.

"Is it brutal?"

"Isn't it everywhere?"

"No kidding."

Then the two of them seemed to remember she was there.

"We've done Mom's bloodwork," Dr. Frankel said, "and we'll have the results in a couple of days. I ordered a CBC because she's a little anemic."

"Is that bad?"

"No," Stephen answered for the doctor. "Just your red and white blood cell counts."

"But do you do that for everyone?"

"Everyone who's a little anemic," Dr. Frankel said. "It's very common. Now, take a look—there."

A gray lampshade—that was her uterus—appeared on the screen, and then something pulsed inside it: a bulb with a glowing halo.

"That's the top of the baby's head."

Kate took a breath. "Where's the rest of it?"

"Come on," Dr. Frankel encouraged. "Turn so we can see you."

The head disappeared, then reappeared, unwilling.

"Give it a push."

"What?"

Dr. Frankel massaged Kate's stomach with her gloved hand, distributing an inordinate amount of cold, blue gel. The head appeared, and then the whole body. First she'd drunk from a tiny bottle; now here was the Cheshire cat.

"There we go. You see the umbilical artery looks good. The brain."

"The brain looks good?"

"The brain and the heart. No cysts or EIF."

"What is that?"

"Sorry," Dr. Frankel said. "Echogenic intracardiac foci— your baby doesn't have them."

"Oh," Stephen said suddenly.

"Yep," Dr. Frankel said.

"What?" Kate said. They had noticed something. "Stephen?"

"It's just that when you're used to looking at ultrasounds—" he began.

"*What?*"

"No, no," Dr. Frankel put a hand on her shoulder. "Nothing's wrong. It's only that this baby isn't very modest."

They were smiling, and finally she understood. But it took a moment for her body temperature to return to normal.

"Well, if you both know, I guess I want to."

"It's a girl." Stephen laughed. "Can you believe it?"

She couldn't, and maybe that was on her face because Dr. Frankel turned to her.

"You thought it was a boy?"

I thought something was wrong with it, Kate did not say.

"A woman in the grocery store told me it was a boy."

"Try to get your groceries delivered," Dr. Frankel said. "Especially now."

"That's what I tell her!" Stephen said. Was he disappointed? He was grinning, but he'd talked about a boy, different from the child he already had. Who didn't want a new start?

"Okay?" Dr. Frankel asked. She was going to turn off the monitor.

"Wait," Kate said. She felt she'd hardly had a chance to look. And now you could see the whole baby, head to toes. The legs and feet seemed like afterthoughts, trailing off from the round abdomen. "Is that hair?" It streamed around her head like some underwater plant.

"She has a lot. But it'll probably fall out. Oh look, she's waving. Can you see?"

She nodded, but she couldn't. The baby was a collection of shadows, a blurry security film.

"All right?" Dr. Frankel said, and she had to say it was.

When she came out of the appointment, she wanted to walk. It was dark and near freezing, but the sharp air was a relief, especially when she pulled down her mask. She thought she might walk over to Fifth and then uptown, look in the windows.

The receptionist had told her to check her email for digital images. At the light, she looked again. There the baby was in black and white, "waving," and there was the 3D version: the alarming sepia-toned alien she remembered from the first visit. *That's just the way sound waves translate into a two-dimensional picture,* Stephen had said, *not the way the baby really looks.* But even this rough representation looked more like a baby now, its hand next to its face, its closed amphibian eyes and soft nose, its lower lip pushed out against its fist. She sent it to her sister, then to Abby. She thought of sending the image to her mother, but refrained.

She reached Fifth, where the doors and windows of the stores were outlined in white lights. People were actually drinking outside at restaurants, laughing and celebrating in spite of the cold, in spite of everything. The heat lamps they had everywhere now were glassed-in pyramids of flame. Waiters in shirtsleeves rushed in and out of the cold, balancing trays, performers of an extreme sport. *Yeah? Watch this.* Up ahead, a wave of yellow taxis streamed down the avenue, presided over by the library's stone lions, garlanded with wreaths.

She crossed Forty-First, walked west toward the lit-up Christmas market in Bryant Park. It was just as busy as it would have been in any other year. She was negotiating a sidewalk crowded with pedestrians, loaded down with bags and backpacks and the occasional suitcase, when she heard the phone buzz in her pocket. She thought Emily or Abby had seen the pictures and was calling right away.

But it was her stepdaughter. "Pia?"

"Hi—I'm still at Maxine's."

But it wasn't a challenge. Pia sounded subdued, almost needy.

"Her mom invited me to stay for takeout."

"That's fine."

She had an impulse. She had her headphones in, and so she glanced down at the phone, pulled up the photo.

"I'll be home after dinner, like eight-thirty."

"No problem. But hey, check your texts."

"Right now?"

"I want to show you something." It was a gamble, but she felt ecstatic. All of a sudden, she felt like she had everything under control. There was a pause while Pia took the phone away from her ear and looked. Kate stopped on the sidewalk. From where she was standing, she could see the skaters cir-

cling the rink in the center of the park. A lush evergreen tow-
ered over them, strung with purple lights.

"Oh wow."

Then she could hear the other girls. Pia was showing it
to them. They asked about the sex, and Pia said they didn't
know.

"We do now, actually."

"What?"

"Your dad could tell just by looking."

"Of course."

"So I let him tell me—it's a girl."

Nothing.

"I mean, gender is a construct."

Pia actually laughed. "Yes, Kate. It is."

Had she ever said her name before? "But it does make things
feel more real."

"It's creepy," Pia said. "But it's cool. Like she's made out of
clay."

"Yeah."

"Her face is so—"

"I know."

"—human," Pia said. "She looks like you."

"I was going to say that she has your mouth—yours and
your dad's."

"Ugh—poor baby."

"I think it looks great on both of you," Kate said. "On all
three of you, I bet."

Some of the skaters were hanging on to the rail; others
zipped expertly around the rink at an angle to the ice, their
hands clasped behind their backs, as if they didn't know anyone was watching. But the largest cohort were methodically
circling, first one foot, then the other.

"Well, um, see you later," Pia said. And then she got off.

Kate went back to the photos. She was standing still, but she
wasn't cold. The baby was like a hot stone in there, completely

still, but full of energy. Her earbuds were still in, as if transmitting a connection.

"Hi there," she said. "Can you hear me?"

The baby shifted position, certainly coincidentally.

"This is—" She couldn't do "mom." "It's me." She hadn't ascended the steps to the shops and the rink, but was standing out of the way of pedestrians, against the library's limestone southern wall. She slid her hand between the buttons of her coat, under the fitted maternity shirt. There was a flutter on her right side, a rearrangement.

"We're doing okay. No need to worry."

People passed them on the sidewalk, none the wiser.

"Okay then," she said. "See you soon."

30

Gunther had told her it was going to rain, and now clouds had sunk down around the island, low and dark over the mountains but with lighter formations higher up. Gunther had also been the one to report that Raffi had taken the blue truck and driven it into the interior. The road ran inland from the coast, continuing straight and flat until you reached the turnoff for the agricultural school. There it wound up toward the Belvedere Lookout, passing a chestnut forest studded with ancient monuments.

"So?" she asked. Anyone with privileges was allowed to sign out the truck for up to two hours.

"There's no name on the board."

"He must've forgotten. I'll mention it."

Gunther didn't say anything, but his expression said that she was more lenient with Raffi than she would've been with him, or perhaps any other member of the team. And what if that were true? The fact was that every student was replaceable, even Gunther, but that she'd never met anyone like Raffi in all her years on the island.

Nathalie checked the *Echinophyllia* and *Pocillopora* recruits in the rearing tanks; at five days old, there was no difference between those from the bleached and the healthy parents. Both types appeared as translucent pale pink rings spotting the concrete tiles, about 5 millimeters in diameter. On the corkboard above the tanks there was a laminated task spreadsheet that still included the names of her two departed doctoral students, Claire and Alan. When something was off, she and Gunther jokingly attributed it to one of them: it must've been Claire who'd forgotten to note recruit growth in b on 2/15, for example; or Alan who had been the one responsible for transferring the wrong settlement tile from c to e. The problem was that it was only a joke: it was impossible to suggest that Claire took ammonium nitrate from the lab without noting it in the log, or that Alan failed to get permission before driving the blue truck out of the station.

She waited until Gunther had left for the day. Then she got in the car to follow Raffi. At first there were open fields on either side of the road, a herd of reddish, shaggy cows scattered on the flat plain, surrounded by mountains. Rotui's long ridge extended out the driver's side window. The mountain was carpeted in green except for one bare triangle, like a nose below two shadowy dark eyes. A few teenage boys, students, yelled as she passed and she slowed down, looked in the rearview mirror: Was it some practical joke? But they had stopped and were pointing at her car, so she pulled over and rolled down the window.

"Bouchon d'essence!" one called out, and she felt stupid as she got out and closed the gas cap. She thanked the boys, who must've been students at the school, and they waved politely.

When she reached the Lycée Agricole, she slowed down again. Raffi had a relative who taught there, but there was no blue truck—only a few compact cars in front of the administration building and some students juggling a football under the thick canopy of a mango tree. She'd forgotten the way the road narrowed after the school, the series of tight turns that led to the lookout. She was concentrating on her driving, and if the truck hadn't been that bright royal blue, she might have missed it. It was tucked into the parking area for the archeological site, backed into the vegetation, as if he expected the dirt lot to fill up with visitors in his absence. In fact the site was not heavily touristed even during the peak season, and in

December with a storm coming, Nathalie was sure they would be alone. What the hell was he doing here?

She heard thunder as she was getting out of the car, but the rain hadn't started. Zebra doves gave their high, broken call from the dust around the great trees, whose lichened roots snaked into the car park. They began like webbing between digits, thin and vertical, some as high as your knees, then sank deeper underground the farther they got from the trunk, making serpentine patterns in the earth. The marae themselves were mostly hidden in the chestnut forest, but you could see one from the road, a long, low stone platform, grown over with moss. They were sometimes referred to as "shrines," but Tahitians would usually correct you. The marae had apparently served many purposes—religious, legislative, agricultural, medical—and now the guides stuck to the anodyne "archeological site." The trees, at least, you could be sure of. They were called "mape," Polynesian chestnut. The last time she'd been here was with a team visiting from Oslo; but before that it had been a long time, maybe not since the year they'd spent on the island when Pia was five.

There were three paths into the forest, and as she hesitated, the rain started. It was punctuated by lightning and more thunder and the tunneling of wind through the trees. You could hear the individual thuds of chestnuts falling. That was the memory she had of the place: following Pia on the narrow trail through the trees, the nuts dropping around them on the ground. They were looking for the marae, but Nathalie had been afraid that one of the heavy chestnuts could strike her daughter, tiny among those massive trees, stumbling over their prehistoric roots. *Attention!* When she'd mentioned this danger to the woman who taught them Tahitian dance on Thursday afternoons, she had said that it sometimes happened—but wouldn't to them. The "mana" of the place would protect them. The word, important in cultures all across the Pacific, meant something like power from nature, a phenomenon

Nathalie respected but was not inclined to entrust with her daughter's life.

When the rain got heavier, Nathalie took shelter under an overhang in the parking area. The shelter was there to protect a set of informational placards, which she read through idly while she waited. On the marae, traditional homeopaths called tahu'a had once practiced their healing arts. A board distinguished between types of illnesses: maladies du corps, de la pensée, and de l'esprit. In Tahitian the final category was called "ma'i vaite": a disease of the soul in which a deceased relative has an effect on a living descendant.

Was that just another way of talking about depression? And if so, was it like syphilis or the clap, one of those diseases Westerners had brought, or was it possible they weren't responsible for everything? If Tahitians had named it, then it had existed before they arrived. It existed everywhere, all over the world, under various aliases: le cafard, the black dog, the dead soul acting on the living.

The mosquitoes seemed to have had the same idea she did. They swarmed under the shelter, attacking her ankles. She bent to slap them away, and noticed another placard, lower and dirtier than the rest, on which was printed an incantation:

> Les marae étaient des lieux à la fois terrifiants et paisables;
> les gens ne s'y rendaient que pour prier, et pour aucune autre
>   raison;
> les Dieux ne pouvaient d'ailleurs être trompés . . .

It was awkward in French. She'd sat politely through enough cultural evenings to know what it was supposed to sound like. The thumping in the original would be like a drumbeat, like nuts falling on leafy ground. The gods were inflexible; to glorify them was the sole purpose of this place. They couldn't be deceived. But on the other placard, it said that the platforms were sites for preparing medicines and making laws. This had always been her frustration with the humanities. Wasn't there a more exact science for examining the past?

Because she didn't believe that it was all in the telling. People had really sat on those platforms—not spirits but real human beings. They had done one thing and not another. At each particular moment something had happened, if only it were possible to know what it was.

She brushed a mosquito from her face, and at that instant she heard the report. Distant, but distinctly not thunder, a sharp crack from the forest. All at once, she had a terrible thought. She left the shelter and started down the closest of the three paths, but there was no way to know which he'd taken. She called his name in the pounding rain that was now soaking through her blouse, dripping down her legs. Was there something she could promise these local gods in exchange for finding him alive—something to do with her work, or her daughter? But she rejected that right away. Everyone had a point past which they wouldn't go, even in their thoughts. She thought of Raffi's mother, his sister, his niece. And then she thought of the black-and-white letterhead from the CIVIN. Ma'i vaite, a disease of the soul, leading him to this sacred place. The spirit inside him, forcing his hand.

And then she saw him. He wasn't on any one path but was making his own way through the thick trunks, one minute absent, the next present. She called out in relief, but he'd already seen her. He was carrying a different case, looking not only displeased but actually furious. She reminded herself that she was the one who was supposed to be angry. He had taken what didn't belong to him. The second case was larger, bright orange, at least a hundred and sixty euros.

"Raffi!"

The rain was still coming down hard. He went straight to the parking area, then put the case in the back of the truck instead of in the cab behind him. What the hell was he doing?

He got in the cab, and she had a sudden fear that he might

just drive off. She ran to the passenger side and climbed in; it did, after all, belong to the station. She brushed water from her forehead, squeezed it from her thin cotton blouse.

Raffi got in but left his door open. He was soaked, his hair slicked off his forehead, his gray Hōkūleʻa T-shirt almost black. "Leaving your car?"

"I just want to talk a minute."

He stared straight out the front windshield. Rain streaked down the glass. He left one foot on the runner, a Japanese-made hiking shoe rather than the clear plastic Méduse local people sometimes wore on the trails. It wasn't as if he were poor. He had a kind of manic energy, in sharp contrast to his usual deliberateness and economy of motion. She was conscious of his body in the humid cab and also of a smell she couldn't place. Was she wrong about the gun? Had he been burning something in the forest? She decided not to mention the Pelican case.

"Veronique saw you leaving." She didn't want to involve Gunther, and the chances that Raffi would check this with the lab's least personable employee were slim. "I thought you might be at the Lycée Agricole."

This observation didn't require a response, and Raffi didn't offer one.

"I was going to hike in, but then the rain—"

"Mosquitoes," Raffi said. It wasn't a complaint or a warning; rather, it was as if he was about to give a lecture on the subject.

"I got stuck under there, so I read about the site."

He glanced dismissively in the direction of the placards. "I don't know what they wrote there."

"It's well done—about local flora, traditional medicine. A little about the marae."

Raffi coughed, took his phone out of his pocket. She was distracted by his shoulders, the crenellated Marquesan design around his right biceps glistening wet. She was suddenly aware of sex, its inconvenient ubiquity. It was the ancient human problem of the forbidden, of accessibility in inverse proportion to desire. She could never get over what a blessing it was that people couldn't read one another's thoughts.

"There's one panel that says the marae had secular uses," she continued. "Government, medicine, fishing—fishing regulations, I imagine. But then there's another that says it was forbidden to come here for anything but prayer. They contradict each other."

He pulled his foot in abruptly, closed the door, and made as if to start the car. "I have to get home. I told Hina I'd take Maeva fishing."

"In the storm?"

"It's stopping."

It was true that the streams on the windshield were gentler now; the sky was lightening.

"I heard a shot."

He was shaking his head already.

"It wasn't thunder."

"I doubt it."

"What's in the case, Raffi?"

Now he did look at her, scornful. His eyes were rimmed red, as if he'd been smoking weed.

"Because if anything ever happened to you—"

Now he looked genuinely startled. "To me?"

"If you're unhappy—"

But she should have known better. Raffi wiped his face again, the back of his neck. Water dripped from his hairline in the humid cab. He frowned at a bug on the windshield, cupped his hand under it and released it into the air. She knew better than to attribute any special meaning to the gesture. It was the same with that expert silence. He could stretch it out until the question that preceded it had been entirely erased.

It wasn't true that the islands had been peaceful before Europeans came. Rather it had been a vengeance society, rigidly hierarchical. Someone killed your brother, you took a brother from their tribe; they took your father, you would come for theirs. The name *Pacific* was a European fantasy.

Raffi put his foot on the brake and pressed the new truck's push-button start.

"Sorry," she said, getting down from the cab. But she was really buying time. "What does Maeva want to catch?"

This question was acceptable.

"Red grouper. Goatfish or soldierfish—'I'ihi." He smiled slightly. "Big fish only now, she tells me."

31

Adults are always saying, we thought X was bad. "We thought Bush was bad, but then there was W. We thought W. was bad, and now we have the ABOMINATION." Frances doesn't say Trump's name, but she thinks there's no limit to how bad things could get. Since I've gotten back, I've only seen Frances outside, because Dad's worried about her. Maybe after the vaccine, he says.

Nuclear weapons use fission to break apart the nuclei of atoms. The nuclei release neutrons, which can set off a chain reaction, making more and more energy. Sometimes scientists make a mistake, like in Castle Bravo, and the explosion gets out of control.

In math we learned that $f(x) \to L$ as $x \to c$. If M. Nagy asks you to read from the board, you say, "the function f approaches the limit as x approaches c." It sounds hard but it isn't. The limit to what you can get out depends on what you put in. You can't get more than you expected. I like math better than science.

12-23-20

At Lycée Corneille, Mlle. Ahmed tried to show us *Hiroshima mon amour* and everyone was like, il y aura beaucoup de sexe! But we missed it because that was the day David saw a mouse under the radiator. When Mlle. Ahmed ran out for the janitor, David fed the mouse three Fraises Tagada from the package. When Mlle. Ahmed got back with the janitor, the mouse was on the floor by David's desk, eating the candy. We thought she'd be happy he lured it out, but she just yelled at us and canceled the film.

The man who ordered Encelade was Vice Admiral Christian Claverie. Clavis in Latin is "key." M. Claverie had a weather report that showed which way the wind was blowing. His office evacuated military officials off the island of Mangareva before the nuclear cloud arrived.

There were 61 children between 4 and 8 years old living on Mangareva when the cloud blew that way. Little kids are the ones who get sickest, because their thyroids suck up the most iodine. Their thyroids don't know if the iodine is radioactive or just regular iodine, like the kind they put in salt. Your thyroid is in your throat and looks like a pair of Fraises Tagada.

12-25-20

On Christmas morning, we sit in the living room. Dad gives Kate a white cashmere sweater that ties above the waist. Kate gives Dad a PSG football scarf. Dad gives me a gift card to Urban, and Kate gives me a pair of black rhinestone climber earrings that I don't hate. Then I give them their gift. Kate opens it, and she's so surprised that she just sits there for a minute. Then she starts to cry.

I wasn't going to get them anything, but at the last minute I saw this store. This was two days before Christmas and I was on my way back from Maxine's—early, because they were doing some holiday thing with her grandmother (the one who didn't get conned and is still alive). I was killing time, walking slowly up Columbus, because I didn't want to go back to the apartment. The blue-and-white snowflakes I loved when I was little were strung across the avenue, junky looking until they light up at night. Some people were shopping, but not as many as in a regular year, and there were moms and nannies with strollers, hurrying because it was cold. A lot of stores had closed, with red retail-space-for-lease signs in the windows, but there were more delivery vehicles than ever: three UPS vans in two blocks, and a huge refrigerator truck, men unloading cardboard boxes of produce onto dollies, blocking the sidewalk.

I wouldn't have stopped if it wasn't for the window, almost as good as the department stores, with a stuffed rabbit in a sweater skating mechanical loops on a glassy rink. They'd really gone all out. Inside there was new age music and a loopy white carpet, and wooden shelves full of the kind of things adults like to buy for kids: wool animals with embroidered faces, painted pull-toys shaped like dogs and ducks, and cashmere blankets in colors called cornflower, apricot, and sage. It smelled good in there, like lavender. The best thing were the mobiles, hanging from the ceiling all over the store, decorated with birds, or hot-air balloons, or stars. A lady asked if she could help, and I showed her the one I wanted. She said, "oh that's my favorite too, and you got the last one. Who are you shopping for?"

ME: My sister
HER: How old is she?
ME: She's not born yet.
HER: Your mom's pregnant! How sweet of you!

I didn't say anything, and she got it down and took it over to the cash register. There were four soft hanging creatures: a pink fish, a blue whale, a green seahorse, and an orange octopus. No coral, but still. She was putting it in the box when all of a sudden I changed my mind.

ME: I think I like the jungle.
HER: ?

ME: With the giraffe and stuff. Sorry.

HER: That's also a great choice! [She went into the back to get the jungle mobile, which was already in a box.] When is your sister due?

ME: In March, but I'm going away before then.

HER: To school?

ME: In France [Not a lie, from some people's POV]

HER: Lucky you! So you'll miss her while you're gone.

ME: Yes

HER: But now she'll have something to remember you.

It wasn't that something changed. I still didn't care if Kate liked me, and I couldn't even make myself hug her after she stopped crying. And I definitely didn't buy it for Dad, who didn't even get home until late on Christmas Eve. It was really that store, where there weren't any impatient parents or whiny kids, where everyone was calm and happy because they were buying something for someone who didn't even exist yet, who was perfect. And I thought that since I wouldn't be here, I wouldn't exist either. And so to the baby, I would be perfect, too.

32

For a couple of days, it seemed like the storm had cleared everything out. Not only the trash in the gutters on Targee, the flattened masks and candy wrappers and plastic bottles, occasionally filled with urine. If not cleared, then covered in snow, which was still fresh when she got home, in big drifts on either side of their front walk, enough for Marcus to make angels and a lumpy snowman in front of the house. Just a head, with a couple of rotten tangerines for eyes and a strange nose that when you got up close turned out to be one of those plastic horns that people blew on New Year's. He was all over her when she got in the door, like she'd been gone a month instead of just four days.

She hadn't wanted to come home, but her mom said they couldn't impose on Anton and Cherisse any longer. Athyna reluctantly agreed; because she hadn't told Krystal what happened, her friend would have thought it was weird if she'd begged to stay. On the ride home, her mom asked about Krystal and her parents in lots of detail: How was her friend doing in school; how many days a week was Cherisse working; did they see anyone else inside; were they planning to get the vaccine when it came? She agreed to stop at the Home Depot on Targee so that Athyna could pick out the sled for Marcus. While they were there, Athyna also found one of those reed diffusers with essential oil that she thought Bree would like, and for her mother a digital picture frame that you could load up with your phone, so that you could look at a different member of your family every twenty seconds, if you wanted.

She was relieved that neither her brother-in-law nor her sister was home when she got there. E had gotten a job at JFK8, the Amazon fulfillment center in the wetlands just south of 278—seasonal but with the opportunity to continue after the holidays. Bree could drop him off before she drove into Manhattan every morning, and her sister's happiness was the kind that overflowed onto everyone around her. The first night when they got home, Bree had hugged her and whispered that she'd missed her, but E had said, "Hey Athyna," using her full name like she was some tiring hassle he'd forgotten about until this minute. In the time she'd been gone, he'd started growing a mustache. It made him look older and less good-looking, but from the way Bree pointed it out—like it was front-page news—Athyna could tell her sister didn't know.

They'd gotten the tree in her absence, but their mom said they'd been waiting for Athyna to decorate. She was taking the whole week off: she was making cookies, and even though their cousins couldn't come from Jersey this year, she was planning a huge Christmas meal for just the five of them. On the twenty-third a package came from Amazon with new stockings, red-and-white fur with their names embroidered in green. Bree made an unboxing TikTok, but Athyna didn't get it until her sister brought her over to the staircase to help her hang them.

"Who's Ava?"

Bree smiled, took Athyna's hand and put it on her belly. "She'll be born in June," she said, "just like Marcus. They'll be five years apart."

Athyna yanked her hand away. She lowered her voice, because their mom was in the next room.

"Are you fucking crazy?"

But her sister had no similar impulse to keep their disagreement quiet. "I told you," she shouted, so their mom would be sure to hear her in the kitchen. "Didn't I say that's what she'd be like?" Then she shook her head at Athyna. "You should've stayed with your bestie in Brooklyn," she hissed. "Let *us* have a nice Christmas."

Then she went up the stairs to the bedroom, clutching the railing as if Athyna had hurt her physically and she needed that support. Athyna went into the kitchen. She was so mad that she could barely speak. Her mom's back was to Athyna as she rolled out the dough for her famous sugar cookies on the counter.

"Where's Marcus?"

"Elijah took him for a haircut."

"Is that safe?"

Her mother turned and gave her a look.

Athyna couldn't help it: "You *knew*."

Her mother rubbed flour on the rolling pin and didn't say anything.

"Why didn't you tell me?"

"You weren't here." Her voice was calm, as if she'd been expecting Athyna to react exactly this way. "And your sister wanted to tell you herself."

She looked at her mom, who was wearing the lavender sweatshirt that said *World's Best Grandma*, fleece pants, and a pair of metallic foam sandals they'd gotten her for her days off, which she said were like walking on clouds. In spite of the sweatshirt she didn't look like a grandma: she had hardly any wrinkles, and her hair had just been done, straight as always, shoulder-length, rich mahogany brown. You could see a few gray strands only at the hairline, where she'd accessorized with a tortoiseshell clip. She was using cookie cutters, and transferring the unbaked rounds onto a greased sheet with a metal spatula.

"Help me, Teena."

They spaced out the cookies on the baking sheet, and then Athyna gathered up the scraps, sprinkled more flour on the counter, and rolled it out again. It was soothing to run the rolling pin back and forth, soothing to press the shapes into the dough. She thought it would have been pretty to use only the stars, but Marcus would like decorating the others: a tree, a candy cane, a snowman. She could hear her sister clomping around defiantly in the bedroom upstairs.

"Yes?" Her mother drew it out.

"I didn't say anything."

"But you're thinking it."

Athyna gave up on one snowman that was sticking, and crumpled it into the scraps. The dough got harder to work with the longer it was out of the fridge.

"A sister will be good for Marcus," her mother said. "And Bree and Elijah want to get their own place. Once they're married."

"When's that going to be?" She meant, when were they moving out, but her mom thought she was talking about a wedding.

"After the pandemic. She's getting a ring for Christmas— don't tell her."

"I'm sure she already picked it out and dropped him off at the store with instructions."

Her mother laughed a little in spite of herself. Athyna pressed her advantage. "You really think he's good for her? You think he's going to keep working and take care of her and everything?"

"Your sister doesn't need taking care of. No girl I raised needs that."

"Okay, but you think she can trust him?"

Her mom looked at her from under her brows, which were beautifully plucked. Athyna could never get her own to look that neat. "I think he's getting there. Why?"

She thought she could feel her whole body expanding, pressing the waistband and the seat of her jeans and the collar around her neck. Bree was the one who was pregnant, but Athyna was blowing up. She was going to explode from the force of what she wanted to say.

"I thought you didn't even like him."

Her mom sighed and picked up the first two sheets. She

tilted her head toward the oven, and Athyna opened it, the blast of warm air in the drafty kitchen. She wished she could climb in there—not like, to die—but just for a rest. She wished there was an oven the size of a closet, where it was warm and dark and you didn't have to come out until you were ready. Her mom slid the cookies in and shut the door. She put down the oven mitts and climbed onto the rubberized step stool to get the bag of decorating supplies from the high cabinet.

"I didn't like him at first," she said. "I didn't think they'd last."

"But you think so now?"

Standing on the stool in the big sweatshirt, her mom suddenly did look older. It was the way she moved, as if she was just a little more fragile than she'd been before.

"Let me do that," Athyna said, but her mom ignored her.

"No one's good enough," she told Athyna, stepping down with the bag of supplies. "When you're a mother. But I wouldn't say anything that would hurt her now. Because he's not just her boyfriend—he's Marcus's dad. And now this new baby."

"Ava."

Her mom sucked her teeth at that. Athyna knew she agreed that it was unlucky to name a baby before it was born.

"You look at it from all sides," she said. "It'll be the same when it's your turn."

"Never gonna be," Athyna said firmly. She knew it was babyish, but she didn't care.

"We'll see."

"No, thanks."

Her mom finally sat down, on the top of the step stool. "Fine with me." But she was humoring her.

"If Bree thinks I'm taking care of another one—"

"Nicole from church told me she's opening a day care—next year at the latest. You'll be in college."

Athyna didn't say anything to that because she didn't want to bring up her essay. She'd told her mom that she'd already finished it. But she couldn't picture herself leaving home, living anywhere else except maybe at Krystal's. And of course that had only worked for a few days.

Athyna suddenly felt dizzy. So far she'd had only one romantic experience, and it had fallen short of her expectations so intensely that she assumed the problem was Javier, or Javier and her. It had felt good to plan to see him, to tell her friends that they were going for pizza after school or that he was coming over to her house to watch a movie. But the actual time alone together had been painful in its strangeness, not only their fumbling make-out sessions but even when they were just talking about something stupid from school—even when they agreed—it was like they were overdoing it, or saying lines from bad TV. When they broke up she was relieved, because she could stop feeling awkward and look for the real thing, the thing in the Baby Rose song that had been stuck in her head all summer. *And your waves pull me deep underwater*—

But now something hit her like an iron weight. Everyone was lying. Lyrics and movies and memes—all of it was about something that didn't exist. There was nothing like that in the world, but everyone kept pretending because it did such a good job attaching all the parts of being an adult—work and sex and babies—into what her teacher would call a "narrative." Without that there was no connection between the random events of your life, good and bad, and the bad things couldn't be explained as the shadow of the good.

It was like when you were a kid and you learned about Santa Claus. It took all the air out of her. Her mom was still sitting on the step stool, giving her a strange look.

"They're never going to be able to get their own place."

"Not for a while, anyway," her mom agreed.

And once Athyna moved out, what would be the point?

This week was one thing. Her mom was home and it was the holidays. But what about January, when everything went back to the way it was before? She had heard all the #metoo stuff about how it wasn't the girl's fault and *believe women* and all that. Everyone had posted something about it. But privately they joked about how there were some girls (Jada, for example, or Angelique) who you'd be stupid to believe. She remembered the way he turned away from her when she got home the other day, like just the sight of her gave him a three-Bayer headache.

The kitchen was too warm with the oven on, no longer cozy but hot and sugary, suffocating. There were two ways out: you could go through the living room, where he'd stood in the doorframe, or out the back, where he'd sat on the steps to smoke. Those were the choices, no way was she going to stay. But how was she going to be brave enough to leave?

33

They did it in the Narcissus room. Afterward she wished she still had her notebook, because there wasn't anyone she could tell. If she told Maxine and Chloe, they'd be like, *WITH SOME RANDO YOU MET ON THE BEACH?* From public school in Queens, they wouldn't say, but would be thinking. And Inès was still grossed out by guys, and Emma would be condescending, like, *Oh—good to get that over with.*

She'd been careful in the notebook, but not so careful that she wanted to risk carrying it with her on the plane. Customs was strict there, even if you had a French passport, and what if they opened the box and had questions? She'd imagined herself in a windowless room, an officer from the Police Nationale flipping through the graph-paper leaves. But she didn't love the idea that she'd left it in the apartment either. She should have used a different initial for Raffi; T maybe, for Tevaihau.

Still she would have liked to put down what had happened with Justin. She knew it wasn't good for girls the first time. She'd heard enough about it in the bathroom at Lycée Corneille. But still she'd been shocked when she opened her eyes and saw the expression on his face, an expression that said he was having a completely different experience than she was on the stiff white sheets, the old quilt down around their ankles, the needles of the stumpy pines brushing the window, the sun-stained brown daffodils on the wallpaper.

Afterward it was so awkward that she was actually glad when

he mumbled something about helping his uncle with a job in Montauk, and took off. She couldn't wait for him to leave. She took a hot shower, and put on almost all the clothes she had with her, and walked down to the beach. While she was down there, he texted: "Sorry I left so fast." Then nothing. What kind of text was that? She wasn't even going to respond, but she didn't want him to think she cared. She held her phone up and stuck out her tongue, like the dumbest selfie ever. She sent it before she could regret it. He hearted it right away, and then was silent again.

It wasn't even the sex that surprised her. It was everything together: the pain—the kind of pain over which she had no control—and the weight of his body on hers in the bedroom. It was the difference between those things and the feeling when he took her earlobe in his mouth. It was the look on the face of the man in the Patagonia vest when he shook his head at her. Maybe he felt okay to look at her like that because of Justin's uncle's truck, but the look was for her alone. He wanted to look, and she was disgusting. She needed protection and at the same time, from now on, she was fair game.

She was coming up the driveway when she heard her name. Her real name, so at first she thought it had to be Maxine and Chloe, showing up at Sandpiper even though she'd told them she needed some time to pack and get ready. Probably they wanted to drink or get high beyond the reach of Gisela. She was thinking of how she could turn them away, when she came to the clearing at the end of the driveway and found Athyna sitting on the back step.

"You came!"

Athyna was wearing a black puffer coat, leggings, and some turquoise socks under high-top Jordans, her big glasses, clear frames. She looked a little offended.

"You invited me."

"I know," Pia said. "I just—you didn't before."

"Sorry I didn't text or anything," Athyna acknowledged. "I was in a rush."

"You took the train?"

"I thought you might not be here."

"I almost wasn't," Pia said. "I mean, I was at my friend's house, and then I came here." What if Athyna had come two hours ago? Found her with Justin? Her face got hot just thinking about it. She tried to remember if she'd shut the door to the bedroom, where the sheets were still a mess, the quilt made by her some-number-of-greats grandmother fallen to the floor.

"I don't have to stay," Athyna said. "I was just—"

"No!" Pia said. "I'm glad you're here!" It was so emphatic that Athyna laughed, but Pia thought she also looked a little relieved.

"I'm warning you, though, it's cold in there."

"Couldn't be any worse than out here."

She took Athyna into the house, kicking off her sneakers. She only did it because she'd been at the beach, but Athyna did the same. They went into the living room, where Pia had forgotten that her suitcase was open on the couch.

"I was thinking about building a fire—" She'd thought of it just that minute. "Sorry the house is kind of gross."

"Oh it's fine," Athyna said politely. She took a step toward the fireplace, jumped and grabbed her foot.

"What happened?" Pia said. "Are you okay?"

Athyna nodded, but Pia could tell it hurt. "I think there's maybe a nail in the floor?"

Pia went into the kitchen, where there was a bag of tools on the shelf above the washer and dryer. She got the hammer to pound the nail into the floor, but it was really to keep Athyna from seeing her face. She didn't know if she was embarrassed or sad. Nothing today was how she'd pictured it.

"My uncle keeps telling my dad to renovate this place. But I guess they're arguing about it. Are you hungry?" There was a menu from Astros pinned to the corkboard by the door. She took it down, leaving the hammer on the windowsill. "We could order pizza? I just have to see if they take cash."

"I have some, too."

"Okay, thanks." Pia tried not to sound relieved. She had eighty-six dollars, which needed to cover her bus ticket to JFK tomorrow, and anything in the airport—in both airports. The minute she used the card, she was finished.

When the pizza finally came, they ate it at the low coffee table in the living room without talking. Pia realized she hadn't eaten since a breakfast bar before Justin came over. She felt as if a week had passed since then; she thought she'd never been so hungry in her life.

"Should I try the fire?" she asked when they'd finished.

Athyna nodded. "Careful, though."

There was a pile of newspaper and one package of those Duraflame starters. She thought you made a kind of pyramid. Her mom would tell her the reason for it, but Raffi would be able to show her how to do it.

"Does your mom know where you are?" she asked Athyna.

"Nope. She was driving me crazy."

"Yeah?"

"Siding with my sister on *everything*. Like, she always says I can tell her whatever. Then I do and she's not hearing me."

She wanted to ask what it was that Athyna's mom wasn't hearing—but the way Athyna spaced out those last three words, a frustrated puff of breath with each one, made Pia think she was done talking about it.

"That sucks," she said instead.

"What about your dad and Kate?"

"What about them?" She didn't mean for it to sound like that.

"Do they know you're here?"

Pia balled up newspaper to go inside the pyramid. The more fuel, the better, she thought.

"They think I'm with my friends, Maxine and Chloe. But I don't really like them."

"So why are you friends with them?"

She looked to see if Athyna was making fun of her. She was standing with her arms crossed over her chest, looking at the fireplace as if she wasn't sure she was going to stay. But from her face, Pia thought she was really asking. It was the same thing Justin had wanted to know. Was she different from Chloe and Maxine? Totally—she had to be. But how she was different, she couldn't exactly say.

"Sometimes it's like I'm one person with them, and another person with my mom, and another with my dad. But I barely see him." That was a stupid thing to say to someone whose dad was dead. "I like being with Raffi."

"Your boyfriend?"

Pia hesitated, but she didn't feel like lying. "No—he's, like, thirty. But he's really nice." "Nice," her English teacher said, was a dead adjective, off-limits.

"For me it was my dad," Athyna said. "Around him I was just, like, relaxed."

"That's what I mean!"

"Yeah."

"But I mean, that sucks."

"Yeah."

Outside, the light was blue; it was already starting to get dark. Would it be weird with just the two of them here tonight?

"You want to look for that place? Sands Point?"

Athyna looked surprised that Pia remembered. "Nah—I think it's far from here anyway."

She glanced around the room, suddenly eager to change the subject. Her eyes fixed on Pia's suitcase.

"OMG I love those things!"

Pia had moved it from the couch to the floor, but it wasn't zipped. "That's just the box," she said quickly.

"You drop the ball, and the ones in the middle don't move.

But then it moves the one on the other side. Momentum equals mass times velocity!"

"Wow," Pia said.

"Yeah—I can't believe I remembered that. Let me see."

"No." Pia jumped up. "I mean, there's something else in there—a present, for Raffi. It's all packed up, so I don't want to take it out."

Athyna sat down finally on the couch. She gave Pia a raised eyebrow kind of look, without raising any actual eyebrows.

"But you can't send it in the mail, so I'm going to take it. I mean, next time I go."

"That sounds kind of dubious, Pia," Athyna said, in an adult voice.

For a second Pia's stomach clenched, but then Athyna laughed.

"That's what Kate always says, if someone's bullshitting," she explained. " 'I'm dubious.' And if you're like, what's 'dubious,' she'll be like, look it up."

"I know what it is."

Athyna gave her a look. "So do *I*. But some kids—" She shook her head disparagingly and looked into the fireplace. The starter was burning nicely, but none of the logs had caught.

Pia took the poker from its iron rack and nudged the flame. "Where does your mom think you are?" she ventured.

"She thought I was with Krystal—my best friend. But she's friends with Krystal's mom, so now she knows I'm not."

"You share location with her?"

"I turned it off."

Pia laughed. "Me too."

But all of a sudden Athyna got serious. "You know they might call the police."

"Missing Hamptons teen."

"Teen *girl*, I bet. With a photo."

"It'll be both of us—teen girls."

"It'll just be you."

There was the kind of awkward silence she'd been afraid of. It happened whenever the subject came up at school, too. She'd thought that was because it was a French school, and the French like to pretend everyone was the same. Liberté, égalité, fraternité, etc., etc. Or maybe it was that uncomfortable everywhere.

"They'll be looking for you, too." But it sounded lame.

"My mom will—she's freaking out."

"My mom couldn't care less." Outside, it had become dark enough that the windows reflected their two figures back at them: Pia crouched in front of the fireplace, Athyna watching her from the slipcovered couch.

"She doesn't want to see you?"

"She's gonna be so pissed—" Pia stopped, because she hadn't meant to confide in Athyna. Maxine and Chloe were the only ones who knew, and only because she didn't know how else to get the ticket. Now she owed Maxine $760.42, and she was going to have to make up something about a waterfall. The whole thing seemed even crazier now that she'd done it with Justin. What did Emma used to say? *Tout dans le monde concerne le sexe, sauf le sexe*—as if she knew everything. That was Oscar Wilde. But what was the rest of the quote?

"Pissed, why?"

"Look," Pia said. "It caught. It's kind of smoky, though."

Athyna was sitting with her legs under her, one foot protruding in its turquoise sock. She looked from Pia to the suitcase and back to Pia. "You're going there, right? To that crazy island?"

There was no point pretending. "Not that one."

"But where your mom is."

"Yeah—you won't tell her?"

"Kate?"

It was weird how they used first names at that school. It made her feel like Athyna knew Kate better than she did, even though they'd been living in the same apartment for months.

"She's just my teacher—it's not like we talk."

"What's it like, your school?"

Athyna shrugged. "It's good—way better than my middle school. It's pretty small, and we have these groups called 'crew.' You get really close with your crew."

"Mine's small, too," Pia said. "But I hate it."

"Could you go to school over there? On the island?"

"My mom says the schools aren't great, after elementary. They barely teach science—I mean, I would be fine with that. But that's why there aren't any Tahitian scientists at the lab, she says. Raffi says the French made the schools bad on purpose, not only in French Polynesia but in Tunisia and Algeria. He says they teach in French to make people forget their languages."

But Athyna didn't seem that interested in schools halfway around the world. "How much does your school cost?"

Pia could feel her face flushing. "I'm not sure." It was true that she didn't know the exact number, but it was more than forty thousand dollars a year.

"They send you even though you hate it?"

"I guess because of the French. And I'm an only child."

Athyna half laughed. "Not for long. You think they're going to send the baby to that school? Or to ours?"

"I don't know," she admitted. She hadn't given it any thought.

"My sister's having another baby."

"Really?"

"That's part of why I left. Like, if they think I'm going to take care of it—"

"That's not fair," Pia agreed.

"And Marcus's dad is a total ass."

"Because?"

Athyna looked as if she was considering. "You can't tell any-one, if I tell you."

"I wouldn't!"

"Especially not Kate."

"You keep my secret, I'll keep yours." She sounded like a little kid, but Athyna nodded.

"So it was right before the storm."

"When we were texting."

"We were home together, just the two of us, and he like . . ." Athyna hesitated, "like . . . jumped me." Pia couldn't see her eyes well enough to guess that she was going to cry, but she could hear it in her voice. That happened to her, too: you didn't know you were going to, and then it just started.

But Athyna recovered herself. "Right on the damn couch, if you can believe it."

"*What?* Did you tell anyone?"

Athyna gave her a look. Dubious. "Like my sister?"

"Yeah," Pia said. "I see what you mean. Did he like—"

"I pushed him off. And he stopped, but—I had to get out of there."

"That is *so* fucked up. And now they're having another baby."

"Right? But you really can't tell anyone—I'm serious."

"I wouldn't. But I mean, you can't stay there."

Athyna hugged her shins, resting her chin on her knees. "The thing is, I love Marcus."

"He's your nephew?"

Athyna nodded. "I even miss him now. Isn't that crazy?"

Pia thought about the giraffe mobile. "I mostly can't deal with kids."

"It's just practice."

"You know what they do over there, when someone has a baby?"

"On the island?"

"They take the—what do you call it—the thing that comes out after?"

"Placenta."

"Right—and they bury it in the ground. You're supposed to bury it on your own land, and then plant a tree right there. Usually a fruit tree, like breadfruit. And then the kid is supposed to learn to take care of the tree, and it's like—her tree—for life."

"That's cool," Athyna agreed.

"But trees can live longer than people. So if someone dies, you might still have their tree. It's like they're still there, inside it."

Athyna was silent, and Pia wondered if she'd gone too far—if Athyna was thinking about her dad. She thought of Raffi's dad, who had a tree for sure, probably in Tahiti where he was born.

"I'd like to see those trees."

Pia had a sudden inspiration. "So come with me." Even as she said it, she knew how stupid it was. She'd barely been able to get one ticket.

Athyna laughed and shook her head. "Girl." Then she sat up straighter and pushed her glasses back on her nose. "So this guy—Raffi. He knows you're coming?"

She'd pictured it so many times. The sound of the metal ramp against the dock, the shaded pavilion where they sold coconuts and ice cream, the driveway where Raffi would be waiting in his white truck.

"I just have to get on the flight," she said. "I mean the second flight—from L.A." It was like a chain reaction: first one step, then another. "Then there's nothing they can do."

Athyna looked at her. "It's not drugs—right?"

"What?"

"In the box."

"Oh—yeah, no."

"'Cause that's stupid, on a plane."

"Yeah."

"So, what?"

Pia looked at the fire. The smallest of the logs was smoldering white ash at one end. Underneath it, bright embers flickered like lava. It was burning but without any flames.

"It's the same over there as it is here," she tried to explain. "I mean, it's way prettier. But the island belonged to the people who were always there—"

"Who planted the trees," Athyna said.

"Yeah. And then the French came, and built military bases in Tahiti and New Caledonia. And proving grounds on Moruroa and Fangataufa—in the Tuamotus, where the black pearls come from. That's where they tested the nuclear bombs."

"What about the people there?"

"They got sick. Raffi's dad died from it."

"Shit."

"Just like the Marshallese from the U.S. bombs. At Kwajalein and Enewetak and Bikini."

The smoke had died down. It wasn't hurting her eyes anymore, and it gave the whole room a good smell—a Mo'orea smell, like when her mom stopped work at a reasonable time and they drove into Maharepa for dinner. The sun went down behind them, and the air was cool and blue. On the lagoon side, white sailboats rocked at their anchors, and on the other, pink, green, and yellow cottages sent up tails of gray smoke from yards where trash and vegetation were burning, or a few brown-and-white cows were nosing the tall weeds behind a barbed wire fence. She could never get over how here and there could exist at once, a watery quarter of the globe between them.

"Now all these countries are talking about sending ships to mine the ocean. For minerals and stuff." She took a breath. "So Raffi wants to fight back."

"And you want to help."

"If I can."

"Because?"

Pia shrugged. She was sitting cross-legged on the floor and the bottoms of her socks were so dirty.

"Because you like him, or because you want to fight back, too?"

Athyna hesitated, like she was going to say something and then changed her mind. She took off her glasses and rubbed her T-shirt on the lenses. The half of Pia's body that faced the fire was hot, but the half facing Athyna was cool, even cold. She thought suddenly of Frances: *cold fire*.

"It's not because of my mom."

"Uh-huh," Athyna said, but it was hard to read her expression. She put her glasses back on. "I'm going too," she said abruptly.

"Where?"

Athyna shrugged, and Pia felt bad for having asked.

"You can stay as long as you want. No one comes here in the winter."

"I'll stay tonight," Athyna said, as if that had been in question. "But after that—" She made a gesture: a wave or the swipe of an eraser. "After that, I'm gone."

34

Kate took out her headphones and dropped them on the counter. One skittered to the floor. Bending left her breathless. The island was otherwise empty and gleaming, because Maria was cleaning the apartment. She spoke mostly Polish; her hair was a startling orange; and her loyalty was probably to the women with whom Kate had just gotten off the phone. The only thing on the granite island was the wooden fruit bowl, now full of lemons and grapefruit, and Kate's loose white plastic earbud, like a knob of polished bone. Or coral.

I know this must be . . . hard for you.

The maddening dropping of the "h." Why was that low class in one accent and sophisticated in another? But the first priority was Pia, whatever Kate felt about her. If Maxine and Chloe had no idea, and Maxine's mother had no idea, then who was the next point of contact? She tried to remember other names but couldn't come up with any. She thought back to the day Pia had told her about the pregnancy tests. But of course that had been a ploy. Even her mother had called her a liar.

Maria was running the vacuum in the hall. She was still on the phone, but she gave Kate a look that lingered on her stomach as she slipped past the housekeeper into Pia's room. Was she imagining censure in the woman's watery blue eyes? The room was picked up, certainly thanks to Maria rather than its occupant. The textbooks were stacked neatly on the desk, along with the school-issued computer. Kate opened the drawer of the nightstand, which contained only a few rubber bands, a lip balm, and, oddly, a paper flyer for a heating and air-conditioning company in Riverhead. She shut the drawer and looked under the bed, in the drawers of the desk, and in the closet. Pia had taken the suitcase with her to Maxine's of course. She sat down for a moment on the bed, because even this amount of exercise now left her winded.

The day Pia found out about the baby, she had been writing in a notebook. Not necessarily a diary, but Kate had assumed because of how her stepdaughter had shoved it under the other books when she came in. Now she got down on her knees and slid her hand under one corner of the mattress: nothing. Rather than hauling herself up again, she crawled around the bed, felt another corner. If Maria looked in again, she could say she was feeling unwell. But from the sound of it, Maria seemed to have opened the front door and was scrupulously vacuuming even their portion of the hall carpet. Kate slid her hand under the third corner and felt something hard. She worked her arm under the mattress and pulled out a beautiful book, from Paris no doubt, with a mottled, pale blue paper cover and a darker blue spine. On the cover there was a legend with spaces for *Nom, Classe, Matière*, although Pia had left those blank. Inside was a surprise: small, meticulous script, which they apparently still taught in Europe—not so different from her own cursive, imparted by nuns, which most of her students couldn't read.

Kate got up and stood at the window. The baby turned in her uterus, like an eel. Her stomach ballooned tight and hard against her chest, and it was suddenly difficult to breathe. Did she remember this feeling? Sometimes she thought she did; other times she was sure she was imagining it. She could see the teenager only from the outside, getting into her aunt's silver sedan. She couldn't remember what she'd been thinking, just the black pine trees out the window of the car, where she rode like a child in the backseat.

She was now the age her aunt had been, when she'd driven Kate in almost perfect silence eight hours from Bay Shore to

Canton. No one but her knew what it had been like when they arrived at the house and her aunt showed her the guest room: an addition to the back of the house, the poor insulation on that damp October day like another punishment. Over her cousin's childhood desk, which she was already too big to use—even if she'd wanted to do the packets of supplementary work her guidance counselor had provided—was a tiny picture of the Virgin in a wooden frame. Had it always been there? Her shame was in the stiff beige curtains hanging over the window, the squeal of the tap in the pink-tiled bathroom, the memory of the exaggerated surprise in her mother's voice when she saw Kate putting her cleats into the bag: *Now what are you going to do with* those? There was no telephone in the room, so no possibility of calling anyone. Not Chris Ferrara, whose parents had grounded him for the entire year—but who was nevertheless still playing baseball and graduating on time—nor any of her girlfriends, who were anyway not thinking about her, but about the senior outing and the League Cup and the colleges where most of them would be freshman by the time she finally got home.

If her aunt pitied her, she hadn't shown it. And that at least was something Kate had appreciated. Her aunt had left her alone in that grim room and shut the door. She'd never felt under the mattress for the pink, spiral-bound diary hidden there, or invaded Kate's privacy in any other way.

Then again, Kate had changed her own sheets. And she had never run away. She'd stayed in Canton and paid for her mistake, as the adults around her had intended. If the price had been steeper than anyone had imagined, well that was a valuable lesson in the way the world worked—one you could never have learned in school.

Fourteen stories down, the traffic was stalled on Seventy-Sixth Street. Someone sat on a horn, and then others joined in. Kate hesitated for only another moment. Then she sat down to read.

35

Pia had warned her. She'd said that Athyna could walk to the beach, but that someone might stop her and ask where she lived. "I bet," Athyna had said. But Pia swore it happened to everyone—everyone who wasn't recognizable to the residents. It was a private lane with beach access, and some of the homeowners were vigilant about outsiders. In the summer, they hired a guard to sit in a beach chair at the entrance to the road.

Well, that was fine because Athyna didn't want to go to the beach. But she hadn't thought anyone would come to the house. When she heard the knock, she was in the bedroom. Pia had left this morning, for her flight. Athyna had said she was leaving, too—she thought she would see if she could spend a couple of days with Tania or Angelique, even Bianca, anyone whose mom her own mom didn't know. Her mom had sent her twelve messages today already—saying that she was staying with a friend wasn't cutting it—and so she had to turn off all the sounds. Periodically her sister broke in to tell her how selfish she was. She fantasized about trading it in for a clean phone, a new number. Starting from scratch.

Maybe she was just tired of looking at her phone, and that was what made her feel around for the watch at the bottom of her backpack. She opened the leather box, freed it from the velvet loop. She'd liked trying it on her wrist when she was a kid, liked its weight, and the glow-in-the-dark bezel, and the words "sapphire crystal" that her father had used to describe the face. Once she asked her dad if he wasn't worried about losing it underwater, and he had lowered his voice and said not to tell her mother, but that professional divers actually didn't wear special watches. They didn't even use a dive computer because there was a supervisor on land who calculated all of that for them. He wore it all the time *except* for when he was diving; before he got to the job site, he always took it off and locked it in the glove compartment of the car. He'd been wearing it when he died.

There was another knock. She hadn't heard a car, so maybe it was one of the neighbors. But she could always say she was Pia's friend. Or even Kate's student. She had more than one solid reason to be where she was. She slipped the steel bracelet around her wrist—it was still too big—and went cautiously to the door.

She was expecting an old white man, with a dog maybe, or a young blond woman in exercise clothes with a coffee. It was a mystery to her why everyone she'd seen so far in the Hamptons was drinking a huge coffee. What did they need so much caffeine for? And so it was weird, to look out the window next to the back door, and see a kid her age. A brown kid, wearing a hoodie and Yeezys, standing not on the step but a few feet away from the door, on the patchy gravel that had once been a path. The sky was blue, but when Athyna opened the door, it was even colder than she'd expected.

"Hey. Um—is Athyna here?"

Vigilant homeowners were one thing. She wasn't going to let some pimply kid who looked like he could go to her school freak her out.

"Who's asking?"

"Sorry, um. I'm Justin."

She gave him her toughest stare. "Athyna."

The boy looked at her like she'd said her name was Beyoncé. Like he'd just realized she was insane.

"What?" His sweatshirt wasn't warm enough for the weather, his hands shoved in the pockets of his jeans.

"A-thee-na—like the Greek goddess."

He stepped back and looked up at the house, like maybe he'd made a mistake. Then he looked back to her. "How do you spell that?"

"*What?*"

He nodded, as if her skepticism was justified. "Because I just met an Athena," he explained. "But she spelled it with a 'y.'"

"Really?" In spite of herself, she was interested. She'd never met another one.

"Was she my age?"

He considered her. "A little younger, maybe."

She was curious whether the other Athyna was Black or white; everyone knew that about adding letters, changing it around. White people dug deeper and deeper into the past for their kids' names, while Black people wanted something brand-new, unique. She'd actually known a girl called Unique in elementary school.

"She said this was her house."

"Well it isn't," Athyna said. "It's not even my house. It belongs to a kid named Pia Davenport, but she's not even here."

"Okay," he said. "Sorry."

She felt kind of bad for him. He looked so cold. She watched as he started back out toward the road.

"Hey!"

He turned around.

"You have a picture?"

"What?"

"Of your friend—the other Athyna."

He nodded, came back. Scrolled through his phone, then flipped it to her. A selfie, tongue out, her crazy two-color hair blowing in her eyes. Athyna wondered why she wasn't more surprised.

"That's her," she said.

The boy waited.

"That's—" She was about to say: *my friend.* "That's her, but her name isn't Athyna."

He frowned down at the photo.

"It's Pia."

"Pia," he repeated. Strangely, he was blushing.

"*I'm* Athyna. Pia left for Tahiti."

"Oh," he said. She was familiar with that kind of look. It was like Hernan when Madison had broken up with him, and changed their name to Maddie, and everyone knew before he did. She almost felt bad.

"She had to get away from her stepmom."

His eyes narrowed, like he doubted her. "How could Athyna—"

"Pia!" Athyna said.

"Pia doesn't have a stepmom," he said. "At least the Pia I know."

"Yes, she does," Athyna said. "She's my teacher for ELA."

This detail seemed to make some impression on him. Maybe he was in senior ELA somewhere, too.

"Her dad just married her—like, a couple years ago."

But Justin was shaking his head. "Pia's dad is dead."

"*Pia's* dad?" Was she going crazy? Justin looked more and more interested. Meanwhile Athyna was starting to feel sick.

"I have some stuff to do," she said.

"Okay," Justin said. "If you see her, could you give her these?" He pulled a pack of ICE BREAKERS out of his pocket and handed them to Athyna.

Yeah, right, she thought. But she took them. She hadn't eaten yet today, and watermelon was her favorite. Justin pulled up his hood. She was letting the cold in the house. The floor was freezing, like ice underneath her socks.

But she couldn't help it. "Did Pia say how her father died?"

"A diving accident," Justin said.

The air, when you breathed it in, hurt your lungs.

"That was his job. He worked underwater, fixing bridges and stuff."

"No shit," Athyna said. She was shaking, but not from cold. The metal bracelet slipped down past the cuff of her sweatshirt, but now her hand was big enough that it wouldn't fall off. She could wear it forever. "You know what?"

He just stood there.

"She's a liar."

Justin looked at his sneakers. They looked like Yeezys, but she could tell they were the fake Chinese kind.

"He was just driving," she said. "He fell asleep."

He nodded, as if that made more sense to him, too.

"It was just a stupid accident."

36

He was distracted, and that was how it happened. After he got Kate's call, he told Craig he needed forty-eight hours. "Don't we all," Craig had said, and so Stephen had needed to explain the situation. His daughter was missing. In addition to being unable to locate his daughter, his wife was barely speaking to him. Meanwhile, it was New Year's Eve. Craig said that he was sorry and that they would manage.

He had been trying not to think about how they would manage, especially in the ICU, when he got to Ronkonkoma. It was stop-and-go traffic across four lanes of the LIE, but he'd almost made it to his exit. He was thinking about what Kate had said. It didn't make sense, because the baby was due in March. They'd even thought about a name: Frankie, for his mother.

But Kate had been so angry that it was almost a relief to pick up the phone and call Maxine's mother, who was apologetic but baffled. It had been her understanding that the girls were having a great time. The housekeeper was there looking after them, but she could possibly have missed the moment when Pia decamped for her own house, which according to Maxine had been four days earlier.

"It's been insane, and I'm actually working this week—"

"Believe me," Stephen said. "I understand."

"I have a friend who can go over to your house now. If you just give me the address? Maxine didn't have it." She sounded irritated by this failure on her daughter's part, rather than surprised or judgmental about the fact that Pia had disappeared. Parenting was something that busy people like themselves were forced to do as expeditiously as possible, without unnecessary self-examination or doubt.

"Never mind," Stephen said. "I could call my brother—but I'm sure she's at the house. I'm driving out now."

"Let me know if we can do anything else to help," Maxine's mother said before hanging up the phone and moving on, he was sure, to her next task. For a moment he had imagined being married to a woman like this one, who seemed to confront her home life with the same practical efficiency she applied to the nuances of corporate securities fraud. Instead of the woman he was married to, who had just told him over the phone that she felt "betrayed," that she wasn't sure if she "could do this anymore." What do you mean, he'd demanded, frustrated, because he'd had to leave a meeting with the cardiology chief to take the call. They were doing it—they were on a highway without an exit, scheduled to arrive in approximately seventy-five days.

But instead of answering his question, Kate had told him that even Nathalie had no idea where Pia might have gone.

"You called Nathalie?" he had said, dread settling in his stomach—but of course that wasn't the point. The point was that his daughter had been missing for four days, and for some reason he couldn't quite understand, Kate thought a partially deaf heating and air-conditioning repairman named Carlos with a business registered in Riverhead might be able to help them.

"Has she said anything about Lloyd's of London?"

"What? No—why?"

"She wants to go back to Tahiti."

"Right," Stephen said. "We knew that. But she doesn't have a ticket."

"I think you should make sure of that."

"Okay," Stephen said. "I should be there in an hour. I love you."

There was silence.

"Keep me posted," Kate finally said.

It was after three, and it would be dark by five. Before five; was it possible that it got dark earlier out here than it did in the city? The day was bright and cold, and the sun was directly behind him, sinking fast, making it hard to see into the rearview mirror. The expressway in front of him was all red brake lights. Pia was old enough not to drown in the ocean. She was in the Hamptons for god's sake—she was fine. He was going to find her at the house. In fact he should've asked Jesse to make the trip; if he had, he would know by now. What had kept him from doing that? One thing at a time, he told himself, but the unfairness of it hit him like the sun in the mirror. If there was anything he wasn't, it was a betrayer. That had been Nathalie's territory.

He was exhausted, and there hadn't been time to get food before he left, only a cup of coffee, which had made him jittery, and possibly was the reason that after thirty-four years of successfully driving an automobile without incident he found himself gliding toward a compact white Honda, realizing he was too close, slamming his foot on the brake several seconds too late. Metal on metal, the dead thud, something orange out his window. Then stillness and the sick certitude of what he'd done.

Only luck and the lightning reflexes of the other driver kept it from becoming a pileup. The oversized, barrel-shaped cones between their cars and the metal divider were like providence. He could see the driver and passenger moving in the front seat, turning to the rear. There was—oh god—a baby seat in back. Not enough space to open the door on his side, so he crawled to the passenger side as the traffic rubbernecked around him. He climbed out into the roaring ethanol haze, and for a moment he felt that they were all watching him: Kate, Nathalie, Pia. Carmen.

"What the hell were you thinking?" The other driver's voice jolted him back: a thin white man with glasses, thick, curly hair, midthirties, in jeans and a Cal T-shirt. Someone he could talk to, maybe.

"Is everyone okay?"

"Okay—no. Jesus Christ."

"My fault," he said, against all the advice. "Completely. I'm tired."

"Then you shouldn't have been driving!"

"You're right. Is the baby—?"

The baby was crying. The woman was on her knees in the backseat.

"I'm a doctor," Stephen said. "I can take a look."

The man glowered at him. "The fuck you will."

His wife, a young Asian American woman with a pink streak in her hair, was worried about whiplash. "Let him look," she said, climbing to the other side of the baby. The father grudgingly stepped aside for Stephen, but kept one hand on the door.

Stephen peered in through the window, and was relieved to see that the car seat held a toddler rather than an infant. The surprise of a stranger getting into their car quieted him, and he looked at Stephen with a face that was tearstained and almost perfectly round. "He's about three?"

"Just." The mother opened the door. "It's okay, now—the doctor's going to take a look at you."

Stephen took his N95 from his shirt pocket and put it on. "Hey, buddy." Behind him, the father made a noise that signified Stephen's inability to be his child's buddy, since he'd almost killed him. "Does anything hurt?" The little boy had fine, black hair with bangs cut straight across his forehead. He was wearing red overalls with cats on them. Stephen held out his phone.

"Could you look here for me?" The child automatically followed with his eyes as Stephen moved the phone up, down, and to each side. "Could I feel his shoulders?" The mother nodded. "Does this hurt? What about this?" The boy laughed, suddenly ticklish. Stephen probed the base of the skull gently with two fingers. He'd forgotten about the softness of baby skin. "Any prickles anywhere?"

"Pickles?"

"Any part of you feeling funny?"

The little boy shook his head with ease. Some of the adrenaline left Stephen's body.

"You're a champion," Stephen said, extracting himself. "He seems fine, but it would be good to see his pediatrician as soon as possible. I don't work with children."

They retrieved their insurance from the glove compartments, and each took a picture. Then he traded phones with the husband, adding his own contact information.

The woman was watching him. "What kind of doctor—"

"I'm a cardiologist."

"Do you take care of Covid patients?"

He was glad he'd put on the mask. "I do, but I've just been vaccinated. I'm really sorry about this. The insurance will take care of it."

She glanced at her husband, who hesitated.

"It looks bad," he said finally. "But I think we can drive away."

"I'll pull out first," Stephen said. "Give you some room."

The man nodded, started to extend his hand and thought better of it. Before they got back in the car, the woman turned back to him.

"Good luck with everything," she said.

It was almost dark when he got to Sandpiper. There had been good visibility in town, but now a fog was rolling in from the ocean. When he opened the car door, the air was cold and damp, thick with salt. He heard deer crashing through the stunted pines behind the house. As he was grabbing his bag from the trunk, a light went on in the bedroom—she was here!

Pia had locked the front door, and so he knocked and called her name. When she didn't come, he used his key. He was grateful to be without Kate, so he could really talk to his daughter. Maybe she would even agree to go to dinner in town. At the same time, he felt more hopeful about his marriage than he had on the highway. It was possible to have a crisis and move past it. He was a good person; if a pair of strangers could see it, wouldn't his wife eventually come around?

"Pia," he called out. "I'm here."

But the bedroom was dark again, the door closed. The Narcissus room, aptly. She must've turned the light off again when she heard him coming. It reminded him of the way she used to hide as a child, half her body sticking out into the room. Did she think he was going to give up?

He switched on the hall light and put down his bag. The familiarity of the black and white linoleum squares, the beadboard walls, the bulletin board with the sun-faded sheet of emergency numbers reinforced his relief. The smell was of mildew and smoke. Had she built a fire?

"I know you're in there. I was thinking we could go to dinner."

Nothing.

"I had an accident on the expressway. I'm a little shaken up. And hungry." And I need a drink, he didn't add.

There was a sound in the bedroom, then the clicking of the lock.

He went to the bedroom door. "You're being ridiculous, Pia."

He heard the squeal of the sash in its warped wooden frame. She was trying to climb out the window.

"It doesn't open more than a few inches," he informed her. "Not since the Clinton administration. But if you open the door, we can talk about it. Whatever it is."

Now that he knew she was safe, he could handle anything. He just needed a meal and a solid night of sleep. But the room remained quiet.

"Goddamnit, Pia." He stepped back and thrust his body against the door. The impact felt good. He was going to break down the fucking door, if that was what it took. He did it again, and there was a scream from inside the room. Then a voice—not hers:

"I'm not Pia!"

He stepped back, startled. Looked down the hall. The voice was female, he thought, almost certainly. But what if she wasn't alone? There was an old hammer with a wooden shaft sitting on the windowsill. He edged sideways toward it, just in case.

He heard footsteps, and then the lock. The intruder was opening the bedroom door. He grabbed the hammer. The living room was dark, and they could come at him from both sides.

"Who's there!"

"Pia's friend," she said. "Don't—"

And then a girl stepped out. Black, about his daughter's age but shorter, her hair pulled back tight in a bun. Scared eyes behind thick glasses.

He dropped the hammer, and they both jumped. His hands were trembling. She stared at the tool on the floor.

"I'm sorry," he said. "I thought you were—"

"She's not here."

"Okay."

"I'm her friend—but I was going."

"It's okay. It's not a problem. I'm—" But did she want more apologies? "I'm her dad."

"I was just looking for a car to the train."

"The train—" He took refuge in logistics. "There might not be another train tonight. And you can use the rideshare apps out here in the summer, but there's probably not anyone driving now. I can take you."

The girl blinked.

"I'm really sorry."

She shrugged. "It's your house." She didn't sound as if she thought much of it.

"I didn't know you were a friend," he explained, but that wasn't what he meant. "I mean, I thought she was with—some other friends. At a different house." Then why had he come here? "At first. And then I thought maybe she was here."

The girl nodded slowly. "Kate is my teacher."

"Kate?"

"Aren't you her husband?"

He recovered himself. "Right—I'm Stephen. Really nice to meet you." It would have helped to shake hands.

"Athena," he heard her say.

He picked up the hammer and replaced it carefully on the windowsill, as if that were its permanent position. "How did you, um, meet?"

She looked at him as if he'd suggested that it was strange that they'd met, strange that they were friends. Or was that his imagination? The interaction was familiar from interactions with patients. Everything was right in his head—he was very careful to guard against bias, had done all the required training—but when he spoke, his words seemed to take on other implications, as if something happened between his brain and his mouth.

"There was a party in the park."

He remembered the party, coincidentally on the day the election had been decided.

"Then we started texting."

"That's nice." What an idiot he was.

"Do you want to call her?"

"Pia?" he said. "I've tried. Many times, actually—she's really not here?" He had the idea that maybe she was hiding in a closet somewhere. Had sent this girl out as a decoy. If that was the case, she wasn't being fair to him. Or to her friend, he amended quickly, in his head. He couldn't help noticing that the friend looked a little messy, as if it had been a while since her clothes were washed.

"I meant Kate," she said. "If you want to check—"

"No—"

She looked relieved. He felt the same way. He noticed that she'd taken her shoes off when she came in, although the floors didn't warrant it. She was wearing a pair of turquoise running socks.

"No," he said again. "That's not necessary. Unless—do your parents—?"

"They know I'm here with Pia," she said quickly, and not quite credibly. But he had to focus on his daughter.

"But Pia—"

"She was here."

"But she left?"

She nodded again.

"To her friend Maxine's?" But he knew before she answered.

"She said she doesn't like Maxine."

"Oh." Somehow the girl wasn't what he pictured when he thought of Kate's students. He always imagined the groups of teenagers he saw on the train, yelling and making a spectacle of themselves. He'd been impressed that Kate could handle it. Whereas this girl was so soft-spoken he could barely hear her. *Soft, gentle, and low*, he heard his mother say, *an excellent thing in women*. It was always a joke, when Frances said it. He had a feeling he was never going to forget the hammer.

"You must be hungry."

"I'm okay."

"Well," he said. "I'm starving. So I'm going to get us something to eat."

She didn't argue.

"I'm not sure if I can drive you back tonight."

She looked up sharply. Was she frightened of him?

"You can stay here, though. And I can take you home first thing in the morning."

"Oh—that's okay," she said quickly. "I'm going to take the train."

"It'll be much faster by car."

Now she looked up at him, and he worried she was going to cry. Or she was trying not to cry. You could see it in her mouth. Her voice pitched a little higher: "Thanks—that's okay."

"Well, we can figure it out in the morning. And for now I'll run out to get—some burgers, maybe?" He wondered if the Grill was open. "I was going to stop by Maxine's, just to talk to the housekeeper. But it sounds like Pia didn't go back there."

She shook her head, looked at her hands. She was wearing a man's watch, bulky on her wrist.

"And you don't have any other ideas, about where she might have gone?"

The girl took an unsteady breath, bringing herself back to their present conversation. For a second she'd been somewhere else.

"Yes," she said, "I do."

37

They flew into the sunrise. The clouds under the plane made a cold, dark topography, but there was a line of fire at the horizon, where the sky went from red to gold to blue. There the clouds rose up in wild dark shapes, tinged with red: a hammer, a shark's tooth, an ancient god with the head of a bird.

The woman next to her woke up. "Oh god," she said, "we're here."

Pia considered pretending she didn't speak French. She didn't feel like talking.

"Back in paradise. But what can you do?"

"It's pretty," Pia said. The box was in her checked bag—you couldn't take magnets in a carry-on—and so she had to be separated from it. They had a thing on the app now that tracked your bag, but the last message before she'd lost service was "prêt à charger." Had it actually made it on the plane? She wouldn't be able to breathe until she got into Raffi's truck.

"That's what everyone says. After fifteen years, though—but what can you do?"

"Were you on vacation?"

"My father's funeral—in Marseille." The woman gave Pia a look meant to convey her error. Not a serious enough error to end the conversation, though. "So that meant three flights. An hour and a half to Paris. Twelve hours to L.A., then the layover, then eight and a half back here."

"I'm sorry," Pia said, unsure if she was apologizing for the death or the inconvenience.

"Do you also live here?"

Pia hesitated. "Back and forth."

"That's better," her seatmate confirmed. "But I have four children, so what can you do?"

If Pia was questioned about the box, she was planning to say she'd found it in the airport. On a seat. She'd thought it was the toy pictured on the outside of the box, and so she'd put it in her suitcase. *I would have to be so stupid*, she thought—but then, people assumed all teenage girls were stupid. Would they have the extra checkpoint before the exit, where you had to put your bags through the machine again?

"Your parents live here?" The woman had shoulder-length, straight brown hair, tied back with a yellow scarf. She was wearing a short-sleeved black sweater and black joggers, and her earrings were shaped like tiare blossoms. She was the kind of woman who put a flower behind her ear and went to the Intercontinental for dinner on the terrace, then complained about all the tourists.

"My mother," Pia said.

"Ah," she said as if she understood everything about it. It was weird because when Pia had been in New York, she kind of missed the French. But as soon as she got back here, she wished for an American sitting next to her, someone who would talk excitedly about snorkeling and the juice factory and how to get *off the beaten path*. Who would assume cheerful, mutual goodwill.

They had come through the clouds and now everything was a shadowy blue color, the water flat as a sheet of steel. As a magnet. The sky was pale yellow behind Tahiti, which was still just a bunch of gray peaks in the early light. It wasn't six in the morning, and Pape'ete was dark. But a cross strung with Christmas lights glittered on the hill above the capital.

"She's not Tahitian, is she?"

Pia shook her head.

"I didn't think so," the woman said. "Neither is my husband."

Pia could hear Raffi in her head on the subject of "local conditions," which meant that teachers and bureaucrats from metropolitan France made twice what Tahitians made in the same jobs and didn't pay taxes. They got to live on the best property, tucked into terraced lots on the steep green mountains, with long views of the turquoise lagoon.

"Of course many of the children's friends are demi."

People sometimes thought Raffi was demi. His skin was dark, but his features were a little different—because of one Chinese grandparent, her mother said. Raffi's mother was as Tahitian as you could be, and taught him all the traditional things; he spearfished and grew tamanu and could braid a hei out of ferns. Last summer he'd made her one, way up on Mou'a Puta, where he'd taken her hiking on a day when her mother was stuck in the lab. Halfway up, they'd stopped and sat on the rocks by a stream to rest. The canopy covered them completely, so you could only see the sky as negative blue space behind the leaves. As usual, Raffi was quiet and she was embarrassed. Even sounds embarrassed her: the rush of the water over the rocks, the sawing of the insects, the groaning of wind in the leaves. It was like someone had put a microphone inside her, like these jungle sounds were being amplified from inside her own body. Raffi just sat there, braiding.

She had wanted to ask him why he did it. Her mother paid him for the diving, but for this? Was he babysitting, or did he want to be here with her? For their hike he was wearing the jelly sandals called Méduse that you could buy in the grocery store, even though she knew he had real hiking shoes. When he finished the garland, he placed it on her head; for a second her face was between his hands. For a second she thought he was going to drag her down into the leaves, put his mouth on hers and his hand between her legs, the way she did at night, thinking about him. But beyond that, she could only imagine, because what he had actually done was to drop his arms and nod critically at his handiwork.

One foot here, one foot there, Ruheruhe, he had said. *That's why we get along.* Then he'd stood up from the flat rock and indicated that they should keep walking.

"The question," her seatmate continued, "is what we're going to do in a few years, when our oldest is ready for university."

"Uh-huh," Pia said, although it didn't seem to matter if she responded or not. She was just a kid. Raffi knew it, too. He had never looked at her any other way.

"My husband hopes he'll go back to France. But I prefer California."

What would it look like for a bomb to explode against the hull of a ship in the lagoon? Unlike the smaller boats, they didn't bob up and down. She could pick them out as they descended, fixed in the water like tiny white islands.

"And you? Where will you go?"

"I don't know," Pia said.

"It's not too early to start thinking about it," the woman advised.

It would be a small explosion, and no one would die. Or that's what she had guessed, from what Raffi was willing to say. He wouldn't talk about it directly, but if she asked about the *Rainbow Warrior*, he would say how it happened. Mitterrand had sent secret agents to the harbor in Auckland, where the Greenpeace boat was docked. The agents included expert frogmen who swam down and attached a limpet mine to the hull of the boat. The limpet wasn't supposed to kill people, just to disable the steering column and stop the *Rainbow Warrior* from traveling to Moruroa, where they were trying to draw attention to the effects of the nuclear tests. (It had killed one person, though—a Portuguese photographer—by accident.) It was the same type of bomb that the American CIA had used in the harbors in Nicaragua. Then the idea had been to hurt

Nicaragua's economy, because no company would insure a ship traveling to a harbor that had recently been bombed. There was, Raffi told her, only one company that insured most ships anyway. And so Pia understood that a research vessel without a steering column would have to be towed to a dry dock to be repaired, in Singapore or the Philippines. That would cost so much money that Lloyd's of London would stop insuring RV *Persephone*, and the company would have to find somewhere else to look for nodules. Maybe all the other mining companies would think twice about sending their boats out looking for metals, if they thought they might get bombed.

"He'll be so far away."

Pia struggled to remember the gist of the conversation—the woman's son, going off to college.

"But what choice do we have?"

"You could go back to France." She thought her seatmate would turn away, at the very least, or chastise her for being rude.

But the woman didn't take it that way at all.

"We could have," she agreed mournfully. "We could have made a life there. But now the kids are used to it—the freedom, and the beaches, and their friends. All the *nature*." She turned her large, dark eyes on Pia, as if she were the adult, capable of dispensing comfort.

"And so what can you do?"

38

It was her friend Ann who dragged her to the New Year's Eve party. Nathalie was going to stay in her room and wait to hear from Stephen, but Ann insisted.

"You're not helping her, sitting here moping," she said. "Come and have a beer, at least. Pia's quite all right. She's punishing you, the two of you, and it isn't fair—but isn't that what they do?"

Ann had two grown children, one making a great deal of money in London and the other pursuing an advanced degree in ethnomusicology somewhere in South America. Clearly her brand of unsentimental British motherhood had produced results, and so Nathalie put herself in her hands.

The party was at one of the villas next to Les Tipaniers, where their colleague Émile was renting. It wasn't far from the cottage where she'd stayed with Pia, although these attached bungalows were more charming, with peaked roofs and outdoor verandas, separated from each other by rattan walls or bamboo roller shades. Inside, where she and Ann went to get drinks from the kitchen counter—a solid piece of polished teak crowded with bottles, beneath a jumbled rack of hanging pots and pans—was a room that had accommodated an endless stream of researchers cycling in and out. Guests sat on a tired-looking couch covered in bright local fabric; under the glass coffee table was a basket of sunscreen and insect repellent and a plastic tub of snorkeling equipment. The bookshelves were crammed to overflowing: travel guides, novels—Philip

Roth in French and Michel Houellebecq in English, a whole shelf of Agatha Christie in both languages—and a row of binders and spiral-bound dissertations. Above them, someone had mounted an old-fashioned wooden spearfishing gun and a collection of hairy, brightly colored lures.

Nathalie followed Ann out to the veranda, checking her phone. She couldn't believe how long it seemed since the dive with Raffi this morning, since the little girls had hailed her from the shore. Presumably Kate had reached Stephen after she spoke to Nathalie; presumably Stephen now had the situation in hand. As she'd hurried to take over from Gunther with the analyst from Pew, she'd thought that "missing" was too strong a word. Pia was taking a break from her alarmist and self-righteous stepmother, a step with which Nathalie sympathized wholeheartedly. In Pia's shoes, she would have done the same.

But she wished her daughter would respond to her messages. When she'd pressed "information" under Pia's name in the past, the GPS would yield a location. Now that service had been disabled. Why hadn't Stephen at least let her know things were under control? Why hadn't he answered any of her messages? But she knew the answer to that. He hadn't responded because he hadn't found their daughter, and she had to admit that in his shoes, she would've done the same. If Pia had disappeared on her watch, she would've exhausted every possible avenue before contacting Stephen. And now it was the middle of the night in New York. Still, she messaged him again: "Nothing??" Ann, not normally demonstrative, reached over and touched her hand.

After the tour was finished, Nathalie had gone back to the lab and worked through lunch, but it had been impossible for her to focus. Then Raffi had messaged—"tout va bien?"—and she knew he was asking about Pia rather than the analyst. Instead of trying to put it in a message, she went looking for him. Of everyone on the island, he was the one who'd spent the most time with her daughter. Had they been communicating over the last few months, while Pia was in New York? She knew from experience that unless she asked directly, and in person, he wasn't going to offer it up.

But by then it was early afternoon, and Raffi hadn't been in the dive shed or on the dock or la dalle. She'd thought he must have gone home, and so she told Gunther that she was taking the rest of the day off. She wasn't going to be able to concentrate until she heard from Stephen, anyway.

Raffi's truck was in the driveway in Paopao, but Monique's little gray hatchback was gone. Nathalie had knocked on the door of the yellow house, just in case, but even Hina and the kids were out. She thought she would find Raffi in his workshop again. The sun was in and out of the clouds, but it was hot either way, and the insects droned in the trees on either side of the path. A rooster of the scrawny Polynesian variety, streaks of green and yellow in its iridescent plumage, ran right in front of her; as if scandalized by her presence, he took refuge with a hen and chicks in a drainage trench. Ripe mangoes and papayas gave off a syrupy, rotting smell from where they lay smashed on the asphalt tracks. There was so much that they couldn't harvest it all.

Nathalie had called out as she rounded the last switchback, but there was no sign of Raffi. His saplings swayed in their tires like self-conscious adolescents, under a shade structure he'd erected from white PVC pipe and green nylon netting. Soon she imagined it would be time to plant them in the ground. The mouth of the shed was black, and when Nathalie entered her eyes took a moment to adjust. She took a step forward, her arms out in front of her. But the blade seemed to come from nowhere, biting her thigh. She gasped and whirled around, protecting her face, expecting another thrust. A raw, rough noise—but it was from her own throat. No one was there.

Relief let the pain in. She'd wiped her eyes in the gloom, and been able make out a table, newly built from plywood, supporting the bright yellow electric handsaw. She must've walked right into the blade, knocking it out of place but not to the floor. It had been careless of Raffi to leave it unsheathed, but she was the one who was trespassing. Her left hand came away from her thigh, slick with blood.

The cut was short but deep, and she'd looked for something to staunch it. Light coming through the space between the walls and the corrugated roof made it possible to see a set of freestanding shelves, quickly but skillfully constructed, like the table. Nathalie was surprised to notice several bags of commercial fertilizer—she'd thought he was making his own—under a row of old paint cans, a red jerry can of spare diesel, an old coffee grinder, and the orange Pelican case he'd been carrying in the woods that day. It had a six-digit combination lock, but she guessed he wouldn't have reset it—and she was right. They used 68-95-99 for everything at the station. Inside was nothing she could use: several coils of double-braided nylon line and a 1000 ml burette still in its protective packaging, something even Gunther hadn't missed. There were also two red cardboard boxes of 12-gauge Fiocchi shells, one of them empty. Strangely, the shells had been disassembled and separated into plastic bags secured with twist ties: casings in one, lead shot in another. Only the primers were missing. And of course, the weapon itself—did he keep it in his truck? The smaller gray Pelican case was nowhere to be found.

On the ground in the corner of the shed was a woven bag she hadn't noticed until now. Nathalie crouched down to look: even a rag or a bit of paper would do. But the only thing in the bag was a white cardboard box, shiny and new, with a picture of a toy on the outside: one of those executive desk toys, with magnetic balls suspended from a metal frame. Someone must have taken the toy, because the box held another type of magnet: eight countersunk ring magnets, 3 inches in diameter, waterproofed with a rubber coating. Nathalie had held them in her hand for a moment—heavy enough that she guessed they were neodymium. Then she'd replaced them in the box and, pressing the fabric of her dress against her leg, made her way carefully back down the hill to her car.

On the veranda, Émile was complaining to the lab director about catajets off the cruiser, *Paul Gauguin.*

"He should be more concerned about the other boat," Ann said, but they were interrupted by one of her students, who drew them into a group that included Gunther, Marc, and the new communications director, Anaïs.

"That's a Danish research boat, I think," Nathalie said. "Raffi and I saw it this morning."

"Nominally Danish, nominally research," Ann said.

"Or research of a particular kind," a postdoc of Ann's put in. "It's one of those exploratory missions."

Ann nodded. "A greenwashing thing."

Nathalie stared at Ann. They'd seen the boat, but Raffi hadn't said anything. Was it possible he didn't know? "It's a *mining* ship?"

"Someone said they're coming from the Solwara site."

"Supposedly an impact study," Ann said. "But it's just a matter of time. The Chinese and the Russians have the largest state-sponsored licenses, but now private companies have exploration rights to the majority—"

Nathalie's phone vibrated in her pocket. She realized, as she scrambled for it, that for a moment she'd forgotten about Pia.

"Excuse me," she said to the director, and took the steps two at a time from the veranda. She jogged away from the music, up toward the road, where she hoped the signal might be stronger.

"Stephen?" she almost shouted. "Can you hear me? Stephen?"

"I'm in Amagansett. She's not here."

He sounded unusually clear, as if he were just across the island. She could see the interior of the house: the brick fireplace and the linoleum floor, the uncomfortable Shaker chairs—like a movie of someone else's life.

"Where is she, Stephen?"

"She was here on Tuesday. Her friend's still here."

"Her friend's there *now*?" Had she somehow mistaken the time? "It's the middle of the night."

"I'm well aware."

The wind made a dry rattle in the palms over her head. Above them, millions of coldly flashing stars.

"Sorry," Nathalie said. "But this is an emergency, no?"

There was a slight delay on the line, which made everything Stephen said sound as if he was hesitating. "I wasn't asleep."

"Her GPS doesn't work. It says 'unavailable.'"

"So she's turned that off."

"What does Maxine say?"

"Not Maxine," Stephen said. "Another friend—Athena."

Pia had mentioned Maxine and the badly behaved boys in her class. No Athena.

"She says Pia left on Wednesday."

Today was Thursday, early Friday morning in New York. New Year's Day.

"Left for where?"

"Tahiti, her friend says."

"That's impossible."

"She said she was taking something to her boyfriend."

"Pia doesn't have a boyfriend," Nathalie said firmly. "At least not here."

"What about Raffi?"

"Jesus, Stephen." As usual, he was jealous of any male within several kilometers of either of them. "He's thirty years old."

"I'm repeating what Athena said."

Every word distinctly clipped, as if she were the one being irrational. And who the fuck was this friend, who supposedly knew more about their daughter's whereabouts than either of her parents?

"*Athena* is confused."

"She seems very certain. She says there was something else in the box."

"What box?"

"The box she was taking him. She said it wasn't the toy."

He wasn't making sense. Had he been drinking?

"What toy?"

"One of those desk toys with the balls that knock together—it's called a Newton's Cradle." Stephen continued to speak—about an airline ticket Pia had tried and failed to buy, and a boy Pia had met on the beach. But Nathalie wasn't following. She was trying to think.

"Are you calling the police, then?"

"I did already."

"And?"

"They're filing a report."

"Call again in the morning."

"Yes."

"Call me back after you speak to them—no matter what time."

"Yes," Stephen said. "Of course."

After they hung up, she stood for a moment on the sandy path to the beach. Her brain was doing the thing it did best, going through every possibility, testing and rejecting:

Raffi had a collection of Newton's Cradles, which he'd never mentioned.

Raffi asked for this specific gift, which Pia recently bought.

The box was intended to trick customs into thinking it was one thing, while it really concealed another. Drugs? Money? Seeds? But it was like when you found two species in unfamiliar partnership, or one that was outside its ecological niche. There had to be some reason for the strange juxtaposition.

She would have returned to the lab if she'd had her own car. Instead she went slowly back to the party, climbed the steps to the veranda, and made her way around some of the guests, who were dancing to ABBA's "Waterloo." Maybe Ann was ready to leave. She found her friend in the living room, talking to one of Émile's Tahitian fishing buddies.

"Nothing yet?"

Nathalie shook her head.

"Tomorrow," Ann said. "As soon as you wake up, you'll have news."

Nathalie was going to say that she was very unlikely to sleep at all, when she heard Raffi's name. She turned and saw Gunther standing at the edge of the party with Anaïs, the new communications director. Nathalie waited until the young woman went inside to the bar before approaching.

"What were you telling her?"

Gunther was leaning against the rattan wall, like a teenage boy at a dance. He had a plastic cup of red punch in one hand. "We were talking about the ship."

"About Raffi, I mean. You didn't mention the lab supplies? Because we cleared that up."

Gunther shook his head.

"I heard his name."

"All I said was that DeepGreen is the company Raphael is always discussing about."

His English was almost as good as hers, and she suspected he wouldn't have made the mistake if he hadn't been drinking. Still, Nathalie jumped on it. "Discussing," she said. "No 'about.'" She was so tired of men and their inane competition. "Why would she care?"

Gunther shrugged.

"Is this still about the sharks? Because ça dégénère—it's out of hand."

Gunther looked chastened, and Nathalie was slightly mollified. He wouldn't admit to being wrong unless he actually knew he was; his fanatical precision demanded it.

Anaïs returned with a beer. A blond, athletic-looking Belgian in her late twenties, she was in her honeymoon period with the island and her new job, thrilled by the adventure of it all. She was the last person Nathalie felt like talking to at the moment.

Anaïs greeted Nathalie effusively in French, then switched back to English for Gunther's benefit: "But who owns the ship?" she asked. "That's what I want to know."

"It's not Danish?"

"The shipping company is Danish," Gunther said, smiling slightly. "They're the ones funding the 'research'—in exchange for shares in the company of course. Through their subsidiary, they own the rights to some of the most productive nodule fields."

"And they contribute ships like the *Athena* to explore them," Nathalie suggested.

Gunther glanced at her. *"Persephone."*

"That's right." She forced herself to focus on the conversation. Maybe Ann was right and all this worry was for nothing, because she would have news in the morning.

"And it's the International Seabed Authority handing out the licenses," Anaïs confirmed.

"But some of them have deep ties to the metals guys," Gunther said. "The ISA is supposed to prioritize the rights of developing nations, especially in the Pacific. And they could've done it, because they were the ones with the survey information about the nodules. Instead private companies mysteriously gained rights to the most productive fields."

"The ISA is notoriously corrupt," Nathalie said. "The companies are just jumping through hoops with these impact surveys. Eventually they know they're getting the licenses."

"Through their subsidiaries," Gunther said, ticking them off on his fingers: "DeepGreen through NORI in Nauru. Allseas with Blue Minerals, Jamaica. And Lockheed Martin created its British subsidiary—that's UK Seabed Resources—because the U.S. isn't a partner to the UN's Law of the Sea and wouldn't have been eligible for a license. The U.S. is obviously a huge market for the metals because of electric vehicle technology. DeepGreen is even thinking of building a processing facility in Texas."

Nathalie turned to him. "Why do you know all this?"

Gunther had the excited look that he got when he had a piece of information in which someone else was interested. He looked from the communications director to Nathalie, hesitating.

"Our *friend*," he said. And when Nathalie didn't get it: "He was obsessing about it."

And just like that, she knew.

The explosion in the forest, the chemicals, the burette.

The shell casings, the magnets, the *Persephone*.

Her daughter.

All of the pieces fit together with perfect clarity, as they almost never did in the lab.

"Obsessing 'about,' or 'over'?" Gunther continued innocently. "Which would be correct?"

She hitched to the lab. Then she took the red skiff. The moon was just past full. People were partying on the *Paul Gauguin*, lights blazing from the passenger decks, and there were lights and music from some of the smaller sailboats as well. But RV *Persephone* was dark. It sat a little distance behind the cruiser, just inside the reef pass, a solid gray mass with only the regulation masthead light illuminated. Maybe the crew was relaxing somewhere on the island, an unlucky few left on board with beer. A limpet would be most effective on the tail end of the hull, at the shaft seal or elsewhere on the running gear, far below the waterline.

The frogmen sent by Mitterrand to sabotage the *Rainbow Warrior* had used rebreathers, but there was no need for that kind of stealth tonight in the lagoon. No one would notice a man slipping from a fishing boat into the water, carrying a case. Inside the case, the bomb that she'd mistaken for a gunshot, a design at least as old as the Second World War. It was simple enough to put together in a basement (or a shed), light enough to attach to a boat with small, powerful magnets. If waterproof neodymium magnets had been hard to find in Tahiti, they would be easy enough to bring from New York—by her daughter, who believed that she could by this action somehow skip over to the side of righteousness. Or at least prove her devotion.

The danger was to the swimmer first, and anyone nearby second. On a boat the size of *Persephone*, the crew wasn't likely to feel a thing. Raffi knew that. The crew wasn't the point. Knowing Raffi, it was instead the beautiful irony of retaliation with a bomb so small: homemade, but powerful enough to rip a hole in 20,000 tons of welded steel. And why? Precisely because of the ocean behind it. The limpet worked because the explosion took the path of least resistance. Above the waterline it would be useless, detonating into the air around it—but underwater it was different. Down there the bomb would drive right through the steel into the hollow hull, because the entire ocean was at its back. The islands were tiny but the sea was vast, and the sea was what would fight for them.

She turned off the motor and scanned the lagoon. The purple-black sky with its swaths of stars, faint music from the pleasure boats. An impossible night for an attack, but every muscle in her body was alive to it. Working underwater, the diver set the chemical fuze. Then he had how many minutes to get out of the way?

There was a shout from one of the decks; she spun around; and that was when she saw them. Chugging out from behind a dark yacht, into the moonlight. A small fishing boat right where you might expect one, coming from the reef where the expert fishermen might go on a night this bright to spear grouper, parrotfish, even the prized unicornfish called ume. His cousin's boat, she was almost sure. She was just close enough to make out two figures, still and erect. She adjusted the rudder in their direction. They would see her now. Two of them: Had she just caught him?

As she got closer she thought she could make out the cousin, short and wide, his long hair in a ponytail down his back. But the other wasn't Raffi. It was a woman, she was almost sure. They were barely moving, maybe a kilometer from the ship. Far enough to be out of danger from a blast, but close enough for a diver to swim back to them.

"Yannick," she called. "Where's Raffi?"

The idiot waved, as if they were out for a Sunday afternoon on the water. The woman seemed to tuck into herself, as if she were afraid. Did she even know what mission she was on?

"Where is he?"

The cousin pointed to the water, and it was at that moment that the woman in the stern turned toward Nathalie. In spite of the dark, the shapeless clothing, maybe just from the way she turned her head, she recognized her.

"Pia!" Her daughter was sitting on a cooler at the stern, a sweatshirt under her life vest, the hood pulled over her hair. She was here, and she was safe. Nathalie's relief was followed by a flood of rage so pure that it seemed to escape language— she didn't know what she was screaming—except that it was the release of every creeping second of this interminable day.

"What is this? This shit! Do you know what I thought? And your father? You know how you made him afraid? He had an accident—he could've been killed! Did you know that? And his wife? And you? You do whatever you want, all the time, without thinking of others!"

Pia's face was white, sick-looking, exhausted. It occurred to Nathalie that she probably hadn't slept in days.

"And for what?"

Pia just sat there, as if stunned.

"What's the reason?"

"I missed you."

The manipulation took her breath away. "Where is he?"

This time, Pia didn't pretend. She knew exactly who Nathalie meant. "Fishing." She was here, and she was fine, but there was no relief, because at any moment—

Nathalie grabbed the rail, pulled the boats together. Yannick leisurely stood to help.

"Goddamnit Pia, it's important!"

"Mom—"

She looked at Yannick. "How dare you? How dare either of you?"

"I was going to—we were going to come find you," Pia said. "After this."

Yannick shrugged. "She came with him."

"I know what you're doing!"

Now Yannick nodded: "A good night for lagoon fish."

"Pia!"

Her daughter at least had the decency to look scared.

"How long has he been down?"

"How long—?" Her voice was faint. "Maybe twenty minutes?"

Twenty was way too long. It was impossible.

"Tell me the goddamn *truth*!"

"I am!"

Did her daughter get it? Did she understand that those people—whoever was left to keep watch while the crew spent New Year's Eve on the island, who couldn't be made out individually from this distance but signaled their presence with light, like certain species in the depths below—were all at risk?

"People could die." And when that seemed to make no impression. "Raffi could die. It's even riskier for him than it is for them."

But Pia made a sudden movement. For a moment Nathalie thought she would dive overboard—anything to escape her mother. But she had turned only to look, because Raffi was surfacing, climbing the ladder. No scuba gear, but a speargun, which he handed up to his cousin, followed by a plastic crate heavy with his catch. He overturned the crate, discharging a haul of silvery reef fish, their colors obscured in the dark.

She was so surprised, she let go of the rail. Their sterns drifted apart, but the boats remained lashed where Yannick had tied them at the bow.

"What happened?"

Raffi bent to remove his fins.

"Where's the Pelican case?"

"I returned it. You can report back to Gunther."

"Fuck Gunther. Where's the bomb?"

Her daughter stood up. "Are you crazy?"

"Am I crazy!"

"Sit down," Raffi told Pia. His wetsuit gleamed in the moonlight. He worked with Yannick, stacking parrotfish and grouper in the cooler until it was full. The remainder thrashed on the deck.

"Is this a fucking cover?" Nathalie said. "Because we have to get out."

"It's not a cover."

"Then where is it?"

He was crouched down over the fish, but now he half turned on one knee, like a man proposing. His wet hair stood up at the crown. "There's no bomb."

For years her government had denied it. The tests moved underground, opening fissures in the rock where plutonium would linger for centuries.

"I *heard* it."

"That was a test."

"A test for *what*?"

Now he stood, left the fish to Yannick. He tossed her a line, pulled her close. Then he turned to Pia.

"Get in the boat with your mother."

For once, Pia did as she was told.

"I'm sorry I didn't bring her to you right away," he said, almost formally. "She wanted to come herself."

She had to tell Stephen—as soon as they got to shore. Pia was with her and she was safe, was all he needed to know. She would make Pia call and apologize for all the worry she caused. She couldn't believe how close they'd come to catastrophe—or that it had been entirely averted. Where were the makings of the mine?

She turned back to Raffi. "What did you do—with the materials?"

He gestured, sweeping it all away. But she couldn't let it go that easily.

"Why ask her to bring the magnets, then?"

But now Pia spoke up. "He didn't ask."

She turned to her daughter, amazed.

"I just thought—"

"You just *thought*—"

"I'm sorry," Pia whispered.

"This is not a fucking school suspension." Pia was looking down. Her hands were trembling in her lap, although it was much too warm to shiver. *Don't cry*, Nathalie thought. *Don't you dare cry*. "This is real!"

A guttural sound escaped from Raffi's throat. It was the closest she'd ever seen him come to losing control. In the dark, his body in the slick black suit, he looked otherworldly—from that other world below them, with which they were both in love. The difference was that it belonged to him in a way it never would to her. And it had been damaged, almost beyond repair. That was what was real.

"But why make it, then? If you weren't going to use it."

Yannick laughed suddenly. "He doesn't have the *balls*." The last word in English.

She tensed, ready for some reaction, but his cousin's comment didn't provoke him. It was almost the opposite. Raffi suddenly relaxed, as if a door had opened.

"I have the balls," he continued softly in that language, "not the stomach."

The fish on the deck were finally still.

"The stomach for what?" Pia said, her voice like a child's. She'd climbed over the gunwale into her mother's boat, but they still hadn't touched each other. Nathalie suddenly yearned to embrace her.

"I'm not like them."

All at once, from the direction of the boats, a collective cry went up. Then a long whistle, a terrific crack, an explosion followed by a flash of light.

All three adults jumped, grabbing the rails, and Nathalie lunged toward Pia. But only her daughter was calm. Seated on the transom, Pia leaned forward slightly, toward the boats.

"Look," she said, pointing. "Fireworks."

39

Kate could have declined Frances's visit, but the fact was that the hospital breastfeeding class had been a joke. She'd had to ride there in a wheelchair because every time she stood up, she felt as if all her internal organs were going to drop out onto the floor. She was also afraid of dropping the baby, who seemed to sense her panic. Her eyes closed and she let out a plaintive whimper; she had squirmed out of the white cap with the name of the hospital in purple, revealing a single thick black tuft of hair, like one of the plastic trolls that had been popular in Kate's youth. She was dizzy, and even once they arrived at the circle of new mothers in the lactation room, she couldn't process the directions the nurse was giving: "Position is key," and "Be sure Baby's tummy faces Mom's tummy." The instructions were simple enough in theory—she'd executed them only a few weeks ago in a newborn care webinar, with a doll—but impossible when you were dealing with a living, writhing infant.

But some people were managing. "He wants to *teach* the breastfeeding class," the nurse said to the woman next to her, whose absurdly giant infant boy had his mouth wide open. To Kate she said, "Baby's mouth should cover your nipple and at least a portion of your areola. Don't let her chomp."

"How can I keep her from chomping?"

But the nurse was already moving on. "Whatever you do, be careful not to press on the back of Baby's head."

How on earth did anyone trust her? But Kate knew the

answer to that. There was no choice, no other more experienced mother waiting in the wings.

This was the reason why she didn't say no when Frances talked her way into the hospital. Stephen's mother appeared in the doorway wearing a white coat over her pleated gray wool trousers and turtleneck sweater.

"It never hurts," she said, winking at Kate. "Oh my—may I look?"

The baby was asleep in the plastic bassinet. Frances moved carefully around Kate's bed. Something passed across the older woman's face—alarm?

"What?"

Frances removed her glasses. "Well this is going to sound silly to you." She wiped her eyes with an actual cloth handkerchief. "I'm moved because I didn't think this would happen for me again. I thought—I've been given three grandchildren and that should be enough for anyone. And now here is this very beautiful girl."

She didn't touch the baby, but sat down in the blue armchair next to the bassinet. The plasticized upholstery protested even Frances's slight weight. It was a gray day, and outside the dirty window, Kate could see the gray and brown hospital buildings. Four stories down, she could hear construction on First Avenue.

"We don't have a name," Kate said. "And I'm having trouble feeding her. The nurse says maybe I should wake her and try again?"

Frances glanced at the door. "Who wants to wake a baby?"

To Kate's mortification, she felt like she was going to cry. She could hardly remember the birth: her baby, born yesterday. Afterward, Stephen had gone home to sleep. When he'd come back this morning, she'd been in the shower, where a clot of blood the size of a plum had fallen out of her vagina onto the floor. The clot was black, but when water ran over it, bright red streams of blood snaked out from the center onto the pink tiles. When she came out of the bathroom, there he was, standing over the baby. He looked up in his gold-rimmed glasses, a stranger. *Mom says she and Dad have been emailing.*

Her mother-in-law looked at her. "The issue is latching?"

The issue is that we might have made a mistake, Kate thought. *The issue is the name.*

"She's not opening her mouth enough," she said. "I'm doing something wrong."

"You're not doing anything wrong. Do you really want to breastfeed?"

She had planned to breastfeed for six months, because they'd conceived the baby at the perfect time. Her maternity leave would dovetail into spring recess, and by the time she had to go back at the beginning of May, the school year would be almost finished.

But now those plans seemed as quaint and antique as a paper map. "I don't know."

"I tell my patients—I used to tell my patients—it's whatever works for you. The more you give, the more they take. It's a feedback loop."

"I read that."

"Not only breastfeeding. I mean all of it." Frances had taken off the white coat, and the shade of her blue silk sweater made her eyes a startling color against her white bobbed hair. She leaned forward in the hospital chair like a much younger woman: "The whole business of raising them."

Had Stephen called Frances when he left this morning? Had he asked her to come? He'd looked concerned when she came out of the bathroom, asked how did she feel. He was a doctor, but she couldn't tell him what she'd just seen on the shower floor. He had picked up the baby and put her on his thighs, on her back, looking up at him. Calm, for the moment. His left hand cupped her head with confidence, and he said things like *look at that* and *is that a yawn* and *how strong you are.* She'd crawled back into the bed with a mixture of horror and relief. She hadn't slept more than an hour or two in the last twenty-four, and the room seemed to buzz around her.

"What do you think of 'Violet'?" Stephen asked.

I know this must be . . . hard for you.

"Too feminine—I thought maybe. But with the 'V'—it's powerful as well."

Violet, *Violeta*. "Are you joking?"

He looked baffled. "It was just an idea."

Did he imagine it as some kind of tribute? Would he ever have told her? He'd told Nathalie all of it, maybe because he felt the need to make Kate more interesting to his ex-wife. Or to impress her with his empathy, which was always for the less fortunate, the less powerful, the types of people to whom tragic things tended to happen.

He was still holding the baby, blithely.

"Careful."

He glanced down. "You know she can't roll?" Surprised at her ignorance. "She isn't capable of it."

"Put her down," she said.

"It's normal to feel strange right now. We don't need a name right away. Of course it's more difficult to do the birth certificate later. But if you want to wait—"

She had misunderstood the French: *parce que l'intimité de mariage n'en finit jamais.* She'd believed foolishly that Nathalie was intimidated by them, their wedding. When in fact it was the reverse. Not wedding in this case, but marriage. Not intimidation, but intimacy. The intimacy of a marriage has no end; it goes on and on.

"Put her *down*."

To her surprise, he did as he was told. The baby lay on her back in the plastic box, a box like a tiny coffin. "Easy now."

To her, or to the baby? The idea that he was humoring her was intolerable.

"I need to be alone."

He stood there, assessing her. But then they heard the nurse in the hall. He waited until the woman appeared, then kissed Kate's forehead.

"Get some rest," he said, neutral. "I'll be back later." She watched his blue-and-white checked shirt disappear around the corner of the door, leaving her with a cold, chest-gripping fear.

"Let's take a look at your vitals," said the nurse.

And now his mother was here.

"He certainly could have been more involved, with Pia," Frances was saying.

Kate wanted to say that she didn't give a fuck about Pia.

"He has this idea that he's being punished." Frances paused, considering: "Everything teaches men that their experience is significant. That they have some kind of destiny. Of course there were Greek protagonists of both genders, but they were queens—Antigone, Electra. The majority of women don't have these problems."

"Punished?"

Frances looked at her directly. "Listen to me babbling about Greeks. And you've just had a baby."

As if she had heard herself being discussed, the baby began waking up. Strange grunts were emanating from the plastic box.

"Let me try again."

"Do you want me to go?"

In many ways she wanted Frances to go. And at the same time, she was terrified. How could they be sending them home?

"They told me the position was wrong."

"Position!" Frances said wonderingly. "Put your pinky in the corner of her mouth."

"Is that sanitary?"

"Just put it in there. Help her open her mouth."

The baby wouldn't stop moving. Her eyes remained closed, but she was ridiculously acrobatic, flailing her arms, twisting in her soft, zippered suit. Her head jerked back and forth, her mouth opening around Kate's breast like a fish. She knew what she wanted, but not how to get it.

"Like that," Frances said. "Exactly."

And then like a miracle, the baby latched, not quite the way the nurse had encouraged, but Kate could feel an unfamiliar tingling. Suddenly her abdomen cramped like it hadn't since she was a newly menstruating teenager.

"All right?" Frances asked.

Kate nodded. It hurt, but something was happening.

Frances went and stood by the window, giving them a minute.

"Of course they aren't all tragic heroes. Some of them don't have a shred of it. Others try to check their own power—but that's only another kind of power, of course."

Finally the baby had relaxed. Her body conformed to Kate's, as if it were still suspended in liquid. Frances was saying something about power.

"Not just men but with other women. Even with children—at first you have all the power and they have all the need. Then it shifts."

The baby turned her head and lost the latch—was that it? It had hardly been two minutes.

"Try the other side," Frances advised.

When she moved the baby awkwardly across her chest, it let out a burp. Frances laughed, and a second later Kate did, too: it was such a loud, rude sound.

It lasted only another few minutes. Afterward, Kate tried to press the small body against her shoulder, careful of her head, rubbing her back as she'd been shown. But she had done it.

"Well now I guess we're naming her after you."

"God forbid," Frances said, but she smiled.

Frankie, Kate thought, they'd discussed it. But how would she know if she were making a terrible mistake?

"It must be so hard," Frances said, "all of a sudden to be alive."

40

Dear Nathalie,

First, I'm glad to hear you think remote is an acceptable option for now. As I always tell Pia (at least when she answers my messages), I miss her every day. But I agree that it's practical for her to stay with you as long as it's working. We have our hands full these days, as you can imagine.

I wonder if Pia has mentioned to you the diary she kept while she was here? It was Kate who found it and suggested that Pia might have gone back to you on her own. Of course it was only the urgency of the situation that made her open it in the first place, and she was reluctant to discuss its contents any further. I've never kept anything more regular than consult notes, but when I looked back through our correspondence over the past year (which I had the occasion to do recently, after another conversation with Kate) I realized that they are the closest thing I have to a record of this extraordinary time. At the hospital so much of our thinking was of the magical variety—if we'd only done this or that. And so maybe there was even a desire on my part to escape into the past, where everything was still possible.

Please feel free to email as often as you like with updates. But I wonder if it's best if we restrict our conversation to what directly concerns Pia? If our extreme circumstances made me uncharacteristically candid in those notes to you, it now seems important to look forward. There's a

way that the chronology gets away from us in writing, if you know what
I mean.

Best,
Stephen

Dear Stephen,

I received your email from the other day, and haven't answered only
because things have been so busy here. I had real luck that the same
cottage was available on such short notice. And at the station there is
an office where the wifi should be adequate for her to log in. It isn't ideal,
but for whom in her generation will these years be ideal?

As for extracurriculars, Pia has expressed interest in assisting a small
group of young scientists from the station with a biofuel project I may
have mentioned. You asked about Raffi's work here in the past and so
I'll just clarify—he was a member of the technical staff, but now has an
additional role as a cultural liaison. Locally extracted biofuel is exactly
the type of thing we should be supporting if we are going to engage with
the community in more authentic ways. If there is an infatuation there
that spurs her interest, then so be it. I have never understood why we
are supposed to put aside our brains when we fall in love.

I agree with what you say regarding our communication. If we stick to
Pia, that is best. I don't know if it is these strange times or the computer
or the act of writing itself that encourages intimacy. But I think that we
make a mistake when we say that this or that is our true self. There
are so many selves, and it is important to be in control of them. This is
something I hope Pia will eventually understand.

Bien à toi,
Nathalie

41

She'd heard her teacher was back, but she didn't have English Language Arts on Mondays. She wanted to tell Kate about Brooklyn College, though, and her scholarship through Macaulay Honors. She'd finished the essay the night before it was due, and no one had read it over, and so when she got the email, she actually screamed, right in the middle of calculus. Their teacher Brandon had frowned at her, but then Javier had looked at her screen and said, *Athyna got Macaulay Honors,* and everyone, even Brandon, started to clap.

She thought Kate might be gone, but she found her in the classroom just as the halls were emptying out. It was May and her teacher had put the wooden pegs in the frosted-glass windows, to let in the fresh air. You could see a sliver of green leaves in the gap, and there was yellow pollen on the sills. Kate was clearing off the tables: left-behind handouts, a scrunchie, someone's Dunkin' bag under a chair.

"What a bunch of pigs."

Kate turned around. "Athyna!"

"Don't clean up after them!" She felt shy so she was harder on her classmates than she might've been.

Kate laughed. "If I don't, Emmanuel has to do it. Come sit for a minute. How's it going?"

Athyna took one of the chairs, and Kate sat opposite. The door to the hallway was open, and people called to each other: "You got it? Hey, Mo!" And, "Maddie, wait!" Inside the classroom, dust floated in the sunlight and the spines of the books she had admired over Zoom were cracked, duller, and less orderly on the shelves. Maybe it was having been home for so long, but she felt as if the classroom was a place from her past.

"You had the baby," she said, although that was obvious. "It's a girl?"

"She's eight weeks old," Kate said. "I should get right home, but the nanny is there another couple hours, so I thought I'd get myself organized." She pulled out her phone and showed Athyna a picture: a bald white baby, strapped into a bouncy seat, an orange bow secured to her head with a band.

"Frances," Kate said. "But we're calling her Frankie."

"She's so cute," Athyna said, to avoid commenting on the name. People with names like "Kate" never got it.

"She's a handful," Kate said. "But we're pretty crazy about her. What about you? How are things?"

"I got Macaulay Honors," Athyna said. "I wanted to tell you."

Kate put both her hands on the table as if she were going to jump out of her chair. "Athyna! That's incredible. Oh my god, congratulations—can I give you a hug? Where are you headed?"

"Brooklyn College," Athyna said. "I'm going to live on campus, in the dorms."

When Kate hugged her, Athyna could smell her shampoo, verbena, and something slightly unpleasant, sour. It took her a moment to remember, but it was the smell of Marcus's head when he was tiny, breast milk. Soon Bree would be at it all over again, but Athyna would be gone.

"My friend teaches music there."

"I'm thinking about studying psychology."

"That's certainly a growth market," Kate said. "I can't believe I never got to read your essay—but I guess you didn't need me!"

"I didn't write about anxiety." But she also hadn't taken Kate's advice to write about Marcus. She didn't like to think about how much he would miss her, or who was going to take care of him when she wasn't around.

"It ended up being about my dad," she told Kate. "How he was the only man in the world who I really admired."

"I'd love to read it," Kate said. "If you don't mind sharing."

"My mom said he wouldn't have minded the pandemic, because his work was outdoors, and he was a homebody. But it's still weird to me that he doesn't know."

Kate took off her glasses, tucked a piece of reddish hair behind one ear. "About the pandemic, you mean."

"About everything."

Kate nodded carefully. "I didn't know that your dad had worked out on Long Island."

"That's where he died." Her husband would have told her— Athyna guessed Kate and her stepdaughter wouldn't have talked.

"He was a diver?"

"Commercial diving." She hesitated a moment, but she didn't feel like lying anymore. "It was a car accident, though. Because he was tired."

"Oh—" Kate looked confused. "I misunderstood."

"That's why I wanted to go out there. With Pia." She felt like she needed an excuse, but maybe Kate thought she'd brought it up because of what happened with Stephen. "I'm sorry—"

Kate's face flushed suddenly, covering the freckles. "You shouldn't be apologizing. It's me—us. Pia invited you, and then it was very wrong of her to put you in that position. Stephen was surprised, but that's no excuse—"

"It's cool."

"Not really," Kate said.

"Is she—"

"Pia?" Her teacher looked relieved to get off the subject of Stephen and the house. "She's spending some time with her mom." Kate started to say something else and then changed her mind. "But I'm more interested in you right now. I need some tips from this year's successful seniors for next year's seniors."

"Write about dead parents?" Sometimes a joke was funny because it was true, and other times it wasn't funny for the same reason. Now she was the one who felt her face getting hot.

"I don't think it's what you write about." Kate got up and started organizing some papers on her desk, which was just another one of the laminated tables, pushed into the corner by the window. "More like how you do it. Israel wrote a great essay about skateboarding, how it got him through the pandemic."

"My mom says everyone went crazy. But I think maybe it made some bad stuff happen faster." Kate looked confused, and so Athyna hurried on: "I mean, stuff that was going to happen anyway. We got it over with."

"Like what kind of bad stuff?"

For a second she thought Kate knew, but Pia wouldn't have said anything. Athyna felt guilty for a moment, having told on Pia—but that was because she was younger, and she might have been in danger, and there was a difference between bad things that hadn't happened yet and the ones that were in the past. She had a slight temptation to tell Kate herself, but quickly squashed it. What if she told, and then her teacher called her mom, because she felt some kind of obligation? You never knew what people were going to do when they thought they were doing good.

"Just, you know, the quarantining and everything."

"We went through hell," Kate agreed. "I think it was hardest on young people—not young kids but teenagers. You need your social lives more than anyone."

Just at that moment her phone pinged, and Kate laughed. "See?"

Athyna glanced down and it was Javier, asking if she was walking to the F. "5 min," she wrote, and he gave it the thumbs-up. People kept asking if they were together again, and she didn't know what to say. They were hanging out all the time, but they hadn't done anything yet. It was like neither one of them wanted to start something because then it was only a matter of time until it ended. In the meantime, it felt easy in a way it never had before.

"I hate when people talk about silver linings."

Kate nodded slowly. "I know what you mean." She was sorting the papers into different-colored folders, putting some of them into a BEST tote bag to take home with her. She would have time, because Pia was gone and there was the nanny with the baby.

"My husband—well, you know Stephen—he does say that it's transformed medicine by forcing it to go digital. And that we know a lot more now about developing vaccines faster. So the next time—I mean, I hope there isn't a next time. For a long time, at least."

Athyna thought Kate was thinking about her baby, hoping there wouldn't be another pandemic while Frankie was a kid. She felt the same about Marcus.

"But worst case, now we've learned what to do."

"What?" She'd been distracted thinking of Marcus, who would start kindergarten in the fall.

"What to do, if it happens again."

"No," Athyna said, "I mean, who?"

Kate stopped what she was doing and looked up. "Who?"

"Who learned?"

"Oh—the doctors, I meant. And all of us. We're more prepared."

"Oh."

She thought about it later, and she wasn't being fresh. She really hadn't understood, because she didn't know what they would do if it happened again. She'd convinced her mom about the dorms without telling her the reason. But Macaulay didn't cover housing, and so they were looking at loans. Her mom and Bree already had fewer hours this spring than they had at the peak, and there had been walkouts at JFK8, where they were organizing for a union. Even Bree agreed that Elijah had to vote yes, but no one knew what was going to happen then.

She could live in her house now that she knew she was leaving. But nothing had really changed—except for one day when she'd found herself alone in the kitchen with E. Her mom and Bree were in the living room sorting through the old baby clothes—what was okay for a girl and what they would give away—and Marcus was watching a show, and E had gone straight to the fridge, ignoring her as usual. But then he'd said something under the noise of Marcus's iPad so no one else could hear: *Sorry, Teeny.* Like he'd dropped something on the floor that she was going to have to clean up. *I was fucked up that day.* Like it had just occurred to him. His back to her. *We cool?*

Kate was standing by the window, looking down at the street. "It's so peaceful," she said. "For once. I almost want to stay here for a bit."

"But you need to get home to Frankie."

"Right," her teacher said, shouldering her bag. Athyna got up too, because Javier was probably standing by the exit with Israel and Kabir, or by himself with his headphones on. He wasn't going to wait forever.

"Are you coming down?"

"In a sec," Athyna said, because it was awkward to walk down all those flights with a teacher.

"Congratulations, again, then," Kate said, smiling back at Athyna, one hand on the doorframe like she could be coming in or going out. "See you tomorrow."

Athyna stood for another moment in the sunlight in the classroom. A school bus for the little kids was idling under the window on Henry Street. "Seven!" the guard yelled: "Last call for bus seven!" Adults always smiled if you talked about feeling old. But it seemed like a million years since they'd lived on Winter Avenue, a million years since her dad had sat on the stoop to keep an eye on them, while she and Bree chalked the sidewalk—playing hopscotch and can you kick it?—and walked them down the hill for a Cyclone or a Two Face when they heard the truck on Jersey Street. Sometimes, before they went in, they would write out their address, taking turns adding one line and then another:

103 Winter Avenue
Staten Island
New York City
New York
U.S.A.
The Earth
The Solar System
The Universe

They'd thought that was so funny, but now she couldn't remember why.

Kate's classroom was near the back stairs, so Athyna went down that way, through the door at the end of the hall with its faded signs from the beginning of the semester: GIRLS VOLLEYBALL TRYOUTS THURSDAY AT 4 PM and THE BEST TIMES NEEDS YOU! The stairway was gloomy and dim, the windows heavily frosted underneath their metal grilles. Only a little light filtered in and so it was like you were underground. There were six echoing flights to the exit and the desk of the security guard, Ms. Angela, who knew everyone's name but called them all "baby."

"Bye, Ms. Angela," she said when she finally got to the bottom. But the guard was busy with a group of boys who'd been up to something. Five or six of them, tall and skinny and bumping into each other, murmuring, "Aw man" and "Sorry, Ms. A" and "But I didn't even," stooping over the guard's not-even-five-foot frame. With her blue uniform shirt puffed out, the gold name tag pinned above her huge chest, Ms. Angela was really giving it to them: "I am *ashamed* . . . at *your* age . . . set an *example.*" From the music room around the corner came the anguished wails of the middle school brass band.

She thought the guard was too distracted by the boys to

have heard, and so she was surprised, on her way toward the last set of double doors, to hear Ms. Angela calling after her, the words accidentally in time with her feet on the last five steps—"Bye-bye, baby, be good"—like a love song, Athyna thought, as she pushed out into the light.

Acknowledgments

I'd like to thank the people who welcomed me to Mo'orea, and made my two visits there so rich and inspiring. I'm especially grateful to Suzanne Mills and her colleagues for allowing me to observe their fascinating work at CRIOBE, from collecting cyanobacteria to feeding the nudibranchs to fish blood sampling. Kevin Berger and *Nautilus* magazine took a chance on sending a novelist to Oceania to write about science. Hannah Stewart, Neil Davies, and the inaugural class of the Island Sustainability Program hosted me at U.C. Berkeley's Richard B. Gump Station, and I remain extremely grateful. Adelina Hanere generously gave insights about Tahitian culture to an outsider, and told a story that made its way into this book. Hinano Teavai-Murphy and Frank Murphy made time for a long interview about Oceania's Indigenous scientists, and Jean Wencélius patiently answered questions about spearfishers and their catch. Heimata Hall spoke frankly about science and politics on Mo'orea. In that vein, I'm very grateful for Titaua Peu's novels, *Mūtismes* and *Pina*, which give readers a glimpse of a Tahiti visitors rarely see, as well as Chantal Spitz's *Island of Shattered Dreams*. I also relied on Christina Thompson's *Sea People* and Anne Salmond's *Aphrodite's Island* for brilliantly written and researched history. I continue to appreciate scientists whose work is accessible to nonscientists online, as well as books like Helen Scales's *The Brilliant Abyss* and Edith Widder's *Below the Edge of Darkness*, which make absolutely clear the enormity of what deep sea mining would destroy. Kathy Jetñil-Kijiner's performance poems from the Marshall Islands were a moving and necessary education about nuclear testing in Oceania. The *Moruroa Files*, from Interprt, Disclose, and Princeton University's Program on Science & Global Security was also enormously helpful. And Alexander Mawyer went above and beyond what could be expected from a friend you've never actually met in person: teaching, editing, and offering indispensable suggestions that changed the direction of this book. Any remaining errors are my own.

John Ismay spent several hours talking me through shipping insurance and limpet mine technology, and Shaun Dozier was similarly generous with the mechanics of commercial diving. Thank you also to Jessica Yager and Rebecca Cogswell for taking the time to share their expertise in infectious disease and cardiology, and to John Berg for all things nautical. And who but Jeffrey Zuckerman would take a friend for Sri Lankan desserts on Staten Island and keep her from making mistakes (or at least fewer than usual) in French?

I'm deeply grateful to Jordan Pavlin for taking on this book in its infancy, for sensitive and timely edits, and for including me in the company of some of my favorite writers. Thank you to Reagan Arthur for welcoming me back, and to Kelly Blair for the cover of my dreams. Amanda Urban, thank you as always for your responsiveness, encouragement, and sense of humor. You're the best agent a writer could hope to have. Jasanna Britton and Emma Freudenberger took the time to read this book when I needed their perspectives most. Julie Orringer, I couldn't write a book without you as a first reader, or negotiate the "writing and mother trade" without you around the corner. I'm so grateful to you and to our community of Brooklyn writers for wisdom, candor, and friendship.

The PEN Writers in the Schools program allows me to meet high school writers of exceptional talent, energy, and promise, and I'm grateful to Andrew Boorstyn and the students at Brooklyn Collaborative Studies for welcoming me into their classroom year after year. This book owes a special debt to Makayla Williams; while this isn't her story, her honesty, intelligence, and strength were a tremendous inspiration, as was her nephew Mason (aka Spider-Man).

Cleo and Nic, thanks for putting up with a mom who prefers lab visits to the beach. Paul, "acknowledging" you would take more words than I have. I love you guys.

Nell Freudenberger is the author of the novels *Lost and Wanted*, *The Newlyweds*, and *The Dissident*, and of the story collection *Lucky Girls*, which won the PEN/Malamud Award and the Sue Kaufman Prize for First Fiction from the American Academy of Arts and Letters. She is a recipient of a Guggenheim Fellowship, a Whiting Award, and a Cullman Fellowship from the New York Public Library. She lives with her family in Brooklyn.

A NOTE ON THE TYPE

This book was set in Janson, a typeface long thought to have been made by the Dutchman Anton Janson, who was a practicing typefounder in Leipzig during the years 1668–1687. However, it has been conclusively demonstrated that these types are actually the work of Nicholas Kis (1650–1702), a Hungarian, who most probably learned his trade from the master Dutch typefounder Dirk Voskens. The type is an excellent example of the influential and sturdy Dutch types that prevailed in England up to the time William Caslon (1692–1766) developed his own incomparable designs from them.

Composed by Westchester Publishing Service,
Danbury, Connecticut

Printed and bound by Berryville Graphics,
Berryville, Virginia